westla

THE FOREST

Ashok Kumar Banker's internationally acclaimed *Ramayana Series*® has been hailed as a 'milestone' (*India Today*) and a 'magnificently rendered labour of love' (*Outlook*). It is arguably the most popular English-language retelling of the ancient Sanskrit epic. His work has been published in 57 countries, a dozen languages and several hundred reprint editions, with over 1.1 million copies of his books currently in print.

Born of mixed parentage, Ashok was raised without any caste or religion, giving him a uniquely post-racial and post-religious Indian perspective. Even through successful careers in marketing, advertising, journalism and scriptwriting, Ashok retained his childhood fascination with the ancient literature of India. With the *Ramayana Series*® he embarked on a massively ambitious publishing project he calls the Epic India Library. The EI Library comprises Four Wheels: Mythology, Itihasa, History, and Future History. The *Ramayana Series*® and *Krishna Coriolis* are part of the First Wheel. The *Mahabharata Series* is part of the Second Wheel. *Ten Kings* and the subsequent novels in the Itihasa Series dealing with different periods of recorded Indian history are the Third Wheel. Novels such as *Vertigo*, *Gods of War*, *The Kali Quartet*, *Saffron White Green* are the Fourth Wheel.

He is one of the few living Indian authors whose contribution to Indian literature is acknowledged in *The Picador Book of Modern Indian Writing* and *The Vintage Anthology of Indian Literature.*

Ashok is 48 years old and lives with his family in Mumbai. He is always accessible to his readers at www.ashokbanker.com—over 35,000 have corresponded with him to date. He looks forward to hearing from you.

Books by Ashok K. Banker

KRISHNA CORIOLIS SERIES

Slayer of Kamsa
Dance of Govinda
Flute of Vrindavan
Lord of Mathura
Rage of Jarasandha
*Fortress of Dwarka**

MAHABHARATA SERIES

The Forest of Stories
*The Seeds of War**
*The Children of Midnight**

---

*Forthcoming

THE FOREST OF STORIES

||Mahabharata Series: Book One||

||Ashok K. Banker||

westland ltd
Venkat Towers, 165, P.H. Road, Maduravoyal, Chennai 600 095
No. 38/10 (New No. 5), Raghava Nagar, New Timber Yard Layout, Bangalore 560 026
Survey No. A-9, II Floor, Moula Ali Industrial Area, Moula Ali, Hyderabad 500 040
23/181, Anand Nagar, Nehru Road, Santacruz East, Mumbai 400 055
4322/3, Ansari Road, Daryaganj, New Delhi 110 002

First published in India by westland ltd 2012

10 9 8 7 6 5 4 3 2 1

ISBN: 978-93-81626-37-5

For sale in the Indian Subcontinent only

Typeset in Adobe Garamond by SÜRYA, New Delhi
Printed at Manipal Technologies Ltd., Manipal

||Om||

We bow first to Nara-Narayana
and Devi Saraswati
before uttering the first word
of this great endeavour . . .

Jaya!

||Invocation||

||Om Ganesha Namaha||

Invoking the power of the infinite om,
with the tip of your ink-dipped tusk
you first recorded this tale of tales
as dictated by the venerable Krishna Dweipayana Vyasa.

May this scribe's humble attempt
to traverse again that great ocean of stories
please you, lord.

||Idam Na Mama||

||Dedication||

For Yashka, who said, 'awesome'.
and is an awesome daughter.
For Ayush, who said, 'do it'.
Ayushmaanbhavya, my son.
For Bithika, who said, 'write'.
and is always right, dearest wife.

This gift of words and swords,
this ocean of endless wonders,
this forest of stories.

||Kshamapana||

To every person I have ever known,
I join my hands in humility,
and beg forgiveness,
for any error I committed,
knowing or unknowing.

Even though you and I
are two distinct individuals,
separated
by walled-in compartments of self,
yet when you lose,
I don't win.

The path to true and lasting peace
begins with unconditional forgiveness.

To end the war without
let us first end the war within.

||Michhami Dukkadam||

||To you, gentle reader||

The song belongs
to they who listen

we had a pact,
you and I,
that I would transport you
on wings of song
from Ayodhya to Lanka
and back again.

Now that journey is done.
and we prepare anew
to embark on another
far greater voyage
across the ocean of itihasa.

Listen now, my friend,
for like the first tale,
this new song I begin,
is not just mine to sing,
it is herstory,
history,
yourstory,
ourstory.

||Jaidev Jaidev Satyamev Jaitey||

CONTENTS

ACKNOWLEDGEMENTS

If you are holding a printed copy of this book in your hands, it's thanks to Gautam Padmanabhan, Paul Vinay Kumar and Renuka Chatterjee of Tranquebar/Westland. They and their colleagues at Westland have successfully shattered the glass ceiling that MNC publishers created to keep Indian authors from competing with foreign imports for so many decades. The fact that Indian authors published by local Indian-owned publishers are able to sell hundreds of thousands of copies after the same books were rejected by every single MNC publishing house in India proves that it takes an Indian village to raise an Indian child. I hope that this is the first of many successful books we publish together!

Their enthusiasm for my work was matched only by the enthusiasm that I receive from my wonderful readers. Over 35,000 of you have written in to date on my website and I welcome your feedback. This is all for you, people.

Bithika, Ayush, Yashka, Willow: You are more than my family. You are the cardinal directions of my life and purpose. Love you always.

INTRODUCTION

This is not an epic fantasy. It's not a sci-fi rendition. It's not a futuristic version. If you're expecting any of those things, you're going to be disappointed.

This is simply the *Mahabharata* of Krishna Dweipayana Vyasa retold by one man.

That man is me, of course.

This is my *Mahabharata*. My MBA, as I like to call it, because Vyasa wrote his *Mahabharata* in three years, which is the same time it takes to complete an MBA course. My MBA has taken much, much more than three years to write. Mostly because I'm not a genius like Vyasa. But also because of the lack of a comprehensive unabridged English-language translation of this great epic. Even today, while you can find literally hundreds of translations of similar epics of western culture, you would be hard-pressed to find a single complete unabridged translation of the *Mahabharata* in print anywhere in the world.

This is just one man's MBA. Done on my own time, without a contract, without any sponsorship or financial support from anyone, without assistants or associates. Just a guy, reading a lot and writing a lot.

In order to write this retelling, I referred to every single available English-language translation and retelling, rechecked the original Sanskrit, then wrote my own rendition. Unlike my Ramayana Series, where I often took great creative liberties, imaginative leaps and ventured into outright fantastical diversions, my MBA sticks very closely to the Vyasa Sanskrit epic. I have kept the structure and order of the parvas and chapters exactly as in the original epic. I have tried to cover all the details in the original as well. I have also tried to stay as faithful to the original as possible.

So what's different about my MBA then?

Me, I guess.

My way of telling the story. My 'voice' as they say in the literary world.

Think of it as a singer covering a familiar song. Some singers nail the track. Others make you cry, not for the right reasons.

There will be *Mahabharatas* after mine. There have been many before this one.

Why should you read my MBA?

I haven't a clue. That's for you to decide.

What I can say is that this is my attempt at reclaiming the world's greatest epic as a great story.

A story.

Not a religious polemic. Not a historical document. Not an itihasa.

Just a great story.

I love this epic. I loved writing it.

And for that reason, and that reason alone, it's possible that you'll enjoy reading it too.

All that I am, all that I know, all that I feel, see, experience, understand, gain insight into, believe, goes into my work. My attempt is not to win literary awards, or become famous or rich, or even to get published. It's taken me eight years to find a publisher willing to publish this book—*after* I finished writing it. I don't know whether it will be a bestseller: I'm pretty sure it won't, and that it won't win any awards or get rave reviews. And you know what? It doesn't matter. I love writing, love the world of ancient epic India, love reconstructing these epic events and incidents, bringing them to life, slowly, patiently, as skillfully as I know how.

As I said in the beginning, it's not a fantasy retelling. It's not a sci-fi rendition. It's not an attempt to gain literary fame and fortune.

It's just a great story that I wanted to retell all my life.

And spent most of my life retelling.

Make no mistake about it: even though I say it's 'my' MBA, this is not some wild off-road rally race version of the original epic. It *is* the *Mahabharata* of Vyasa, in the same narrative sequence as the original epic, each passage verified against the original Sanskrit and cross-referenced with all available translations, then narrated in my own style.

Where do 'I' come in? The same place 'you' come in, I guess. Just as you, as an individual, bring to the story your own viewpoints, perspective, background, personality, culture, that whole bundle of mindmeld, so also I bring to the retelling of this great tale, my unique khichdi-pulao curd-rice melange of feelings, nuances, insights, personality quirks, dramatic devices and if I may say so, a few writing skills I may have acquired, incidentally, over the course of a lifelong writing career.

And having said that, I'll take my leave now.

From this point on, you will not hear from me again or see me anywhere in this long odyssey. My work here is done. You're on your own. But my voice is here. My heart. My soul. My passion for story-telling, for living. My love for this great epic. My fascination and obsession with this magnificent world, this great game of words and swords, this towering itihasa that dwarfs all of world literature. I'm the voice in your head, the omniscient narrator of the 'movie' you're about to experience, the singer whose rendition of a great classic evergreen you're about to hear.

But ultimately, it's the song that matters.

The story.

The epic.

The grandeur, the majesty, the horror, the wonder.

Turn the page. Start the journey. Discover the impossible. Remember the forgotten.

And I guarantee that within a few pages, you'll forget all about me. And you'll see only the story itself.

Because, bloody hell bugger, it's one mother of a story.

If epic wasn't already a word, it would have to be invented in order to describe this monster saga. This great game of gods and men. This epic itihasa.

Go on now. Get out of here. There's the pathway ahead, winding through the forest. Follow it. Go where it takes you. Don't come back here again, you hear? You have a long way to go and this is barely the beginning of the beginning.

But before you go, here's a hug and a kiss and warm breath on your cheek and a gruffly given wish in parting:

Happy reading!

ASHOK K. BANKER

Andheri, Mumbai
November 2011

||Paksha One||

SAUTI'S TALE

||One||

Deep in the heart of the great forest Naimisha-van lay the ashram Naimisha-sharanya. The head of the ashram was Kulapati Shaunaka who was so titled because he fed and taught ten thousand brahmin acolytes. To reach the ashram one had to detour far from the nearest trade road, enter the dreaded Naimisha forest and traverse a great distance through that wild and dense jungle with no clear path or markings to indicate the route. If one did not lose one's way entirely or fall prey to the prolific fauna of the forest, one might perhaps, almost by chance, happen upon the narrow winding path that, eventually, after many turns and twists and circumlocutary detours, brought one into a clearing of unexpected size and extent. Here lay the ashram, bounded on all sides by dense woods, an island of meditative study in a verdant emerald ocean. It was a place not likely to be found by casual wayfarers. The only visitors who undertook the hazardous journey here were long-bearded rishis herding new batches of fresh-faced brahmacharyas recruited from across the land, walking in long lines with hands interlinked, chanting shlokas officially intended to placate the Lord of the Forest, but also to warn away any lurking lions or other hungry predators. Once here, they stayed in solitary splendour for years, absorbed in their studies and oblivious to the outside world.

When on a summer's evening a visitor appeared, one could hardly blame the young brahmacharyas seated beneath the banyan trees for starting and exclaiming. Nor could one admonish the young brahmins for interrupting their sandhi recitations to run clamouring to their gurus to announce the arrival of a stranger. Even their gurus, those venerable ancient sages with admirable control of their emotions, could not conceal the surge of interest that lightened their faces as they turned towards the lone figure that had emerged from the shadowy pathway and was making his way steadfastly across the clearing. The visitor appeared to be carrying nothing but the copper lota that was the mark of a travelling brahmin, and a stout staff.

'That is no stranger,' said one particularly learned and widely-travelled guru as his sharp gaze observed the approaching visitor. 'It is none other than Ugrasrava, son of Lomarsana, known as Sauti to one and all. The name derives from the fact that he is the son of a Suta and therefore himself a Suta too. Who knows what that means?'

Everyone knew: a Suta was the son of a Kshatriya father and a Brahmin mother. The name was synonymous with the profession of Sarathi or charioteer, because most persons of the Suta gotra turned to the profession of charioteering. This prompted one of the lesser sparks among the brahmacharyas to exclaim aloud that if the visitor was a Suta, then where were his chariot and horses?

'Hidden in his lota!' cried one of his brighter companions, immediately ducking his bald pate in case the guru might smite it.

The guru did not smite him; he even permitted himself a ghost of a smile. For humour was not forbidden to brahmins, nor was the simple taking of pleasure in little everyday things. But Maharishi Gyanendra, for that was his name, did turn a stern face to the quick wit to warn the boy against passing further commentaries on a learned and respected visitor. The message successfully communicated and acknowledged by the boy's shamefaced grin, the guru continued: 'Some Sutas tend toward the profession of kusalavyas.' This too needed no explanation. Kusalavyas were bards, poets, storytellers, raconteurs, so named for their vast wanderings across fields of kusa and lava grass, which they used as sleeping pallets. The guru added: 'Ugrasrava Lomarsana is a kusalavya of such renown that even our kulapati honours him.'

At this the young acolytes oohed and aahed in chorus, for any visitor whom their own kulapati honoured must truly be a great personage.

'Will he recite a poem for us?' asked the excited students.

'A war poem!'

'A battle epic, with devas and asuras!'

'And dev astras deployed and maha-mantras!'

'And fantastical creatures and faraway lands!'

The guru laughed at the enthusiasm of his shishyas, his beard wagging. 'That is for him to choose if our kulapati deigns to ask,' he said.

His eyes twinkled as he looked at their shining hopeful faces. It was not often that a visitor came to remote Naimisha-sharanya, much less a great Suta and he well understood their eagerness. He shared it as well, for katha-vidya, life-lessons encoded in the form of parables, was the essence of all Vedic lore. In particular he hoped that the visitor would recite one special poem that was fabled among brahmins the world over and which was considered holier than the holy Vedas themselves. To hear the great epic Jaya told by a Suta of such prowess would truly be a blessing.

But first, the visitor would have to be received with due honour and ceremony as befitted a fellow brahmin of his stature. Already he could see that the Kulapati had been informed, judging by the movement among the rishis clustered around the centre of the ashram. That was where the great yagna was being performed. Except for a few dozen gurus such as himself who must need continue their education of their brahmacharya acolytes, the majority of Naimisha-sharanya's rishis, maharishis, sadhus and other brahmins were all engaged in the performance of the yagna.

As the visitor came closer, trailing hordes of curious and excited young acolytes in his wake, the guru saw that the Suta looked immensely weary and well-travelled. He was covered with fragments of leaves and dust and there were even wood chips stuck in his dhoti and in his matted hair. The guru sighed. Evidently Naimisha-van had attempted to thwart the pilgrim's progress. Even more evidently, the pilgrim had succeeded in pushing through. The Suta may be a charioteer only in name but he was no less adept at travelling in whichever direction he pleased. The guru permitted himself another faint wisp of a smile. He greatly wished to get to know this Sauti better now, and, if Brahma willed it, to hear the great epic from his own lips.

||Two||

Samantapanchaka.

A plain well chosen for battle. Vast, flat, desolate.

The ground firm beneath their feet, bleached clean by the northern sun, scoured by the wind until there was barely dust enough to blow in their eyes. No undulation broke its sullen monotony, no tree took root there, no hillocks or ravines impaired the horizon. Every inch was visible, every acre of hard-trodden soil naked beneath the searing northern sun, devoid of obstruction, concealment and diversion. A perfect container for the five lakes of blood spilled by Parashurama, from which it took its name. Parasu-Rama, literally Rama of the Axe, so named because as a brahmin boy who had witnessed atrocities committed by errant kshatriyas upon his own family, young Rama had taken up the axe he used for his wood-chopping chores and set out to seek and kill every kshatriya he found on earth. Twenty-one times he had cleansed the earthly plane of every last living kshatriya, warring with them en masse until this vast plain had been filled with five lakes of their blood. Finally, weary of slaughter, he had set down his parasu and retired to a life of meditative contemplation. And in time, the blood had soaked into the earth, leaving behind only this vast plain, burned sterile by the northern sun.

A plain where a senapati seated astride an elephant could view the lay of the land for yojanas in every direction; could shield his eyes from the slanting sunlight and easily view the dark, shuffling shape of the enemy body, armour and weaponry gleaming beneath the relentless sun; turn from the waist, lean back, and view even the farthermost extremities of his own forces.

It was a site perfectly suited to a great war. Vast enough to encompass two of the greatest armies ever assembled. Eighteen days they fought here. Till all but five were dead. Eighteen akshohinis of men and beasts. A number greater than any assemblage in the history of warfare, before or after. Brothers, clansmen, kinsmen, locked arms here in bloody civil strife. And the result was the end of an era, and of a dynasty.

The traveller stood and contemplated the horror of that conflict. Finally, he raised the hardy staff, gripping it with both hands, and began walking. He left a trail of triple prints in the fine dust of the plain that, in time, was erased by the gentle but incessant breeze that traversed the land, just as it had covered over countless trails before.

||Three||

The sun was still high by the time he reached the outskirts of Naimisha-van. He did not pause but plunged right in, and in an instant, his slender, gaunt form was no more than one of countless shadows within the embrace of a forest of shifting shapes.

An errant breeze curled around the traveller's neck, nuzzled him as tenderly as a gandharva's caress, and whispered sweet indecipherables in his right ear before flitting away coyly. He heard it rustling leaves and brushing past dense foliage as it danced wantonly through the deep forest. As it fled farther away, it reminded him, a lifelong sworn celibate, of the faint tinkling of silver anklet bells and the soft teasing laughter of a courtesan in a rajah's seraglio.

He shivered and glanced up. He was dwarfed by the boles of enormous trees, rising high above to form a dense canopy that blocked out the sky and shrouded the heart of the forest in perpetual twilight. Craning his neck, he could just spy the tips of the highest leaves glistening as they caught the occasional rays of the noonday sun. It was only a little past the noonday hour. But if he looked around him, he might well be deceived into believing that darkfall was imminent.

He hastened his steps, bare feet pressing steadily into the mulch and leaf-strewn forest floor where no human feet but his own had traversed for unknown ages. Something slithered through the undergrowth nearby, hissing sibilantly. He knew better than to slow his pace or turn his head. Eyes fixed resolutely ahead, he strode onwards. He did not think he had much farther to walk; he prayed he did not have much farther to walk.

He had walked unstintingly for days, stopping neither for food nor rest. Accustomed though he was to a rigorous pace, a life spent on the open road, the forest unnerved him. There were tales told of Naimisha-van. Rumours of strange inhabitants who resided within its shadowy depths. Not all were human, it was said. Not all were benign. There were tales of horror, wretched stories of hapless travellers who had spent the night within the vaulting embrace of these formidable boles, and had never been seen or heard from again.

He had always laughed off such tales, not being one to succumb to superstition or fireside entertainments, but it was one thing to laugh at a tale in the gaudy light of noonday, or even by the crackling heat of a fire with twenty companions beside you, and quite another thing to recall them when striding alone through the same darkling woods themselves. Especially when that darkness was not a natural one.

His face, pinched and terse with concentration, had no smile upon it now. All he cared about was reaching his destination before the day ended and real darkness descended completely and the forest swallowed him within its nocturnal embrace.

He shivered again as another gust of breeze whisked past him. This was not the playful caressing gust that had teased him moments earlier. This was a rough blow that shoved at the small of his back with the force of a man's hand, forcing him to open his mouth in a moue of surprise at its strength, then shook branches to rain down twigs and leaves upon his person, and then went on to raise dervishes of dust and debris on the forest floor, first to his left, then to the right, then straight ahead, in an almost sentient pattern. Abruptly, a pile of writhing leaves and dead branches rose up in a frenzy, whirled violently, and flew directly at him. It struck him with the force of a minor sandstorm, blinding his vision, enveloping him in a pillar of dust, leaves, rotting wood and mulch and something that reeked like the sour urine of some jungle predator.

He cried out in momentary confusion as the dervish assaulted him, its fury stinging his ears like the outrage of a cuckolded husband. Counterpointing its rage, the soft teasing tones of the earlier gust that had caressed him returned, whispering in nervous agitation. The voices rose and fell in debate.

A twig with a sharp point scratched his shoulder hard enough to nick and draw blood. And with that, he lost his patience.

|*Om Namay Shiva*|

he cried.

And invoked the name of the lord of the forest. Indeed, the lord of *all* forests, and all their denizens, living or otherwise, Pashupati himself, who of course was none other than Mahadeva in one of his infinite forms. He continued chanting invocations to Shiva in his various forms, amsas and avatars, ending with a japa recitation of a powerful mantra:

|*Hara Maheshwara Shulapani Pashupati Shiva Mahadeva*|

The birdsong and insect-noises that had been so shrilly loud only moments ago were instantly hushed. The breezes died away.

Unsupported by the dervishes, all the assorted debris—leaf fragments, dust, rotting wood—fluttered down to the forest floor to lie still. The light, so dim and murky, seemed to relent, growing a mite brighter—just a mite, but it was enough.

The forest waited; watching, listening.

He looked around, dusting himself off with brisk efficient movements, took up his staff, and, in the moment of still, waiting clarity, saw that he had been approaching his destination in an elliptical curve, taking far longer than was needed. A small ray of sunlight gleamed through the close-growing boles, marking the correct way he ought to go, and he smiled.

He reached the clearing only a short while later.

||Four||

Their eagerness was palpable through the arghya—the customary washing of the visitor's feet—and through the other necessary formal rituals of greeting and hospitality. At moments, he could almost read their well-contained curiosity in minute clues. But they were tapasvi sadhus, ascetics of the deep forest who had renounced all worldly cares, and they wore their patience well, their bearded, care-lined visages composed in the preternatural placidity that came from a lifetime of brahmanic contemplation.

They watched him patiently through his partaking of some welcome refreshment—simple ascetic food and plain water though it was, it seemed the best meal he had eaten in ages—and refrained from needless conversation.

But once he was done with the refreshments and the oblations, and the oil lamps were lit and the chores finally over for the day, they gathered around the fire built in the heart of the clearing. Aging rishis and munis, young acolytes and brahmacharyas, every last one of the denizens of this remote outpost of brahmanical learning and ascetism. Even a little fawn with an injured forelimb that seemed to have become an honorary member of the ashram. The warm rays of the setting sun bathed the clearing in luminescence.

They sat around in a circle, the firelight limning their bearded faces and hair piled in matted buns upon their heads, casting into sharp flickering relief their sage features, and as he warmed his tired limbs in the glow of the fire, he saw their gazes, turned inwards from decades of contemplation upon the mysteries of existence, grow bright and clear as chestnuts in fire, lit from within with the burning desire to learn. To *know*.

He saw the young acolytes with their chottis wagging as they turned their heads, some barely out of boyhood, their smooth unlined cheeks shining ruddily in the fire's glow, eyes round and innocent as the eyes of the tame fawn that sat docilely by their side, chewing on a stalk of kusa grass, watching him with large, wet, innocent, doe-eyes. They could scarcely contain their eagerness for their elders to broach the question that was on every tonguetip. Formal matters all discussed, conversation ceased eventually. The silence grew, filling the sunset hour, making every shifting of a dry log within the fire and every insect call or cricket chirring or whipoorwill's note seem preternaturally loud, as if the denizens of the wood were gathered around the clearing as well, watching and listening from the deep shadows of the jungle, waiting, as the rishis and munis and acolytes waited . . .

Kulapati Shaunaka spoke at last, his voice smoothened by some fourscore years of daily rote recitation into a gentle tenor.

'What of the Dark Islander?' he asked simply.

Dark Islander.

Krishna, meaning dark-skinned. *Dweipayana*, meaning Island-born. Hence the descriptor, Dark Islander. Add the family name Vyasa at the end and there you had it. Krishna Dweipayana Vyasa. 'I bring you the news that he has surrendered this mortal form and transcended to the next life,' Sauti replied, keeping his voice level and reverential, to convey his sadness yet without exhibiting a mite more emotion than was necessary. For here in the extremes of civilization, they followed the old ways. News of a death was to be stated in a particular fashion. Sanskrit was a precise, poetic language. Within its paradoxically simple yet complex grammar, there were no movements that were not dance, no phrasing that was not lyrical. All was precise and aesthetically balanced, beauty and precision perfectly entwined.

They took the news equitably. None had known the ancient sage closely, though, like any seeker of knowledge in the present era, they had all lived in the shadow of his immense achievements and body of work. What Sauti saw now upon their faces was not sadness, regret or pain; it was simple reverence. They spoke for several moments more about the great one, and those who had known others who had encountered him spoke of those incidents and memories. Sauti listened without commenting, for he knew this was their humble way of showing their respect for the great departed.

Finally, the question he had been waiting for—they had *all* been waiting for—arrived. It was spoken by Maharishi Gyanendra. The old sage seemed no less eager than his gathering of fresh-faced bald-pated brahmacharyas. 'We hear you were present at the sarpa sacrifice of Maharaja Janamajaya,' he said. 'That you were one of those privileged to hear the recitation of the great itihasa from the lips of the great one and his disciple Vaisampayana themselves.'

He nodded. 'And from the lips of Krishna Dweipayana himself. 'For despite the overall perfection of their rescencions, the master would often correct the disciples when they strayed, however minutely, from the body of the narrative, and bring them back upon the correct path. Indeed, there were times when he himself ventured to recite whole portions of the work, primarily the core poem he once called Jaya.'

At this revelation, the eyes of the brahmacharya acolytes grew so large and round that the firelight reflected in them caused them to glow like fireflies. Even the rishis forgot themselves and blurted out stammeringly: 'Vyasaji himself recited portions of the epic? In your presence?' They added reverentially, 'Gurudev?'

'He did,' Sauti replied calmly. 'And it was an experience like none other. His voice, ancient and cracked with age and with the burden of over a century of harsh ascetic living . . . although, I have heard it said after his demise that he lived a millenium *and* a century . . . his voice was rich and febrile, as eloquent as the Ganga roaring in spate herself, as clear and pristine in its enunciations as the Gangotri emerging from its secret cranny in the high Himalayan glaciers, and as headlong in its profligacy as the river when it tumbles down the great ranges to crash upon the foothills of the northern plains. Such was the power of his recitation that at times, they say, the devas themselves came by to listen, planets slowed in their courses, suns paused in their burning, and comets hung motionless to listen.'

There was silence in the wake of this description. Awed, adulatory glances. They were seated in the presence of one who had heard the recitations of the great Ved Vyasa himself! For that was how Krishna Dweipayana had come to be known, for his gargantuan achievement in compiling the Vedas, the secret repository of all the sacred knowledge of the Bharata race since time immemorial, collected into four volumes of immeasurable worth. Ved Vyasa.

Finally, he himself volunteered the information he could see they all hungered for, yet hesitated to ask openly. 'And I had the pleasure of hearing him recite his greatest work of all, the great poem that is his life's supreme achievement.'

'The *Bharata*!' said Maharishi Gyananendra.

Kulapati Shaunaka softly muttered 'Sadhu! Sadhu!' to emphasize the auspiciousness of the great epic.

Sauti inclined his head. 'The *Bharata* itself. Although, it has since grown into a far greater epic than even the great Vyasji envisioned.'

'How so?' the rapt expression on the faces of the aging rishis and smooth-skinned acolytes was so similar, they might all have been siblings in that moment of shared curiosity.

Sauti explained. 'The original poem he composed was some 8,800 shlokas. In that form, it was known simply as *Jaya*, which aptly suited its contents, covering the history of the war between the two factions of the Kuru family as it did then. However, over repeated retellings, he himself expanded it to a larger work numbering 24,000 shlokas, which he then renamed *Bharata*, for it was no less than the history of the Bharata race itself, and while the great war was the central matter, it was preceded and afterceded by several other narrations as well. But today, after the great retelling consuming twelve years of the sarpa sacrificial ritual of Raja Janamajaya, it has burgeoned to the mammoth size of a hundred thousand shlokas. In this epic form, the poem is now known by one and all as *Maha-bharata*. Or the Great History of The Bharatas. And it is by this name that Vyasa has consented to have it known, although he himself preferred the original title of *Jaya*.'

The fire crackled greedily, chewing upon a new log. A consumed length of wood, eaten in the centre, collapsed upon itself, sending up a shower of sparks that rose high into the air, like a cloud of fireflies rising up to join their remote siblings, the stars themselves, starting to glimmer here and there on the grey canvas of the dusky sky. For a moment, the entire assemblage was illuminated richly, and so were the environs immediately surrounding the clearing. Sauti's eyes blinked as he glimpsed—or thought he glimpsed—forms, shapes, silhouettes, wisps and shadows, clustered thickly in the dense woods, like an army of watching, listening hordes gathered around in the shadowy depths. Then the cloud of sparks diminished and dissipated and he could spy only his immediate environs, the gleaming faces of his brahmanical companions. He sighed softly. What had he thought he had seen? The spirits of the dead, gathering around to hear their own history? The legends of the Naimisha-van claimed that the souls of those killed in the great Kurukshetra war came here to reside, to find solace for and understanding of the events that led to their demise. Could it be that by listening to the history composed by the sage Vyasa they might finally find that solace? He shrugged off these errant thoughts with an effort. Surely he was letting his imagination run riot.

And yet, why else had he felt compelled to come directly here from Janamajaya's sarpa ceremony if not to start his avowed mission of retelling the epic poem to all those who would listen? For that had been Mahaguru Vyasa's last wish, that this immense compendium of knowledge and narration be passed on to as many as possible across the civilized world, that all might know how the greatest war of all had come to pass, and might be warned against future wars waged against their own neighbours and brothers. For that was the only purpose of a tale of war: to ensure that, by hearing of the horrors and heartbreaks of that most awful of human endeavours, future generations may be persuaded against attempting it themselves. And what better place in which to start the cycle of narration than in the heart of this war-haunted wood where so many had lost their lives. Yes, perhaps the souls of the dead would gather round to listen, and in listening, find the peace that had eluded them for so long. He could sense their uneasy energies as they crowded the darkness at the fringe of the firelight's circle, murmuring restlessly in the back of his mind.

He addressed his next words not only to the sages and acolytes seated before him, but to the forest at large.

'Will you hear the tale?' he asked. 'The song which the great preceptor called Jaya, and which I have come to refer to as The Great Bharata epic? Before you answer, I must inform you: It is a compendious work, massive in scope, unrivalled in ambition, and unequalled in length. Not till the end of mankind's days upon this earth in this cycle of the Ages will this work be rivalled. No person hearing it and imbibing its virtues will ever be found wanting in spiritual prowess. While it is called the Fifth Veda, it is at once equivalent to *all* the Vedas. Indeed, it is an education in itself.'

He paused, locking eyes with each one of his listeners in turn, ensuring that they understood the pact they were about to make. 'To begin *The Mahabharata* is to pledge fealty to it to the very end. This is a task that once begun, ought not to be left unfinished. Such is the pact I must demand of each one of you before I begin. Let me also tell you that it took my esteemed colleague Vaisampayana and Mahagura Vyasji twelve long years to recite it in its entirety to Maharaja Janmajeya. No doubt that was often interrupted by the necessary daily duties of running a kingdom as well as the rituals of the sarpa sacrifice itself, not to mention countless other minor or major distractions. I do not know how long it shall take me to repeat it here, and can only pledge that, once begun, I will not brook even a fragment of a part remaining untold. It is my sworn vrata, my sacred vow taken at Ved Vyasa's samadhi itself, that I would recite only the full, unabridged tale in its entirety. If you would hear it told thusly, I shall be greatly desirous of reciting it. Tell me, does it please you to have me do so?'

The answer to his query came not only from the lips of the mortal listeners seated before him, but, it seemed, also from the forest itself. The excited but soft acquiescence was echoed by a fervent sibilance from the darkness bounding their circle of light.

'Yes,' the entire ashram of brahmans said, resoundingly, without an instant's hesitation.

'Yesssss . . .' the forest seemed to echo, the sound carrying round and round until whirled by the wind to fill the entire forest itself, reverberating deep within those murky woods.

Sauti resisted the urge to shiver despite the warmth of the log fire.

'So,' he said, 'It is decided. It is given unto me, Ugrasrava Lomharsana Sauti, to deliver unto you this vast assemblage of itihasa. Know ye that this vast work is as infinite as human history itself, for it *is* in fact human history in its entirety. What is not within it is to be found nowhere else. And all that is elsewhere is here.

'Let us then begin by invoking the sacred name of Ganesha, Lord of Beginnings and Scribes, and Remover of Obstacles.'

And without further ado, he said simply:

'Here is the tale known now as *Mahabharata*.'

||Paksha Two||

THE BOOK OF CREATION

||One||

In the beginning all was darkness.

Light itself did not exist, not a single ray was visible on any side.

From the darkness emerged a Great Egg.

Resplendent.

Brilliant.

Indescribable.

This was the Seed of all Creation at the beginning of all Yugas. The inexhaustible Brahman, upon which all things rest, the fount of all worlds, basis of all matter, eternal, true and beautiful beyond description.

In perfect balance, carrying the inscrutable laws that govern all existence, it was the most perfect manifestation of purest energy.

That which is and is not.

Paramatman.

From this great Egg of Brahman was born the only true Creator, the sole Lord Prajapati, Brahma Suraguru—Preceptor of the dynasty of the Suras, whom you know now as Devas, the race of the Gods—therefore Guru to the Gods themselves, also known as Sthanu Manu: the primordial Man, Ka, and Parmesthin.

From Brahma the Creator sprang Daksha, son of Prachetas. Then Daksha's seven sons.

Then the twenty-one prajapatis, lords of creation.

There also came the Maha Aatma. That Being of immeasurable soul whom all the seers and sages know, whose depths can never be fathomed and whose infinite bounds remain beyond the measure of mortal minds, and who is to us mere mortals the Universe eternally expanding.

Then were birthed the Vishwa Devas, the Adityas, the Vasus and the Ashwins.

Also the Yakshas, Saddhyas, Pisacas, Guhyakas and the Pitris, our forefathers.

After them came the wise and learned Brahmarishis. Brahmins who spread knowledge and praise of the eternal force Brahman and almighty Brahma.

Then came the Rajarishis, royal seers of Kshatriya birth who acquired knowledge of all-pervasive Brahman through their diligent study and are living proof of the ability to transcend one's mortal station through acquisition of knowledge.

The primordial elements were created: Water, Heaven, Earth, Wind, Sky, the cardinal and lesser directions and the earthly forces that govern them, the years, seasons, months, fortnights, and days and nights in turn, and all else that was witnessed by the world.

As it was in the Beginning, so shall it be at the End.

All that now exists, movable and immovable, shall be drawn together again at the end of Existence, when the decay of Entropy overcomes all.

As one season begins and ends, thus at the beginning of each era, all is destroyed and created again anew.

Thus the Great Wheel of Existence turns endlessly as it has always turned without any beginning to its motion, bringing about the ceaseless cycle of Creation and Destruction.

This is the sum of all Creation: Thirty-three thousand, thirty-three hundred and thirty-three gods were created: 33,333.

Here is their accounting in summary:

From the son of the sky, the great Surya, Vivasvat, source of the eye's light, the resplendent one, came many sons who are themselves no less than the sun himself: their names are Savita, Richika, Brihadbhanu, Chakshus, Atma, Vibhavasu, Arka, Ashavaha—Bringer of Hope, Ravi, and Mahya. Of these, Mahya was the youngest son and his son was Devabhrata—He Who Shone Like a God, hence also known as Subhraja, the Shining One. Subhraja had three sons who gained great fame in their time, named Dashajyoti, Shatajyoti and Sahasrajyoti, each of whom gave birth to great numbers of offspring. Great-spirited Dasajyoti had ten thousand sons. Self-possessed Shatajyoti fathered ten times ten thousand sons. And Sahasrajyoti had ten times that number.

From them were descended the dynasties of the Kurus, the Yadus, the Bharatas, Yayati, Ikshwaku and all the Rajarishis. Many other lineages were also birthed as well as diverse living beings in abundant diversity, each a house unto themselves.

Then were born the three mysteries of knowledge: Veda, Yoga and Vignyana.

Veda is the coded repository of all knowledge gleaned through direct and indirect means.

Yoga is the communion between our mortal souls and the Paramatman Brahman.

Vignyana is knowledge gained through self-realization.

Then was created the threefold path: Dharma, Artha and Kama.

These are set out in various shastras that explain the application of the principles of Dharma, Artha and Kama to provide a code of conduct for worldly affairs.

And the Puranas, the ancient itihasa with their nirukta, their commentaries and the shruti, texts of secret revelations.

All this immeasurable wealth of knowledge is contained here, within this great epic itihasa named *Mahabharata.*

The sage Krishna Dweipayana-Vyasa has distilled all this knowledge, and made a summary and index of it all, for the convenience of those who wish to memorize its salient features, as well as the unabridged exposition for those who desire to imbibe the whole rich erudition.

After immense penance and austerities, the son of Satyavati divided the eternal Veda into four distinct parts. For this epic endeavour he is known as Ved Vyasa, Classifier of the Vedas. Once this was accomplished, he then set out to compose this holy history. Rising every morning for three years, he wrote daily until it was complete and in the form we now possess. Most remarkable of all is the author's own role within the great epic. The learned brahmarishi, son of Parashar, at the behest of his mother Satyavati, matriarch of the Kuru dynasty, and her stepson Bhishma, son of Ganga, acting under law, ploughed the field of Vichitravirya to reap the heirs of the Kurus—to put it another way, he sired three sons by the wives of Vichitravirya.

These three Kurus were Dhritarashtra, Pandu and Vidura. They blazed with the heat of three fires.

His part accomplished, the great sage Krishna Dweipayana retired to his ashram to continue his life of austere existence. Only after the three sons sired by him were birthed, grew to adulthood, lived out their lives and eventually departed on their last journey, did the great seer unveil *The Bharata* to the world of mortals.

It was at the bidding of King Janamajaya and thousands of

brahmins attending the twelve-year course of the sarpa-yagna that the great seer recited this composition for the first time. His shishya Vaisampayana was present at the sacrifice and from time to time, he took up the narrative at his guru's urging. Thus, both master and pupil recited in turns. Vyasa faithfully recited the genealogy of the Kurus in detail, the dharmic virtues of Gandhari, the sagacity of Vidura and the equanimity of Kunti. The blessed sage also extolled the magnanimity of Krishna Vasudeva, the trustworthiness of the Pandavas, the unscrupulous acts of the Kauravas—Vyasa said it all.

First, he composed his poem in twenty-four thousand shlokas, without the minor narratives. This core work he called *The Bharata*. It is the heart of the epic. He then summarized and indexed all the events, contents and individual parvas in one hundred and fifty shlokas. He taught this index first to his own son Suka, later passing it on to other shishyas he deemed fit for the task. Sage Narada recited it to the Devas, the sages Asita-Devala to the elders, the pitris and Suka to the gandharvas, yakshas and rakshasas.

Let me now describe the primary characters of this wondrous epic with an analogy. This great Bharata itihasa is as a tree of history to future generations who shall be the inheritors of its plentitude:

To the Kauravas, Duryodhana was the passionate tree itself, Karna its trunk, Sakuni the branches, Duhshashana its abundant fruit and blossoms, the blind king Dhritarashtra its root.

To the Pandavas, Yudhishtira was the tree of dharma, Arjuna its trunk, Bhima its branches, Nakula-Sahadeva its plentiful blossoms and fruits, Brahma and the brahmin race its root.

Now let me summarize the central events of *The Bharata* proper, the original tree from which spread the forest of stories that is now the epic *Mahabharata*:

After a lifetime of war and conquest, Pandu retired to the forest with his wives, intending to live amongst the rishis of the woods, spending the rest of his days in the pursuit of his favourite pastime, the hunt. This very passion became his undoing when he cruelly killed a stag while it was in the act of mounting its mate. Cursed by the hapless doe, Pandu was forbidden to perform the conjugal act himself on pain of death. Resorting to boons from the devas and in keeping with the law, his wives Kunti and Madri conceived sons from the gods Dharma, Vayu, Indra, and the twin Ashwins. Raised by their mothers and the holy sages of the forest, the five sons of Pandu grew to manhood. While they were still brahmacharyas with tufted hair, the rishis decided of their own accord to take them to Dhritarashtra and introduced them as 'the sons of Pandu, your sons, brothers, acolytes and friends'. Whereupon the sages of the forest vanished. On seeing the five Pandavas, an excited outcry rose from the assembled people of Hastinapura. Some insisted that these could not possibly be sons of Pandu since Pandu had long since been dead and had produced no offspring. Others insisted they were and must be welcomed with due ceremony. Voices were heard across the city, clamouring loudly as the Pandavas entered the city. An enormous rejoicing arose, not just from the people of the city but from invisible multitudes, raising their voices in a tumultuous explosion of sound. Flowers showered down from the skies, delicious fragrances filled the air, and the auspicious music of conchshells and kettledrums sounded from all four directions. The controversy over their parentage was drowned out in the hue and cry as the people rose up to welcome the Pandavas whose fame spread rapidly and widely.

From that day on, the Pandavas lived at Hastinapura without

threat from anywhere or anyone, continuing their studies of the holy Vedas and other shastras. They were honoured, respected and loved by all. The dharmic strength of Yudhishtira, the resoluteness of Bhima, the bravery of Arjuna, the discipline of the twins and Kunti's immaculate behaviour toward her elders grew famous throughout the known world. Years passed.

At the swayamvara of a princess who shared the same birth name—Krishna—for she was as beautifully dark-skinned as he, Arjuna performed a gigantic feat to best all challengers and was chosen by her as husband. That day he won a name for himself as a great archer, a reputation he would uphold and enhance over time as he conquered every king and champion who challenged him, and became as difficult to face in the battlefield as the sun in his domain. Thus did he pave the way for his elder brother Yudhishtira to perform the Rajasuya sacrifice and lay claim to declare himself monarch of the known world. On the advice of Vasudeva Krishna and flanked by the strength and valour of his brothers Bhima and Arjuna, Yudhishtira then went forth and slew Jarasandha and the prideful Sisupala, king of Chedi, thus earning the right to initiate the Rajasuya and reap a rich reward of treasure. When his stepbrother Duryodhana attended the sacrifice and saw the immense wealth the Pandavas had acquired—the sacrificial offerings, the rich bounty of victory, precious gems, gold, jewels, cows, elephants, and untold treasure, a mighty anger born of envy rose within him. When he saw the magnificent Sabha Hall designed to resemble a gargantuan celestial chariot by the brilliant Maya, architect to the gods, Duryodhana's jealousy knew no bounds. Even as he seethed and fumed, he stumbled due to his ill-contained emotions and at the sight of his pratfalls, Vasudeva Krishna and Bhima laughed and mocked him as being one of common birth.

It came to Dhritarashtra's ears that his eldest son and heir had turned wan and yellow and was wasting away. Out of fatherly concern for his son's well-being, the blind king granted Duryodhana his wish to enter into a gambling match with the Pandavas. When Vasudeva Krishna came to hear of this, he grew angry. But despite his displeasure, he did nothing to halt the fatal game and looked on as a succession of unjust and undesirable events transpired, even as the quarrel between the Pandavas and Kauravas escalated into a full-blown conflict. Indeed, despite the best efforts of Vidura, Bhishma, Drona and Kripa to play the part of peacemakers, it was Vasudeva Krishna himself who was solely responsible for encouraging the two halves of the Kuru dynasty to slaughter one another in the great war that ensued.

Later when he received the news that the last of his sons had perished and the war was ended, at terrible cost to the Kuru race, Dhritarashtra poured out his heart in a long tormented lament to Sanjaya, son of Gavalgana, and expressed his desire to give up his life at once. Then did Sanjaya console him with wise and significant words.

Krishna Dweipayana has composed a work that is no less than a holy Upanishad. Those who acquire knowledge of even a single line of a single shloka of *The Bharata* epic are absolved of all sins. Here are extolled the performers of great deeds, the devas, the deva-rishis or divine seers, the brahamarishis and the rajarishis, one and all, as also the Yakshas and great Nagas. The Eternal One, Vasudeva Krishna, is lauded here as well, for he is the amaranthine everlasting truth, the essence of dharma personified, and the immortal light. He is the boundless fount of Brahman, wellspring of all that is and is not, that which shall continue unto infinity as well as the unstoppable force of entropy, the Beginning and the End of all things. In this itihasa is described the sacred spirit who embodies the five elements of earth, water, energy, wind and sky, the three qualities of sattva, rajas and tamas, and who transcends the very idea of that which is manifest and who can never be described as un-manifest. The reader who follows the path of dharma without wavering and reads this work shall be eternally blessed. The true believer who reads this first chapter of the *Bharata* from the very beginning shall never suffer from obstacles. Anyone who reads any part of this introductory chapter at the time of sandhyavandana in the morning or evening shall be cleansed of any sin acquired the preceding night or day. As butter is the cream of the curd, as the cow is the choicest of four-footed beings and brahmins are the best of two-footed beings, and as the ocean is the greatest of all bodies of water, thus in the *Bharata*, this introductory chapter is like the cream, the truth and the ambrosial amrit. He who offers a brahmin a single shloka of this great work at a funeral ceremony shall find his offerings of food and drink to the ancestors multiplied infinitely. It is said that the Vedas should be complemented by a thorough study of the Puranas and the two Itihasas. But the Vedas are wary of those of little knowledge, lest that knowledge be flawed. But this Veda composed by Krishna Dweipayana, once read by a person of learning, shall lead to infinite gain. Even the ultimate sin of killing an embryo within the womb can be nullified by reading this work. A pure person who reads this chapter sincerely at the turn of every moon phase will acquire the auspicious worth of having read the epic entire. That person who reads it daily shall attain long life, fame, and entrance to heavenly realms. In eons past, the devas and rishis once placed the four Vedas on one side of a scale and the

Bharata on the other side. The *Bharata* proved heavier. For it is superior in substance and content and thus came to be known as *Maha-Bharata*. You who persist and understand its true meaning shall be freed of sin forever. The froth of tapasya, the froth of rote-learning, the sacred laws of the Vedas, these are not sins. They only become sins when abused.

||Paksha Three||

THE TALE OF PARASHURAMA

||One||

The fire burned high, sending out eruptions of sparks and soot from time to time as logs settled. Dusk had succumbed to nightfall and the dark of the jungle had emerged and enshrouded the clearing. The eyes of the rapt ashramites of Naimisha-sharanya glittered and gleamed for dozens of yards beyond the spilled circle of firelight. Ugrasasrava could not see the end of their numbers. Had there been so many when he began speaking? Had their numbers swelled as other ashramites joined them? Surely they had waited until everyone was seated before urging him to begin. Yes, he was quite certain of that. Yet there were many more present here now than there had been at the outset of his preamble. He dismissed these thoughts firmly; it was the firelight and the woods, playing tricks on his eyes.

'O, Son of a Suta,' said Kulapati Shaunaka warmly, his voice and lined face revealing his great respect for the teller of the Bharata epic. 'Pardon my interruption. I see that you are at a natural pause in your great narration. Thank you for that accounting of the Creation of the world as well as the epic of Vyasa. Now, pray, tell us of the place Samantapanchaka from whence you came. It is a most holy region and as such it bears great value for us. In particular our younger brahmacharyas would benefit greatly from your narration of its history and the reason for its fame.'

Ugrasrava was about to answer when a young acolyte raised his hand, apparently asking to be heard. Maharishi Gyanendra who was seated nearest to the boy, looked taken aback and admonished him firmly: 'Shishya, it is not your place to speak at this forum. Your job is merely to listen. Leave the queries and discussions to us elders.'

Ugrasrava smiled and said to the head of the ashram: 'Kulapati, if I may take a moment before responding to your request.' When Shaunaka nodded readily, Sauti turned to Maharishi Gyanendra, 'Gurudev, forgive me as I do not mean to hinder the immaculate education of your shishyas, but I would hear what the young man has to say, if you permit it.'

Gyanendra frowned at the offending brahmacharya but nodded curtly.

The boy spoke up in a surprisingly quiet and calm tone, betraying none of the breathless excitement Sauti had expected. 'Mahadev, I only wished to say that we are all aware of the reason for Samantapanchaka's fame. It is on account of the very Maha Bharata battle that occurred there, whose history you are about to recite to us.'

Sauti shook his head. 'You are incorrect, young man.'

He saw the young acolyte's face fall and kept his voice soft rather than admonishing: 'It is true that Kurukshetra as a whole is famous for being the battlefield where the Kuru war took place. It is also true that Samantapanchaka is a part of that vast rolling plain where the most terrible battle in human history was fought and more lives were violently ended than in any other conflict of disaster since the beginning of creation. But a part is not the same as the whole and thus Samantapanchaka is renowned for a reason far greater and older than even the Maha Bharata war. Indeed, it is a holy place and its history plays an important part in your own presence here—as also the presence of everyone of us. For it is the story of the near-extinction and brave survival of the Bhrigu race and where would all brahmins be today had the Bhrigus not survived?'

Sauti bowed his head respectfully in the direction of Shaunaka. 'Kulapati Shaunaka in his infinite wisdom has requested me to narrate that very tale, and this young man has unwittingly proven that every young shishya must hear the same story as well, in order to understand the history of his people.'

He smiled one final time at the young brahmacharya who looked chastened and contrite now: 'Lack of knowledge is a temporary ailment easily remedied; it is only when it is not remedied that it becomes a permanent condition. Listen carefully, along with your fellow brahmacharyas, to one of the seminal tales of our itihasa.

'Once, when the world was still young and the race of men only recently civilized, a conflict raged between those who believed in the power of the word and those who ruled by the sword. Most men acknowledged those among them who had curated the collected knowledge of generations as being men of superior learning and wisdom. Many even desired to ascend to that level and become men of knowledge themselves, joining ashrams and becoming brahmacharyas as so many of you did. But some among them would not set down their swords and believed only in a life of violent oppression. These few ruled by fear and intimidation and the indiscriminate use of weaponry. In time, their numbers swelled and they became a force to fear. They slaughtered brahmins only because they were *brahmin*, regarding them as symbols of the word and therefore to be hated and killed whenever possible. They forbade their fellow warriors from following the path of knowledge, killing even their fellow kshatriyas when they would not do as they bid.

'This was not a conflict of kshatriyas and brahmins alone: for many kshatriya clans and lines were wise enough to understand the superiority of the word over the sword, of knowledge over weaponry, of wisdom over war. They knew that while the brahmin varna protected, preserved and accreted the store of human knowledge, they were brahmin not merely because of an accident of birth but by dint of their rigorous education and dedication to knowledge. Many such enlightened kshatriyas sent their own children to follow the path of knowledge, seeking to end the ceaseless wars and conflicts that plagued humankind. But a few kshatriya lines lived in perpetual hatred of all things brahminical and regarded knowledge and learning as their enemy. In time, these kshatriyas grew isolated and in conflict with their own fellow kshatriyas as well as with all brahmins. They were led by one kshatriya line in particular, the Haihayas, whose king was Arjuna Kartavirya and who swept across the world as a pestilence across the population.

'Among brahmins, few were as enlightened or as masterful in their accumulation of knowledge as those of the Bhrigu clan. This is a tale of their forebear who lived in the time of Arjuna Kartavirya, the Bhrigu sage Jamadagni, and his fifth son, Jamadagneya, better known to itihasa by another, more fearsome name . . .'

||Two||

The great sage Jamadagni was absorbed in his meditation when the calm of his ashram was disturbed by the thunder of a thousand hooves. Frowning at being disturbed from his tapasya, he rose and went to see why mounted men had come to this remote place. His wife Renuka was hurrying back from the river, bearing a heavy earthen pot filled with fresh water. Her face glowed with excitement.

'It must be my father,' she said to her husband as she approached the stoop of their thatched hut where he stood. 'Or at the very least my mother come to visit me! Only a king or queen would travel with so many mounted men.'

She set the pot of water down on the stoop, spilling some. He noticed that the pot was barely half full and a trail of splotches marked her route across the clearing. He did not comment on it. He already knew that to his wife, a visit from her family far outweighed the daily drudgery of her domestic chores. Not for the first time, he wondered if he had indeed done the right thing by marrying a kshatriya woman and bringing her away from her palatial city life to spend her life as a hermit's spouse.

Yet there was great love between them, he knew, and he sensed it even now as she clutched his hand and tentatively squeezed it, conveying her happiness as the sound of hoofbeats grew closer. It was true that as a daughter of the Suryavanshi Ikshwaku dynasty, she could not help displaying strong emotions or desiring the hustle and bustle of her former life, but it was his arm she squeezed in excitement and to him that she turned her smiling face to share her joy. He smiled and patted her hand.

Jamadagni looked around for his sons. She noticed him looking and said, 'Vasu and Vishwasvasu are collecting herbs and fruit for our meal. Sushena and Rumanvanta have gone to fetch firewood. Parashurama is gone to his guru to study.'

He nodded and thought to correct her. After all, their eldest son's given birth name was Rama, a simple and beautiful name on its own, and one often favoured by her lineage. But ever since that axe—*parasu*, in Sanskrit—had been bequeathed to him by his guru Shiva, he carried it everywhere he went, even to the river when he bathed, so much so that everyone had taken to calling him Parasu-Rama, Rama of the Axe. Or colloquially, Parashurama. Not a very appropriate name to call a brahmin.

But he decided to say nothing. People who came to be known by their most distinguishing characteristic were people to whom fame came naturally. There was little point in objecting to something that was natural. Besides, there was no doubt that Parashurama took after his kshatriya mother far more than his brahmin father. It was the reason why he had been gifted the axe by his guru, none other than Shiva the Destroyer himself.

The thundering swelled to a deafening pitch then broke into a ragged explosion of beats as the clearing filled with mounted armed riders. The frontrunners drew up their mounts at the sight of the ashram hut and the seer and his wife standing before it, but their faces remained hawkish and their weapons stayed in hand. The dust raised by their arrival clouded the air for several moments, even as the thundering of hooves dwindled and finally died away. Even before the dust could settle, a trio of tall hard-faced kshatriyas dismounted and strode towards the hut, swords in hand.

'Who lives here?' one asked, raising his sword insolently to point at Jamadagni. One of his companions turned his head, hawked and spat a gob of phlegm. Jamadagni resisted the urge to ask the man if he would spit thus in his own house but held his tongue. Judging by the loutish appearance of these men, it was possible they thought nothing of spitting or worse even in their own house. Palace, more likely. For the three of them were clad in richly-filigreed armour and finely made garb beneath the armour. Even their swords had icons on their hilts. And even through the settling dust he could see the coloured dhvaja on the pole of their flagbearer.

Kshatriyas. Brothers. Princes. And if I am not mistaken, that is the symbol of the Haihaya line. Jamadagni knew at once that if he did not carefully heed everything he said or did from this moment on, his wife and he would be slaughtered without a second's hesitation. And if these men were to learn that his wife was of the Suryavansha Ikshwaku line, even their sons would not be spared. A brahmin had no cause to have enemies, being a person of Vedic study and peaceful meditation. But these kshatriyas were no less than mortal enemies to Jamadagni.

'My wife and I,' he replied.

The sword remained in the air, its pointed tip aimed at his throat. Jamadagni glimpsed the sword-bearer's brothers looking at Renuka with more than casual interest and suppressed the surge of anger that rose in his gullet.

Finally, the sword dipped and the kshatriya turned away rudely, showing Jamadagni his back. 'Only an old brahmin's hovel,' he said to someone beyond Jamadagni's field of vision.

The person spoken to came walking slowly into view, an attendant brushing the dust from his rich anga-vastra and armour with a peacock-feather duster. Another attendant followed close behind in perfect step with his master, holding up an umbrella palkhi with the distinctive coloured fabric and embroidered sigil of a royal seal that left no doubt about this stranger's title and position. The man himself was exceedingly tall, powerfully built, and moved with the lithe grace of a predator. He was perhaps a decade and a half older than the three loutish kshatriyas before him and clearly their forebear. They all shared his hawkish features and cream-wheat complexion, and most of all, they all moved and spoke with a similar arrogant sense of entitlement.

Jamadagni realized with a shock that he knew exactly who this personage was—there was no disputing it. *Arjuna himself, King of the Haihayas! At my ashram! Great and merciful Brahma, why do you bring me this test of my resolve and endanger the lives of my loved ones?*

King Arjuna Kartavirya, son of Kritavirya, glanced at the thatched hut, passing his gaze condescendingly over both Jamadagni and Renuka, seeming to find nothing of the slightest interest in anything he saw.

He pointed his chin toward Jamadagni. One of his sons immediately spoke on his behalf. 'Brahmin, we seek rebels fighting for Sagara. Have any come past?'

Jamadagni bowed his head. 'My Lord, we have seen not a single other person in this remote aranya for months.'

King Arjuna Kartavirya glanced at him, seemed to find no reason to contradict his claim, and gestured with his eyebrows at his son.

'We are in pursuit of a band of warriors loyal to Sagara, son of Bahu. Have you heard or seen any such forces moving through this part of the forest in the past three days?'

Jamadagni shook his head. 'Nay, my Lord. It is as we said. The forest is quiet and undisturbed. These warriors you speak of have not passed this way.'

One of the other princes spoke up—the one who had pointed his sword at Jamadagni. 'Bear in mind that allies of the Suryavansha Ikshwaku dynasty are enemies of the Haihayas. This is King Arjuna Kartavirya of Mahishmati, our father. He defeated the Naga army of Karkotaka Naga most recently, but ten years ago, he sacked Kashi when it was under the reign of King Haryaswa and later King Sudeva, both of whom attempted to oppose him and were killed. He also fought and killed King Divodas of the Vatsa, and defeated his son Pratardana who still seeks to regain the Vatsa kingdom. In addition, he deposed King Bahu of the Ikshwaku and claimed Ayodhya as well. Since you are brahmins and no doubt unaware of the lineages of raj-kshatriyas, I shall enlighten you. All these kings my father opposed were of the Suryavansha dynasty, the solar line. He, as well as all of us, are of the Chandravansha dynasty, the lunar line. Our allies in battle are the Talajangha kshatriyas and we are supported by the Panchagana, the five armies of the Shakas, Yavanas, Kambojas, Pahlavas and Paradas. We are indomitable and cannot be confronted in battle. We will rule the entire world soon. It is futile to oppose us.'

Yet Bahu, son of Sagara, does oppose you. And soon he will defeat your great Panchagana and take back control of Ayodhya, seat of the Suryavansha Ikshwaku line. In fact, he must be near victory for King Arjuna Kartavirya and his heirs to be chasing him through the forest on their own with such desperation. You may posture and preen as much as you please, but the circumstances belie your words.

Jamadagni dared not say any of this aloud. For not only would it give these ruthless Haihayas an excuse to cut him and Renuka down on the spot, it might lead to their learning that Renuka herself was a princess of the Suryavansha Ikshwaku line, their sworn enemy.

As if sensing his thoughts, Renuka turned her head in Jamadagni's direction. He shook his head very slightly, just enough to indicate to her that she should remain silent. She did.

One of the other princes, the one who had spat so brazenly, asked in a peevish tone: 'Brahmins, have you any food? King Arjuna Kartavirya requires nourishment.'

Jamadagni bowed his head again. 'We are poor brahmins. We have no possessions or wealth. Our repast is simple herbs and roots from the forest. It is not fit for a king, or even any kshatriya.'

The princes looked at their father.

He shook his head with a derisive expression on his face.

The prince who had spoken before said, 'Then go back to your chanting and meditating, brahmins,' in a tone that made both chanting and meditating sound like vulgar activities. He glanced at his brother princes as he said this, and both sniggered briefly in response before suppressing their amusement in the presence of their father.

The king shook his head with infinite weariness, started to turn away, then paused, looking up at nothing in particular, as if considering. Jamadagni tried not to look at his arms, the famous arms of Arjuna Kartavirya. Finally, almost as an afterthought, the king turned back. He spoke in a baritone that was deceptively mellifluous and pleasing to the ear. 'Search the place anyway.'

The princes emitted eager grunts and rushed forward. They shoved past Jamadagni and Renuka, followed by a score of kshatriyas. Jamadagni took hold of his wife by the shoulder and moved her aside, out of the way of the armed and armoured men tramping across their threshold, and stood to the side with his arm around her. The sounds of the Haihaya soldiers and their princes rummaging through their meagre possessions came from inside the hut. Two of the princes had gone around the hut and were exploring the rest of the ashram premises. There was nothing for them to find, Jamadagni knew, but the sooner they finished the sooner they would leave.

He whispered to Renuka: 'When they find nothing, they will leave.'

Renuka nodded her head to show she understood. Jamadagni realized she was shivering with fear. He was glad it was fear and not anger. As a kshatriya herself, a warrior-princess of the Suryavansha Ikshwaku line no less, Renuka could easily have lost her head and begun berating the Haihayas. The result would have been certain disaster. But mercifully, she had grasped the peril of their situation and was holding her pride in check.

Jamadagni prayed they would finish the search and leave as quickly as they had come.

||Three||

'Look, father!'

One of the boorish sons of King Arjuna Kartavirya came around the hut dragging a cow by a string attached to its nose-ring. She was a lovely animal, white and brown, with the firm flesh and level back of a young bovine, not yet humped with old age, or marked with the scars and bruises of the yoke, her large eyes doe-like and striking, the nose-ring in her nostrils adding to her feminity, as did the mincing way she walked. She caught sight of Jamadagni and mooed pitifully in protest at the manner in which she was being treated, her eyes wide and rolling. The other two princes prodded her in the flanks with their sheathed swords when she tried to resist. One even put his boot to her rump and shoved. She lurched forward squealing.

Jamadagni clutched Renuka's shoulder tight, silently warning her not to move or make a sound of protest. Even speaking might betray her, for though she was a dutiful brahmin wife and mother in every respect, she had been raised a warrior-princess and speaking deferentially to other kshatriyas, particularly under hostile circumstances, might well bring out the warrior in her as well. After all, these were the arch enemies of her own lineage, the killers of her distant cousins and kin. The best thing she could do was stay silent.

'A cow,' King Arjuna Kartavirya said dispassionately, glancing at the terrified animal. 'I am too old to fill my belly with milk, and I am no brahmin to desire ghee. What would you have me do with this beast?'

'Eat it!' said one of his sons, grinning.

'We shall slaughter it and roast it here on a spit, and we can all feast and regain our strength before continuing the chase.'

'Yes, father!' said the third son eagerly. 'It would take too long to go back home to Mahishmati and we need meat to regain our strength. This is a good plan.'

Jamadagni felt his stomach sicken, nauseated with fear and rising anger. Kill a brahmin's cow just to make a meal? Slaughter and roast it on consecrated ashram soil? What wanton beasts were these Haihayas? Yet he dared say none of these aloud for the consequences would be certain death. Instead, he stared at the back of the king's head, waiting to see his response. He knew that anything these young princes and the soldiers said or did was only by leave of their liege. It was this man who was the dangerous one. The one to watch.

King Arjuna Kartavirya seemed to be pondering his sons' suggestion. 'Why not,' he said at last. 'It is a young cow, her flesh will be tender and nourishing. There seems to be no other source of nourishment in this wretched aranya. Very well. Slaughter the cow and baste it. Salt it well.'

And he began to walk away.

Jamadagni could remain silent no more. He released his wife's shoulder and moved her behind him before stepping forward. 'My Lord,' he cried in the most pathetic voice he could manage. 'I beg your leave to speak.'

One of the princes raised his sword as if to strike Jamadagni down for his insolence.

'No,' said the king, his back still turned. How had he seen his son's action? Arjuna Kartavirya was renowned for his arms in battle, perhaps he had eyes that matched the arms in supernatural prowess. 'Speak, brahmin,' he said, still facing toward the clearing, where his soldiers stood in tired rows, awaiting their next command. 'But heed what you say and remember to whom you address your words.'

'Great one,' Jamadagni said, keeping his head bowed low and his hands joined. 'If it is food you seek, this cow will provide it. There is no need to kill her.'

The king's back seemed to laugh at Jamadagni. 'Did you not hear me say that I am grown too old to sup on milk. I do not care for butter and cheese either. The cow's flesh, on the other hand, makes a fit meal for fighting warriors. I have already decreed that the cow be slain. You, on the other hand, shall be executed for questioning my command. Let it not be said that a judgement pronounced by Arjuna Kartavirya, emperor of the world, can be overturned by a brahmin! Kill him.'

At once the swords slipped free of their sheaths and the arms of the princes rose eagerly as they advanced on Jamadagni. Renuka's scream rang out from behind, shrill and piercing. Jamadagni saw the way the prince nearest to him turned his grinning face to leer at her eagerly and knew that once they had slain him, they would have no reason to leave her alive—or untouched. He had a fraction of an instant in which to act and only one recourse. He took it.

'*Kama-dhenu!*' he cried.

His voice, trained by a lifetime of sandhi recitation and chanting of shlokas and mantras, rang out across the clearing like a temple bell, electrifying the very motes of the air itself:

|*Namo devyai Maha devyai*|
||*Surabyai cha namo nama*||
|*Gavam Bheeja swaroopaya*|
||*Namasthe Jagad Ambike*||

The oncoming swords had halted at the utterance of his first word, the uncouth Haihaya princes bearing the weapons of slaughter had frozen still, startled by the authority and power in his voice. If there was one thing kshatriyas feared, even if briefly, it was the brahmin power to summon and manipulate the forces of brahman to work his will. Even without looking at them directly, Jamadagni saw the fear on their moustached faces.

His own eyes were directed at the cow, as were the shlokas he was reciting, the *Gomatha Stuti*. It was but a prayer to Mother Cow, recited by all brahmins to honour and please the four-legged givers of the essential items that sustained a brahmin's life. But by simply prefacing it with the title 'Kama-dhenu' he had rendered it a special invocation, infused with the power of all the tapas he had accumulated over his lifetime of meditation and penance. Dhenu was the cow's given name, so named by her rightful owner. Kama meant desire. Kama-dhenu therefore meant Dhenu who fulfilled one's desires.

Even as the last echoes of his recitation died away, the cow mooed long and loud. Her cry filled the clearing. Jamadagni saw the Haihaya princes react, backing away from the cow, even though it was but a harmless bovine and they were strong warriors armed with drawn swords. At the periphery of his vision, he sensed the other soldiers also react, made nervous by his chanting of the mantras. This was the Treta Yuga: the world was still young, words still had their full potency, and the utterances of a man of brahman could move mountains and redirect rivers if he so desired. It was the reason why many kshatriyas, particularly those openly hostile to brahmins as the Haihayas were, struck before they spoke, deeming it safer to kill a brahmin on sight rather than wait and chance being struck down by his mantras. There was even a term for it: astra. A mantra of such potency, it could be wielded as a weapon. Which was literally what the term meant, *weapon.*

What he had just recited was no astra. Far from it. But these brutes did not know that. Already they were backing away from him, the cow and the hut as if all were ablaze and the fire threatened to consume them as well.

Only King Arjuna Kartavirya stood his ground, although he had turned to face Jamadagni once again and was watching him with an expressionless face that was all the more menacing for not revealing any emotions even as everyone around him was displaying conflicting emotions and expressions.

Dhenu lowed again, raising her head and turning it from side to side, eyes looking downwards, whites showing. She was still afraid of the men with swords, she sensed their bestial intentions. But the mantra compelled her to obey. The lowing she had just issued was her reply to Jamadagni, informing him that she was now ready to fulfil his desire.

Jamadagni turned to look at the Haihaya king. 'It is food you desire, is it not?' he asked. 'Food suitable for the nourishment of men at war? You shall have it.'

He spoke the next part of the *Gomata Stuthi*, the smriti—

secret—part that was not known even to his fellow brahmins. It was a complex mantra, dense and difficult to understand let alone recite. He had never spoken it before, only heard it once when the owner of Dhenu had recited it in his presence. But he was a brahmin. It was what he did. He recited the shloka perfectly.

The cow lowered her head and snorted. It was an unlikely sound from a young female, the kind of snort that might be expected from a grown bull instead. Straining, forceful, aggressive. She stamped her feet, kicking her hind legs. The princes backed further away, increasing the distance between the cow and their precious selves. The other soldiers watched with rising alarm. Only King Arjuna Kartavirya observed both Jamadagni and the cow with dispassion.

Dhenu issued a deafeningly loud bellow that Jamadagni felt strike the bones of his chest and reverberate within his lungs.

He saw the kshatriyas close their eyes for an instant, no more than a blink and a wince. When they opened their eyes again, there was a great feast spread out across the clearing.

They exclaimed, backing away in great alarm, as if they were witnessing the appearance of armed men or a horde of elephants rather than just food. A few moments passed, during which they looked at each other, then at the repast that lay before them, unsure of what they were witnessing or what to do next.

A great length of cloth, some ten yards long and five yards wide, enough to take up one whole side of the clearing, had appeared. Upon this cloth were arrayed a rich variety of victuals of every possible description, along with nectar, juice and wine of every kind, all arranged in fine pots, jugs, bowls and ornate containers. It was a feast fit for a king—or for several dozen kings in fact.

And it was real, as even Jamadagni's olfactory sense told him.

The soldiers and princes realized it too, for even if their eyes were deceiving them, their noses could not mistake the aromas of such rich food and drink.

They looked around at their leader for guidance.

He was looking at Jamadagni, eyes cold and face devoid of any discernible emotion.

'What manner of brahmin trickery is this?' he asked in a voice that was almost a growl of warning. His hands hung by his sides, flaccid and unmoving. Jamadagni kept a watch on them, for he knew from all he had heard of the Haihaya King that it was those arms that were the real threat.

'It is no trickery, my lord.' Jamadagni kept his head bowed and his hands clasped. 'You desired a meal. I provided it.'

'But how? From where did this feast appear?' King Arjuna Kartavirya's queries were sharp and pointed, as was his tone. If his face and eyes did not betray emotion, his voice more than made up for the lack. That mellifluous baritone voice conveyed an infinite range of subtle nuances. There was awe present, a little fear as well, and much suspicion, doubt, and distrust. 'And what part did the cow play in this magic feat?'

'It was not magic, raje, merely the miraculous product of Gomata.'

The Haihaya king's voice added a touch of speculation to the mix of audible emotions, even as his face remained resolutely inscrutable. 'All cows cannot produce entire feasts on demand. Magically. Out of thin air. What manner of being is this in the shape of a young cow?'

Jamadagni swallowed. He had hoped that the appearance of the meal would distract the ravenous kshatriyas from all other thoughts. And he could see that the warriors as well as the sons of the king were already staring with gaping mouths, already fallen under the spell of the delicious aromas that filled the clearing.

'Answer me, brahmin!' King Arjuna Kartavirya's voice cracked as sharply as a whip.

Jamadagni dipped his head. 'The cow is no ordinary cow. Her name is Dhenu.'

'Dhenu,' repeated the Haihaya king, as if tasting the word, rolling it on his palate to savour its meaning. 'The Giving One. An appropriate name for a cow. Yet I recall you calling out a somewhat different version of that name earlier, before you began chanting your brahmin gibberish. What was it?'

Jamadagni felt a bead of sweat burst forth on his forehead. He did not like the alteration in the voice of the Haihaya king. Arjuna Kartavirya sounded less afraid and anxious now that the initial shock of the sudden feat had worn off, more . . . calculating, more shrewd. 'Kama-Dhenu,' he replied, deciding it was wisest to say as little as possible.

'*Kama*-Dhenu!' King Arjuna Kartavirya said aloud.

At once the cow reacted, mooing. The two princes nearest to it—though still a good ten yards away—both reacted as well, stumbling into one another in a bid to retreat farther from the animal. Their armour and swords clashed noisily as they extracted themselves from one another's arms, each cursing the other softly so as not to be heard by their father.

'A most unusual name for a cow,' King Arjuna Kartavirya said, ignoring his sons. 'Kama meaning desire. Dhenu meaning The Giving One. Therefore Kama-Dhenu must mean the One Who Gives You Your Desire.'

His face remained as inscrutable as always, even as his voice ranged through a variety of emotions. Pleasure at his decoding the Sanskrit names, relaxation as he began to see that this was not a threat to be feared, and most disturbing to Jamadagni's ears, wily calculation as he began to understand the full measure of what he had discovered.

'A Cow That Fulfils One's Desires,' he said, playing with the Sanskrit words as a musician might play with a lute. 'Fascinating!'

He pointed a finger at his sons. 'Eat. Everyone. Eat and drink to your heart's content.'

There was the barest moment of hesitation. Then every last man in the clearing fell upon the arrayed food and drink like a pack of hungry wolves upon a solitary doe in deepest winter. The rude sounds of lips smacking, liquid being gulped, food being chomped, crunched, torn to shreds, and otherwise consumed by two hundred and fifty uncouth hungry kshatriyas were the only ones to be heard for the next several moments.

Jamadagni waited for King Arjuna Kartavirya to join his men in their feast. But the Haihaya king stood where he was, watching, listening, waiting.

After a while, he called out to his sons. He had to call more than once to distract them from their frenzied eating and drinking. They appeared to be in a contest to choose who among them could eat and drink the most in the shortest time possible. Jamadagni wondered if perhaps they thought that because the feast had appeared so suddenly, it might disappear as fast. The thought was an amusing one, and he might have smiled, had the circumstances not been so dire.

When the father finally had his sons' attention, he asked them roughly, 'Is it good?'

They turned ecstatic faces to him, smeared with food and wine stains. They babbled answers but the visual evidence was sufficient to answer the Haihaya king's query.

He turned back upon Jamadagni that same cold inscrutable gaze. 'What else can she provide?'

Jamadagni kept his head low and his hands joined. 'Does my lordship crave more food? Speak your appetite's desire and I shall ask Gomata to provide.'

King Arjuna Kartavirya's voice suggested a sneer. 'I possess wealth enough to feed the world thrice over every day. What if my appetite desires things other than food? Can Kama-Dhenu provide them?'

Jamadagni swallowed again. This was the very thing he had feared might come to pass. 'I have never had occasion to test her, my lord. In fact, this was the first time I made any demand of her.'

The King of the Haihayas snorted. 'Typical brahmin austerity. But you do possess the mantras that will invoke her giving nature, do you not? So ask her for something other than food.'

Jamadagni spread his hands in apparent bewilderment. 'What shall I ask for, sire?'

'Ask for gold. Precious gems. Women. Anything. I merely wish to see what she is capable of producing through her magical power.'

Jamadagni felt his hands trembling despite himself. 'My lord,' he said.

Renuka came up behind him and put her arms around his shoulders, comforting him by adding her strength to his own. He glanced sharply at her, indicating with his eyes that she was to continue to remain silent. She blinked and held her eyes shut an instant longer than needed, to communicate her understanding.

He was glad for her presence, for her touch. He prayed that their sons would not return until this nightmare was ended. The sooner he answered King Arjuna Kartavirya's queries and the Haihaya was satisfied, the sooner he would leave the ashram with his vile kshatriyas.

You delude yourself. Now that he knows the power of Kamadhenu he will not simply leave here. You heard the greed in his voice just now. He lusts after her for what she is, a being of power. Earlier, he was about to spare our lives because there was no reason to waste even the energy needed to kill us. Now he has a powerful motive to do so.

'Do it,' the Haihaya commanded. 'Demand extraordinary wealth. A king's ransom.'

Jamadagni knew this was the beginning of the end. Once the kshatriya saw what Kamadhenu was capable of, he would never be able to simply leave here. Yet he had no choice but to comply with the Haihaya's request—even using the wrong mantra was not possible. As a brahmin, he could no sooner mispeak the words than he could forget his own identity. Truth above all. This was Treta Yuga, also known as Satya Yuga, the only Age of Truth in the history of the world. A brahmin must speak every shloka immaculately, and speak nothing but the absolute truth.

Trying to ignore the growing dread within his heart, he recited the mantra that would compel Kamadhenu to fulfil the desire of King Arjuna Kartavirya.

||Four||

Sauti paused and partook of the refreshment offered him by the brahmacharyas. The air was electric with anticipation as the rishis of Naimisha-sharanya waited to hear the rest of his narrative. After a short respite, he continued.

'What followed next was as tragic as it was inevitable. Kamadhenu produced all that Rishi Jamadagni commanded. At the sight of the great piles of gold and gems and other precious objects, King Arjuna Kartavirya was filled with lust for more. He kept demanding that Jamadagni compel Kamadhenu to produce more and more, each time naming some new item that he desired until a small hillock of treasure lay in the centre of the clearing. Then, as Jamadagni had feared all along, the Haihaya realized that if he possessed Kamadhenu herself, he would be the richest, most powerful man in the world. When this realization came to him, he took the calf by force and left with his sons and soldiers and returned to his capital city Mahishmati. Before leaving, he compelled Jamadagni to instruct him, and him alone, in the mantras of command, and once the Bhrigu had finished teaching him the powerful shlokas, he struck him aside and rode away with the magic calf.'

Sauti looked around. The night had grown quiet and still. The insect songs of twilight had given way to the calm of the night. In the deep jungle, predators roved and fauna continued their nightly game of survival, but here in the sanctified shelter of Naimisha-sharanya, the peaceful brahmins and brahmacharyas listened with rapt attention to every syllable of Sauti's narrative. They had all heard some part or version of the legend of the Bhrigu before, but never before recited in such poetic detail.

'The only reason why the Haihaya did not kill Jamadagni was because he thought he might have need of his knowledge later. Not all kshatriyas need be ignorant or illiterate. Indeed, many are among the wisest and most knowledgeable in their own right, often vying with the wisest brahmins in the quest for Vedic enlightenment. But the Haihayas were ignorant to a fault and hostile to all forms of learning, and like all ignorant beings, the Haihaya lived in perpetual self-doubt. King Arjuna Kartavirya thought that there might yet be something that needed to be known in order to keep the calf of plenty producing the endless supply of treasures he envisioned, and so, until he could be sure of that plentiful supply, he decided to leave the brahmin and his wife unharmed.

'Later that same day, the sons of Jamadagni and Renuka returned home and learned of the events of the day. They were outraged and furious at the abuse meted out to their parents by the Haihaya king. But being brahmins, they could do nothing about it. Except for the fifth son, Jamadagneya, whom, as we have learned, was also named Rama and had come to be better known as Parashurama, Rama with the Axe.

'Now, Parashurama was no ordinary brahmin boy. In fact, he shared more than some of the best qualities of a warrior. His great-grandmother Satyavati was a kshatriya who married Sage Richika of the Bhrigu clan. Satyavati was concerned that due to her kshatriya parentage, her children might display warrior tendencies as well. So she appealed to her husband to use his divine knowledge to ensure that her offspring would turn out to be knowledge-seeking brahmins who worshipped the word, not the sword. At the same time, Satyavati's mother, the wife of King Gadhi, lacked a son and heir who would inherit Gadhi's throne and continue his lineage. She in turn desired a child who would be disposed towards war and weaponry or in other words, kshatriya-like tendencies.

'With this in mind, Sage Richika performed a yagna and divided the payasam sanctified from the yagna into two parts. One part he gave to his wife Satyavati to consume, the other part to her mother. But mother and daughter accidentally exchanged their portions and each consumed the other one's share. Only after they finished did they realize their error. Satyavati appealed to her husband to do something. As the wife of a brahmin, she could hardly raise a kshatriya son! Nor would having a brahminical son solve the problem her mother faced.

'Sage Richika could not entirely alter the potency of his mantras. But he took steps to ensure that the effect of the payasam would be delayed by one generation. Thus, Satyavati gave birth to a son with perfect brahmanical tendencies and who became an emblem of the brahmin varna, Jamadagni. While her mother had a son who was the perfect heir for Gadhi. Thus both mother's and daughter's dilemmas were resolved.

'But as predicted by Richika, the effect of the payasam was delayed, not cancelled. Thus it was that Jamadagni's son, Jamadagneya, was born with kshatriya tendencies. In acknowledgement of this fact, Jamadagni and his wife Renuka named him Rama, a favoured name in her kshatriya dynasty of

Suryavansha Ikshwakus. However, they hoped that at worst he would be a brahma-kshatriya, one who was conversant in the arts of war but chose to follow the path of knowledge and peace. As for Satyavati's mother, she gave birth to a son whom she named Vishwamitra, and who grew up as a kshatriya with a keener interest in learning than his father might have wished.

'Young Rama grew up honouring his parents' wishes to the letter. He was a dedicated brahmacharya and a devout seeker of Vedic wisdom. Thanks to his parents' enlightened upbringing, he did not suppress or deny his kshatriya side but kept it in check by training under one of the most austere and disciplined gurus possible, the mighty Lord Shiva himself, Destroyer of Worlds. Shiva's training demanded impossible penance and discipline which no ordinary kshatriya—indeed, no ordinary mortal—could dream of achieving. Simply by gaining Shiva's acceptance as a guru, Jamadagneya Rama proved himself to be a formidable brahma-kshatriya, that rare enlightened being who possesses the best qualities of both brahmin and kshatriya varnas. It was in acknowledgement of this very austerity and pacificist approach that Lord Shiva gave his divine Parasu to Rama, thus earning him the epithet Parashurama by which he was thereafter known.'

Sauti looked around at his audience. Despite the utter blackness of the forest background and only the flickering light of the oil lamps and torches around the ashram, he was certain that once again their numbers had swelled. He did not know how this could be possible, nor did he think that merely attempting to recount his listeners would yield satisfaction. In any case, once launched upon his mammoth recitation, he could not permit himself to be interrupted or distracted by such minor considerations. If the myth was true: if the dead of Kurukshetra indeed resided in Naimisha-van: if those dead souls now gathered around to hear his recitation of the *Mahabharata* epic, then so be it. What better motive to study itihasa than to learn the causes of one's destruction?

'There is an episode involving Rama that will better enable you to understand his dual nature. When he was but a boy, an incident happened involving his mother. Rama and his brothers were away in the forest, collecting fruit and herbs, chopping wood and performing other daily chores. Sage Jamadagni was preparing to perform his ritual ablutions so he could begin his day's meditation. As usual, Renuka went down to the river with her pot to fetch water for her husband's ablutions. As she walked the path that led down the Ramshrung mountains to the Malaprabha river, she heard unusual sounds and laughter. Through the close-growing trees and foliage she glimpsed someone splashing about in the water below, making a great deal of noise. It was King Chitraratha, lord of the gandharvas, the artistic and musical entertainers of the devas, dallying with his lovers. Innocent as she was of such activities, totally isolated and secluded in her life as a hermit's wife, Renuka had no experience of such a sight. At first, she did not even know what was transpiring on the banks of the river below. The closer she came to the riverbank, the more she saw and heard, and the more these titillating sights and sounds aroused and inflamed her curiosity. Finally, she stopped and watched from a discreet spot behind a tree.

'King Chitraratha was a magnificent specimen of masculine perfection, endowed with great physical beauty and artistic talent. He sang and recited lyric poetry, danced and cavorted with his gandharvas in a display of amorous art performance such as only gandharvas and apsaras can demonstrate. Any mortal observor would be powerfully aroused by such a scene. To Renuka, innocent and pure of life and thought, it was an erotic assault that engulfed her completely. She felt as if her entire being was aflame, and was overcome by her passions. Watching the other-worldly lovers engaged in the oldest pastime of all, she could not help but fantasize about participating in those arcane acts herself.

'The sound of the pot striking the ground as it fell from her hand brought her back to her senses with a jolt. The gandharvas hardly heard or noticed, absorbed as they were in their pursuit of ecstasy. But she was powerfully embarrassed by the extent to which she had lapsed and the thoughts that had consumed her and she ran all the way back to the ashram, hardly noticing or caring that she was catching her garments and ripping them on branches and roots, or that her neatly knotted hair had fallen open to loose her tresses in wanton abandon. She arrived back at the ashram of her husband in a state such as he had never seen her before, dishevelled, glistening with perspiration brought on as much from her fantasizing by the river as from her reckless run uphill, her hair loose and tangled, her clothes torn and dirty—and no pot of water in her hand.

'Jamadagni was startled beyond words. As a man of great wisdom and insight, he instantly knew what emotion assailed his wife. After all, she was his wife and consort and he of all people recognized the signs of arousal upon her face. Her dishevelled state and frantic guilty manner were a great shock. To make matters worse, she blurted out an explanation of what had transpired in a feeble attempt to gain his sympathy. But the more she said, the deeper she sank into self-incrimination. Her description of the physical beauty of King Chitraratha and the acts she had witnessed him performing with the female gandharvas were sufficient to enrage her husband.

Sage Jamadagni was not a man given to a loss of temper easily and he loved his wife dearly enough to overlook almost any transgression. But this was a shameful lapse and somehow her mental adultery seemed no less than the actual act, so deeply had she given herself over to the emotional and psychic details of the self-seduction. What he did next was as much the reaction of a jealous husband as that of an outraged brahmin penitent.

'One of their sons had returned home during this time. Jamadagni ordered him to take up a weapon and kill his mother at once, as her crime, in Jamadagni's view, was beyond tolerance or forgiveness. He would not debate the right or wrong of such a terrible penalty, and insisted that the execution be carried out without question or argument.

'Reluctantly and with great distress, the first son refused. Shamefaced, he asked his father's forgiveness for he was unable to follow his instruction.

'Thereupon, Jamadagni asked his first son to go fetch his brothers.

'When all five of his scions were before him, he ordered each of them in turn to follow his bidding and execute his condemmation of their mother.

'One by one, each of them refused him. Shamefaced and recalcitrant, they were terrified of their father's wrath but unable to do as he bid.

'Except for Parashurama. He was the last to return home as he was performing his usual chore, chopping wood for the yagna fire. He saw his mother's weeping distress, heard his father's enraged commands, sensed his brothers' shameful impotency, and listened to the terrible pronouncement.

'Without a single word or hesitation, Parashurama raised his axe and with one smooth blow, beheaded his mother.

'His father stared, his anger silenced at last. Parashurama's brothers broke out into grievous weeping. Parashurama knelt before his father, bowing his head. Jamadagni stared down at his son and was filled with admiration for him.

'Impressed by Parashurama's obedience, he told his youngest son that he could have any boon he desired. For though a brahmin hermit lived in utter poverty and in a state of near destitution, these were the result of his vows. In point of fact, he possessed the power to grant almost any desire or wish through the use of the powerful mantras he knew. He now offered to grant his obedient son any wish he demanded.

'Parashurama thanked his father and touched his feet in devotion, then said that all he desired was for Jamadagni to restore his mother to life. Indeed, it was because he knew that Jamadagni possessed knowledge of the mantra that restored life to the dead that he had willingly executed his own mother. Now that her punishment had been meted out, it was only fair that Jamadagni should give Parashurama and his brothers their mother back again.

'Jamadagni was left speechless by his son's intelligence and his obedience. His anger dissipated by now, he agreed that being executed was punishment enough for his wife. Uttering the potent mantra of resurrection, he restored Renuka back to life, and when she was whole and breathing again, embraced her and accepted her unconditionally once again.'

Sauti stopped and looked around. 'So you see what a resolute boy Parashurama was? He respected and loved his parents so much that he could behead his own mother at his father's bidding, but he only did so because he was certain he could resurrect her again. He could do such a thing because unlike his brahmin brothers, he was born with the heart of a warrior. The kshatriya part of his being enabled him to commit that terrifying act of maa-hatya, killing one's own mother, as well as to think beyond that terrible act to its aftermath, whereupon he knew his father would agree to resurrect her. Only a kshatriya could conceive of and then act upon such an unspeakably violent plan, all within the space of the few seconds it took for his father to order him to execute his mother.

'That same quality, the ability to see the need for violence and act upon it without hesitation, was what led to the events that followed the theft of the calf Kamadhenu. Had Parashurama been an ordinary brahmin boy like his brothers, he could never have done what he did next. Then again, perhaps the generations of suffering inflicted upon countless pacificist brahmins, and the Bhrigu line in particular, had naturally evolved a descendant of that line in whom all the collective righteous rage of those who were wronged and killed had converged. It was as if all the sufferings of his Bhrigu ancestors at the hands of kshatriyas had been brewed into the cataclysm that walked the earth by the name of Parashurama.'

||Five||

When Parashurama returned home and found that his father's calf had been stolen, and stolen by none other than the king of the very Haihaya kshatriyas who had been slaughtering brahmins for decades, he did not hesitate. He took up his axe and set out on the road that led to Mahishmati. He did not stop to think of the consequences of what he was about to do, nor of the odds against him. For while a brahmin's disciplined meditation and learning compel him to consider carefully before embarking upon any venture, a kshatriya's very nature is predicated on swift reflexes and instinct. Parashurama only knew that his father and mother had been insulted, their sanctified home and ashram defiled, and a precious calf stolen. What Jamadagni had not mentioned to the Haihayas, as it would hardly have mattered to them, was that the calf actually belonged to Lord Indra. The king of the Devas had graciously given it to Jamadagni for safekeeping. Bad enough that King Arjuna Kartavirya had stolen the calf; worse still, the calf had not belonged to Jamadagni in the first place.

In those days, kshatriyas were masters of the realm. Brahmins cloistered themselves in deep aranya ashramas, on unattainable mountain peaks, or in the most uninhabited locations possible. There, in their ashrams and caves, they reigned supreme over the worlds of learning and inner space. But the developed world of cities and towns and villages was dominated by kshatriyas who roved the land, taking whatever they desired and fighting for anything that was disputed.

Mahishmati, the capital of the Haihaya nation, was a land overrun by the kshatriya way of life. Violence was omnipresent, and considered a way of life. Sadly, it was the people of other varnas, those who were merely living their lives or going about their tasks, who suffered the most. Some fell victim to rapacious kshatriyas like the Haihayas, others were innocent bystanders who came in harm's way accidentally, and many unfortunates died or suffered only because they happened to work with or work for one or other group of warring warriors. Many tradesmen, craftsmen, artisans, artists and even poets set aside their tools and implements and took up weapons only to defend themselves and their families against the incessant threat of violence. Fights erupted at any moment, every day there was a battle, and life itself was one endless war campaign.

It was to this violent and ruthless city that Parashurama came in search of his father's lost calf. A young man barely grown to adulthood, hair matted and tied in a knot on top of his head, clad in the simple white anga-vastra and dhoti of a brahmacharya, bearing the ash smears that declared him a brahmin, he walked the dusty road that led to the city. Even before he reached its high gates, he encountered trouble. A band of Haihaya warriors were returning from a skirmish in which they had fared badly against the forces of Bahu, son of Sagara. They were talking bitterly amongst themselves of Bahu's inroads into Haihaya territory and how the tide appeared to be turning against their army as well as the Panchagana. Everyone of them agreed that it was only a matter of time before King Arjuna Kartavirya lost control of Ayodhya and once that great stronghold fell, it would be a great blow to their cause. It was while they were in this foul mood that they chanced upon the young brahmin boy walking steadfastly along the raj marg. 'Brahmin!' said one of them, tapping the hilt of his sword on his shield. 'Do you not see kshatriyas on the road? Bow at once to us!'

'Show some respect for your superiors!' said another, deliberately taunting Parashurama.

Parashurama did not even notice that they were addressing him. Completely absorbed in his goal, he walked at a rapid pace, intent on reaching the city. The Haihayas took his quick walk as an indication of cowardice and thought he was scurrying away from them. Irritated, they rode after him and one of them raised his sword to strike Parashurama down from behind.

His eyes on the dusty road, the sun above and behind him, Parashurama saw the shadow of the Haihaya horse rider with his raised sword swooping down on him. Without a second's thought, his axe flashed upwards. A man's cry rang out. And the arm holding the sword fell with a clattering thump, severed arteries and veins splurging life fluid onto the earth below. The injured man swung his horse around, screaming in pain, and his stump spewed blood onto his comrades, drenching their armour and faces. He fainted away from the shock and loss of blood, falling to the ground as his horse milled about in confusion.

Parashurama continued to walk on towards the city. He had not slowed his pace even when he defended himself against the Haihaya's attack. He flicked the blood from the axe's edge as he went, but did not return it to its place in his waistcloth; he let it stay in his hand by his side, swinging as he walked, its finely honed blade catching the noonday sunlight and reflecting it in bright dazzling shards.

After a moment in which the other Haihayas gaped at their fallen friend, and other pedestrian and horse-mounted passers-by on the raj marg continued on their way with eyes averted from what they assumed was just another routine instance of kshatriya violence, realization set in of what had just occurred.

A brahmin had killed a kshatriya.

A brahmin boy, no less, on foot and armed only with a woodchopper—for Shiva's parasu appeared deceptively ordinary in appearance at first sight—attacked from behind by a veteran Haihaya warrior, one of King Arjuna Kartavirya's own.

It was unheard of. Unthinkable. Impossible.

Yet it had happened. There lay the fallen kshatriya, severed stump bleeding out the last of his life onto the dust of the road, who only moments earlier had been talking and laughing with the rest of them.

Without thinking further, the rest of the band of veterans roared with fury and spurred their horses, riding after the brahmin boy, who had already left them several dozen yards behind as he continued his resolute journey up the raj marg. Swords drawn, they rode down at him from behind, hell-bent on avenging their fallen comrade. Others on the raj marg drew their horses aside, leaped off the road, or stopped their chariots or uks wagons to let the Haihayas pass. Nobody paid much attention to the intended victim of their rage. When kshatriyas were on a rampage, it was best to continue about one's business and ignore them completely—unless of course they expected you to bow or serve them. Only a pair of brahmacharyas, trekking back to the city with herbs collected from the woods, paid heed. As fellow brahmins, they knew they were about to witness a familiar sight: the murder of one of their brethren for no fault other than the mere fact that he was a brahmin. Even though they were both boys with hairless chins, they had seen scores of such assaults and massacres; it was a part of daily life under Haihaya rule. The world belonged to the men who wielded swords, and that meant kshatriyas. The only weapons they possessed were words.

But not the brahmin boy. He was armed with something more than words. And unlike his brahmin brethren, he was not afraid to use it on kshatriyas if compelled.

As the band of Haihayas rode down on him, Parashurama raised the hand holding the axe before his face. He did not slow his walk or turn his head. He kept walking towards Mahishmati. The blade of the raised axe was as clear and mirrored as still water. Upon the surface of the blade, he could see a clear reflection of the raj marg behind him—and the Haihaya riders bearing down on him with swords drawn and ugly expressions on their bearded faces. He gripped the axe by the leather thong that hung from the base of its handle with his other hand, then, as the riders came within striking distance, he swung it.

What followed next was a blur to the watching brahmacharyas across the road.

While they had witnessed any number of acts of violence in their youthful lives, almost all involving kshatriyas slaughtering brahmins or, less frequently, one another, they had never witnessed anything akin to what they saw on the raj marg that noonday.

Parashurama's axe swung around in a looping blur as the first Haihaya bore down on him. The blade of the axe seemed to glide through the torso of the kshatriya, as if it came close to his body but did not actually touch him. This was because it did not strike with any impact, merely spun a full looping turn without any indication of having struck the rider.

The first rider swung at Parashurama, appeared to miss him by an inch, and rode past.

Parashurama's axe continued to twirl around the leather thong, which was spinning on his forefinger held up in the air like a man launching a discus, crooked just slightly at the tip to keep the thong from slipping off. By the time it was on its third looping turn, the next horseman came within striking distance. Parashurama moved his hand at blurring speed, and once again, the axe continued spinning as it cut through the space which the rider occupied, apparently without touching the rider himself.

The second rider also swung at him, missed, then overshot.

Parshuarama then stepped sideways, moved the spinning parasu to adjust for the new angle at which the next rider was approaching, and spun it at this third Haihaya as well, with much the same result. Except that this time, there was a brief red glitter, as though red rubies had been tossed in midair and caught the sunlight.

The axe spun round without interruption, and the rider hacked downwards, missed, and rode past.

Now, a peculiar thing happened to the first rider.

He had stopped his horse and had begun to turn its head, to ride back at Parashurama for a second pass. But he barely managed to twist the reins once, then doubled over in apparent agony . . . and fell off his horse to the ground.

Except that only the top half of the Haihaya fell off. It slid off the man's torso, as neatly severed as a joint of lamb struck cleanly by a butcher's blade, and fell with a wet thump to the road. The rest of the man, everything from about midway down his chest downwards, remained seated on the horse, gaping bright red and terrible in the gaudy sunlight.

A moment later, the same thing happened to the second rider. The angle of the severance was slightly different, the second man having been cut a little lower than the first man, but the effect was much the same.

The axe had cut them in half.

The third rider paused, appeared to gag on his own blood, then toppled off his horse—but the cut was not complete in his case, which was why the brahmacharyas had glimpsed the ruby red blood winking in the sunlight, and the top half of his body hung down, still partly attached to his lower body. It was a nauseating sight. The horse was drenched in the blood of the rider and whinnied in alarm and disgust.

The remaining Haihayas suffered much the same fate.

For about the space of ten or twelve normal breaths, Parashurama swung his axe round and round on his upraised finger, as each warrior rode down at him, and in that time, as many warriors died.

Moments later, the raj marg was strewn with the severed bodies of almost a score of Haihaya veterans, butchered like chopped meat.

Parashurama turned back towards the direction he had been going, and continued on his way.

He flicked the axe as he went, sending a few drops of blood flying from its blade. But oddly enough, not all the blood was flicked off. The gore upon the edge and sides of the blade seemed to seep into the shining metal face, like water absorbed by parched earth.

Parashurama flicked a drop or two off, but the rest seeped into and was swallowed by the blade itself. The axe literally drank the blood.

Even thirty yards away, the brahmacharyas across the road could hear the blade sing.

It was a keening shrill metallic sound, like the sound a knife blade makes when set to a rapidly spinning grindstone. It was so high-pitched, it set stray dogs to barking for miles around, and along the length of the raj marg people looked up and frowned, sensing rather than hearing the sound before shaking their heads and continuing on their way.

Parashurama continued walking towards Mahishmati. Already, the gates of the city were within sight. The encounter with the veterans had taken barely a few moments of his time. Seventeen experienced and battle-tested warriors lay dead in the dust behind him. There was not a scratch upon him.

||Six||

Parashurama approached the gates of Mahishmati. The kshatriyas milling about the gate were mostly inebriated louts spoiling for a fight. The gatewatch duty was a lucrative assignment as it came with the power to stop any visitors, seize contraband as well as levy the city toll. Few dared pick a fight with the gatewatch of Mahishmati because they represented the official might of the Haihaya empire. Over time, this had led to the sentries abusing their positions of power, preying on travellers, demanding a higher toll than was official, pocketing a portion for themselves, taking bribes from the richer merchants, smuggling contraband out or in, confiscating items for their own personal use or as gifts, and generally doing as they pleased. They mostly spent their duty hours under the influence of one or other of the many intoxicants that came into their possession, playing bone-dice games to decide who went home with the day's spoils of confiscation, or, when they needed some diversion, harassing the female or weaker travellers passing through the gates they watched.

They might have let Parashurama pass by unmolested, taking him to be what he was in fact: a brahmin boy from some remote ashram come to the city on some errand or other. Strictly speaking, brahmins were not expected to pay any tolls or taxes, being as they were, bereft of worldly possessions and wealth. But this was Mahishmati, seat of the Haihayas, and the very existence of a brahmin was an affront to any kshatriya.

So, just as Parashurama was about to pass resolutely through the vaulting gates of the city, he was challenged by a drunken guard.

'You there. Pay your toll.'

The sentries at the gate, hearing their colleague call out and seeing the brahmin boy, crossed their spears, barring Parashurama's way.

Parashurama slowed, then came to a halt. His dark face glowed with an energy that belied his unattractive features, lending him an extraordinary aura of strength and charisma. His features were not handsome, far from it, and his body was squat and dwarfish in proportion. But the fiery black eyes, high prominent cheekbones, bristling black beard and crow-black brahmin hair matted in a knot atop his head, with the powerful neck and shoulders, all created a sense of great power and menace when seen from close up.

The gatewatch guard who had called out the challenge felt and saw this menace as Parashurama halted close before him and had a tiny moment of misgiving. It was gone as soon as it had arisen. After all, this was no kshatriya; he was merely a brahmin from the aranya. A naïve young acolyte who was sworn to ahimsa, the philosophy of non-violence and would sooner cause himself to waste away in self-punitive austerities than lift a finger against another living being. There was no menace or danger here!

'Toll,' said the gatewatch curtly. 'Pay.'

Parashurama merely stood his ground and glowered. He was not looking directly at the gatewatch guard or at any of his colleagues. His gaze was set beyond them, upon his destination, the city within. This lent him a peculiar air of distraction, the look of a man not entirely in his senses. And this was true: Parashurama was inhabiting a mental space that was not the rational realm of most mortals. Certainly not the warped morally corrupt world that these predatory sentries inhabited. He was following his own sense of dharma.

He gave no answer to the guard.

The gatewatch looked at his colleagues with amusement. 'A silent one we have here, men.'

'Maybe he's taken a maun-vrata,' said one of the others, drinking from a jug of soma they had confiscated from a wine-vendor passing by. 'A vow of silence.'

His colleague, seated on the wall above the gate, called down: 'Brahmin fool won't have a penny to his name anyway. Beat him and kick him on his way.'

Another sentry pointed to the shining blade of the axe hanging from Parashurama's cloth waistbelt. 'He could pay the toll with that. That looks like it could be worth something.'

'Or useful at least,' said the first man who had spoken.

He reached for the axe, intending to examine it more closely. 'Let's take a look at this, young'un, shall we?' he began. 'I have always wanted—.'

He never finished—either his words or his action.

Even before his fingertips touched the hilt of the axe hanging from the brahmin boy's waist, Parashurama had taken up the axe, and cut off the gatewatch sentry's arm. It fell with a soft thud to the ground, knocking over the jug of soma. Thick honey wine spilled into the dirt, mingling with the blood from the severed arm.

The other sentries reacted quicker than their compatriots on the raj marg had earlier. For one thing, being on gatewatch meant they dealt with all manner of ruffians and foreigners. Corrupt they were, but fit and skilled at violence as well, or else they would not survive a day of being on gatewatch. The instant they saw blood spilled, they drew their weapons and attacked without further comment or discussion. Spears and swords in hand, they moved in on Parashurama, intending to kill him without wasting a single breath on asking a question. He had maimed one of their own, that was all that mattered. He had to be brought down at once.

Parashurama raised his forefinger, twirling his axe on its leather thong. It spun at an amazing speed, the edge of its blade producing the same keening song it had made earlier. The sentries heard it and noted the blurring speed at which the axe spun round the brahmin boy's finger, but moved in anyway.

It was not long before they all lay dead, or horribly maimed and dying, at their post.

Visitors coming and going gawked at them and reacted to the extraordinary sight of so much Haihaya blood spilled at the very gates of the city. They had never before seen such a thing, not in Mahishmati.

Nor had they ever seen anything like the brahmin boy who stood over the butchered corpses with the axe in his hand. The axe that seemed to have almost no bloodstains on its blade, and which produced a sharp high-pitched sound that physically hurt their ears and set dogs barking across the city.

Parashurama raised both hands, shaking the axe at the krtavardha banner which bore the sigil of King Arjuna Kartavirya.

'Haihaya! I am come to reclaim my father's calf. Come out and return our property to me, or I shall enter and kill every last kshatriya within these walls today!'

As the echoes of his challenge faded away, the citizens who had witnessed the slaughter of the gatewatch turned to one another, unsure whether to laugh or to wonder at his audacity. Surely he was suicidal, insane, deluded. To stand at the gates of Mahishmati and challenge the entire Haihaya dynasty? What hubris! In moments more soldiers would come—scores, hundreds, thousands if need be—and put an end to this ingenuous youth.

They waited to watch the foolish young brahmin die.

||Seven||

Parashurama did not have long to wait. It so chanced that King Arjuna Kartavirya had not yet reached his capital city. The Haihaya king had set off from Jamadagni's ashram with his prize, intending to come straight home and experiment further with his new possession. But on the way, a thought had occurred to him. He realized that if Kamadhenu could grant any desire its owner asked, then there was no reason to restrict one's demands to treasure alone. He had demanded uks carts to carry the treasure he had already conjured up back at Jamadagni's ashram and now a veritable grama train of uks wagons followed his band of warriors on the raj marg, laden with more wealth than he had brought home from most military raids or campaigns. And that was what made him realize that if he could ask for uks carts to carry his treasure, he could ask for other things as well, things not inherently of value but of great strategic and tactical use to a warlord.

For instance, at this very moment, he was chasing Bahu, son of Sagara, with a band of about 250 of his finest soldiers. He commanded great armies, massive military forces, but it was not practical to mobilize them all quickly enough to give chase to a small band of rebels. What he needed was a way to track down and find Bahu and his band of marauders quickly and efficiently. He needed a small force of expert trackers who perfectly knew the region of the aranya into which Bahu and his warriors had taken refuge and were capable of flushing them out and slaughtering them on sight.

And so this was what he asked Kamadhenu for next. Stopping on the road itself, he uttered the mantras of command and compelled the calf to produce his demand. A blink of an eye later, a whole company of lean-faced men, accompanied by dogs as lean-faced and lithe-bodied as their masters, stood before King Arjuna Kartavirya, ready to do his bidding. He set them upon the trail of Bahu and soon enough, the hunt was on.

Hours later, he had rounded up and slaughtered Bahu's band of rebels and captured Bahu himself. He decided to take the rebel leader back to Mahishmati to be tortured and publicly executed as an example. There were still some packs of rebels loose across the wilderness, for they had split up and fled to the four quarters. The Haihaya king sent his three sons after them, using the trackers and their dogs. He ordered his sons not to return home until they had tracked down and eliminated every last one. Then he turned the head of his own horse and started back for his capital city.

And thus it was, only a little while after Parashurama stopped at the gates of Mahishmati, King Arjuna Kartavirya came riding up as well, bearing in tow the very thing that he had stolen from Parashurama's father, the precious calf Kamadhenu.

King Arjuna Kartavirya was taken aback by the extraordinary sight that met his eyes at the city gates.

Parashurama stood alone before the gates, with a large and growing crowd of travellers, merchants, citizens and other brahmins standing across the way and watching with great interest. His axe was in his hand, still singing after the slaughter of another round of victims. And the bodies of those he had killed lay strewn all around him.

Even at a glance, King Arjuna Kartavirya estimated there must be at least two hundred corpses lying around the brahmin boy. It was difficult to tell exactly because the corpses were mostly hacked apart, but there appeared to be body parts corresponding roughly to that number

He looked around, frowning in the afternoon sunlight, trying to fathom who else had assisted the brahmin boy in this slaughter. Where were his allies? Surely there must be a sizable contingent of kshatriyas fighting alongside him, to have produced such a death toll?

It took him some time to absorb and accept the fact that it was only one man, a boy at that, and that too a brahmin, who had accomplished all this, entirely on his own. With a single axe.

Parashurama recognized King Arjuna Kartavirya from his burnished armour and the banner-bearer and umbrella-bearer that flanked him. He raised his axe and hailed him loudly.

'Kshatriya! You have stolen something that is not your property. Return unto me that which you took from my father's ashram.'

King Arjuna Kartavirya grinned at his men, then permitted himself a hearty chuckle. 'The boy has spirit. Clearly he was struck too hard on the head when yet an infant. Cut him down where he stands.' He raised a finger, adding, 'Use archers first. He seems to be fairly effective with the axe, but it won't be any use against arrows.'

Several shortbows appeared in the hands of the Haihaya horsemen. Accustomed to shooting from the saddle, this was an easy target for them. They loosed a volley of several dozen arrows at once at Parashurama.

Parashurama twirled the axe on his finger as he had before. The blade blurred. He stood rock still. The hail of arrows flew at him, lethally aimed, and almost all found their mark—and were chopped to splinters by the spinning axe.

The watching crowd oohed in amazement. This was something new.

King Arjuna Kartavirya frowned. 'Try javelins. All at once.'

They did.

The result was the same. The axe chopped every last javelin to fragments. The splinters fell in a pile around Parashurama, yet not a scratch marked his body.

The audience cheered and applauded. Despite the presence of the Haihayas and the knowledge that this charade could not possibly continue forever, they felt an overwhelming joy at seeing the brutal kshatriyas bested at their own game: use of weapons. The watching brahmins cheered loudest of all.

Parashurama let the axe slow, then lowered it. 'Surrender the calf to me now, Haihaya, and you may yet live. I will not warn you again.'

King Arjuna Kartavirya bared his teeth. He was no longer amused by the brahmin boy. 'Kill him,' he said shortly to his warriors. 'Attack him with everything you have, all at once, and do not stop until he lies dead.'

It was easier said than done.

A short while later, every last man of King Arjuna Kartavirya's contingent lay dead on the ground, butchered by the unrelenting axe.

The crowd had swelled to the size of most of the city's population by now. Word was spreading far and wide. A brahmin boy had challenged the Haihayas—and he was slaughtering kshatriyas by the hundreds, single-handedly. Already, the poets would be composing their lyrics.

King Arjuna Kartavirya stared coldly at the insolent brahmin boy who stood before his gates, barring him entry to his own city, his own kingdom, his own home.

It was intolerable. An example must be made.

But how? Clearly the boy was possessed of some extraordinary astra. That axe was no ordinary wood axe. Nor was its wielder merely a brahmacharya: he displayed a skill comparable to the greatest champions the Haihaya king himself had seen in combat.

He thought of asking the calf to produce a greater champion than the boy.

To produce the greatest axe-wielder that ever lived.

Or even, a stroke of brilliance, the guru who had taught the boy! That personage would undoubtedly be able to best the youth, surely?

But there was another factor to consider.

The watching crowds.

Had this encounter taken place within the palace compound, or in a remote forest clearing, it would not matter what means Arjuna Kartavirya resorted to in order to secure victory. He could summon up entire armies of champions from Kamadhenu to destroy the son of Jamadagni. Ironic, considering that the calf itself was Jamadagni's!

But he needed to set an example. The boy was fighting alone. And to throw armies against him would suggest that Arjuna Kartavirya himself was the weaker one, to need such great numbers to best a mere brahmin boy. It would engender any number of rebellions across the land. Every brahmin boy would be inspired to take up an axe or a hoe or a yoke and attack kshatriyas. Parashurama would become a legend for all brahmins to follow.

He needed to set an example.

He needed to best this boy himself.

Man to man.

In single combat.

To prove that he, Arjuna Kartavirya, was the greatest warrior of all. And nobody else, brahmin, kshatriya or otherwise, could challenge him and live.

Nobody.

And so, the king of the Haihayas dismounted from his horse, and walked towards the spot where Parashurama stood, swinging his axe.

||Eight||

Parashurama mistook the kshatriya king's action for capitulation. He thought that he had made his point effectively and the Haihaya had decided to cut his losses and surrender the calf to its rightful owner. As Jamadagni's son, he had been raised to the highest standards of morality. Dharma dictated that the kshatriya acknowledge defeat and return the calf willingly. So Parashurama expected that this was what the Haihaya was doing. He watched as the kshatriya approached, then stopped about one score yards from the place where Parashurama waited.

Parashurama noticed that the calf was farther ahead, tethered to an uks cart, one of several in a long grama train of heavily laden wagons. The men on the uks carts made no move to dismount, untie the calf or bring it to their king. Perhaps the Haihaya king intended to speak with Parashurama before having the calf fetched, or perhaps he intended to tell Parashurama to take the calf himself and return home with it. Either option was acceptable. Parashurama had killed a number of kshatriyas here today. He had taken no pleasure in the act. It had been mindless butchery, no different from the practice sessions with his guru Mahadev where he was expected to wield the sacred Parasu until he no longer thought about each action or gesture, but merely acted. It was thanks to those rigorous training sessions that he had acquired the ability to wield the axe relentlessly, moving with the automatic repetitive actions of a man chopping wood or cutting down a tree.

Parasu was partly responsible of course. The axe was no mere object made from wood and metal. It was a living thing, created and consecrated by Mahadev himself, Lord of Destruction. This was why it sang when it worked, just like any woodcutter might sing as he chopped down trees. And it was why it drank the blood of those it slew. Shiva had warned his shishya about that last part. Parasu loved the taste of blood; the more it drank, the more it desired. If its wielder permitted it to drink too much, it might not be able to stop. Then a point might be reached whereupon the axe drove the bearer to fight on, so that Parasu could continue to drink more blood. An endless cycle of thirst and slaking would follow and there might be no limits to how many Parasu would slay. Its thirst could never be fully quenched and that meant it could drink on forever, until its owner reached a point where he might no longer care whom he killed, so long as Parasu could drink. In exchange, Parasu granted its wielder a sense of invulnerability—nay, not merely a *sense*, but invulnerability *itself.* So long as Parasu was given the blood of new victims to drink, its wielder could not be harmed or killed. He would effectively be immortal.

After all, it was a weapon of a god.

Parasu had drunk a fair amount today, more than it had ever consumed in Parashurama's hand. Parashurama could feel the power surging from the axe even now, singing in his veins, filling his being with a sense of supreme power. *Immortal. Invulnerable. Unassailable . . .* Parasu sang these thoughts to him silently, giving him a sense of complacency. This must be what it felt like to be a deva. Yet, it was important to remember what Lord Shiva had taught him: *Use Parasu only to accomplish your given task, no more. You must wield the axe, not let the axe wield you.*

He was glad that the Haihaya was capitulating. He felt that already Parasu had drunk too much, that the axe was intoxicated with the blood it had consumed, and he could hear it singing out to him silently, craving more, pleading for more . . . *demanding* more . . .

King Arjuna Kartavirya began swinging his arms.

Parashurama blinked.

What did this mean?

No words, no offer of conciliation, no acknowledgement that he had stolen the calf and was now willing to return it, just this peculiar . . . windmilling motion of his hands?

What was the Haihaya doing?

As Parashurama watched, the kshatriya's hands began swinging around in a diagonal motion that did not appear plausible by human standards, let alone physically possible. That angle, the way those shoulders bent and those elbows twisted? Had he broken his arms? How was he swinging them so rapidly? And why was he doing it?

Then a remarkable thing occurred.

King Arjuna Kartavirya's arms elongated, stretching out impossibly long and far, yards long, then a score of yards long . . .

Then, they divided, splitting into multiple arms, all different lengths, thicknesses, different in form and function . . .

In moments, there were hundreds of arms stretching out from the torso of the Haihaya king, sprawling across the raj marg and the surrounding area, like the vines of some great banyan tree, flailing about madly, still forming and shaping themselves, solidifying into a variety of forms. As Parashurama watched in fascination, each arm began to pick up a weapon from the several hundreds laying about. With several hundred men lying dead around, there were any number of weapons present. The elongated arms of Arjuna Kartavirya began taking up various weapons and wielding them.

Parashurama was astonished by the sheer number of arms that now sprouted from the body of King Arjuna Kartavirya. The Haihaya king's torso and body remained exactly as it was, standing rooted to the ground with surprising stability, anchoring the morass of flailing arms that covered the ground for tens of yards around him. There must be easily hundreds of arms, for every single weapon laying about had been taken up and still there were many arms seeking more weapons. Parashurama saw some arms simply reach out and close fists over rocks, rusting metal objects and anything that lay within reach.

The watching crowd gasped and emitted sounds of awe. Yet it was evident from the nature of their reaction that they had witnessed something like this before. Apparently, King Arjuna Kartavirya had displayed this astonishing ability on earlier occasions.

Parashurama was fascinated. He had never seen a man with a thousand arms before. For surely that was how many arms now swung about in the air, bearing weapons, swaying like cobras preparing to strike.

What a fascinating sight. And what an interesting challenge. If only his guru were here to watch this, Shiva would undoubtedly take great interest in observing his pupil engage with such an unusual opponent.

Clearly, King Arjuna Kartavirya had no intention of returning the calf amicably to Parashurama. He intended to fight. And from the looks of it, he intended to kill Parashurama himself. That was honourable, to do his own fighting instead of having his endless supply of lackeys do it for him. Parashurama respected him for that much at least. Whether or not the kshatriya succeeded in his goal was another matter. What concerned Parashurama was that the Haihaya had challenged him and had started by demonstrating that he possessed an ability far superior to that of his fellow kshatriyas.

If nothing else, it would make this one fight more interesting at least than all the earlier ones—he barely remembered those, blurring as they all did into one another, an endless succession of slaughter in which Parasu gained more satisfaction than he did.

Now, at least he had a worthy opponent.

Parashurama hefted his axe and began to swing it around on its leather thong.

Parasu began to sing again as it swung around, faster and faster, until its movement was a blur even to Parashurama, and its song a sharp keening at the farthest limit of hearing.

Across the city, the dogs resumed their barking.

The crowd oohed and aahed, anticipating the clash of the brahmin with the axe and the kshatriya with a thousand arms.

Parashurama waited for the enemy to attack.

||Nine||

The yagna at Naimisha-sharanya demanded a great deal of attention from the rishis as well as the acolytes. Coupled with the numerous daily chores, sandhi recitation lessons and other kul learning, it was always evening by the time everyone finished their sandhyavandana and assembled in the clearing to hear Ugrasrava Lomarsana Sauti resume his narration of the epic. Everyone looked forward eagerly to each day's narration and everyone felt more than a little disappointed when it ended for that evening. In this, there was little difference between the oldest maharishis and the youngest acolytes. Everyone wanted more.

Sauti smiled apologetically each night as he rose after declaring that day's narration ended, taking in the sea of wistful expressions and disappointed sighs. As the days passed, he grew certain that his audience expanded daily and in time, it seemed as if their numbers extended beyond the clearing itself, into the deep recesses of the jungle, until he felt as if the entire Naimisha-van was listening, each tree representing a dead soul in the Kurukshetra war, eagerly listening to hear the itihasa of their ancestors and to know the events leading up to the great war that caused their demise. If there is one question that has always haunted the human mind, it is this: What is the point of living? What is our purpose here on earth?

Why were we put here on this mortal plane? Is there a larger plan?

Phrase it any way one wishes, they all come back to the same question: *Why are we here?*

It was a question that everyone hoped the great epic *Mahabharata* would answer. After all, it was called the Fifth Veda for good reason. It not only told a great tale, but also illuminated the essence of the human condition through the events of that great tale. And no question was more essential to the human condition than knowing why one existed.

||Ten||

The fire crackled as Sauti resumed the tale of Parashurama and the history of the Bhrigu clan:

'Parashurama slew King Arjuna Kartavirya and returned home with the calf. The Haihaya king's thousand-armed attack was formidable and was capable of routing entire armies, for each arm could function independently of the others, extending longer or shorter, stronger or leaner, and fight separately of the rest of its sibling limbs, thereby confounding any number of the enemy. King Arjuna Kartavirya could plough through an enemy force like a pair of uksan dragging a yoke through soft earth, leaving a trail of churned bodies and sods of flesh. He was an unstoppable force.

'But against a single opponent, and that too Parashurama, his power proved futile.

'Parashurama's ability to wield the Parasu at blinding speed enabled him to chop off every last one of Arjuna Kartavirya's thousand arms. It was pure butchery. A thousand arms on one man or a thousand arms on five hundred men, it made no difference to Parashurama. Or to Parasu. They hacked off every last limb, evading every attempt to strike, cutting through every weapon, eliminating every threat, until the Haihaya king lay standing on the raj marg before the gates of his own city, shoulders spouting blood in thick, viscous jets. He slumped to the ground, lifeless and lay staring blindly up at the sky.

'Parashurama stepped over him and untied the calf from the cart to which it had been tethered.

'He took the calf home to his father, who was pleased and relieved to see it. He intended to return it safely to Indra at the earliest possible moment. Some things were too powerful to remain in the possession of mortals.

'But that was only the beginning of the conflict.

'King Arjuna Kartavirya's sons returned home soon after, their mission successfully accomplished, and the last rebels dead. They found that their father had been slain in a humiliating encounter, cut down at the gates of his own city by a mere brahmin boy. The enemy their father had captured and brought home, Bahu, son of Sagara, had taken advantage of his captor's death to make good his escape. Now, Bahu was raising a great army and preparing to wage all-out war against the Haihaya and the Panchagana, to stake his claim upon the throne of Ayodhya once and for all. And when he was done reclaiming Ayodhya, he had promised, he would take over Mahishmati and the possessions of the Haihaya and their allies as well. With Arjuna Kartavirya gone, it was likely he would accomplish his goal. What was more, the slaying of the Haihaya king at the hands of a mere brahmin boy had already become the stuff of legend, and across the land, kshatriyas were taking up arms and declaring war against the Haihayas and the rest of the Chandravanshis.

'The sons of Arjuna Kartavirya were not capable of standing up to the might of a full-blown opposition. With their father gone, their own kingdom would crumble quickly. He had held the conflicted forces of their allies together through brute strength. Now, they would be lucky if their own army remained loyal to them long enough to fight one battle.

'Seeing the end of their dynasty, brought down so suddenly and shockingly, they laid the entire blame at only one man's feet. Jamadagni. After all, it was he who had demanded his calf back. He had sent his son forth to reclaim her. And so he was responsible for their father's death.

'They rode towards Jamadagni's ashram. As it so chanced, Parashurama was away at that moment. The sons of Arjuna Kartavirya fell upon Jamadagni like wolves on a lamb, and tore him apart. They did to him what Jamadagni's son had done to their father, severing his limbs and then chopping his body into multiple parts and pieces.

'Then they rode away to try to piece together the fragments of their own disintegrating legacy.

'Parashurama returned home and saw the fate that had befallen his father.

'He recalled the sufferings of his Bhrigu ancestors over generations at the hands of kshatriyas such as the Haihayas and other enemies of the brahmin varna.

'He saw that the violence that existed in the world at present was all the work of these very kshatriyas, who, despite their so-called code of kshatriya dharma, were wanton, ruthless, immoral beings who did nothing but shed blood and spread violence like a disease upon the earth.

'He saw them as a pestilence upon the mortal realm.

'And he resolved to cleanse them from the world.'

||Eleven||

Three times seven Parashurama scoured the world of every living kshatriya. Twenty-one times he travelled the earth, seeking out warriors he had missed before, who had hidden away out of cowardice, or disguised themselves as brahmins or sudras or even vaisyas rather than fall prey to his terrible axe. Twenty-one times in all, he slaughtered every last warrior and cleansed the earth of every last person of the kshatriya varna.

He would have continued endlessly perhaps but the spirits of his pitrs, including his grandfather Sage Richika, appeared before him and appealed to him to cease his campaign of vengeance. Only then did he stop.

Weary of slaughter, his task done, he decided to go home.

Crossing the river Malaprabha on his way home, he paused to clean his axe. Parasu had drunk far too much blood. Twenty-one generations of kshatriyas had died under its perennially sharp blade. Now there was no more left for it to slake its thirst. Parashurama dipped it into the cool waters of the river, meaning to rid it of its burden, for the blood it drank added greatly to its weight and Parashurama had borne that weight too long.

The axe relented, also weary of bloodthirst, and began to purge itself of the blood it had consumed. Like a man who has consumed too much will vomit up the excess, Parasu began to spew forth the blood of its countless victims.

The river began to turn red with blood.

Parashurama realized that if he allowed Parasu to relieve itself here, the entire Malaprabha would be filled with the store of its accumulated blood. And eventually, all that blood would be carried down to the great ocean which would also be tainted. He lifted the axe out of the river.

He went in search of a suitable place to relinquish the blood of his victims.

He found it in the great northern plain. There he unleashed the blood from Parasu, once, twice, thrice . . . five times in all, the blood flowed from the axe, like a roaring tide. When it was drained, five enormous lakes of blood lay upon the land.

Samantapanchaka was the name given to this place.

Over time, the land absorbed the blood.

But was forever tainted.

It was on that very site that the great Maha Bharata war took place an Age later, when eighteen akshohinis of the Kauravas and Pandavas clashed on that field and stained that tainted soil once again with fresh blood.

||Twelve||

The rishis of Naimisha-sharanya asked Sauti to explain what the term akshohini meant. He replied that an army was broken into various units, and each of these was called an akshohini. He then explained what an akshohini consisted of, how many elephants, horses, chariots and foot soldiers.

Perhaps in keeping with the motif of eighteen, Sage Vyasa had also compiled his epic poem in eighteen parvas or sections, Sauti said. He then explained how he had taken Sage Vyasa's original eighteen parvas and divided them further into a total of one hundred sections or books. He briefly outlined the contents of each of the hundred sections. He then praised the epic, saying:

'Even he who is well-versed in the Vedas, the Vedangas and the Upanishads but has not read the *Mahabharata*, cannot be said to possess any real knowledge. For once a person has heard this epic, no other tale will seem as pleasing, and will be as the harsh cawing of crows after listening to the sweet singing of koyals. Just as the three realms of heaven, earth and the underworld have been created from the five elements of earth, water, brahman, wind and sky, thus is all poetry inspired by this supreme poem. Just as we know of four manner of beings—those born alive from wombs, those born from eggs, those that are plants, and those that are born from exudations and which we call insects, thus are all the Puranas derived from this greatest purana of all. As the five senses are dependent on the functioning of the mind, all events hereafter are dependent on this history. There is no story that can be told without taking inspiration from this ur-story, for it is to story-telling itself as food is to a living body. All poets shall take inspiration from it in order to pursue their professions. This Bharata epic which flowed from the lips of the great Krishna Dweipayana Vyasa is incomparable, beyond measure, purifying, sanctifying and a cleanser of all sins. He who wades into its divine ocean of stories has no need to bathe in the waters of Pushkar to cleanse himself.'

||Paksha Four||

THE SARPA SATRA

||One||

All day long the sacrificial fires burned, fed by an army of brahmins. Janamajaya son of Parikshat sat with his brothers Shrutasena, Ugrasena and Bhimasena on the field of Kurukshetra, performing the formidable sarpa yagna. An island of activity in the vast desolate plain, the yagna was attended by many pre-eminent brahmins who became ritvijas or officiating priests, and sadasyas or participants in the ritual sacrifice. The hotar, the brahmin who recited the essential Vedic shlokas uninterrupted, was the great Vedic scholar Chandabhargava, a Bhrigu descended from Chyavana. The udgatar, who chanted shlokas alongwith the hotar, was the wise old Kautsarya Jaimini. The adhvaryu, the officiating priest of the ritual, was Bhodhapingala. And Shargnarava was the brahmin of record for the yagna. The great Krishna Dweipayana-Vyasa was a sadasya, along with his sons and disciples: Uddalaka, Shamathaka, Shwetaketu, Panchama, Ashita, Devala, Narada, Parvata, Atreya, Kundajathara, his associates Kutighata and Vatsya, an old scholar named Shrutashrava, Kahoda, Devasharma, Maudgalya and Samasaurabha. These were but a few of the many illustrious Vedic gurus and brahmins who attended as sadasyas at the sarpa yagna.

It was but the start of the ceremony. As of now, only the initial offerings and mantras had begun and the main purpose of the ritual—the extermination of the entire species of serpents on earth—was yet to start. As the brahmins had explained, it would be some time before the yagna accumulated sufficient brahmanic potency to start drawing in snakes from around the world, literally pulling them from wherever they existed, into the sacrificial fire, there to burn to ashes. It was an ambitious undertaking and required every ounce of concentration on the part of the officiating and attending brahmins, and Janamajaya and his brothers knew this well. They too were focussed on the yagna's immaculate execution, and were deep in concentration as the purohits poured endless ladles of ghee into the flames and recited the powerful shlokas from the Vedas uninterrupted. The roar of the fire as it was buffetted by the winds across the Kurukshetra plain was like the voice of Agni personified, underscoring the rhythmic chanting of the priests.

The site of the yagna also weighed heavily on the minds of the king and his brothers. It was not that long ago that their own forefathers had assembled here in prodigious numbers, waging the greatest war ever known in the history of the human race. When the blood-speckled dust had settled on that gruesome tragedy, only a handful of survivors remained alive on this field of battle. Of them, only one had left an heir: Abhimanyu, who had died in the notorious chakravyuh formation, had left his wife Uttara with child at the time of his demise. Abhimanyu himself was the son of Arjuna, one of the five Pandava brothers, from his union with his wife Subhadra, sister of Lord Krishna himself. This made Parikshat the great-nephew of Krishna and the grandson of Arjuna. Parikshat in turn sired Janamajaya, and it was in fact for his father's sake that Janamajaya was performing this sarpa yagna. In a sense, this ceremony and those sponsoring it, were causally linked to the

Maha Bharata war itself. These thoughts were no doubt on the minds of King Janamajaya and his brothers that day as they sat on the field at Kurukshetra as the yagna fire blazed and the brahmins challenged the wind with their ritual chanting. Who knows what anxieties and emotions filled the hearts and minds of the four Kurus as they sat upon the very spot where their entire dynasty and the vast part of the population of their nation had been exterminated, in a battle with their own brethren and kin?

It was at this moment that a sarameya happened to stray into the consecrated site where the yagna was taking place.

The sarameya was, as his name suggested, a progeny of the celestial bitch Sarama herself, from whom all dogs are descended. He was but a pup, and merely exploring. Sniffing with his whiskered nose to the ground, as pups will do, he had followed his nose to the site of the satra, forgetting his mother's warning not to stray too far from her nest. The eldest of his litter, he was bolder than his siblings, and twice as tall and long as they, but still no more than the length of a man's hand. His brindled fur bristled sharply as he smelled myriad rich exotic scents in that place, his little tail rod-stiff and pointing directly upwards as he snuffed and sniffed his way along. So low was his nose and so intense his concentration, he failed to notice that he was coming close to a place of human activity. The countless lives expended on that alluvial plain had left a morass of lingering scents that were like an explosion of sensory experience to the little canine. Through the power of scent alone, he could almost imagine in his dog's mind what terrible slaughter and violence had transpired here, and the effect overwhelmed him.

He stumbled into the innermost area of the yagna, nose still to the ground, tail raised high, and might well have blundered past the preoccupied brahmins who were all intent on their chanting and feeding of the fire, passed onwards and never been noticed. He was a tiny thing after all, no more than a handful of fur, and all but invisible to most humans. But his zigzag pattern of movement, caused by his following a path dictated by his nose rather than his sense of sight, happened to bring his little furred head in contact with the foot of one of Janamajaya's brothers. Unfortunately for the little tyke, the foot in question belonged to Shrutasena, not known for his sense of patience or tolerance.

Without even looking at the pup, Shrutasena swatted him aside.

The pup yelped and stumbled.

Then he picked himself up and wagged his tail, lifting his little head to stare up at the tall human whom he had apparently offended in some unknown way. He came closer to the human, wagging his tail, and attempted to lick Shrutasena's foot to show that he had meant no offence and would happily be friends if Shrutasena wished.

Once more, Shrutasena kicked the pup aside. The little ball of fur weighed no more than a few hundred grams and flew several feet away, tumbling over and over in the dust, squealing in distress. He regained his feet, yelping and calling out to his mother for help, unable to understand why he should have been treated so roughly when all he had sought to do was apologize and proffer a paw in friendship.

The pup's crying caught the attention of Janamajaya's other brothers, Bhimasena and Ugrasena. While it is true that a little sarameya can easily slip by unnoticed through a human camp, yet once he begins crying out, he can wake the whole camp.

Janamajaya's three brothers all came up and began beating the pup with their lathis. Blow after blow rained down on the little sarameya. Fortunately for him, he was small enough to dodge and avoid most of the blows, or else he would certainly have died that day. But a few of the blows did catch him and caused him great pain and bruising, even cracking a rib and a thigh bone. He yelped pitifully and when that did not stop the shower of blows, he howled his distress.

Somehow, he slipped out of the circle of pain and fled, limping and howling loud enough to alert the entire contingent of brahmins. They looked up, frowning, but did not pause in their ritual activities for once begun a satra or yagna must be seen through immaculately. Even a syllable misspoken or the wrong herb proferred to Agni can render the entire enterprise invalid. Once they saw that there was no cause for alarm, merely a stray dog being chased away, they forgot the incident instantly.

As did Janamajaya's brothers, who resumed their seats and returned to their thoughts, dire and dark as they must have been.

Limping and crying pitifully, the little pup made his way homewards. After a considerably longer time than it had taken him to reach the yagna site, he finally managed to limp his way back to the nest where Sarama guarded the rest of her new brood. On seeing his mother, he began crying louder than ever, and limping more pitifully. His mother exclaimed and rushed to his side to comfort him. After licking his wounds and bruises and after a close examination of his injuries, she finally asked him what had happened. Speaking in their canine tongue, he communicated to her how he had come by his injuries.

'You must have done something to provoke them, my son,' she said.

'But I did nothing!' he wailed.

'Perhaps you licked the sacred ghee? Or soiled the sanctified site?'

'No!' he insisted. 'I did nothing. I never even looked at anything. They just beat me for no reason at all.'

Sarama was outraged. She went at once to the site of the sarpa yagna and confronted the king himself. His brothers attempted to bar her passage but as Mistress of all Dogkind, Sarama was a giant among her kind. She towered above all three of Janamajaya's brothers and could have swallowed the trio whole if she chose. She glowered at them, baring her fangs and snarling, and they stepped aside to let her pass unmolested. The priests glanced in her direction, puzzled, but continued their rituals. The day's session was still in progress and they could not afford to pause or interrupt their work for even a moment. Janamajaya rose from his seat and was taken aback at the sight of the huge dog looming above him, snarling menacingly.

'Raje,' she said angrily. 'Your brothers beat my son for no reason at all. He did nothing wrong here. Why did they attack him, a poor defenceless little whelp?'

Janamajaya had no answer to offer. He looked at his brothers who also looked away, avoiding his gaze. They had been too harsh with the pup and realized it, but would not say so aloud. After all, he was a mere dog! And they were princes of the Kuru line.

'He did not lick the yagna ghee,' Sarama went on. 'He did not even look at it! Yet your brothers attacked him and beat him—with lathis! This is unjust violence. Have you of the Kuru race not yet learned to rid yourself of the evil of violence? Has the slaughter of countless millions of your people not taught you anything?'

Janamajaya hung his head in shame. He had nothing to say that would appease the angry mother. And Sarama was an angry mother, reacting no differently from the way any mother would had her child been beaten so brutally and without cause.

Sarama's anger was fuelled further by the silence of the Kuru king and his brothers, for she knew then that they were guilty of needless violence against a helpless, defenceless little creature. Her rage knew no bounds. 'I curse you, Janamajaya!' she barked. 'As you have unjustly beaten my child, so also shall evil befall you without cause or reason, when you least expect it!'

And she turned, showing the Kurus her hindquarters, flicked her tail, and departed.

On hearing the curse of Sarama, Janamajaya was very disheartened. To be accused—justifiably—found guilty, and then cursed, by a dog, even if she was the mistress of all dogkind, was not something anyone could claim to be proud of achieving. He buried his face in his hands and wondered why tragedy seemed to befall his line time and time again.

Later, when the day's yagna session had ended, he returned home to his palace in the capital city of Hastinapura, seat of the Kuru nation, and gave word to his people that he desired a priest, one so honourable and devout that he could counter the effect of Sarama's curse and absolve Janamajaya of his sin. For though his brothers had struck the blows that harmed the little sarameya, it was under Janamajaya's rule and at his sarpa yagna that the misdemeanour had been committed, therefore he held himself responsible. But though his people searched far and wide for such a priest, none could be found. For though just a dog, Sarama was a powerful being in her own right. Many myths and legends even considered the celestial bitch to be one of many forms that the Eternal Goddess herself, sometimes known as Devi, other times as Durga or Kali, or an infinite variety of names and titles, chose to take at certain times. Some even believed that Janamajaya had transgressed against Kali herself and would now have to suffer the consequences of his actions. This was ironic since the very cause of the sarpa yagna was to mitigate the effect of an earlier transgression against the demon king Kali by Janamajaya's late father Parikshat. The king Kali was in no way related to the goddess Kali, and the commonality of name simply referred to their shared darkness of complexion, a common trait among people of the Arya race, but it was nonetheless a matter of some significance. What good was performing a ritual to expiate the sins of the father if the son himself committed further sins in the course of the ritual?

Time passed.

One day, Janamajaya went on a hunt. His quest for prey took him to a remote neck of the jungle at the farthest extent of his domain. In the course of his search, he lost sight of his prey but chanced upon an ashram deep within the jungle. A rishi named Shrutashrava resided there and seated beside him was his beloved son Somashrava. After discerning that the son was a rare enlightened soul as well as possessed of precisely the qualities he sought, Janamajaya appealed to Rishi Shrutashrava to permit his son Somashrava to accompany him back to Hastinapura and act as his preceptor. The father agreed but felt it was his dharma to inform Janamajaya about certain facts concerning the son.

'Bhagavan,' said the rishi, for he regarded the king of the Kurus as no less than a god incarnate in stature and dignity. 'My son is a great ascetic and has acquired much knowledge. But he was not born to me in the usual way. Rather, he was the result of my semen being consumed by a snake who then brought him to term in her womb. Due to his unusual nature, he possesses the power to absolve you of sins against any being, with one notable exception: He cannot help you if you transgress against Mahadeva. Moreover, he has sworn a secret vow that requires him to grant a brahmin anything he asks for. If you can accept these unique characteristics of his personality, by all means take him with you and may he serve you dutifully.'

Janamajaya was so pleased at having found the perfect preceptor, he was undaunted by these revelations. He joined his hands together and addressed the rishi with the same respect afforded to himself: 'O Bhagavan, it shall be as you say.'

Janamajaya returned to Hastinapura with Somashrava and introduced him to his brothers. 'Henceforth, this is my guru. Kindly regard him as your teacher as well, and obey his every command.'

Shortly thereafter, a rebellion rose in the kingdom of Takshashila that demanded the king's attention. Janamajaya rode out at the head of his army to suppress the uprising and do battle against the Takshashilans.

||Two||

Around the same time, there was a rishi named Ayoda-Dhaumya who had three shishyas named Upamanyu, Aruni and Veda. One day, the seer called upon his disciple Aruni, who hailed from the region of Panchala. 'Aruni,' said the sage, 'there is a breach in the levee. Go and stop the flow of water.'

The pupil did as his teacher bid and went to the levee. He found the hole in the embankment but could not find a way to stop the breach. After exhausting all other methods, he finally lay down and used his own body to block the flow of water. Time passed but as nobody else was aware of his plight, nor could he find any other way to keep the water from escaping, Aruni remained there in the levee, using his own body to keep the hole closed.

Days passed.

One afternoon, Rishi Ayoda-Dhaumya wondered at Aruni's absence. 'Where is Aruni of Panchala?' he asked his other shishyas. 'Bhagavan, you sent him to repair the hole in the levee,' they replied. 'He has not yet returned.'

Rishi Ayoda-Dhaumya, accompanied by his other two disciples, then proceeded to the embankment. Unable to see Aruni anywhere, the rishi called out, 'Aruni, where are you? Show yourself, my son.' At the sound of his guru's voice, Aruni rose and presented himself.

He explained his absence by showing his guru the hole and demonstrating how he had lain down to block it himself, to prevent the water escaping. With the aid of the other pupils, he was now able to repair the breach and made no complaint of the time he had spent lying in the muddy embankment, alone in the cold and dark, without food or respite. Rishi Ayoda-Dhaumya was greatly impressed by his disciple's discipline and sense of duty.

'Aruni of Panchala,' he said, showing his pleasure, 'since you blocked the breach with your own self and therefore acted as a stopper to halt the flow of water, you shall henceforth be known as Uddalaka!' The guru smiled at his own wit, as did his pupils. 'And since you obeyed your guru's instructions so well, you shall attain all that you desire in life. All the wisdom of the Vedas shall be known to you and all the dharmashastras as well. Go forth and prosper. Your education is done.' Overjoyed, Uddalaka who was formerly Aruni, departed the kul of his guru and set out into the world.

One day, Ayoda-Dhaumya said to his second pupil Upamanyu, 'My son, go and take care of my cows.' Upamanyu did as his guru said. Each day, after caring for the cows, he returned to the guru's ashram at sundown and respectfully greeted him. One evening, the rishi observed him, then frowned and remarked, 'Upamanyu, you appear to be quite fat. How do you derive nourishment?' To which the student replied, 'Guru, I support myself by begging for alms.' Rishi Ayoda-Dhaumya said disapprovingly, 'You are not to use alms you receive by begging without first sharing them with me.' Thereafter, the disciple surrendered all his alms to his guru each day.

Some days later, Rishi Ayoda-Dhaumya again observed

Upamanyu looking as fat as before. 'Upamanyu, I take all your alms away from you. How then do you continue to sustain yourself so well?' Upamanyu bowed his head and answered, 'O Bhagavan, after handing over the alms for the day to you, I go out and beg for more. Those alms I use to feed myself.' Rishi Ayoda-Dhaumya was upset at his pupil: 'This is not the way to obey your elders! You are circumventing the letter of my instructions. I commanded you to give all your alms to me, yet you keep some for yourself. When you act thus, you deprive others of their sustenance. You are a glutton, Upamanyu!'

Ashamed of his lapse, Upamanyu continued to care for the cows but now surrendered everything he received as alms to his guru without keeping anything for himself. But again Rishi Ayoda-Dhaumya observed him and asked, 'Upamanyu, you give all your alms to me, and do not collect more for yourself as I forbade it. Then why do you still appear so fat?' The pupil quailed at his preceptor's disapproval and hesitantly admitted, 'I drink the milk of the cows.' Rishi Ayoda-Dhaumya waxed angrily again. 'These cows belong to me, Upamanyu. It is wrong for you to drink their milk without asking for my permission. I forbid you to do so henceforth.'

Upamanyu promised he would no longer drink the milk and continued herding the cows. Days later, his guru looked at him again and still found him as fat as before. 'Upamanyu, how is this possible? You do not eat alms or beg a second time for more alms for yourself. You do not drink the milk from my cows. Yet you appear as fat. What do you survive on?' The shishya replied, 'Bhagavan, your cows are suckled by their calves. Even after they finish suckling, they spit out generous quantities of froth. I drink the froth they spit out and thus I am fed.' Rishi Ayoda-Dhaumya shook his head in despair and said, 'Upamanyu, you do not understand. The calves throw out more froth than usual because they pity you. But by consuming their froth you deprive them of their rightful sustenance. Henceforth, I forbid you from drinking the froth.'

Once again Upamanyu left his guru's ashram and took care of his cows. But acting under his guru's instructions, he no longer kept any part of the alms he received, nor did he beg a second time for more alms for himself, nor did he drink the milk from the cows, nor even the froth spat out by the calves after they suckled at the udders of the cows. He began to suffer the pangs of hunger. Starving and desperate, he saw a bush in the forest and found its leaves desirable. He ate the leaves, not knowing that the bush was a sun-plant named arka. The acrid raw juice from the leaves caused him to lose his eye sight. Blinded, he wandered through the forest until he stumbled and fell into a well. At day's end, the cows found their way home by instinct without Upamanyu. When Upamanyu failed to return, his guru said to his other pupils, 'I forbade Upamanyu every form of sustenance or nourishment. He must be starving and angry. That must be why he has stayed in the forest rather than return home with the cows.' Concerned for his shishya's well-being, Rishi Ayoda-Dhaumya went into the woods to search for Upamanyu. He cried out his name loudly as he went, searching for hours. 'Upamanyu, where are you, my son? Come to me!' Upamanyu heard his guru's voice and called out weakly, 'Master, I am here. I have fallen into a well.' The rishi found the mouth of the well and leaned over it, peering into the dark pit. 'How did you happen to fall into this well?' he asked. Upamanyu sobbed in shame. 'I could not bear the hunger any longer, my guru. I ate some leaves and went blind. I know now that they must have been leaves from the arka sun-plant. I cannot see a thing now. I have lost my eyesight forever and cannot climb up from this well.'

The guru heard his pupil and advised him gently, 'Upamanyu, my son, you must pray to the Ashwins. Pray long and hard, sing their praises sincerely and with all your heart. Those divine healers will restore your eyesight.'

Upamanyu took his guru's words to heart. He knew that it was through his repeated flaunting of his guru's instructions that he had come by this sorry pass. Had he heeded his guru and done exactly as bidden at the very outset, none of this would have happened. He wished with all his heart for an opportunity to prove that he was a good shishya and worthy of the guru's faith in him. Praying to the Ashwins—or to any god for that matter—was no easy task. The fact that Rishi Ayoda-Dhaumya believed that he, Upamanyu, could summon the Divine Twins through the power of his prayers alone was a great show of faith.

Summoning up his reserves of strength, Upamanyu began to sing the praises of the Ashwins. He recalled the appropriate shlokas from the Rig Veda which served exactly this purpose and chanted them from memory, with perfect inflection, rhythm and cadence.

Upamanyu's voice sang out from the pit of the well shaft, through the forest, and rose to the heavens, until, finally, it reached the ears of the divine Ashwins themselves.

Those celestial Twins manifested themselves before Upamanyu, appearing in physical form at the bottom of the well. He sensed their presence and greeted them with appropriate reverence and adulation. They spoke with a single voice that was doubled in sound and intensity.

The Ashwins said to Upamanyu: 'We are pleased with your recitation. Take this cake and eat it. It is yours to enjoy.' And so saying, they handed him a delicious cake.

The cake smelled wonderfully aromatic and enticing to starving, blind Upamanyu. He reached out eagerly, desiring to take it and consume it at once. Yet he paused.

'Nay,' he said to the divine Twins. 'I cannot accept anything without first offering it to my guru. I thank you kindly for your gift but you must allow me to present it to my guru. He will decide whether or not to share it with me.'

The Ashwins said: 'Many years ago, your guru prayed to us just as sincerely and we gifted him a similar cake as well. He ate it all himself without offering it to his preceptor. You would only be doing exactly as he did.'

Upamanyu shook his head. 'Forgive me, great ones. I know you only speak the truth therefore everything you say must have happened exactly as you say. Even so, I cannot eat this cake without first offering it to my preceptor. Perhaps he will permit me to partake of a piece.'

The Ashwins were impressed by Upamanyu's fortitude and said to him, 'Your devotion to your guru is unassailable. We are pleased by your choice. Your guru has teeth of black iron. Your teeth shall be golden. Your sight will be restored in full and you shall be granted good fortune as well.'

The instant they pronounced these words, Upamanyu found himself able to see again perfectly, with no trace of the pain or discomfort caused by the eating of the arka leaves. He was blessed with a brief glimpse of the shining Ashwins before they faded away, departing for their heavenly realm. He bowed and joined hands to thank them as they vanished. Feeling refreshed and strengthened, he was then able to climb out of the well easily.

Standing before his guru, he touched his preceptor's feet and told him all that had transpired within the well. Rishi Ayoda-Dhaumya nodded, smiling happily, and said to him, 'It shall be as the Ashwins said to you. You will have perfect knowledge of the Vedas. And you shall attain whatever you desire in life. This was your test, and you have passed it successfully. You are now free to go on your way.'

Rishi Ayoda-Dhaumya's third pupil was named Veda. One day, the guru instructed him, 'Veda, my son, stay here in my house. I am leaving on a long journey. Consider this house to be your own and reside here until I return. You will be forever blessed for doing this.'

Veda did exactly as his guru bade him. He lived in his guru's house and took care of all the daily chores without respite. Like a bullock yoked to a heavy plough, he pulled his load of responsibilities without complaint, enduring the extremities of cold, heat, hunger and thirst, and never leaving that house for any reason. After a much longer absence than anticipated, Rishi Ayoda-Dhaumya returned and relieved Veda. Pleased with his pupil's rigorous sense of responsibility and strict adherence to his every instruction, the guru praised him, blessed him and sent him on his way, having obtained perfect knowledge and great good fortune. This was the trial of the third pupil, Veda.

||Three||

Veda then went forth and in time, embarked upon the grihastha-ashrama stage of existence, which is to say, he became a married man and a householder. In time, attracted by his reputation for being a man of great learning, three students came to study with him as well. But because of the deprivations and austerities he and his fellow shishyas had suffered in Rishi Ayoda-Dhaumya's ashram, Veda resolved never to test his students as cruelly. Not once did he order them to observe rites rigorously, nor mete out punishments for non-compliance, nor did he expect perfect obedience from them. In time, two kshatriyas named Paushya and Janamajaya—a quite different person from King Janamajaya of the Kurus—came to Veda's house and asked him to be their preceptor. He accepted.

One day, Veda had to leave home to officiate at a ceremony for one of his patrons. He requested one of his disciples named Uttanka to look after his house. He told Uttanka: 'Do whatever needs to be done to take care of the household. Ensure that nothing is lacking.' With these simple instructions, Veda left. As it transpired, his journey took him to a faraway foreign nation and his absence from home was far longer than expected. Uttanka obeyed his guru's request dutifully. Some months later, the women of the household gathered together to speak to him. They told him that Rishi Veda and his wife had been desirous of having offspring for a long time. Now, the preceptor's wife was in the ideal period for conception, based on her biological factors as well as the astrological signs and other omens. If this time passed, who knew when she might conceive again. As the man of the house, it fell to him to impregnate her and ensure that her period of fertility did not go to waste. Uttanka was troubled by the request of the women. He said to them, 'I hear your demand but it is not proper that I should do this on your word alone. I take my instructions only from my guru and he has not asked me to do any such thing.' They urged him, saying that the preceptor had after all told him to do whatever needed to be done and to ensure that nothing was lacking, therefore he would only be performing his duty to the guru by filling his wife's barren womb. But Uttanka held firm and refused to do as they said.

In time, the guru returned home from his long journey. He heard all that had transpired in his absence, and was pleased with Uttanka's decision for he would not have approved of another man inseminating his wife. He said to Uttanka, 'My son, you have fulfilled your dharma admirably while using your own judgement wisely. This is a great service you have done for me and I am deeply grateful to you. In return, name anything you desire and I shall do everything in my power to return the favour. Do you wish to leave my service and pursue your own fortune? If so, then I grant you leave to go and bless you with a certainty of success in any endeavour you choose.'

Uttanka considered his guru's words and replied, 'Gurudev, it is well known that when a shishya completes his education he must give his guru a dakshina, otherwise if one person asks for something without offering anything in return and the other person gives without rightfully receiving anything in exchange, there shall be enmity between those two, and one shall inevitably die. You have already granted me the greatest gift any guru can give his shishya: you have given me leave to go forth into the world, declaring my education complete. In exchange, I wish to give you your guru-dakshina as it is only fair that I repay you for your gift of learning to me.'

Rishi Veda was impressed by his pupil's answer and said, 'In that case, Uttanka, give me some time to consider what guru-dakshina to ask.' Uttanka was sanguine and continued to stay peacefully at his guru's ashram.

Some time later, Uttanka came before his preceptor and asked him once again, 'My guru, command me what guru-dakshina you desire that I may give it you.' Rishi Veda said, 'Uttanka, my son. So many times have you asked me already what guru-dakshina I desire. I am still unable to think of anything. Yet you deserve an answer, therefore go to my wife and ask her if she desires anything. Give her whatever she demands and I shall consider it as my guru-dakshina.' So Uttanka went to the guru's wife and joined his hands before her. 'Shrimati, my guru says I have completed my education and may go home. But I must give him guru-dakshina before I take my leave. He has sent me to you. Command me what you wish and I shall bring it to you as a guru-dakshina.' The preceptor's wife thought briefly and replied: 'Go then to King Paushya, your guru's patron. His queen possesses a certain set of earrings that she wears often. Ask him to give you those earrings and fetch them to me. In four days, there shall be an important ceremony and I wish to appear most radiant before the brahmins who will attend. Bring me the queen's earrings and you shall have the blessings of your guru as well as my own good wishes!'

Happy to finally have a task to perform, Uttanka set out at once for Raja Paushya's palace.

||Four||

It was a long distance to the palace and while he was walking, Uttanka saw upon the road the largest bull he had ever seen in his life. Seated atop the bull was the largest man he had ever seen! Intrigued by this extraordinary sight, Uttanka slowed to stare at the enormous bull and the giant seated atop it. As he was staring at them curiously, the man called out to him. 'Uttanka!' He was startled to hear his name shouted by a stranger. The man called out to him, 'Uttanka, eat the dung of this bull!' Uttanka recoiled in disgust at the very thought. Naturally he did not comply with the giant's request. Once again the giant called out, 'Uttanka, eat it without hesitation. Your guru himself has eaten it in his time.'

Despite his disgust, Uttanka felt a powerful urge to do as the stranger said. Somehow, he overcame his repulsion and ate the bull's fetid dung and even drank its urine.

Soon afterward, Uttanka reached the palace of Raja Paushya and went before the king. He introduced himself and announced, 'Raje, I am the disciple of your guru Rishi Veda.' King Paushya replied warmly, 'Then you are as a god to me. Speak. What can I do for you?' Uttanka told him about the earrings his queen possessed, which were desired by Rishi Veda's wife, to wear for the ceremony before the brahmins. 'I beg you to give me the earrings that I may present them to my guru's wife as my guru-dakshina.' Paushya answered without hesitation: 'Of course. Go directly into the queen's palace and ask for my wife. Tell her I sent you and you shall have what you desire.'

Pleased to hear this, Uttanka went into the inner apartments of the palace of the queen. He searched everywhere but could not find the queen. Returning to the king, he said with some irritation: 'Raje, you ought not to have lied to me. You said the queen was in her palace but I looked everywhere and could find no trace of her.' Paushya was taken aback at first, then thought for a moment. Finally he said, 'There can be only one explanation. You must be somehow impure or polluted. Since she is a faithful wife to me, she cannot be seen by anyone who is not immaculately clean. Somehow, you must have consumed stale food or in some way rendered yourself unclean. Think and try to remember.' Uttanka thought back and realized the king spoke the truth. 'Indeed, it is as you say. As I was in a hurry to come here and reach back to the guru's house before the ceremony, I performed my ablutions on the road, while walking.' Paushya nodded. 'That would explain why you did not see the queen. Ablutions must always be performed while sitting, never while standing or walking.' Uttanka saw the wisdom of the kshatriya's words and performed his ablutions again. He sat facing the east, then first washed his hands, face and feet thoroughly and without making haste. Then, maintaining absolute silence, he sipped just enough clean water, ensuring it was completely free of scum or froth, in precisely the right amount that was required to reach his heart. Then he washed twice and cleansed his orifices with water. Only when he had duly completed these ablutions to perfection did he rise once more and enter the queen's inner apartments. At once, he saw the queen, seated where she had always been, now made visible to his senses.

At the sight of Uttanka, the queen rose and greeted him appropriately with respect befitting an acolyte of her husband's guru. 'Great one, command me. What can I do for you?' Uttanka said to her gently, 'Good queen, I ask that you give me the earrings that you are wearing. I wish to give them as guru-dakshina.' Without hesitation, the queen removed her earrings and proffered them to him gladly. But as she gave them she cautioned him in a whisper: 'Good man, know this. Takshaka, Lord of Nagas, dearly desires these earrings. He would do anything to possess them. Carry them carefully.' Uttanka thanked her for the earrings and for her warning and assured her, 'Shrimati, do not fear. This is my guru-dakshina. Even Takshaka, King of Snakes, cannot take them from me now!'

He bid the queen farewell and returned to Paushya. The king asked him if he was satisfied now and Uttanka replied, 'Oh yes, raje, I am very pleased. I shall now take your leave.' Paushya bade him wait, saying, 'Great one, you are clearly a person of great learning and note. I have been waiting to perform an important shraddha. By your grace, we may now perform it before you leave.' Uttanka was reluctant but felt obligated to the king for his gracious treatment and generous gift. 'Very well, raje. I shall stay a short while. But I ask that rather than prepare special food which will take a great deal of time, let us consume whatever food is already prepared.' The king agreed and sent for food for Uttanka at once.

When the food arrived and was served to Uttanka, he was upset to see that it was brought cold and there was a hair in the food. Angered by this extremely rude slight, he threatened Paushya: 'You dare offer unclean and cold food to a guest? I shall curse you with blindness!' Paushya reacted equally sharply: 'In that case, since you wrongly accuse me and spoil food that was unspoiled, you shall lose the ability to have offspring!' But as the host, Paushya felt obliged to investigate his guest's complaint. On examining the food closely, he found that it did indeed contain a hair and was quite cold; he enquired further and learned that this was because the food had been prepared by a woman who was careless and had not braided her hair. Apologizing for this grave lapse in his hospitality, he joined his palms before Uttanka and said in a contrite tone: 'Great one, the fault was entirely my own. You spoke truly. The food served to you was indeed cold and unclean. Please forgive me for this error. Please do not curse me with blindness.' Uttanka sighed and shook his head regretfully: 'What I pronounced shall surely come to pass. You will go blind but I shall counter the effect to ensure that you regain your eyesight soon. Now that you admit your fault, you must also take back your curse. Do not render me incapable of bearing offspring.' Paushya rubbed his face in misery. 'Great one, would that I could. But as you know, a brahmin's heart is soft as ghee even though his words may be sharp as razors. A kshatriya is the opposite: our words may be soft as ghee but our hearts are sharp instruments. Even now, my anger has not been quelled completely. I cannot take back my curse. Please, just go.' Uttanka rose and said, 'I spoke the truth. The food was impure just as I said. Yet I allowed myself to be appeased by you. Earlier, you cursed me saying that I had wrongly accused you and spoiled food that was unspoiled. But my accusation *was* true and the food *was* spoiled, therefore your curse is ineffective. Let the matter end here.' So saying, Uttanka left Raja Paushya's palace, taking the earrings with him.

||Five||

Uttanka was eager to return to his guru's house and complete his mission. He put aside all thoughts of the events preceding and pursuant to his procuring the earrings and kept his mind set on reaching home at the earliest. But after walking a fair way, he saw a peculiar sight. There was a man on the road ahead who kept appearing and disappearing. As Uttanka approached, he was able to make out that the man was a kshapanaka, either a Buddhist or Jain mendicant, given to wandering naked and begging for alms. One moment, he could see the kshapanaka quite distinctly, standing on the road, the next moment, the kshapanaka was nowhere to be seen. Uttanka was vexed by this sight, remembering the equally bizarre incident that had occurred when he was en route to Raja Paushya's palace. 'I shall ignore this phenomenon completely and concentrate only on reaching home quickly,' he told himself.

He continued walking. But instead of passing by the kshapanaka, somehow the man always stayed several yards ahead of him on the road, continuing to appear and disappear in random flashes. Tense and disturbed by this vision, Uttanka found himself exceedingly thirsty. Due to the altercation with King Paushya, he had been unable to eat or drink anything since leaving his guru's home days earlier and was desperately in need of refreshment. Spying a pool just beside the road, he bent down to drink. As his simple garb contained no compartment, he was compelled to set the earrings down beside him for a moment while he cupped his hands to drink the water. The instant he set them down, the kshapanaka appeared in a flash beside him, snatched up the earrings and disappeared.

Uttanka sprang up and chased after the kshapanaka. At first the mendicant continued his vanishing act, but as Uttanka gained on him and began to grasp hold of his limbs and struggle to get the earrings back, the being finally gave up his disguise and assumed his true form. He showed himself to be Takshaka, king of snakes, and in his true body, it was impossible for Uttanka to grasp hold of him. Uttanka struggled manfully with him for a while, but Takshaka slithered out of Uttanka's grasp and slipped into a chasm in the ground that had miraculously appeared. Uttanka understood at once that the queen's warning had come to pass. If he allowed Takshaka to escape now, the lord of the Nagas would wriggle all the way home to the realm of snakes and Uttanka would never recover the earrings. His only chance was to plunge in after the lord of snakes. Determined to fulfil his obligation to his guru, he leaped into the chasm moments before it closed.

Uttanka tumbled through empty space for what felt like an endless period of time. Finally, he found himself on solid ground with no recollection of having suffered any impact on landing. He was in a rock tunnel deep underground. Hearing a slithering sound from ahead, he moved in that direction and spied Takshaka's tail swishing from side to side as the serpent lord slipped away. He followed the Naga for another endless period of time, through tunnel after tunnel, through bifurcations and intersections, through small narrow tunnels where he had to slide sideways to avoid striking his shoulders or elbow and through enormous vaulting tunnels where the ceiling was too high overhead for him to see and his footsteps echoed cavernously. Through all this pursuit, he could barely see anything, the entire journey being in darkness. Only the sound of Takshaka slithering ahead guided him. He was in perpetual fear of the Naga lord slipping through a tunnel before he could follow, leaving him at a loss to know which way to go next. By some instinct, he was able to avoid striking his limbs on the rocky outcroppings as he went, and to avoid the numerous pitfalls and yawning abysses that lay at every turn. After an unknown duration, he finally saw light up ahead and emerged to find himself in a wondrous place.

At first, he thought he had somehow emerged into the upper world again, and was standing on a vast plain beneath the open sky. By degrees, he realized that he was in fact farther underground than any mortal had been before. Many miles, certainly several yojanas beneath the surface of the earth. The place he had emerged into was a vast underground cavern, so enormous that he could barely glimpse the roof of it, high, high above. The cavern's other dimensions were equally epic: from one side to the far end was a distance so great, he could not accurately judge how many yojanas it might cover. There were entire townships nestled on the ground of the cavern, gleaming cities and individual nests where Nagas lived in uncountable profusion. Lakes, even oceans, mountains, valleys, hills and dales, it was a world unto itself, but all formed of the craggy black rock of the underworld, and lit by a luminescence alien to the illumination of daylight and sunlight. It was perpetual night here but without stars or moon or celestial orbs visible, only utter blackness beyond the phosphorescence of the inhabited regions.

He climbed down from the tunnel's entrance and walked to the nearest city of the Nagas. He began to see many of the denizens of the underworld, some in anthropomorphic form with only some vestige of their snake-like nature, others more serpent than human in appearance, and still others neither snake nor human but something else entirely. There were as many varieties of Nagas as there were species of living creatures on the surface of the world. Uttanka marvelled at their profusion and variety and despite their fierce outlook, he found himself curiously without fear.

As he stopped in the centre of the city, he felt certain shlokas form in his mind unbidden. Following his instinct, he recited these aloud:

|Beautiful sarpas, subjects of Airavata!|
||You victors of wars, you wielders of lightning!||
|Handsome and many-shaped with chequered coils,|
||Adorned with jewels of shining hues||
|You shine as the sun shines|
||In the great cavern of the sky||
|Myriad are your pathways on the banks of the Ganga|
||Who dares march against your assembled might?||
|I salute you who salute the great Takshaka, Airavata of the Nagas|
||I salute you Takshaka son of Kadru and your son Ashvasena||
|By the banks of the river Ikshumati in Kurukshetra, you lived|
||Along with your youngest brother Shrutasena||
|Who lived in Mahadyumna and coveted your throne|
||May you march with 20,000 men at war and always find victory!||

After he finished chanting these shlokas in Sanskrit, Uttanka was able to pass unmolested through the land of the Nagas. But although none obstructed his way or threatened his well-being, he also did not find that which he sought, namely, the earrings he wished to carry back home to his guru's wife. Continuing to search doggedly, he began going from chamber to chamber in the great city of the Nagas. He saw many wonderful sights. Among these, he saw two women weaving a length of fabric mounted upon a loom worked by hand. The fabric was formed of black and white threads. He also saw a great wheel being turned by six boys. And a man who was handsome beyond description.

Inspired yet again to poetic heights, Uttanka chanted the following shlokas:

|Three hundred and sixty spokes in this wheel,|
||Moving in a cycle of twenty-four divisions||
|Turned constantly by six young boys|
||Representing the hours of the day and the days of the year||
|Two young women who are the weavers of time|
||Weave black and white threads eternally||
|Representing the past and the present|
||Creating and destroying worlds endlessly.||
|O master of the vajra, protector of worlds!|
||Slayer of Vritra, destroyer of Namuchi!||
|The man in black who commands truth and untruth|
||He who once rode the great steed Ucchaihshrava||
|Avatar of Agni, as he emerged from the amrit-manthan|
||Lord of three worlds, great Purandara!||
|Before thee I bow eternally!|
||You are master of the universe||
|All fortresses fall before thee|
||Mighty Indra, accept my salutation!||

The man who was handsome beyond description turned his gaze upon Uttanka. It was as if the sun had emerged from a cloud-blackened sky to shine its light directly upon him. He felt the heat and radiance of that great being shine upon him and enlighten his soul.

'I am pleased by your praises,' said the man. 'Speak. Ask me for something you desire.'

Uttanka bowed to him and said meekly: 'Lord, let me have power over the Nagas.'

The man commanded, 'Blow into the anus of this horse.'

Uttanka did as he was told. At once, a great rush of flames and smoke billowed forth from the horse's orifices. As he watched with amazement, the smoke spread through the world of the Nagas like a living thing, scorching every creature, entering every crevice, burning every last living being and habitation. Before his very eyes, the great wondrous world of the Nagas was turned into a place of ruin and ashes, awash in smoke and soot.

Faced with devastation, Takshaka emerged out of his hiding place. Still carrying the earrings, he threw them back at Uttanka, eyes weeping copiously from the smoke and flames. 'Take back your earrings! I no longer want them!'

Uttanka took the earrings with great delight. But the instant he received them his thoughts turned back to his given mission. This was the fourth day since he had departed his guru's house. It was the very day the ceremony was to be performed for which the guru's wife had desired to wear the earrings to impress the attending brahmins. It was quite impossible for him to climb all the way up from the realm of the Nagas and reach his guru's home in time. And if he did not give them to her in time, all his effort would be in vain.

He only thought these things but the man knew his thoughts and spoke aloud again: 'Do not fret, Uttanka. Mount this horse. It will transport you to your guru's house in an instant.'

||Six||

Uttanka accepted the offer gratefully. Mounting the horse he turned its head and found the horse riding of its own accord. Its hooves clattered on the rocky floor of the underground cavern and as he looked back, he saw sparks shooting out each time it touched the stony ground. The city of the Nagas fell far behind astonishingly quickly. The horse entered the tunnel through which he had come and thundered up at blurring speed. It was all Uttanka could do to hold on and keep his seat. In no time at all, he found himself on the surface once again, and back on the road home. Shortly thereafter, he arrived at his guru's house and dismounted with relief. He saw the preceptor's wife had just bathed and was dressing her hair. As Uttanka entered, he heard her saying to her husband, 'Uttanka has not returned as promised. I must curse him.' Just then Uttanka bowed before her and presented her with the earrings.

She exclaimed and took the earrings, admiring them joyfully. 'Uttanka, you could not have come a moment too soon. In another instant, I would have cursed you! You have performed your duty admirably and given your guru-dakshina. May good fortune smile on you always!'

Uttanka's guru greeted his pupil warmly and asked him what had taken him so long. Uttanka narrated his experiences to his guru. In his excitement and his relief at having succeeded in his mission, the episodes of his travels tumbled forth in the wrong sequence and he described things that had occurred last, first, and those that had occurred first, last. But his guru sorted the incidents easily in his enlightened mind, stroking his beard as he contemplated. 'These events have a profound meaning,' he told Uttanka. 'You have already fathomed some of their significance, I shall explain the rest.'

The two women Uttanka saw weaving the loom, Rishi Veda told him, were named Dhata and Vidhata, the Giver and the Creator; one transposes and the other disposes. The black and white threads stood for night and day respectively. The wheel with twelve spokes was a solar year, the six boys turning it were the six seasons. The handsome man was Parjanya, Lord Indra in his incarnation as god of rain. The horse was Agni, lord of fire. The mammoth bull that Uttanka saw on the way to Raja Paushya's palace was Takshaka, alias Airavata, king of snakes in yet another of his many disguises. The giant who rode it was Indra, signifying his control over Takshaka. The bull's dung which Uttanka ate at Indra's request was Amrit, the nectar of immortality. It was because he ate it that he was not killed in the kingdom of Nagas. Rishi Veda smiled as he finished, saying, 'Indra is my friend and it is by his kind grace that you were able to return with the earrings. Now, my son Uttanka, you have achieved all you desired: you have given the guru-dakshina you promised. You have my leave to depart with good fortune.'

Touching his guru's feet to take his blessing, Uttanka left his preceptor's house for the last time. Now he was truly free of brahmacharya-ashrama, the first major stage of his life. He had graduated to full adulthood and could go anywhere he pleased, pursue any occupation or vocation, marry and be a householder, it was entirely his choice. And he intended to do everything, live his life as fully as he could.

But first he had to perform one more task, this time not for his guru but for himself.

He set out for Hastinapura, capital city of the Kurus, for he was angry with Takshaka and desired revenge on the lord of sarpas.

At Hastinapura, he sought an audience with King Janamajaya, who had only just returned victorious from Takshashila, after quelling the rebellion and annexing that kingdom. Uttanka, filled with the confidence of having graduated from his guru's kul after gifting him his desired guru-dakshina and by dint of the knowledge and experience he had acquired, stood before Raja Janamajaya. The king was seated on his throne, surrounded by many advisors for his great victory had enhanced his power and position and the prestige of the Kuru nation. As was required by protocol, Uttanka first pronounced the appropriate blessings and auspicious shlokas praising the king's victory, then, carefully choosing his words and intonation, said, 'O king among kings, why do you squander your time in puerile pursuits when a vital duty demands your attention?'

Now this was an extraordinary thing to say and other kings might easily have taken umbrage at this bold rebuke. But Raja Janamajaya was no ordinary king and he understood that no brahmin would speak thus without good cause.

Unperturbed by Uttanka's rebuke, Raja Janamajaya greeted him with full saluations and then said, 'O king among brahmins, I perform my kshatriya dharma and care for the security of my people. Tell me, what else should I have done? I seek your wise counsel.'

Uttanka explained himself: 'Raje, it was Takshaka who inflicted violence upon your father, the mighty Parikshat. Therefore you must wreak vengeance on that evil-souled king of serpents. The time has come to take revenge and acquit yourself of your debt to your noble-souled father. Parikshat lived like a king ought to live, causing no offence, but despite his innocence this dastardly Takshaka bit him and struck him down like a tree struck by lightning. Arrogant with power, he committed heinous murder when he killed your great sire; it was nothing less than an assassination of a great monarch. When the sage Kashyapa tried to restrain him, he killed even that great seer. It is only fitting that you seek to burn this vile serpent lord in the blazing agni at your Sarpa Yagna. This is most vital. Continue with this yagna until Takshaka is destroyed and avenge your father. In so doing, you will also gain my deepest thanks and blessings. For I too was waylaid, obstructed, and cruelly set upon by the same vile Naga when I sought to do nothing more than fulfil my obligation of guru-dakshina.'

After hearing Uttanka's eloquent appeal, Raja Janamajaya's wrath at Takshaka waxed greatly. As ghee fuels the yagna fire, so did Uttanka's words inflame him. Until now he had only possessed the most general notion of how his father's death had come about, but after Uttanka's impassioned speech, for the first time he insisted on knowing every last detail of that macabre tragedy. When he heard the full story of his father's demise, his heart was flooded with grief.

||Paksha Five||

TALES OF THE BHRIGU

||One||

The day's rites, chores and lessons had been completed and all were assembled yet again. By now a familiar pattern had set in. Nobody needed to be told, reminded or called to the narration sessions. Sauti's daily recitation of the *Mahabharata* epic was as much a part of everyone's routine as breathing or bathing. Eager faces turned shining eyes toward him as he stood before the maharishis and rishis of Naimisha-sharanya. They were standing too, as were all the brahmacharyas. They could not be seated until he, their guest, was seated. And he would not take his seat until his host urged him to do so. He waited patiently but there was still no sign of Kulapati Shaunaka. It was not proper for him to enquire why the kulapati was taking so long to join them. Yet he was eager to continue the recitation as he had barely begun and there was yet a great sea of stories left to navigate.

He joined his hands and enquired gently, 'Honoured brahmins, tell me, what part of the great *Bharata* should I recite to you next?'

In response they replied with equal politeness, 'Honourable son of Lomarsana, we are eager to hear every last shloka of the excellent epic and we know you will regale us with many more great tales of adventure and history. But our master Kulapati Shaunaka is busy in the sacred chamber of Agni, preserving the sacred fire. As you know, our guru is also learned in the Puranas. He knows the tales of devas and asuras. He also knows the stories of mortals, nagas and gandharvas. Son of Lomarsana, the venerable Shaunaka is the chief brahmin at this sacrifice, most able, faithful to his vows, a reservoir of wisdom and lore regarding the sacred Vedas as well as the *aranyakas*, the forest books. Scrupulously truthful and greatly revered by us all, his presence is awaited to grace us before we continue. We pray that you wait as well. Once our guru has taken his seat, we shall be most pleased to listen to whatever he asks you to recite next.'

Ugrasrava, son of Lomarsana, said, 'So shall it be.' And it was agreed from that day on that only when Kulapati Shaunaka himself was seated and urged Sauti to continue, would the poet proceed with his recitation.

Sauti expected his audience to show signs of impatience, restlessness. After all, the vast majority of those waiting were young brahmacharyas. But such was their love for their preceptor and so great their respect that none displayed the slightest hint of impatience. Everyone waited patiently until the kulapati completed his ritual in the house of Agni to his full satisfaction and in perfect accordance with the prescribed order of the rites, and only then came to the clearing where Sauti waited with the rest.

Once he seated himself, Shaunaka said, 'My son, in times past your father was renowned as a scholar of the Puranas. His knowledge of those great ancient anthologies was prodigious, and it was our good grace, a long time ago, to hear many of those fine tales from his lips. Tales of the divine, of the ancestors . . . As his son, I know that you too must be well versed in that ancient lore. Today, I have a great yearning to know the tales of the Bhrigu, in whose line I am descended. Pray, tell me those tales.'

In his request, it was implicit that he apologized for deviating from the main narrative that Sauti was recounting. And now Ugrasrava understood why the rishis had bade him wait for their guru, not only on account of their respect for him and because Shaunaka did not wish to miss a single word of narrative, but also because the kulapati was eager to learn the history of his ancestors from Sauti. In a world where the only way one could know one's history was through the recitations of other people, each man and woman was as a closed book filled with an unknown amount of knowledge. Kulapati Shaunaka hoped that perhaps Sauti possessed some version of his ancestor's itihasa that would help him understand them—and by extension, himself—better. It was an honourable request and Sauti was pleased at the comparison the guru had made, equating him to his own father, for it was the highest compliment possible. He replied with great warmth.

'Great one, you honour me. It is true, I have indeed studied the Puranas at my father's feet and he passed on his vast store of knowledge to me. But the same tales you speak of are also incorporated in the great epic of Krishna Dweipayana Vyasa and I learned them from Vaisampayana as well. Of all the tales in that great epic, the itihasa of the Bhrigu is revered by the devas themselves, by Indra, Agni and the Maruts. I am privileged to narrate the same history to you now. I begin with Bhrigu, the first of your line, who sired a son named Chyavana Bhargava. Chyavana in turn had a son named Pramati and Pramati in turn married Ghritachi and they had a son named Ruru. Ruru and his wife Pramadvara had a son named Shunaka, a righteous and learned man, famous for being well-versed in the Vedas and the Shruti, dedicated to ascetism, truthful, honourable, wise in his understanding of the brahman that guides the universe and master of his own senses. Shunaka was your great-grandfather and it is for him you are named Shaunaka, or scion of Shunaka.'

Kulapati Shaunaka leaned forward, his crow-black eyes gleaming in his age-lined face framed by his white beard and matted hair. 'One question, O son of Suta, and then I shall not interrupt your narration. Why was Bhrigu's son Chyavana given that name? It is one thing I have long desired to know. I would be grateful if you could tell me.'

Sauti smiled. 'It shall be my honour to share the knowledge. Listen, great one, to the tale of your ancestors.'

||Two||

Bhrigu had a wife, greatly beloved to him. Her name was Puloma. Through the natural act between man and woman, she conceived from Bhrigu's sperm and her womb flowered with his child. One day not long after, Sage Bhrigu left home as usual to perform a consecration ceremony. While he was gone, a rakshasa came to the ashram. This rakshasa stopped short at the very sight of Puloma. He gazed at her like one besotted. The sage's wife, disconcerted though she was at his relentless gaze, performed her duty by honouring the guest, offering him a simple ashram repast of fruit and roots. But the rakshasa had eyes only for Puloma, and was filled with lust for her. Now among rakshasas, when one desires a mate, one is entitled to abduct her and marry her by force. This rakshasa desired to do the same with the wife of the sage. This rakshasa was named Puloman.

Unable to contain his lust yet driven by a desire to know more before he committed any hasty act, he entered the room where the holy Agni was enthroned and addressed the sacred fire. 'Mighty Agni, I ask you under oath to tell me, whose wife is this woman. Tell me honestly, great Pavaka! Is this not the same woman who was engaged to be my own wife? It was her father who gave her hand in marriage to another man, this Bhrigu—who therefore committed a crime against me. Now that I have found my beloved Puloma again, I desire to take her with me and make her my own as is my right. It infuriates me that Bhrigu should possess my slim-waisted beauty when she was betrothed to me first!'

The fire crackled and spat and hissed but spoke no response to Puloman's questions. So the rakshasa repeated his queries even more passionately: 'O Agni, I hail thee. You always bear true witness. You dwell in all creatures as an observer to the best and worst deeds. You are wise in knowledge of all karma. If you tell me that this woman who calls herself the wife of Sage Bhrigu is indeed the same Puloma who was betrothed to marry me first, then I shall consider Bhrigu to be her abductor and unlawful oath-breaker. I shall be entitled to carry her away and make her my own. You shall bear witness to this and settle this matter by revealing the truth. Answer me, great deva!'

Again and again did the rakshasa ask Agni to reveal the truth. But how could Agni reply? The sacred fire the rakshasa was questioning was nurtured and fed by Bhrigu himself, in his own chamber within his ashram. Therefore it owed Bhrigu fealty. Not to mention the fact that even Agni deva who was in that fire as in all other fires everywhere, feared the wrath of Sage Bhrigu, who was strong in austerities and powerful in knowledge of brahman. If Agni spoke in the rakshasa's favour, Bhrigu might well curse Agni. And a sage's curse was a terrible thing. Yet if he took Bhrigu's side and lied to the rakshasa, then he would betray his own true self, for as Puloman had rightly pointed out, fire never lied and could only speak with a true tongue. Therefore the sacred Agni desired only to keep silent and attempted to make only those sounds that fire makes and to speak no comprehensible words to the agitated rakshasa. But in its distress, it released a sound that could at best be described as a whispered incomprehensible word and at worst as a sigh. But so infuriated and desperate was the rakshasa that he took that inscrutable sound as affirmation.

||Three||

Having heard Agni affirm his belief, Puloman, being a rakshasa, altered his guise to take the form of a boar and using supernatural power, abducted Puloma forcibly and carried Bhrigu's wife away with the speed of the wind. Angered at the violence done to his mother and at being carried away from his father's hermitage, the unborn son of Bhrigu fell from his mother's womb. Thus was he named Chyavana, or the Deprived, for he had been deprived of his rightful place in his mother's womb for the allotted period. When he witnessed the self-induced abortion, Rakshasa Puloman was shocked into releasing Puloma. Chyavana Bhrigu, just emerged from his mother's womb well before his due time, nevertheless was filled with the power of righteousness. He blazed forth like a newborn sun, turning the rakshasa who had abducted his mother to ashes. Torn apart with pain, his mother Puloma fell down, weeping copiously. She struggled to regain her feet that she might carry her newborn son back to his father's home, but she was in no condition to make the journey. As Bhrigu was one of the prajapatis, the forebears of humankind, and created by Brahma himself, thus was Puloma the daughter-in-law of the Creator. Hearing his daughter-in-law's cries of pain, Brahma consoled her and collected her tears to form a great river. The river swelled and retraced her journey back to the ashram of Bhrigu, to mark the path of her abduction. In her honour, Brahma named that waterway Vidhusara, or Bride's Run.

On his return home, Sage Bhrigu was alarmed to find his wife missing. He was equally surprised to find the new waterway that passed by his ashram. Following the course of Vidhusara, he traced it back to the place where Puloma still lay, Chyavana beside her and the burnt skeleton of the rakshasa nearby. Through his knowledge of such creatures and occurrences, Bhrigu immediately surmised that this was the rakshasa Puloman and that he had attempted to abduct the woman to whom he had once been betrothed while Bhrigu was absent. But he could not understand how the rakshasa could have known for certain that Puloma was indeed the same woman without someone confirming this fact. When Puloma regained consciousness, he asked his wife: 'Who was it who told the rakshasa about you? For without confirming the truth of your identity, he could not have abducted you thus. Someone must have told him that you were indeed the same woman who was betrothed to him earlier. Who was it?' Puloma was greatly weakened by her ordeal but saw her husband's anger and replied, 'My lord, it was our own sacred fire. Agni himself told the rakshasa. For a great length of time the rakshasa ranted and raved in our agni chamber. Only when Agni confirmed his suspicions did he kidnap me. He would have spirited me far away from here by now, but thanks to your unborn son, his plan was thwarted. Our child aborted himself and left the safety of my womb to use his power to scorch the rakshasa to ashes. It is only thanks to him that both he and I are still here.'

Furious at this betrayal, Bhrigu stormed into the chamber where he preserved and honoured the sacred fire. 'For your betrayal, I curse you,' he cried to Agni. 'Henceforth, you shall be an omnivore and shall devour anything that is fed to you with no regard or respect!'

||Four||

Agni was outraged at Bhrigu's curse. 'Great brahmin, why do you act so rashly today? I always adhere to dharma and tell the truth impartially regardless of the consequences. When pressed, I could not help but answer truthfully. What did I do wrong? A witness who is questioned and despite knowing the true facts bears false testimony condemns both his ancestors and descendants for seven generations! Failure to speak is not an option either, for he who knows the truth about any crime but wilfully refuses to give testimony becomes an accessory to that same crime! If I desire, I too could curse you for wrongly accusing me. But I serve brahmins and hold your varna in high esteem. Therefore, I shall remind you of my qualities that you appear to have forgotten in your rash haste. Listen well!'

Agni continued in a fiery tone: 'Through my yogic penance, I take many incarnations—in the form of agnihotras, sattras, and other rituals and ceremonial sacrifices. What oblation is offered to me in proper accordance with the precepts laid down for those rituals as described in the Vedas shall please the devas and the pitris. The former, the gods, are as water and so are the latter, the ancestors, and like all water upon this earth are therefore governed by the moon. The offerings at the new moon are for the devas and those of the full moon are for the ancestors. On all other phases of the moon, they are worshipped variously as one or individually. Since the devas and pitris eat what is poured onto me, therefore I am as their mouth to the Thirty-three Gods and all the ancestors. On the day of the new moon the ancestors, and on the day of the full moon the devas, all eat through me the sacred ghee that is offered. How can I therefore become omnivorous?'

In great anger and in response to Bhrigu's curse, Agni withdrew himself from the world. He disappeared from the agnihotras of the brahmins, from sattras, and all other ritual ceremonies and sacrifices everywhere. Deprived of omkaras, vashatkaras, svahas—the initial exclamations made when offering oblations, the oblations themselves, and the concluding exclamations—all beings on earth became most miserable. In desperation, the seers of the world appealed to the devas themselves: 'The loss of fire has deprived the three worlds of all sacrificial rituals. We beg your swift intervention.' The devas in turn went with the seers to almighty Brahma. They told him about Bhrigu's curse on Agni and Agni's subsequent protest. They supported the plea of Agni saying, 'How can the very mouth of the devas and eater of prime portions of sacred oblations become omnivorous?'

Brahma heard all arguments before summoning Agni. In gentle words, with great respect and honour, the Creator addressed him thus: 'You are the maker of the three worlds and their destroyer. For all things are born of fire and shall return unto fire at the end of their days. By preserving all sacrifices and ceremonies, you preserve the three worlds as well. You are the being that births himself. You are the supreme form of energy. Your sovereignty cannot be disputed! How then can you behave thus childishly and withdraw yourself?

You are pure and incontaminable and shall remain so eternally. You can never become an omnivore in your entire body, irrespective of the curse. Only flames that are meant for the acceptance of oblations shall consume everything offered to them—and yet, in consuming, you shall nevertheless render them pure as well! Just as the sun's rays purify all things they touch so also shall you purify everything offered to and consumed by your flames meant for oblations. Do not fear the sage's curse. Accept it! Let it come true. Accept the portions of the devas as well as your own when offered into your mouth. But purify everything you consume! Thus both the power of the sage's curse as well as your own purity shall be upheld!'

Agni heard the words of almighty Brahma and replied without argument: 'So shall it be.'

He obeyed the instructions of the Paramesthin thereafter.

The devas and sages returned to their homes, delighted, and the sages resumed their ceremonies and oblations. All creatures on earth rejoiced. Freed from any taint, he consumed all things fed to him and remained pure eternally.

This was the history of the curse and the reason why Agni consumes all that it is given, as well as the story of the destruction of the rakshasa Puloman and the birth of Chyavana.

||Five||

Chyavana, son of Bhrigu, grew to manhood and wed a lady named Sukanya. In time, they had a radiant and great-souled son named Pramati. Pramati in turn wed Ghritachi and birthed a son named Ruru. And Ruru with his wife Pramadvara sired Shunaka. There is a great story concerning Ruru, he of resplendent might.

In ancient times there was a sage named Sthulakesha who had earned himself great power through his austerities and learning and was famous for his concern for the welfare of all creatures. One day, the king of Gandharvas, Vishvavasu, sired upon the apsara Menaka, a child. When time came for her child to be born, the apsara Menaka delivered the baby, which was a girl, on the bank of a river and then abandoned her there. Sage Sthulakesha heard the cries of the child and discovered her there, alone and bereft. He was overwhelmed by her blazing radiance and knew her at once to be the child of an immortal. Driven by his great compassion for all living creatures, he adopted her and raised her in his own ashram. She grew up to be a woman of great physical beauty, and in acknowledgement of her superiority to all others in this respect, he named her Pramadvara, literally meaning The Most Beautiful.

Now Ruru, grandson of Chyavana and great-grandson of Bhrigu, lived in that same ashram. When he set eyes on Pramadvara, he fell madly in love with her. Through his friends, he sent word to his father of his passion, and when Pramati heard of his son's desire, he went to Sage Sthulakesha to arrange the match. The sage happily engaged Pramadvara with Ruru, and fixed an auspicious date for their nuptials, selecting the phase when the nakshatra, or star, named Bhagadaiva, also known as Uttarphalguni, would be in the ascendant. All concerned were filled with great anticipation and joy at the joining of these two young persons.

A few days before the appointed date of the wedding, the beautiful Pramadvara was playing innocently with her friends. Involved in her play, she failed to notice a sleeping snake coiled in the bushes and stepped on it accidentally. Driven by instinct as well as by the inexorable power of Time, the snake sank its venomous fangs into the careless girl's foot. Pramadvara fell down senseless. Her beauty, so alluring when she was alive, became even more alluring when she lay dead, for the venom of the snake enhanced her beauty manifold, and she appeared to be simply asleep on the ground. Her adoptive father and the other sages of the ashram quickly gathered around her motionless body, lustrous as a lotus in bloom. Svastyatreya, Mahajanu, Kushika, Shankhamekhala, Bharadvaja, Kaunakutsa, Arshtisena and Gautama were present, as were Pramati, his son Ruru, and other inhabitants of that part of the forest. Overcome with grief, they sat in a circle and began to lament her passing. But Ruru, unable to bear his pain, left that place.

||Six||

Unable to bear the grief of losing his beloved Pramadvara, Ruru wandered aimlessly through the forest, weeping piteously. His thoughts kept returning to his last sight of Pramadvara, looking even more beautiful in death than she had in life. Mourning and lamenting, he called out loudly, 'My beloved Pramadvara lies on the ground, dead. She is gone from this world. And in her absence, the world fills up with pain and grief. But if I have been scrupulous in my austerities and vows, if I have given alms and helped the needy, if it be true that I have honoured my elders and shown them all due respect, as I have been true and righteous from the day I was born to this day, then why do I suffer thus? Why has my Pramadvara been taken from me? Let her rise up again! Let her stand and live once more!'

Moved by his pain, the devas sent word to Ruru through a dhoot, an envoy of the gods. 'Ruru, your grief-stricken words can accomplish nothing. Once life has fled a mortal body, it can never return. Tragic as it is, Pramadvara's time on this earth has run out. This daughter of the gandharva and the apsara is dead now. Waste no more time in mourning.' And then, seeing Ruru's grief increase rather than abate, the dhoot said quietly, 'You persist in your grief. Very well then. A great age ago, the devas devised a loophole in the iron law of life and death. If you choose to resort to it, you may find some solace and regain your Pramadvara.'

At once Ruru pounced on the dhoot's words. 'Tell me at once! What is this loophole? If there is any way at all to get back my Pramadvara, I will do it. I beg you, grant me this deliverance, messenger of the gods.'

The dhoot nodded sombrely and said, 'Then hear me well, scion of Bhrigu. Bestow half your life upon your beloved and she shall rise again and be your bride.'

Ruru stared at the dhoot. 'Is that all? I would give all my life for her! What is one half? I agree at once! I surrender half my life to Pramadvara that she may live again. Let my slender beauty rise once more and be exactly as she was in life, for she is love itself personified.'

The dhoot bowed low to Ruru and left his presence. He then went to the netherworld, realm of Yama, lord of death and dharma. When he came before Yama, the lord of death instantly knew him, for the dhoot was none other than the king of Gandharvas, Vishvavasu, father of Pramadvara. He folded his hands before Yama-dev and said: 'Dharmaraja, if it please you, let Ruru's beautiful beloved Pramadvara, rise empowered by half her beloved's life which he has granted her of his own free will.' He bowed low and added, 'If you deem it fit.'

Yama's response was brief. 'Dhoot of the devas, king of the Gandharvas, if you deem it so, then it shall be so.' And he gestured powerfully, saying 'Let Ruru's beloved Pramadvara rise with half of Ruru's life empowering her body.'

At that very instant, back in the ashram of Sage Sthulakesha, in the centre of the circle of mourning and chanting rishis and forest dwellers, the beautiful Pramadvara stirred, opened her eyes, sat up, then rose to her feet as if rising merely from a restful slumber, to the amazement of all present.

Thereafter, Pramadvara continued to live as normal, her life extended by the exact duration of half of Ruru's allotted lifespan. In balance, Ruru's own life was shortened by exactly half its allotted length. But these were things noted and verified only much later, once both had lived out their lives normally and fruitfully.

At that time, Ruru and Pramadvara went ahead as planned, and were joined in sacred matrimony in accordance with all rites and ceremonies and prepared for a life of great mutual happiness, bringing joy to all who knew them.

But in his heart, Ruru swore an oath. Having come so close to losing his beloved Pramadvara—having in fact lost her forever if not for the intervention of the gods and his own sacrifice—he swore a terrible vow to destroy the species of snakes at every chance. And from that day on, that resolute keeper of vows slew snakes at every opportunity, using any and every means or weapon at hand. His anger was terrible and could not be appeased.

One day he was travelling through a large forest when he came upon a dundubha, a snake that was not poisonous. As he was wont to do, he raised up his staff and tried to strike it dead. The dundubha escaped the first blow but was injured painfully. Ruru raised his staff again, this time intent on striking a death blow. But the dundubha cried out in anguish, 'Brahmin, I have done you no harm! Why do you wax wrathful against me? Why have you attacked me for no reason at all?'

||Seven||

Unnerved by the snake's appeal, Ruru paused in his attack. A good-souled man, he replied, 'My wife, who is as dear to me as life itself, was bitten by a snake. For that reason I swore a vow that I would kill every snake I saw. I cannot spare you. Prepare to die.'

But the dundubha cried out angrily: 'Brahmin, there are many kinds of snakes. Some do kill humans, I do not deny it. But I am of a kind that is only related to them by smell, called dundubha. We share the same misfortunes as our venomous brethren but not their poisonous aggression. We share their sorrows but have our own ways of seeking joy. It is not right that you should kill dundubhas like myself. You should learn to differentiate between us and our venomous brethren.'

Taken aback by this passionate eloquence, Ruru lowered his staff. He feared that the snake might be a sage in disguise. Seeking to appease the great soul, Ruru said, 'You do not seem like an ordinary snake. I believe you must be some other being only temporarily occupying this form. Tell me then, how did you come to be a snake?'

The snake's response was astonishing. 'Alas, what you say is true. I am reduced to being a snake only on account of the curse of a brahmin. In fact, I am a rishi named Sahasrapata.'

Intrigued now, Ruru set his staff aside and sat on a log. 'Tell me, good snake. Who was this brahmin and why did he curse you, and how long are you condemned to occupy this present form?'

The dundubha said, 'Listen then and I shall tell you my story.'

||Eight||

Long ago I had a friend, a brahmin named Khagama. He was sincere, honest and possessed the power of tapas, gained from his austerities. I was still a child then. One day, while he was engaged in the agnihotra sacrifice, I mischievously wove lengths of straw together to resemble a snake and startled him with it. Frightened, he fainted.

When he revived, he was furious with me. With the fury of a righteous man, he swore to me, 'Because you made a powerless snake to scare me into fainting during my ritual, so by the force of my anger, you too will become a powerless snake!'

Trembling with fear, for I knew what a brahmin with his power could accomplish through such vows, I beseeched him with folded hands. 'Khagama! I am your friend! I only meant to make you laugh with my prank. Please, my friend, withdraw your curse.'

Seeing me so agitated, his anger reduced by degrees. Drawing several deep breaths for he was still recovering from his fright, he finally said, 'A brahmin's curse once uttered can never be taken back. But I will grant you a means of escaping your curse. Listen to me carefully and hold this in your memory forever. There shall be a sage named Pramati and one day he shall raise a son named Ruru, a man pure of heart and mind. When Ruru appears before you one day, you shall be immediately freed from my curse.'

And even as the dundubha finished his story, Ruru saw that he had been transforming back into a man by degrees. As the son of Pramati watched incredulously, the dundubha stood before him, his mortal form regained.

Rishi Sahasrapata joined his palms together and bowed before his saviour. 'Best of beings, since you have saved me from my curse, I offer you some words that may prove beneficial to you. Know this: the only righteous path is ahimsa. For only by not destroying life can we ourselves live peacefully. Therefore, a brahmin should never take the life of any living creature. The sacred texts have already expounded upon this, emphasizing that a brahmin's dharma is to always be peaceful, truthful, learned in the Vedas and Vedangas, never give any creature cause to fear him, and should be ever willing to forgive those who transgress. This law of ahimsa is therefore the highest dharma of a brahmin. Not for you is the dharma of a kshatriya, who holds the danda of punishment, who wields it against transgressors in order to protect his people. Leave that to the kshatriyas. You know of the snakes destroyed at Raja Janamajaya's sarpa satra, do you not? Those frightened snakes were saved by a brahmin performing this highest dharma. His name was Astika, and he was a brahmin among brahmins.'

||Nine||

Ruru heard Sahasrapata's words and replied, 'Good brahmin, I do not know anything about this sarpa satra of Raja Janamajaya but I am intrigued. Tell me more. Why did this King Janamajaya seek to destroy snakes and how did he set out to destroy them? And how did this Sage Astika save them? Do tell me the story.'

But Sahasrapata, whose body was now fully anthromorphised, replied only, 'Ruru, you will indeed hear the story of how Astika saved the snakes, but not from my lips. Another brahmin shall recount the tale to you.'

And having said this, his body faded away completely. Nonplussed, Ruru searched around in that part of the forest, but could find no trace of the rishi who had been a snake. Exhausted and hungry, he went home and eventually, heard the story from his own father.

||Paksha Six||

THE BOOK OF SNAKES

||One||

Kulapati Shaunaka seated himself and addressed Sauti. 'I too am curious to know the story behind Raja Janamajaya's sarpa yagna. Pray tell us, why did that tiger among kings seek to destroy all snakes on earth? Whose son was he, what was his family history? And what of this brahmin Astika of whom we have just heard? Who was he and what was his family history? Tell us all, good Suta.'

Ugrasrava replied: 'Great one, I shall recount to you the tale of Astika, answering all your questions.'

Shaunaka's age-lined face beamed in the firelight. The sage looked around at his fellow sages and the assembled brahmacharyas and rubbed his hands in evident enthusiasm. 'Yes, tell us the tale of Astika! We look forward to it.'

The son of Lomarsana smiled in response at the kulapati's enthusiasm. 'Itihasa. This is what was spoken as history by the ancients and retold by Krishna Dweipayana Vyasa to the sages of Naimisha-sharanya.'

At the mention of their ashram, the brahmins looked at one another, surprised and pleased.

Sauti went on. 'Indeed, my own father, the learned Lomarsana, himself a disciple of Vyasa and a suta as well, narrated it to the sages of this great ashram, in your own presence, Kulapati Shaunaka. I was but a child and present on that occasion. And now it is my great privilege to continue in my father's tradition and narrate the same tale to you once more, kulapati, as well as the other denizens of your ashram.'

||Two||

Astika's father was a lord as powerful and renowned as the legendary Prajapati Daksha himself. Celibate and always dedicated to austerities, he ate sparingly and never spilled his seed. He was known by the name Jaratkaru. Famous among yayavaras, he lived his life as a mendicant, and remained ever righteous and rigid in dharma. Once during his wanderings, he came to a great cave and saw many beings hanging upside down from the roof of the cave. He saw that these people were suspended by a single string of grass and that this string of grass was being gnawed at steadily by a rat who lived in a nest of rats in the cave.

Alarmed at this unusual sight, he enquired of them, 'Who are you and why are you left to hang thus from the roof of this cave? Do you know that the rope from which you hang is made of grass and it is being gnawed on by rats and may break at any time?'

To his amazement, they responded: 'We are a clan of rishis rigid in dharma who pursued our living as yayavaras, by which name we are known. We suffer this fate because we are bereft of descendants save a solitary heir named Jaratkaru. Unfortunately for us, he too pursues the same path as we did, that of the yayavara. He will grow old without a wife and die childless. That is why we are condemned to hang upside down in this cave, because our clan is dying and literally descending into the earth for want of heirs. But who are you who comes to this desolate place and why do you show so much interest and concern for us, brahmin?'

Jaratkaru replied emotionally. 'Strange though it seems, I am Jaratkaru, your sole descendant! All that you say is true. You are my forebears. Now tell me, what should I do to help you?'

Conferring among themselves, his pitris replied, 'You must have offspring, Jaratkaru! Sire an heir for your own sake as well as to continue our line. This is your given dharma. All your virtuous deeds and the accumulated tapas of your austerities are worthless without an heir to continue your line. Go forth, marry, have children. You are our only hope now!'

Jaratkaru bowed his head in acceptance. 'Earlier, I had resolved never to take a wife because I had chosen the path of a yayavara. But for your sake I am willing to forego that resolution and take a wife. But, my great forebears, if I take a wife, it must be according to certain conditions I set down. I will only take a wife who has the same name as I, and whose family willingly gives her hand to me in marriage. Moreover, she must be an unspoiled girl and we must marry exactly according to prescribed rites. These are my conditions and difficult as they are, I will not deviate from them. I shall go forth and seek out such a wife and if such a woman gladly accepts even a penniless mendicant as myself as husband, then I shall marry her and continue your and my lineage and you shall then be freed of this state of limbo and attain to moksha at last.'

Having pronounced these words, Jaratkaru the yayavara then went forth into the world and sought high and low for a suitable girl. But search as he might, he could not find a girl who met the conditions he had set down. One day, he was travelling through a forest and in those deep woods, he felt overcome by his failure. Sinking to the ground in despair at the thought of his suffering ancestors, he called out for alms, and asked for the hand of a young girl in marriage from anyone who might be listening.

The earth shook and the forest was filled with a great commotion. Animals ran helter-skelter and a fierce wind blew and rain lashed Jaratkaru's face. As suddenly as it had begun, the chaos ceased and when he opened his eyes again, Jaratkaru saw a great Naga before him, towering high, its uncoiled length stretching away farther than his eyes could see. As he gazed at this astonishing sight, the Naga reduced himself to a less fearsome size and assumed the partial aspect of a man to speak to Jaratkaru. When he spoke, his voice was a sibilant hiss that lashed through the jungle like a monsoon gale.

'I am Vasuki. I heard your plea for alms, yayavara,, and I came here to offer my own sister in marriage to you.'

At the mention of the Naga's name, Jaratkaru was struck dumb momentarily. Vasuki was the legendary king of the Nagas who had once aided the devas and asuras in the great amrit-manthan, offering his own body to be used as a rope to be entwined around Mount Mandara so the mountain could be turned to and fro like a churning ladle in the great ocean, to produce the Amrit, elixir of immortality. He was among the greatest of snakes, son to Sage Kashyapa and his wife Kadru, creators of the species of snakes, brother to Anantha and Takshaka. Kadru and her sister Vinata were the daughters of the great Prajapati Brahma, who gave both daughters in marriage to the Sage Kashyapa. The sisters later became bitter rivals and when Kadru's own children refused to side with her against their aunt, she cursed them to burn in the sacrificial fire of a raja named Janamajaya in a future age. Vasuki's brother Anantha was the same great serpent on whose coils Lord Vishnu the Preserver himself sat in his yogic posture of perpetual transcendental meditation called yoganidra or ananthasayana. Anantha, Vasuki and Takshaka were each distinguished by the title of Nagaraja, King of Snakes. Vasuki's usual place was coiled around the blue throat of Lord Shiva himself, and it was the great Destroyer who had lent him to the devas for the amrit manthan an eon ago. His power was unimaginable, second only to that of his bhraatr, Takshaka, the fearsome one who possessed the deadliest venom of all snakes. Faced with such a fearsome being, unimaginable as a brother-in-law at first glance, Jaratkaru's instinct was to say no outright, but he could not simply refuse without some justification. A thought struck him. He had sworn a vow that he would only marry a young girl whose name was the same as his own. All he had to do was ask Vasuki his sister's name and deny her on the grounds that her name differed! Reassured, he addressed the Naga respectfully.

'Great Naga,' he said aloud. 'What is your sister's name?'

Vasuki answered sibilantly but with obvious grace and respect, 'Jaratkaru, I know of your vows and conditions and come to you well aware of them. My younger sister's name is also Jaratkaru, the same as your own. I waited only until she was of sufficient age to be given away in marriage, preserving her carefully for you. Take this slender-waisted beauty as your wife.'

And Vasuki stepped aside to reveal, standing behind him, a beautiful young girl who exactly met Jaratkaru's conditions and demands for an ideal wife. Thus did the forces of brahman conjunct to ensure that the same snakes who had been cursed by their own mother to burn some day in a sacrificial fire of a king named

Janamajaya married one of their siblings to the yayavara Jaratkaru, that they might set into motion the events that would countermand the curse upon their species.

Pleased with Vasuki's offer, Jaratkaru married the Nagaraja's sister in accordance with all due rites. In time, they had a son named Astika, who grew up well learned in the Vedas and Vedangas. He was impartial to all beings in the three worlds. His presence dispelled all fear from the hearts of his mother and father and they were both content. Jaratkaru's lineage had been continued and his ancestors, freed from their descent, rose upto moksha, showering blessings upon their descendant and his heirs.

||Three||

Kulapati Shaunaka was pleased with this account but requested Sauti, 'Son of Lomarsana, you are most gracious. Your eloquence and felicity of narration are incomparable. Your father would be very proud of you, for you match even his own prowess in reciting these ancient tales using perfect metre and phrasing. I know there is far more to the tale of Astika than you have narrated until now. I entreat you, pray tell us the entire tale without leaving any detail out, with all diversions and deviations as it contains.'

Sauti bowed to Shaunaka. 'Great tiger of the Bhrigu line, how can I refuse you? I told you the abbreviated version of Astika's story. As you will it, I shall now narrate the unexpurgated tale in its entirety exactly as my father taught it to me.'

||Four||

Many years ago, in the Age of the Devas, there lived the Prajapati Daksha. He had two beautiful daughters. Their names were Kadru and Vinata. Daksha married both daughters to the Sage Kashyapa. One day, feeling generously disposed to his wives, Kashyapa told each of them that they could avail of any boon they desired. Both sisters were overjoyed. Kadru was the first to ask for her boon and she demanded one thousand nagas as her sons, each fiercer than the other and equally splendid. Goaded by her sister's demand, Vinata also asked for sons, but demanded only two, specifying that they must both be greater than Kadru's sons in strength, form, energy and courage. Kashyapa gladly granted his wives their requests and sired upon them the sons they desired. 'Care well for your sons to be!' he cautioned them, then left for the forest on a task.

A great length of time passed.

Finally, Kadru gave birth to one thousand eggs and Vinata birthed two eggs. Their maids kept the eggs separately in steaming vessels as instructed and waited for the eggs to hatch.

Five hundred years passed.

After five hundred years, Kadru's eggs hatched and as promised, one thousand sons emerged. But Vinata's two eggs remained unhatched.

Unable to tolerate her sister having gained her promised sons without she being similarly blessed, the impatient Vinata broke open one of her eggs. She saw that the upper half of the body was fully grown but the lower half was as yet unformed. Enraged, the unborn son opened his eyes and glared at his mother in anger: 'Mother, by cracking open my shell before my time, you have doomed me to be thus deformed forever. As punishment for your rash act, I curse you to be the slave of the woman you sought to rival for five hundred years! Only your other son may set you free from that enslavement, but only if you wait another five hundred years until he is fully developed and breaks open his shell of his own accord.'

Having issued this curse, the unformed son of Vinata rose into the sky and became the phenomenon we now call Aruna, the red sky of dawn, who is also the charioteer of the sun-god Surya and heralds his imminent arrival.

A further five hundred years passed.

And then the second egg cracked open and Vinata's second son was born, fully formed and resplendent, a being of incomparable power. This was Garuda, king of birds. As soon as he was birthed, he took flight into the sky to search for the food that had been preordained for him by the Creator, abandoning his mother.

||Five||

Shortly after Garuda's departure, the two wives of Kashyapa saw a great horse approaching the sage's ashram. This was no ordinary horse. A great stallion, this was the jewel of the species, the best of all horsekind, so radiant that even the devas cheered when he arose from the great churning of the ocean which we know as amrit-manthan. This was Ucchaihshrava himself, supreme among all horses, greatest of his kind, possessed of unsurpassed strength, radiant with divine splendour, and born with all the auspicious marks. He was one of many magnificent things that emerged from the amrit-manthan. He was king of horses.

The great mountain Meru blazes with energy, turning resplendent beneath the rays of the sun when they fall upon its glowing golden peaks. Arrayed with ornaments of burnished gold, frequented by devas and gandharvas, the peak is unnattainable and its base unfathomable to anyone who has committed sins against dharma. Terrible predators roam its slopes; divine herbs illuminate it. This great peak rises to cover even the vaults of swargaloka, the highest heaven. To most beings it is unreachable even in their wildest imaginings. Boundless rivers and scented groves resound with the sweet song of every kind of bird. It has stood aloft through the eons. It was up to this same mountain's bejewelled peak that the most venerable devas once ascended. These great divinities, austere and faithful of oath, assembled and began deliberations on how best to obtain the sacred ambrosia named Amrit, elixir of immortality. For once they obtained and consumed the Amrit, they would become immortal and therefore immune to the assaults of their enemies, the asuras.

It was Narayana, our great Lord Vishnu, who advised them on the best method, addressing his words to his fellow member of the holy Trimurti, Lord Brahma: 'This is not a task for us devas alone. We must enlist the aid of the asuras as well. Together, we must churn the pot of curdled milk until the best of herbs and precious treasures are released, and finally the Amrit itself will emerge. This is the only way to obtain the sacred ambrosia.' The pot he spoke of was of course the great Sagara, the vast ocean.

Acting on Narayana's instructions, the devas went to Mount Mandara. Their goal was to uproot the great mountain and use it as a churning pestle to work the ocean, for it was the only thing that could suffice for the task. Now, Mount Mandara is a great peak among mountains. It rises up 11,000 yojanas, which is a length equivalent to 44,000 kroshas, or 99,000 miles! This is only the height of the mountain—its foundation descends many more thousands of yojanas into the earth. Moreover, the mountain is gargantuan in weight and proportion, with innumerable nets of creepers covering its vast jungles filled with many fierce-fanged beasts of prey. Even the best attempts of the devas failed to uproot it. In desperation, they returned to stand before Vishnu and Brahma with joined palms. 'Aid us in uprooting Mount Mandara, great ones. You have but to will it and it will be done.'

'So be it,' said Vishnu. And on his word, the great Nagaraja

Anantha unwound his epic coils and rewound himself around the vast bulk and length of Mount Mandara. Exerting a mighty effort, the king of snakes uprooted the mountain with a deafening sound and dragged it behind the congregation of the devas and asuras, all the way to the ocean. There they called upon the lord of the ocean, Sagara, and requested, 'We wish to churn your waters, great one. Grant us leave to do so that we may produce Amrit.'

Sagara agreed, saying, 'You may do so, but only on condition that I too shall receive a share of the ambrosia.'

Then the devas and asuras together went to fetch Akupara, the great turtle upon whose shell rests the world entire. 'Kurmaraja, none except you can bear the mountain on your back for the purposes of the churning. Pray act as the base.' The king of turtles agreed and using elaborate tools and ingenuity, Lord Indra undertook the task of fixing Mount Mandara to the back of the great turtle at the bottom of the ocean. Finally, all was in readiness for the churning to begin.

Working together in collaboration for the mutual goal of obtaining the elixir of immortality, the devas and asuras all joined hands to share in the epic task. With Mandara as the churning rod, Vasuki the rope, and Akupara as the base, they began to churn Sagara, the pot of curdled milk as Narayana had called it. The asuras and danavas grasped the head of Vasuki, while the devas took hold of his tail. Vasuki's brother Anantha stayed by his lord Narayana, and repeatedly raised his brother Vasuki's head as it emerged from the great waters, then hurled it down again with force, to aid the churning. Vasuki's enormous length wound up and down, up and down, repeatedly, until sparks, then flames, then puffs of fire and black smoke began to belch forth from his maw.

From this black smoke were created clouds with lightning in their belly and thundershowers raged down upon the devas, refreshing them and washing them clean of their fatigue from time to time. From the top of the spinning mountain, great quantities of flowers were set free by the force of the churning, and these blossoms rained down as well, also refreshing both devas and asuras. The churning increased in frenzy. A terrible roar began to issue from the depths of the ocean, like the loudest thunder ever heard. Untold hordes of oceanic creatures and submarine life forms were crushed by the mountain and their habitats destroyed forever. From the whirling mountain Mandara, great trees were snapped loose by the force and fell off, killing the birds that nested in them. The wood of the trees began to catch fire from the friction produced by the churning motion. Wildfires blazed unchecked, adding to the chaos and peril. The animals and predators that dwelled on the mountain were driven out, some scorched by the fires, others flung loose by the churning, and died with terrible screams. All manner of creatures perished. Mount Mandara began to resemble a black thundercloud within which lightning flashed and fires raged. The fires spread everywhere, endangering all living beings on earth.

Indra saw the danger and used his power as lord of storms to quench the fires with a thunderous downpour. The rain, lightning, fire, and the force of the churning began to squeeze out the juices of countless herbs and the resins of trees caught in the maelstorm, producing a juice with no less potency than the elixir itself. Drinking of this juice, the devas attained immortality. The rest of the juice ran into the ocean and mingled with its milky depths, and from the continued churning, this milky mixture turned into the purest of ghee, which in turn floated up to the surface, redolent of the finest essences.

The devas called out to Brahma who was seated and watching the Amrit Manthan. 'Great Brahma, we are weary with effort. As are the asuras and danavas, daityas and both the Nagarajas Anantha and Vasuki. Yet the Amrit itself has not yet appeared, even after eons of churning. We cannot continue thus forever. We beseech you, entreat Lord Vishnu to aid us and give us strength to complete the task.'

Brahma spoke to Vishnu: 'Vishnu, only you can help them complete this task. Lend them a portion of your divine strength.'

Vishnu replied: 'They shall have the strength they desire. I grant this energy to all those who have devoted themselves to this task. Now there is only one last phase left to complete: Insert Mandara into the ocean once more and turn it around the other way!'

At Vishnu's words, all those participating in the Amrit Manthan felt themselves rejuvenated and energized. They did as Vishnu said, bending their backs to one mighty effort as they inserted the mountain down into the oceanic depths once more, then turned it around the other way. Now they churned with a new frenzy, and the noise of their effort filled all the three worlds. Once more the maelstorm spun.

And from the depths of the maelstorm there arose the following things of power:

First came the Sun, radiating a hundred thousand rays.

Then came the Moon, whose bright cool light was as tranquil as the sun's was fierce.

Next came Sridevi, the goddess Lakshmi, clad in pale white.

Following her came the goddess of wine and the white horse, Ucchaihshrava.

Then came the celestial gem Kaustubha which eternally adorns Vishnu's chest.

The radiant Sun, Aditya, swift as thought itself, blazed a trail and was followed by Lakshmi, the moon and Ucchaihshrava, to land before the devas.

Then from the manthan there rose the resplendent god Dhanvantari, bearing a white gourd pot in his hand, in which was contained the Amrit itself, elixir of immortality, divine ambrosia.

At this extraordinary sight, the danavas produced a great outcry, saying: 'It is ours!' and surged forward to claim Amrit for themselves.

But Lord Vishnu used his power to assume the shape of a beautiful and seductive woman Mohini who bewitched the danavas with her beauty into giving her the gourd full of Amrit. He then gave Amrit to the devas. Enraged at this betrayal of their pact, the asuras swore a war oath against the devas and prepared for battle.

||Six||

Upon the same shores of the vast body of salty water where they had so recently worked together in perfect coordination to churn the ocean and produce Amrit, the daityas and danavas assembled, clad in their strongest armour and armed with their fiercest weapons and shields. Great was their number and terrible their rage. Outnumbered and outmatched, the devas had no hope of victory by ordinary means. But thanks to the duplicity of Vishnu, they now had possession of the elixir of immortality, the sacred ambrosia, Amrit. Even as the asuras clanged their swords against their shields and worked themselves up into a fury for battle, Naryana, our Lord Vishnu, still in his beguiling form as Mohini, handed the gourd of Amrit to Nara, his twin form with whom he sometimes merged or divided from as required, who passed it to each of the devas in turn so each one might drink from it and become immortal.

But the asuras did not lack for craftiness either. Unnoticed by the gods, a danava named Rahu assumed the form of the deva named Buddh, who is the celestial body closest to the sun. Disguised as Buddh, Rahu took the gourd of Amrit and began to drink it. But the sun and moon, being celestial bodies themselves and therefore better able to recognize their colleague, saw through Rahu's disguise and knew that this was not their companion planet Buddh. They set off a hue and cry, alerting the other devas. Acting with the speed of thought, the great god Vishnu flung his deadly weapon, the celestial chakra, and the discus sliced off the head of Rahu before the ambrosia could pass down his throat. However, his head had consumed Amrit and therefore became immortal. Severed from its body, that jewel-decorated head gave out thunderous roars of outrage and ever since that day, a perpetual enmity began between Rahu and his betrayers, the Sun and Moon. Even today, when his rage becomes too great to control, he swallows one or other, even though they soon reappear as they slip through his severed throat.

When all the devas had drunk of Amrit, they turned immortal. And it was not a moment too soon for the asuras were worked up to a frenzy and rushed at the gods with an enormous earth-shaking roar and thundering of feet, hell-bent on revenge.

Then Vishnu shed his beguiling Mohini avatar and transformed back into his awe-inspiring true form as Hari deva. He returned their roars of rage with a great bellow of his own, drowning out their cries and proclaiming his supremacy. The hearts of the asuras quailed at the great war cry of Vishnu and the sky and ocean blackened on that great field of battle by the shores of the vast ocean which still frothed and seethed from the recent churning. Then upon those ploughed shores there commenced the greatest battle ever waged between the devas and the asuras.

The raging of the ocean, the thunder of the skies, the howling of the asuras, the battle cry of Vishnu, the roaring of the devas, all blurred and melded to form one deafening sound. The blackness of the sky dimmed all sight, until the only things visible were the white froth raging on the surface of the wild seas, and on the shore, the gleaming of thousands of raised weapons—swords, axes, tridents, spears, javelins, lances, metal clubs, chakras. In the gloamy dimness the armies clashed. Javelins flew through the air, punching through breastplates, penetrating heart and lungs and gristle, severing the spine to emerge with an explosion of blood and gore. Spears pierced flesh and shattered bone to splinters. Swords laid open torsos, severed limbs. Chakras spun through the air, gleaming malevolently as they found their targets, decapitating, maiming. Clubs pounded down, smashing skulls like ripe fruit. Blood spewed from open mouths, through shattered teeth and smashed jaws. Bodies were trampled underfoot, eyes crunched to pulp beneath boot heels. Jewelled earrings, silver nose rings, engraved armour plates, filigreed shields, gold crowns, ruby signets, precious ornaments worth a world's fortune lay trampled and marred in the muck of the battlefield. Asuras fell in great numbers, their corpses piled high in red streaked mounds that resembled copper-veined mountains. The cacophony of blood lust rang out, cries of 'Slice!' 'Kill!' 'Chase!' 'Throw!' 'Cut!' 'Attack!' ringing out like an insane battle chant.

Last to enter the field were the great ones Nara and Narayana.

In those ancient days, weapons were celestial devices summoned by the utterance of a mantra. Nara summoned his divine bow which appeared at once, gleaming darkly in his fist. Narayana thought of his danava-destroying chakra, Sudarshana. No sooner had he summoned it than the dark skies, veiled by crow-black stormclouds, blazed with a blinding bright light, causing all those engaged in combat to pause and gaze up in surprise and awe. From the peak of the sky, through the clouds, descended the Sudarshana, radiant as the sun itself, impossible to look at directly, rock-steady in its path. Like a device fixed to a rigid pole, it descended, unwavering and blinding in intensity, to hover above Vishnu the immitigable. A golden discus of a mysterious metal unknown to mortal science, it spun with a speed impossible to measure, its bladed tips spinning rapidly enough to form the semblance of a continuous edge, producing a keening sound like a living being. Vishnu, in another of his infinite variety of forms as Achyuta, the Imperishable One, received it with an upraised forefinger around whose tip its centre spun, empowered by his mighty consciousness. Blazing with his own divine fire, Achyuta was indistinguishable from the sun-bright Sudarshana. With the strength of a thousand elephants, he unleashed the Sudarshana Chakra and with a shrill screeching cry of unmistakable delight, the dev astra descended upon the field of battle. In thousands died the progeny of Dit and Danu then, unable to counter the power of Vishnu's Chakra. At times it blazed like fire, its celestial energy exploding to send flying outwards the shredded scraps of hundreds of asura bodies. At other times it descended to ground level, spinning underfoot as it travelled along the field, scything enemy bodies and reducing them to mangled pulp. It drank the spilled blood like a vampirical beast, screaming with terrible delight. Everywhere it went, it caused havoc and slaughtered the enemies of the gods in great numbers.

But the asuras were powerful as well. Undaunted, a thousand demons rose up bearing mountains on the palms of their hands which they flung down upon the lines of the devas, crushing them on impact with booming explosions. The world was filled with the crashing of thousands upon thousands of mountains as the asuras retaliated with fearsome rage. The earth herself, great and tolerant Prithvi-Maa, began to tremble beneath the force of the impact and waver in her course. And still the asuras continued to shower down mountains upon the overwhelmed devas.

Then great Nara plunged deep into the ranks of the asura hordes, mingling with them unnoticed at first. Using his divine bow, he loosed a hail of powerful arrows with tips of unknown golden-hued metal and feathered shafts, like a rainstorm rising up from the ground to the skies. The sky grew dark with the profusion of arrows, released at such blinding speed by the magnificent bow of Nara that they appeared to be issued from an army of archers rather than a single bowman. The arrows struck the mountains still in the hands of the flying asuras as well as those peaks still plummeting earthwards, and shattered them with terrible force, reducing each one to fine powdered dust. The dust fell like a benediction upon the laughing devas who applauded their fellow god.

Then did the tide turn against the asuras. Nara and Narayana in the field used their divine bow and magnificent discus to wreak a terrible toll upon the enemy. The rest of the deva forces attacked from high and low, flank and van, until the asuras, harried and disordered, knew not where to turn to make a stand. Frustrated and despairing, some burrowed their way into the earth, eating through the soil and stone and roots to bury themselves deep within the body of the planet. Those closer to the shores of the ocean plunged into the salty waters, seeking refuge in the darkest depths. Soon the field was clear of all except the victorious devas.

Producing a mighty cheer of triumph, the gods celebrated their undisputed victory.

Afterwards, they restored things to their natural places. Mount Mandara was hauled back to its original site and set firmly in place. Akupara was released from his task to go back to bearing the universe upon his shelled back. Indra led the devas in a great celebration that lasted for an untold time and filled the heavens with their gaiety and jubilation. When all was done, Indra, the slayer of Bala, acting for the devas, handed over the gourd pot containing Amrit to Kirti, the Crowned One.

||Seven||

Meanwhile, back at the ashram of Kashyapa, the sisters Kadru and Vinata saw the great steed Ucchaihshrava approach. The celestial stallion had only just then emerged from the Amrit Manthan and its route took it past that site where the wives of Kashyapa lived. But the great horse's aura glowed so radiantly, it was not visible in the manner of an ordinary horse. Observing its supernatural brilliance, Kadru asked her sister, 'Sister dearest, what colour is the horse Ucchaihshrava? Tell me at once!' Vinata replied graciously, 'Blessed sister, there is no question about it. The celestial horse is white from nose tip to tail tip, of course. Why? Do you believe it is another colour? Come then, my pretty one, let's have a wager!' Kadru said with exaggerated politeness, 'My sweet-smiling sister, you are quite wrong. I say the horse has a black tail. But you are the prettiest one, are you not? Don't spoil your beauty with a sour look. If it's a wager you wish, I am game for it. I bet you that the one who is mistaken about the horse's colour will become the other one's slave. What say?' To which her sibling Vinata replied at once, 'Agreed!' Then, as it was late in the day and the light insufficient, both sisters agreed to return the next day to examine the horse by the clear light of day.

Back home, Kadru was determined to win the wager by any

means necessary. She commanded her one thousand sons: 'Turn yourself into horse hairs as black as kohl and cover the celestial horse's tail completely.' When they refused, she urged them again, saying, 'If you do not do as I say, I shall lose the bet and become her slave!' But still they would not agree to deceive their aunt. Finally, frustrated with their non-compliance, she cursed her own sons: 'You shall all perish in the sarpa satra of the Kuru, Raja Janamajaya!' This terrible curse resounded as far away as Brahmaloka, where the great Father heard Kadru's words and mused on the cruel utterance. But after consultation with the other devas, he agreed to let the curse stand, for the sons of Kadru had multiplied manifold and were increasing in numbers at an unprecedented rate, and were moreover virulently poisonous in their venom, fearsome creatures, and rapidly exceeding all bounds of his control. They bit anyone they chose, intimidating with their lethal venom and running rampant where they pleased. But, out of his love for all living creatures, he countered the curse by bestowing upon Kadru's own husband and the father of these same snakes the knowledge of how to neutralize their venom.

The next morning, the sisters rose with the sun, driven by their mutual jealousy and each eager to better her sibling, and set out to view the horse Ucchaihshrava who had taken shelter in a certain grove. Their route took them first to the ocean. Arriving at the shore, they gazed out upon that vast watery expanse. They saw thousands of species of the waterworld coexisting. There were untold varieties of fish. There were enormous timi, also known as whales. And there were timingila, those creatures that devoured whales. There were sharks, crocodiles, turtles and also the mythical makaras. Land creatures hesitated to approach it because of the presence of these awe-inspiring predators. Yet it was also a treasure trove of precious stones, the abode of Varuna, the beautiful home of the Sea Nagas, mother of all rivers, home to the submarine fire, and hiding place of the asuras. Eternal and immeasurable, filled with unimaginable wonders and fearsome reverberations, source of terrible calamities and awash with maelstroms spinning above bottomless abysses. It was also a source of great succour and rich treasures, trove of Amrit, producer of quakes and storms, at once both sacred and supreme. Its shoreline changed constantly, altered by its turbulent moods, slapping the land with waves like raised hands, buffetting the earth with powerful forces and washes. Its tides waxing and waning with the shifting moon, it was the resting place of the Panchajanya, that great Conch belonging to Lord Vishnu, and an endless supply of pearls. In ancient times, Lord Vishnu in his avatar as Varaha, the boar incarnation, plunged into the depths of the endless ocean and churned up the waters with his furious quest for land, finding it at the very bottom of the waters. However, the brahmarishi Atri, despite seeking the same earth for one hundred years, failed to find it. At the beginning of each Yuga, or the Eon which is one part of the Day of Brahma, the lotus-navelled Vishnu falls into the sleep of Yoga-nidra, this same milky ocean becomes his bed. Its waters then resemble the tongues of Agni in the sacrificial yagna, holy, boundless, immeasurable and eternal.

The sisters looked upon this great ocean, saw the thousands of rivers that rushed toward it as eagerly as lovers into each other's embrace. They heard the cries of the untold species that lived and preyed and died within its unplumbed depths. And they flew over the great world of Varuna and Sagara and passed to the other side.

Arriving at the grove where Ucchaihshrava loitered, the sisters Kadru and Vinata looked at it in clear daylight. To Vinata's dismay there were indeed many black hairs on the white tail of the horse, thus proving Kadru's observation to be true. Vinata grieved even as her sister gloated. Having lost the wager, Vinata then became her sister's slave.

||Nine||

Meanwhile, Garuda, the second son of Vinata who broke open his own shell and emerged without his mother's interference or help, flew through the sky, greatly expanded in size and strength from the fledgling that had come out of the shell. Resplendent as a mass of blazing flame and possessed of fearsome aspect, he appeared as the pure energy of fire itself, striking awe and fear into the hearts of even the powerful devas. Awed at this inexplicable sight, the devas all cried out in alarm and sought out Vibhavasu, he of many hues. 'O Agni, a part of thy energy flies through the sky threatening to set ablaze all the worlds. It is enormous in size and too brilliant to behold. Do you seek to destroy us all with this weapon of flame?' Agni replied reassuringly, 'Devas, it is not what you think. That is the mighty Garuda. His brilliance equals my own but he is not of my making.' Awed by the power and appearance of Garuda, the devas and all the great sages then followed Garuda and sang his praises from a distance. 'Lord of birds. You are a great force unto yourself. Your aspect is no less fierce than that of Agni, host of the sacrificial flame. You are no less than a deva. Be our supreme protector. You are an ocean of might, you are purity incarnate. Your qualities are beyond number. You possess great ferocity and can perform impossible deeds. You are unconquerable, possessed of full knowledge of all that has been and all that will be. Your heat surpasses that of the sun, you engender all things permanent and transient. Even the sun pales in comparison with your splendour. If you choose to rage, you can destroy all things as the sun does in his outbursts. You fly through the sky unbounded, you soar above the clouds themselves. Surely you can grant all boons and achieve the mightiest feats. You are no less powerful than the great fire of entropy which consumes all matter at the end of each Yuga. O king of birds. We approach you as friends and allies. Be not harsh with us. Do not scorch us with your power, we entreat you.'

Preening with pleasure at this exaltation from the devas, Garuda, the beautiful feathered one, controlled his heat and radiance out of consideration for them and continued on his way. After a great flight across the vast ocean, Garuda came to his mother's house. Having lost the wager over the horse, Vinata was enslaved by her sister. She served Kadru daily, living a life of constant humiliation and despair. Kadru, proud in her newfound role as mistress and commander, summoned Vinata imperiously. Vinata appeared and bowed before her, asking her orders. Kadru ordered her sister to transport her to the legendary abode of the Sea Nagas at the bottom of the ocean, Ramaniyaka. Compelled to obey, Vinata lifted her on her back and carried her to the ocean. At his mother's request, Garuda carried the sons of Kadru. Now, Garuda was wont to fly very high and as he rose up into the sky, the snakes upon his back began to suffer the fearsome heat of the sun. Scorched and tormented by the heat, the snakes suffered great pain and fell unconscious.

Seeing the state of her sons, Kadru cried out to Indra by his various names. 'O Shakra, husband of Shachi, king of the gods, slayer of Bala, destroyer of Namuchi. I bow before you. My sons are being burned to death by the heat of the sun. You can save them. Purandara, you are a destroyer of cities, you can produce a deluge and save them. You are lord of the wind, clouds, fire and lightning. You are thunder and monsoon, the sun and the fire, you are all things wonderful and magnificent. You are Vishnu, you are the thousand-eyed, you are the last resort of all who hope. You are soma, drink of the devas. You are muhurata, the crucial instant of auspicious action. You are the tithis, the lunar days. You are kshana, the time it takes for a twinkling of an eye, four-fifths of a second, and you are lava as well, one-sixth of a kshana. You are shuklapaksha, the brighter half of the moon month, and you are krishnapaksha, the bahula or darker half of the lunar cycle. You are kala, the daily waxing of the moon, and a fractional measure of time. You are kashtha, one-thirtieth of a lava. You are truti, half of a lava. You are time in all its aspects, from the greatest to the most minute. You are the solar year, the changing seasons, the months of the calendar, the nights and days themselves. You are the earth sublime, its mountains and forests. You are the clear sky with brilliant sun. You are the vast ocean and its billowing energies, the timi whales as well as the timingalas that devour the whales, the makaras. You are justly famous. You are worshipped by the greatest seers, the enlightened maharishis. You are the drinker of soma offered at sacrifices. You are He whom brahmins worship when they desire anything. Your fame extends to the sacred Vedas, where you are praised extensively. It is to ensure their pleas reach your ears that the twice-born study the Vedangas diligently.'

At this passionate entreaty by Kadru, Lord Indra rode his bay horses across the sky, veiling the sun with a dense blanket of stormclouds. Crackling with lightning, the clouds unleashed a deluge of epic proportions. Thunder crashed and wave upon wave of torrential rain washed across the earth, submerging it in water across its length and breadth. Overwhelmed with delight, the Naga sons of Kadru revived and were refreshed by the water and praised the great Vasava for his aid.

Soon after, the beautiful feathered Garuda arrived at an island. This was the place known as Malaya, for its sandalwood trees, surrounded on all sides by endless ocean and filled with the cries and songs of numerous birds. There were rows of wooded groves rich with fruits and blossoms, where well-constructed houses stood by beautiful lotus lakes. Apsaras and gandharvas frolicked in the flower-strewn groves. The island was refreshed by cool scented breezes. Blossoms and petals showered down from the high Malaya trees, and the Naga sons of Kadru were charmed by the beauty of the place. They lived there awhile and took great pleasure in its natural wonders. After some time had passed, the pannagas called to Garuda who flew down and folded his great wings, bending his mighty head low that he might hear their words. 'Take us to another beautiful island as charming as this one, Garuda. You must know many such places from your travels across the sky.' Irritated at their abrupt orders, Garuda asked his mother: 'Must I obey their every whim?' Vinata sighed and replied, 'Yes, my son. For under the terms of the wager I lost, I am enslaved by my sister, your aunt. And as my son, you are therefore enslaved as well.' Curious, Garuda enquired further and learned for the first time all the details of the lost wager. After he heard the full story, he was unhappy. Appealing to the sons of Kadru, he asked them, 'Tell me one act that I may perform that will appease you forever. No matter how great a deed, I shall perform it, if only you will agree to release my mother and I from this state of slavery.' At this, the sons of Kadru hissed sibilantly and answered, 'Bring us Amrit! And you shall be freed from your bond!'

||Ten||

Garuda went to his mother and asked for her blessings. 'I shall go and fetch Amrit and end our enslavement.' Upon which his mother urged him to eat something before he went that he might gain strength for his mission. 'What shall I eat, mother?' he asked her dutifully. Vinata thought awhile, then said, 'Far from here, in a remote bay, you shall find the Nishadas, hunters of creatures who dwell in the ocean. Their diet makes them strong and their flesh shall give you strength as well. Eat as many of them as you can, consume them by the thousands, and you will be well nourished for your task. But remember, you must never eat a brahmin or kill one. Among all living creatures, a brahmin is like fire itself and can never be eaten or killed. Just like fire, a brahmin angered can blaze like the sun and destroy you by the tapas heat of his austerities. A brahmin is the first to eat at a sacrifice for he is supreme among the varnas, a father and a preceptor.'

Garuda bowed to his mother. 'In that case, Maatr, tell me, how do I recognize a brahmin from among other persons? By what signs is he distinguished?'

Vinata answered, 'My son, a brahmin may appear similar to any other mortal being, but if you eat one by accident, when he passes down your throat, it will feel as if you have swallowed a live coal. If you try to swallow him, he will stick like a fish hook. And you will know at once that you have tried to eat a brahmin!'

Eager that her son not make any error, Vinata again repeated her instructions carefully. Garuda listened attentively. When it was time for him to leave, Vinata pronounced a blessing over him, out of her maternal love: 'May the Maruts, those gods of wind, protect your wings. May Chandra, the moon, protect your back. May Agni, the lord of fire, protect your head. May Surya, the sun god, protect your entire body. Go now, my son. I shall perform a ceremony to pray for your well-being until the time you return.' Garuda bid goodbye to his mother and spread his wings, soaring up into the sky.

In time, he found the bay where the Nishadas resided and fell upon them like great Kaal itself, the almighty Lord of Death Yama in the form of Time. His mighty wings beat up a great dust storm that covered the sky, dried up the ocean and caused even the adjoining mountain ranges to shake. Then, moving stealthily through the twilight of the dust storm, he opened his beak wide. Stampeding in panic from these unusual phenomena, the Nishadas unwittingly ran right into the open beak of Garuda. Just as birds rise from a jungle in thousands when startled and fly up into the sky, thus did the Nishadas run along their only escape route—directly into the maw of the great bird. Garuda scooped them up by the thousands and consumed them, eating their flesh, strengthened by their diet of fish. The slaughter of the Nishadas was relentless.

Then, as was inevitable, a brahmin and his wife happened to be among those that fell into Garuda's beak. Even as they fell, screaming, into his throat, Garuda felt himself scorched as if he had swallowed a live coal. Remembering his mother's instructions, at once he opened his beak and released the brahmin, saying, 'O great brahmin. You are free to go. I have sworn an oath never to eat a brahmin, even if he lives among those who are wrongdoers.'

Relieved, the brahmin scurried out of the beak, then paused to look up. 'Mighty one, the woman with me is my wife. She is a Nishada but I pray you, spare her as well.'

Garuda said, 'Take her then, and go. Hurry before you are both consumed by the energy in my belly for once it touches you, there is no escape.'

Without wasting a moment, the brahmin took his Nishada wife by the hand and both escaped from Garuda's beak.

Garuda spread his wings and took flight once more. Flying to his father's ashram, he came before Sage Kashyapa and greeted him with appropriate plaudits. When his father gave him leave to speak, he said, 'I am on a mission to steal the Soma of immortality, Amrit. Once I hand it over to the Nagas, my mother shall be freed from her enslavement. Requiring energy for the task, she advised me to eat the Nishadas. I did so, but even after consuming thousands of the fisherfolk, I am still not sated. Great father of mine, pray advise me on what else I can eat that I may grow strong enough to steal the ambrosia.'

Kashyapa pondered the matter then said, 'My son, in ancient times there was a maharishi named Vibhavasu. He was prone to losing his temper easily. Vibhavasu had a younger brother named Supratika who was also a great ascetic. Both brothers jointly owned certain possessions and properties of value. Supratika wished to have his share of these things to possess independently. He constantly urged his brother to divide their possessions. One day, angered by his brother's constant demands, Vibhavasu told him, 'Many people foolishly believe that dividing property is the best way. But once it is divided, these same deluded fools are then driven apart. The more they think about wealth and possessions, the more they wish to ensure that they have received their fair share, and obsess over dividing their properties and possessions, while retaining a semblance of friendship. In time, this leads to enmity and selfish greed and eventually, utter ruin. Knowledgable persons like us should be wiser than to pursue such selfish and deluded goals. Partition can only cause unhappiness and ruin. Supratika, your constant demands have exceeded my patience. Despite all my advice, you are obsessed with acquiring your share of the property. Your bullheadedness is intolerable. On this account, I curse you to become an elephant who constantly pushes his head against a tree, determined to bring it to the ground!'

In retaliation, Supratika said, 'If that is so, then I curse you to become a turtle that lives in the water and is unable to take any action, no matter how vital!'

Thus, each of them turned into an elephant and a turtle. And until this very day, they continue to maintain their enmity towards one another, feuding and brawling constantly. Look upon this great lake before us. Do you see the large majestic elephant that comes toward us, trumpeting its anger? That is Supratika, transformed by his brother's curse. And there, responding to the elephant's challenge, Vibhavasu the turtle rises from the bed of the lake to the surface. Watch how the elephant curls his trunk in fury and plunges into the lake to do batttle with the turtle, attacking it with his trunk, tusks, tail and feet. The turtle is no less indignant and agitates the water mightily as it retaliates. These are no ordinary turtle and elephant: Vibhavasu the turtle is three yojanas tall and ten yojanas in girth! While Supratika the elephant is six yojanas high and twice that in length! They are both joining together in a battle royale as we speak. Scoop them up and eat them whole and you shall gain all the strength you desire to accomplish your chosen task!'

At his father's words, Garuda eagerly leaped into the sky, turned in a wheeling flight, and swooped down to grasp hold of the elephant with one enormous claw and the tortoise with the other claw. Gaining height again with powerful flaps of his great wings, he flew to the tirthsthan named Alamba where a grove of celestial trees flourished. These were divine trees, hung with gold and silver fruits and branches of lapis lazuli. Being a bird, he sought only to perch upon a tree branch that he might eat his meal of turtle and elephant. But, buffetted by the gale-intensity of his wings, the magical trees trembled in fear, afraid that Garuda's immense weight would crack their golden boughs. Garuda was able to understand the concern felt by the divine trees and he had no desire to shake free their magical fruit which were capable of granting any wish to those who ate them. So he went in search of a more suitable perch.

He found a great and ancient fig tree with immense branches, its roots spread far and wide over the course of its historic life. The tree saw and understood Garuda's need and called out to him: 'Great bird, I bid you welcome. Come perch upon my mighty branches which extend for one hundred yojanas and eat your meal in peace!' Garuda, enormous as any mountain, descended with a great flapping of his wings, bearing his prey, and perched upon the giant branches that had housed a thousand birds for as many years. But the instant his claws touched the branch, it broke with a loud crack and the entire tree shook.

Instinctively, moving as quickly as thought, Garuda snatched up the bough he had broken and held it in his beak before it could fall to the ground. He saw that the bough had a large number of tiny humanoid creatures hanging from its underside, their heads facing downwards. On closer inspection he realized these were the valakhilyas, the austere rishis who had been generated from the body of Brahma himself in a great age past. Each of them was the size of a man's thumb and they preceded the sun's chariot on his daily journey. Unwilling to let the bough drop and crush the valakhilyas to death, Garuda held that great bough in his mighty beak and flew up to the sky again. Unable to find a suitable perch, he flew on for a great distance, often circling for ages in search of a landing spot, without finding any. Across countless nations he flew thus, carrying the giant elephant in one claw, the turtle in his other claw, and the giant bough in his beak. But nowhere on earth could he find a place strong enough to bear the combined weight of himself and his burdens.

At last he came to the great mountain Gandhamadana atop whose peak his father Kashyapa was standing on one leg in a yogic asana. Sage Kashayapa saw his son and understood his plight at once. He called out to Garuda: 'My son! Be careful what you do! The valakhilyas drink the energy of the sun to sustain themselves. If angered, they will turn their solar power upon you and burn you instantly!' Having cautioned his son, Kashyapa then turned his attention to the valakhilyas themselves. 'Great ascetics, my son Garuda has embarked on a noble mission. Pray, grant him your permission to proceed.'

Acknowledging their fellow sage, the valakhilyas acceded to Kashyapa's well-phrased request and relinquished their hold on the giant branch. Descending to the ground, they travelled on to the Himalayas to seek out another place to complete their austerities.

But Garuda still had a problem. 'Father,' he said to Kashyapa, 'advise me where I can drop this branch without harming any brahmins. For my mother Vinata cautioned me never to harm a brahmin. Is there a country where no brahmins reside where I can go to discard it?'

'Tarkshya,' said his father, using an affectionate epithet for his son, 'in a distant land there is a mountain uninhabited by humans. It is remote, inaccessible, and in a place where no man can reach, with caves buried in snowdrifts. Mortal men do not know of its existence even in their imagination. I will communicate its location to you with the power of my mind.'

Thus instructed, Garuda rose up again, carrying the giant branch, giant elephant and giant turtle and using the power of his mind alone, entered the base of the mountain instantly. Thus, he covered a distance of one hundred thousand yojanas in the wink of an eye. Seeing the mountain, he let go of the branch with great relief. With a terrible sound, the branch crashed and fell, causing the entire mountain and the surrounding countryside for many hundreds of yojanas around to shudder. Trees shed their fruit, leaves and flowers showered down, and the snowdrifts and glacial ice clinging to the peak and slopes of that mighty mountain were shaken loose and crashed down in a great avalanche. Alighting atop the summit of that same mountain, Garuda finally rested his weary body and feasted on both the elephant and the turtle, eating both with great relish. As soon as he finished, he was filled with immense energy, and was ready to undertake his ambitious mission.

Once again travelling at the speed of thought, he flew from that mountain peak to the land of the gods to steal the ambrosia of immortality.

But the devas are gods and they saw portents and signs of the impending threat. Indra's vajra, that divine thunderbolt, released itself with an ominous sound even without his bidding. Meteors blazed trails across the sky. The various clans of the gods—Vasus, Rudras, Adityas, Sadhyas, Maruts and their kith and kin—all began attacking one another and fighting for no apparent reason. Things occurred that had never taken place before, even during the war of the devas and asuras. Tumultuous winds roared, cloudless skies produced thundering sounds, and even the God of the gods, he who has ever been and shall ever be, rained showers of blood. The flower garlands around the necks of the devas withered and wilted. Swirling dust and grime darkened the gleam of their crowns. The light of the stars was extinguished.

Indra, who was also the performer of a hundred sacrifices and therefore known as Shatkratu, was disturbed and bewildered, as were his fellow devas. He appealed to the preceptor of the gods, the great sage Brihaspati. 'Gurudev, what is the cause of these phenomena? Such portents can only serve to forewarn us of a great enemy's approach. But I see no one who threatens our well-being.'

Brihaspati replied, 'King of the gods, it is through your own negligence that this has occurred. The valakhilyas, through the power of their austerities, have created an extraordinary creature. This giant bird, son of Kashyapa and Vinata, is powerful and possessed of maya, the power of illusion. He comes here now to steal your precious Amrit. Do not underestimate him. This feat is well within his ability. He is capable of doing the impossible.'

Disturbed by his guru's words, Indra in his form of Shakra spoke to the other devas, fellow guardians of the sacred elixir. 'These portents are signs of the approach of a great and powerful bird. He comes now to steal our Amrit. We must prevent him from doing so.'

On Indra's instructions, they took up pre-arranged positions around the gourd pot of Amrit, weapons in hand. Indra armed himself with his vajra. Each of the devas was clad in his best armour and armed with his fiercest weapons—chakras, balas, trishuls, parasus, and every other projectile imaginable. Armed and armoured thus, the army of devas stood there waiting, determined to protect the nectar of immortality at any cost. What army would dare challenge such a divine host, armed as if for a great war, capable of facing even the largest gathering of enemies ever assembled?

||Eleven||

Kulapati Shaunaka joined his palms together. 'Suta, forgive my interruption. What did Brihaspati mean when he blamed Indra for his negligence? How was the great Indra negligent? And what did he mean when he said that Garuda had been created by the austerities of the valakhilyas? But even before that, I wish to ask an even more basic question: How did Kashyapa, a brahmin of great knowledge and austerity, come to have a bird for a son? And how did this bird-son, Garuda, possess such incredible powers and strength, including the ability to travel at will through the power of thought? If you possess knowledge of any of these answers, I would hear them.'

Sauti nodded. 'Indeed, Kulapati. All these questions are answered in our ancient Puranas and contained within the body of the *Mahabharata* epic. I shall answer them briefly here before resuming the tale of Garuda and Amrit.

'Prajapati Kashyapa once undertook a sacrifice in order to obtain a son. He was aided by the rishis, the devas and the gandharvas. He appointed Indra in his form of Shakra, the other devas and the valakhilya sages to bring firewood for the sacrifice. Because of his immense strength, Shakra picked up a load of firewood as large as a mountain and carried it easily. On the way, he saw some rishis as tiny as the joint of a thumb, struggling to carry a single leaf of a palash tree. These were the valakhilyas. Emaciated from lack of food, bone-thin, they were very weak and barely able to walk straight. Unseen by them, a cow's hoofprint had filled up with murky water, and they fell into it. Amused by the sight, Indra burst out laughing and instead of offering to help, simply stepped over them and continued on his way. Angered by Indra's behaviour, the valakhilyas resolved to punish the king of the gods. When they finally reached the site of the yagna, they poured offerings into the sacred fire and chanted mantras which would cause the creation of a being equal to Indra in strength, power and capable of travelling anywhere simply by willing himself there. Additionally, they specified that this new being would cause great fear and pain to Indra himself and when the two clashed, the new god would be one hundred times as strong and fierce as Purandara. On hearing their invocations, Indra turned pale with fear and appealed to his host, Kashyapa, to protect him from the being created by the valakhilyas.

'Kashyapa went to the valakhilyas and asked them if they had indeed succeeded in creating the being they desired. They answered in the affirmative. He attempted to arbitrate and began by referring to the word of their own forebear, Brahma. "Indra was appointed by Brahma himself as the lord of three worlds. By invoking the creation of another god equal to him, you run the risk of offending Brahma himself and undermining his words. This is not right. On the other hand, I have no desire to thwart your wishes. Therefore, let the being you invoked be like another Indra, more powerful and supreme, but let him be an Indra among the winged creatures, not mortal or deva. In this manner, your words as well as Brahma's injunction shall be upheld."' The valakhilyas were not malevolent nor vengeful by nature. They bowed to their host and fellow brahmin and said graciously, "Prajapati, it is true that we desired to create a new Indra to replace the existing one. But because we were attending your ceremony to obtain a son, it was to that same future son that we poured our oblations and offered our invocations. Now, the rest is entirely up to you, for the being we invoked shall be your own son, and you its father. Therefore, whatever you desire shall come to pass."

'At this time, Dakshayani Vinata was most desirous of having a son and had been performing austerities and rites to achieve this goal. Pleased with her efforts, Kashyapa told her that her austerities would bear fruit and her wishes would be answered. "You shall have not one but two valiant sons. Through the auspices of the valakhilyas and my own efforts, both sons shall be blessed and worshipped everywhere." Then Kashyapa son of Marichi cautioned his wife to take great care when she carried the seeds of life in her womb. "One of these shall be a great and powerful winged being, Indra among birdkind, capable of great feats and bestowed with nopareil powers." Once the children were seeded within his wife's womb, Kashyapa spoke to Indra, reassuring him. "Purandara, you need have no further cause for fear. I have ensured that both my sons from the daughter of Daksha will be winged creatures, not mortals or devas. They shall be as brothers to you. You may cease your worrying. But you should learn a lesson from this incident. Never again insult or mock those who have knowledge of the brahman. Their words are as weapons, their fury terrible." Relieved, Indra returned to his home world, Indraloka. In time, Vinata gave birth to two sons, both bird creatures, in the manner I have already described to you. The first son, the unformed one, became Aruna, who comes before the sun. The second who was fully formed and omnipotent, was Garuda, whose story I shall now continue . . .'

||Twelve||

The devas were prepared to repulse any foe, however powerful. Undaunted, Garuda arrived at the site where they were protecting the sacred elixir. At the sight of Garuda, the gods began to quail. Some of them sought to surrender their arms as they believed Garuda to be indomitable, and their fellow devas grew furious at them and fights broke out among the gods themselves. In this chaos, Garuda began his assault. The first to bar his way was Vishwakarma, that famous architect among the gods, also known as Bhouvana. Determined to guard the soma with his life, he prepared to fight valiantly. But with a single flick of his claw, Garuda ripped Vishwakarma to shreds, then tore out his innards with his beak and flicked them aside with a beat of his wings. Then Garuda flapped his wings faster and faster, stirring the very earth itself into rising in a maelstrom. So great a quantity of dust churned through the air that nobody could see anything. Moving through this turmoil like an avenging force, Garuda slashed, bit, jabbed, pierced, and tore apart the devas as a raven tears worms from the ground.

Indra rallied the Marut named Vayu, Lord of the Wind. 'Clear this dust away instantly!' he commanded. Shaken by the great bird's attack, the god of the wind heard Indra's command and obeyed. In moments, the dust cleared and all could see one another and Garuda again.

Then Indra led the devas in an assault on Garuda. Stung and nicked by their weapons and blows, he roared, filling the three worlds with his fearsome cry. Beating his great wings, he rose up into the sky above the heads of the devas. The gods attacked him on every side, with every weapon at their disposal, flinging spears, javelins, lances, arrows, cutting with swords, axes, chakras, jabbing trishuls, striking powerful blows with hammers, iron maces, clubs and weapons of every kind and description. Garuda withstood all their blows without coming to harm. On and on the battle raged, but Vinata's son fought on relentlessly, showing no signs of weariness or pain. Even though he was but one, and they were many, and immortal, yet it was the devas who grew the worse for wear. For he tore into them with savage ferocity, mangling bodies with his deadly beak and talons, sending entire scores of them scattering with a single flutter of his wings. Immortal though they were, they were not immune to pain and began to suffer grievious injuries and wounds. Then, unable to bear the assault of the king of birds, the defending line of the devas disintegrated. They began a phased retreat to save their own lives. The saddhyas and gandharvas retreated eastwards, the vasus and rudras to the south, the adityas to the west and the ashwins, who are also called the nasatyas, went north. They did not simply flee but fought every step of the way, rallying any number of times. But it was to no avail. As the field cleared, individual champions began to try their best to hold off the invader so that their fellows might retreat safely. The great Garuda fought in single combat with the brave Ashvakranda, killing and rending him apart. He battled the bird Renuka and reduced her to feathers, bones and blood. The valiant Krathana was ripped to shreds. The bird Tapana fared the same. Uluka, Shvasana, Nimesha—also a bird, Praruja and Pulina all died fighting valiantly but hopelessly. Like Shiva at the end of each yuga, in his final form as Pinaki, wielding his celestial bow, Garuda wreaked havoc in the ranks of the once omnipotent gods.

Finally, the devas routed thoroughly, the battlefield his and his alone, the best of birds went to claim his prize. There lay the gourd pot, only a short distance away, unguarded now and his for the taking. He screeched with joy and flew towards it. To his surprise, as he approached, a great wall of fire sprang up. It covered the world from ground to sky, and raged with violent winds, buffetting the flames in every direction. The entire world seemed to be ablaze and the intensity of the fire was equivalent to the heat and brightness of the sun itself at its prime.

But Garuda was not about to admit defeat. Able to change his form at will, he assumed ninety times ninety mouths and flew down to earth. There, he scooped up the water from countless rivers, filling every one of his beaks, then flew back to the heavenly realm at the speed of thought. Driving the raging firestorm before him by beating his wings to form a perpetual set of bellows, he sprayed the water from his eight thousand one hundred giant beaks at the flames with unimaginable force. That jet of water quenched the fire wall long enough to create a small gap. Instantly, Garuda reduced himself to the size of a fly, and flew through the gap, passing through the wall of fire.

Jetting through the gap in the wall of fire with lightning speed, Garuda approached the gourd pot containing the ambrosia. He saw a chakra near the gourd, edged with sharp blades and spinning at frantic speed, blazing with an emanation of terrible heat and blinding light. Any creature attempting to subvert it would be instantly chopped into fine bits. Garuda reduced his body further, to the size of a pin point, and slipped through the spokes in the chakra.

Past the chakra, he saw two enormous Nagas standing guard over the Amrit. They were not ordinary snakes, for their jewelled scales glittered brightly and their tongues shot lightning bolts as they flicked out of their fanged mouths. Their eyes glinted malevolently and shot out firebolts that would sear anyone that approached. Garuda threw dirt into their eyes, blinding them as well as rendering their firebolts useless. They shot fire and lightning at him but as they were unable to see, he was able to avoid every blast. Then, enraged at being blinded, they began to spit venom like acid and lunged repeatedly. A single strike of those venomous fangs could render him senseless, perhaps even kill him, but Garuda was able to evade those attacks as well. Then, creeping in beneath their hoods, he attacked them viciously. With the eternal enmity of birds towards snakes, he tore into them and shredded their scaled bodies to strips of bloodied meat. Finally, nothing lay between him and the Amrit.

Vinata's son seized his prize with his beak and flew up into the sky at the speed of light. So swift was his passage that the gourd pot containing the sacred elixir shattered instantly. But he caught every last drop of ambrosia in his beak, without drinking any of it. He carried it thus to his destination, still as strong and radiant as when he had first set out on his mission.

A shadow came between him and the sun, taking him by surprise. He looked up and saw Vishnu hovering before him. Vishnu joined his palms in the gesture of respectful greeting and said, 'I am not here to do battle with you. Rather, I admire your sacrifice. You could have consumed the Amrit yourself just now. Instead, you only held it in your beak to carry back home to your cousins, the Nagas. This is a commendable act of self-denial. In return for this great sacrifice, I wish to offer you a boon. Name your desire.'

Garuda replied, 'I wish to always be above you. Immortal, free from the decay of age, yet without drinking a single drop of Amrita.'

Vishnu laughed at this and granted Garuda's wishes. Then Garuda surprised the great Hari by announcing that he wished to confer a boon upon *him*!

The Black-skinned God smiled mischievously, and asked that Garuda should always be his vaahan, or carrier. Garuda agreed. Vishnu then emblazoned the effigy of Garuda upon his krtadhvaj and showed the bird the banner, saying, 'Thus shall you always be above me!' Garuda smiled in response and nodded, acknowledging the greatness of Hari, the evergreen one. But Indra was not willing to accept his defeat. As Garuda flew on, still carrying the Amrit in his beak, Purandara attacked him with his vajra. Struck by the lightning bolts time and time again, Garuda said to Indra in an ironic tone: 'I feel no pain at your attack nor have I suffered any harm. But because I respect the rishi from whose bones your weapon was originally constructed, therefore I shall shed a single feather. You will never be able to find its ends.' Thereupon, Garuda cast off a solitary feather, more beautiful than anything else on earth. Seeing the beauty of that feather, the devas exclaimed and renamed the bird Suparna, One with Beautiful Feathers. Even arrogant Indra was humbled by this magnanimous gesture.

Acknowledging the greatness of Garuda, the Lord of Storms joined his palms in acquiescence and asked Garuda to make him his friend and ally, as he desired to know the limits of Garuda's strength and abilities. Garuda agreed graciously. 'We shall be friends henceforth, Purandara,' Garuda said, 'but as for knowing the limits of my strength, it is not right for me to boast of my own prowess or praise my own qualities. Still, Shatakratu, since you are now my friend and you have asked me this question in friendship, I shall attempt to answer. Hear me, Shakra. On any single feather on my body I can bear the entire world, with all its mountains, forests, oceans, all things that move and those that do not move—you can even add your own weight to it, and I shall bear it all easily, upon that single feather. Therefore judge for yourself the extent of my strength.'

Indra was grateful to the king of birds. 'Thank you for sharing this confidence with me. Now that we are friends I wish to say something to you. If you give this soma to those who asked for it, they will become immortal and wage war against us devas. As king of the gods, it is my dharma to prevent that from happening. Therefore I request you as a friend now, kindly return the Amrit to me.'

Garuda was amused by Indra's request. 'God of a thousand eyes, I cannot return this Amrit to you now for it is my sworn mission to fetch it. Yet I resent my cousins the Nagas who demanded this task of me, for they enslaved my mother and caused her to suffer many humiliations. There is still something we can do to prevent their drinking it and benefitting from its magical properties. I shall set down the soma before them and fulfil my mission. But you may accompany me and pick it up at that exact moment and bring it back! That way, both our purposes will be fulfilled.'

Indra was pleased at this plan and agreed at once. In return for Garuda's aid in returning the Amrit to the devas, he granted the bird king any boon he desired. Garuda dipped his beak and answered, 'Great Shakra, I possess power enough to do anything I please. Yet grant me this one boon: Make the Naga, the mightiest snakes of the world, my natural food.' Both sealed their pact and Suparna proceeded to his destination, where the Nagas eagerly awaited his return, Indra following discreetly.

At the sight of Garuda descending from the sky, the Nagas sent up a great hissing in jubilation. Landing with a flourish of his mighty wings, Garuda emptied the Amrit from his beak into a receptacle of darbha grass. At once the Nagas sought to pounce upon and drink thirstily of the elixir of immortality. But Garuda cautioned them, 'Surely you must first bathe and purify yourself before partaking of this divine nectar, that it may be most efficacious in its results.' The Nagas paused, realizing the truth in Garuda's words. Suparna went on, 'As you can see, I have accomplished the impossible task you set me. Now fulfil your part of our bargain. Set my mother free this instant.' Happily, the Nagas agreed and freed Vinata of her enslavement, then went to cleanse and purify themselves before partaking of the ambrosia. The instant their backs were turned, Indra descended like the vajra that was his trademark, took the Amrit, and returned to the heavenly realm. After they had bathed and performed their purification rites, the snakes returned but saw they had been deceived. Out of desperation, they began to lick the darbha grass on which the nectar had been placed, in the hope that there might still be some traces left. But Indra had used his power to carry away every last droplet and the snakes only succeeded in cutting their tongues on the razor-sharp darbha grass. Thus did snakes get their forked tongues and darbha grass become sacred thereafter.

Returning home with his mother, Garuda and Vinata lived happily in the forest. As decreed by Indra, snakes became his natural food thereafter and he devoured them in great quantities, sharing them with his fellow birds as well and enjoying great fame. This is his story and all who know it will be eternally graced by the great-souled lord of birds.

||Thirteen||

Kulapati Shaunaka asked, 'Sauti, among many wonderful things, you have also told us the names of two birds born from Vinata. But what were the names of the snake sons of Kadru? Pray, tell us at least the names of those who were foremost among the Nagas.'

Sauti replied, 'Great one, the number of the snakes runs to thousands, hundreds of thousands, ten hundred thousand or prayuta, and even a hundred million or arbuda, or more. It is impossible to recount all their names. I shall relate to you the chief genealogy of the first snakes to be created. First was Shesha. After him came Vasuki. Then Airavata, Takshaka, Karkotaka, Dhananjaya, Kaliya, Maninaga, Apurana, Pinjaraka, Elapatra, Vamana, Nila, Anila, Kalmasha, Shabala, Aryaka, Adika, Shalapotaka, Sumanomukha, Dadhimukha, Vimalapindaka, Apta, Kotanaka, Shankha, Valishikha, Nishthayunaka, Hemaguha, Nahusha, Pingala, Bahyakarna, Hastipada, Mudgarapindaka, Kambala, Ashvatara, Kaliyaka, Vritta, Samvartaka, two known as Padma, Shankhanaka, Sphandaka, Kshemaka, Pindaraka, Karavira, Pushpadamshtra, Haridraka, Aparajita, Jyotika, Shrivaha, Kauravya, Dhritarashtra, Pushkara, Shalyaka, Virajas, Subahu, the mighty Shalipinda, Hastibhadra, Pitharaka, Kumuda, Kumdaksha, Tittiri, Halika, Karkara, Akaraka, Mukhara, Konavasana, Kunjara, Kurara, Prabhakara, Kundodara and Mahodara.'

Shaunaka thanked Ugrasrava Lomarsana and said, 'What happened to the snakes after they were cursed by their mother for not aiding her in deceiving her sister?' Lomarsana then told him the story of Shesha and Mother Earth.

||Fourteen||

Shesha left the home of his mother Kadru and went to Mount Gandhamadana to practise severe penance and austerities. Existing only on air, he travelled to other holy sites such as Badri, Gokarna, the aranya of Pushkara, and the slopes of the sacred Himalayas. In these sacred tirthas he observed his vows scrupulously and lived a life of self-deprivation. Brahma watched him thus for a long time, then finally could bear it no more and appeared before him. 'Shesha, why do you suffer thus? What is your desire?' Shesha bowed to the mighty grandfather of humankind. 'My brothers who shared my womb are wicked. They are constantly jealous of one another. Even though Vinata is our kin and her son is our brother, yet they have treated him unkindly. They have shown much cruelty to both our aunt and cousin. In turn, he too shows them great hatred. I cannot bear to see my own brothers fight thus. I have no desire to reside with them. Let me live alone and pursue my own existence independently. Our great father Kashyapa was a superior being, of great fortitude. I wish to follow his example and continue my austerities until this life is ended. Pray, let me do so.'

Brahma was saddened by Shesha's words. 'What you say is true, Shesha. Your brothers are liable to suffer great consequences for their mother's offences and their own. But I do not wish to see you suffer for their fault. I entreat you, stop grieving and punishing yourself thus. Ask me any boon you desire. If you seek to serve dharma, then ask me a boon that will enable you to serve dharma even more effectively!' Shesha saw the wisdom in Brahma's appeal and said, 'Divine forebear, in that case, let my boon be simply to achieve all delight, joy and satisfaction through this same peaceful pursuit of dharma through austerities!' Brahma was impressed by Shesha's modest demand and blessed him profusely. 'Shesha, your stability and fortitude is unmatched in the three worlds. Your tranquil nature and peaceful independence is awe-inspiring. There is much instability and violence in the world today. I ask you therefore to bear the world itself and hold it stable that humankind may find peace and tranquillity and all life may remain in balance.' Shesha agreed readily, asking Brahma to place the world upon his head. Brahma then instructed Shesha to burrow deep inside the earth, where Prithvi Maa herself would open a passage specially for him, placing him at the perfect spot to provide maximum stability to the world. Shesha entered the passage in the earth and took the burden of the world upon his head. He remains there to this day, carrying the Devi named Prithvi which is our mortal planet, upon his head, surrounded by a girdle of oceans. For this great undertaking he was praised effusively by mighty Brahma himself, who then instructed Vinata's son Garuda to always aid his cousin Shesha—or Anantha as he is also known—in his time of need.

||Fifteen||

Vasuki, now the eldest and most senior of the Nagas, had heard of the curse pronounced by his own mother. He called a meeting with Airavata and all their other siblings. 'Brothers, as you know our own mother has cursed us. Anyone who is cursed by his own mother has no hope of remedy. What is more, Brahma himself was witness to this curse, which makes it immutable. Now, we are all doomed to die in the sarpa satra of Raja Janamajaya which is but the same curse of our mother Kadru brought to fruition. Still, I know that we are wise beyond measure and by combining our wisdom, we may yet find a loophole in dharma which enables us to survive the ill effects of this curse. I invite your suggestions.'

Some snakes suggested that they turn themselves into brahmarishis and exhort Janamajaya to call off the sacrifice. Others expounded on this strategem: 'We shall travel back in time to insinuate ourselves as mortal brahmins among his advisors. Over time, we shall gain his confidence and respect. When the time comes to start the sacrifice, we shall advise him against initiating it in the first place. Thereby, the sacrifice shall never begin therefore it can never succeed in destroying our species!' The suggestions continued: 'If all else fails and the sarpa yagna still goes forward, we can go to the chief preceptor and bite him with venom, killing him before he initiates the sacrifice. We shall kill all priests who dare to officiate at the sacrifice!' But some of their brothers objected saying, 'This is the very reason why we are facing this calamity today! We cannot resolve our problem through further violence. Killing brahmins will only compound our sins thousandfold. The only way to resolve the situation is through peaceful means. At all times, we must adhere to dharma. Adharma will only lead to death and destruction.' After further thought, a suggestion was offered: 'Let us become rainclouds and shower torrential rain to extinguish the yagna fire.' Yet another was made: 'Let us sneak into the site of the yagna under cover of night and steal the ladles for the sacrifice.' The more violent Nagas shouted again: 'Let us go in great numbers and kill everyone present!' Other angry ones suggested, 'Let us defile the yagna offerings of food with our dung and urine, rendering the yagna itself worthless!' Someone proferred: 'Let us become officiating brahmins at the satra and demand an impossible guru-dakshina in order to proceed with the sacrifice!' Someone cried out, 'Yes, and let the dakshina be that Raja Janamajaya does not perform the yagna at all!' Another group suggested: 'Without violence, let us kidnap the king and hold him ransom until the yagna is cancelled!' Still others said, 'The only way to be certain is through violence—let us bite Janamajaya as we bit his father before him. With the Kuru king dead, there can be no sarpa satra!'

Vasuki heard the clamour of suggestions and considered them all carefully. Finally, after much thought and consultation he said, 'Brother snakes, I am sorry but none of our ideas seem practicable. I am not satisfied with any of our plans. We must still think further. I take full responsibility and blame if we fail in this endeavour but I cannot go ahead with any of these suggestions.'

In the gloomy silence that followed Vasuki's announcement, Elapatra raised his hood and hissed, 'This talk of preventing the sarpa satra from beginning is pointless, as is the idea of kidnapping or killing Raja Janamajaya. Let us first accept these two facts: One, Raja Janamajaya is determined to host this yagna, and two, the yagna will take place as scheduled. But there is something I heard once that may be of use to us now. Soon after our mother pronounced our curse, I overheard the devas speaking to Lord Brahma. They were amazed that a mother could curse her own children so harshly and not be reprimanded by the great Creator. This is how he answered them: 'The snakes have become too numerous, too venomous, and too violent. They threaten the existence of all life on earth. For their sake, I permitted Kadru to pronounce her curse and the curse to take effect. But it is not as cruel as it sounds. Only the most venomous and vicious snakes shall actually perish in the sarpa satra of Raja Janamajaya. Once they are dead, the other snakes who are peaceful and observe dharma diligently, may still escape. A great rishi will rise in the line of the yayavaras named Jaratkaru. He shall marry a woman bearing the same name as his own, and their son will be named Astika. Rishi Astika will be the one to halt the sacrifice and ensure the survival of those snakes who are virtuous, peace-abiding and follow dharma.' Elapatra then pointed out, among their gathering, their sister named Jaratkaru. 'Since Jaratkaru's wife is to bear the same name as himself, and there sits our sister of that name, let us offer her as wife to the rishi, that he may cohabit with her and produce a son named Astika. Thus shall one of our own kith and kin become our salvation.'

The snakes were delighted to hear this excellent plan. Vasuki undertook the task of taking their sister Jaratkaru, who gladly volunteered, to the rishi when the time came. Soon after this congregation of the snakes, the Amrit Manthan began and Vasuki was used as the rope for the churning. In the course of that momentous event, he learned that almighty Brahma was in fact well aware of the plan suggested by his brother Elapatra and had in fact been the one to plant the seed of the idea in Elapatra's head—that was how Elapatra came to overhear Brahma's conversation with the other devas. Brahma exhorted Vasuki to delegate his snake brethren to always keep watch over Jaratkaru so that when the time came, they would be ready to fulfil his desire for a wife by offering their sister to him in marriage. Wherever Jaratkaru travelled, he was watched by snakes.

||Sixteen||

Shaunaka asked, 'What does the name Jaratkaru mean? Why was the rishi given that name? And how was it that the sister of the snakes came to have the same name?'

Sauti answered, 'Jara means destroy or decay. Karu means that which is huge or enormous. Jaratkaru was born with a gigantic body but over time through his austerities, he reduced it considerably, causing it to wither and decay. Thus he was named Jaratkaru. Vasuki's sister was also born with a huge body which she retained for much of her life. But she too caused her own body to reduce until it reduced to a fraction of its original size. Thus she gained the name Jaratkaru as well.'

Shaunaka chuckled openly at this answer as did all of the other brahmacharyas and rishis present in Naimisha-sharanya for they were familiar with the process by which even the largest-bodied reduced in size over time through constant self-deprivation and self-control. Many broke out openly in laughter as they looked around at the younger, still wide-bodied acolytes who had yet to attain to the title of Jaratkaru. 'Very fitting!' said the kulapati at last as the laughter finally died away. But tell us more about these two persons of the same name? How did Jaratkaru and his wife Jaratkaru fare together? You have told us only about their offspring and their stories. Tell us about Jaratkaru and his marriage. Also tell us about how his descendant Astika halted the sacrifice of Raja Janamajaya. Leave nothing out when you relate their stories.'

Ugrasrava bowed his head. 'I shall do so, great one. In order to accomplish my task as a suta effectively, I must shift between stories at the appropriate time. Permit me to do so without offering an explanation or warning at each transition. As you hear the stories unfold, their connections will become amply clear to your enlightened mind and you will enjoy the beauty of this great narrative of Sage Krishna Dweipayana Vyasa. For it is a masterwork of itihasa, containing all the devices of poetics and aesthetics employed in their finest grain.'

'Sadhu! Sadhu!' said Kulapati Shaunaka, and he was echoed by the great congregation around him. The echoes reverberated across the clearing, and yet again Ugrasrava Lomarsana Sauti felt certain that the auspicious exclamations were repeated even within the distant depths of the great jungle, as if the entire forest of Naimisha-van listened to and approved of his narrative prowess.

||Seventeen||

Once there was a king named Parikshit. Born in the Kuru line, he was son of Abhimanyu and the great-grandson of Pandu. Like his great-grandfather, he was a dedicated hunter, devoted to the thrill and joy of the hunt. Strong of limb and keen of eye, he was an excellent archer and if he set his heart on hunting any creature, it never escaped his aim. Wild boar, deer, hyena, buffalo, every manner of creature that was fit to be hunted was pursued and brought down by his eagle eye and steady hand. One day, engaged in his favourite pursuit in the deep jungle, he shot a deer with a distinctive tuft of fur. Pierced by the arrow, the deer ran screaming into the deep woods. Like Lord Rudra seeking the sacrificial deer in swargaloka, Raja Parikshit pursued the deer relentlessly, bow ready to snap off a second fatal shot the instant he laid eyes on his prey. 'I have never failed to bring a deer down once I set my sight on it,' he thought, 'and I shall not fail today.' His pride drew him ever deeper into that jungle as the deer, even though wounded and in pain, tested his stamina to the limit. Tired and thirsty, Raja Parikshit chanced upon a humble hovel, barely a shelter beneath which stood a milch cow with calves suckling. There sat a rishi engaged in deep meditation. His name was Shamika although Parikshit did not know it. Relieved to see another human being in that desolate place, Raja Parikshit stopped before him. 'Brahmin, I am Raja Parikshit, son of Abhimanyu. I shot a deer and it ran this way, pierced by my arrow. Did you see which way it went?' The rishi opened his eyes and looked at the king but because he had undertaken a maun-vrata, a sacred vow of silence, he could not answer. Parikshit was a king and accustomed to being answered instantly. When the rishi continued to stare at him without answering, he was offended. But he tried to ask the question again, keeping his voice level and his manner respectful, because he had been brought up to always show respect to brahmins and elders. Still the rishi refused to answer. Parikshit was certain the deer had passed this way only moments earlier. Soon he would lose its trail and fail for the first time in his life. He was tired, hungry, thirsty and eager to end the chase quickly. When the rishi continued to ignore his queries and closed his eyes to resume his meditation, Parikshit took this as a personal affront. He lost his temper. A dead snake happened to be lying nearby. Picking it up with the end of his bow, he draped it around the rishi's neck, intending to provoke him into speaking. But the rishi adhered to his vow and remained silent. He only opened his eyes and glared at Parikshit again, this time showing his own anger and displeasure. As Parikshit stared at the absurd sight of a rishi meditating with a dead creature draped around his throat, the Kuru king realized what he had done and felt ashamed. In his desperation to get his quarry, he had committed a grave transgression against a brahmin. Not wishing to compound his error of judgement, he quickly left that place and returned to his city, the hunt abandoned.

Now, unknown to Parikshit, a neighbour of the meditating rishi had observed the whole incident. His name was Krisha and he was a friend of Shringi, the son of the rishi around whose neck Parikshit had placed the dead snake.

Some time later, the rishi's son Shringi returned home. On the way home, he met Krisha who smirked and said, 'Shringi, you are always so proud and superior. But I just saw your father, wearing a carcass around his neck like a necklace. Is that any way for a brahmin to act, meditating with a corpse on his body?' Shringi was a self-righteous young brahmin, austere in his views and his vows, and given to great fits of rage. He was a devotee of Brahma and it was on Brahma's urging that he had cut short his trip to come home. He was offended by Krisha's tone and manner of speaking. He refused to believe his friend. 'What nonsense is this? There must be some mistake. Why would my father wear a corpse around his neck?' Krisha laughed. 'The only mistake was made by Raja Parikshit. The Kuru king was hunting a deer which had passed this way. He asked your father to point out the direction the deer had gone, but your father refused to answer him.' Krisha blinked, trying to take in this information and replied crossly, 'My father has taken a vow of silence. He cannot speak to anyone for any reason until his vow has ended.' Krisha shrugged, still grinning. 'Raja Parikshit must not have known that. He lost his temper at your father's silence, picked up a dead snake and wrapped it around your father's throat. Now look at your father, still sitting there with the carcass!' Shringi caught hold of Krisha, who took one look at Shringi's furious expression and stopped laughing at once. 'Where is this King Parikshit now?' asked Shringi. Krisha gestured with a nod of his head. 'He left some time back. Probably went back to Hastinapura.'

Shringi pushed Krisha aside and ran the rest of the way to his humble hermitage. He saw his father seated in the cowshed, the dead snake around his neck. Shringi's anger swelled until his eyes turned red and his face glowed with rage. He could not bear the sight of his father, so devoted to his austerities that he survived by only drinking the froth discarded by the calves after they had suckled at their mother cow's teats, and who spent his days in utter silence under the force of the maun-vrata. His father opened his eyes and saw his son standing before him, staring at the dead snake and Shringi saw his father's eyes turn away in humiliation. Tears sprang to Shringi's eyes. His father still did not speak but in his mind, Shringi could hear his father's voice saying, 'Son, we are men of brahman. We possess nothing of value except the virtue gained by our austerities. Always remember that. Poor though we are in wealth and belongings, we are rich in austerities and can always hold our heads high with pride, for few even among brahmins can claim to be as devoted to their vocation as we are.' It was this same approach to life that made Shringi equally proud and righteous and his heart could not bear to see his virtuous father, who had suffered and surrendered everything, humiliated in this fashion by a wealthy raj-kshatriya from such a great dynasty.

Taking up water with his fingertips, Shringi vented his anger in a terrible curse against Parikshit. 'I curse this evil king, defiler of brahmins, disgrace to the Kuru race, for his sin of abusing my old, feeble father. Seven nights from today, the great Takshaka, king of snakes, shall hunt down and find Raja Parikshit no matter where he hides, and shall pierce him with his fangs, using his lethal venom to send the vile kshatriya to the abode of Yama.'

Shringi's father Rishi Shamika heard the curse and stirred, breaking his vow of silence. 'My son, what have you done? This is not what I have taught you? This is an act against dharma!'

Shringi could not believe his father. 'But look at how he treated you! I could not let him commit such an insult and walk away without consequence! I stand by my curse: Within the next seven days, Raja Parikshit will be bitten by Takshaka and sent to Vaivasvata's realm.'

Shamika shook his head. 'What he did was wrong. But what you do is wrong as well! He is a king and a kshatriya. It is the duty of such persons to protect brahmins like us. If they act rashly as he did, then we must somehow find the strength in our hearts to forgive him.'

'But he acted against dharma too!' Shringi cried. 'He insulted a brahmin whom he ought to respect and protect!'

'True. But one cannot wipe out one transgression with another. If a kshatriya fails in his dharma and does not protect a brahmin, if he insults one instead, then we must show ourselves greater than he, and forgive him his lapse. By violating our own dharma and seeking violence against him, we commit a greater crime!' Shamika shook his head, upset with his son's outburst. 'You do not understand the full story. Parikshit was exhausted, near collapse, he had not eaten or drunk a drop of water, nor rested for who knows how long. His determination to finish off the deer and succeed at the hunt was his undoing. He had no idea I was under a maun-vrata. He thought I was the one being rude and insolent by not answering him. He thought it was my dharma to answer, to offer him food and water and shelter, as our king. Even if he acted wrongly, he did so out of exhaustion and while in an improper state of mind. You had no cause to issue such a terrible curse against him!'

Shringi saw the point of his father's argument at last. But he spread his hands in despair. 'But father, there is nothing to be done now. Because I only speak the truth, my curse will be effective. I cannot stop it now, once spoken.'

Shamika sat beside his son and pondered the matter with some gravity. 'Very well then. I shall do what I can to try to mitigate it somehow. But, my son, I have some advice for you. There is a lesson to be learned from this incident and your reaction. Even though you are a grown man and are dedicated to your given varna, devoting your life to austerities and the gaining of knowledge, yet you have still much to learn. In this instance, you behaved not like a man but like an impetuous child! You must give up this anger, or it will destroy you one day. There is no use pursuing austerities and controlling your urges and desires for decades, if in a single moment you allow anger to overcome you. Anger is an emotional motivation, just like lust, greed, hunger, thirst. If you can control those others so perfectly, then you must learn to control your anger as well. A man who cannot control his anger is no different from a man who cannot control his lust, greed or other instincts. The only way to gain true maturity and progress as an ascetic is through peace and non-violence. Any action or word that causes, or permits to be caused, harm to other living creatures, is against dharma. There are no exceptions to this rule.'

Shringi listened to his father's words and asked, 'But what does one do when someone commits such a transgression, insulting or humiliating oneself or one's loved one?'

Shamika put a hand gently on his son's shoulder. 'One forgives.'

While Shringi considered what he had done and what his father had said, Shamika sent his disciple Gauramukha to Hastinapura. Obediently, Gauramukha travelled straight to the Kuru capital and requested an audience with the king. Raja Parikshit received him with full respect and honour. Enquiring after the king's welfare as his guru had instructed, he then came to the real purpose of his visit. Acting on his guru's orders, Gauramukha told the king, in the presence of his advisors, the history of the incident in the forest, ending with the curse spoken by Shringi son of Shamika and his guru's instructions to himself.

Listening to the disciple's story, Raja Parikshit was overcome with remorse. Mortified at what he had done, he regretted how he had behaved with poor Shamika. Hearing that the old, feeble rishi had been under a vow of silence, he was overwhelmed with self-recrimination. He barely heard the disciple repeat the curse. To Raja Parikshit, all that mattered was that he had behaved unforgivably toward an innocent, old, impoverished and frail brahmin who had only been constrained by his own vow of silence. He thanked Gauramukha for his message and asked him to beseech his guru Shamika for his forgiveness, for he was deeply ashamed at his actions. Gauramukha informed the king that the guru had already forgiven him his error, and that was why he had sent his disciple here to warn Parikshit.

After the disciple left, Parikshit sat in counsel with his ministers. Still focussed more on his own mistake than on the curse, he nevertheless understood that as king, he had a responsibility to his people and dependents. Acting on the advice of his counsellors, he had a palace be built overnight, standing on pillars to make it impossible for any snake to climb, with every entrance heavily guarded day and night. He placed brahmins, vaids and men of science around the palace to use warding off mantras, herbs and potions to dissuade any serpents from approaching. The moment the palace was constructed, Parikshit took up residence within it, surrounded by his protectors, and continued with his royal duties.

The next six days passed uneventfully.

On the seventh and last day, Sage Kashyapa was on his way to meet the king. As he was a brahmin possessed of great knowledge of various sciences, he had been summoned. His special knowledge lay in the preparation of antidotes to snake venom. It was his given mission to ensure that in the event that Raja Parikshit was bitten by a snake, he would be on hand to adminster an antidote to counter the venom at once. Aware of this, Takshaka, king of snakes, assumed the form of a brahmin and appeared before Kashyapa on the road. 'Where do you go in such a great rush? What task is so urgent to make you travel so quickly?' asked the old brahmin. Kashyapa replied politely, 'Good brahmin, today is the last day of Raja Parikshit's curse. If Takshaka, king of snakes, does succeed in biting the king, I will administer an antidote to his venom. It took me these many days to prepare the perfect antidote. Now that it is ready, I must rush to the king's palace to be present in case the serpent lord succeeds in his endeavour.'

Takshaka then laughed and revealed his true form. 'Kashyapa, look upon me now! I am that same Takshaka you speak of. Turn back now. Once I bite someone, he can never be saved. Your mission is useless.'

Kashyapa did not flinch or blanch before the king of snakes, not even when Takshaka enlarged himself to his full size and towered menacingly over him, swaying proudly. 'You may believe that to be true, Naga. But I have faith in my own scientific knowledge as well. I am certain I can cure the king of your bite—if you are able to bite him at all.'

Infuriated by Kashyapa's response, Takshaka hissed and dripped venom, showing his long fangs. He indicated a very large and old fig tree nearby. 'Do you see this fig tree, brahmin? It has existed here for hundreds of years. Yet I can wither it in moments with the toxin from my venom, destroying it as swiftly as fire itself would consume the wood! Even your great knowledge cannot save it then!'

Kashyapa shrugged. 'If you want to bite the tree, bite it. Then let us see whether or not it withers.'

Provoked further by the brahmin's challenge, Takshaka lunged at the tree, twisting his hooded head sideways to sink his fangs deep into the ancient wood. At once the sap of the tree began to sizzle and dry up as the powerful venom from the snake lord's pouches entered the veins of the tree. The trunk began to turn grey, the leaves lost their colour, the fruit blackened and the whole tree withered before Kashyapa's eyes just as if it had been set ablaze by an invisible fire. In moments, it was reduced to an ashen state. Even the ground for miles around began to wither and die. Takshaka had injected enough venom into the tree to slay a thousand trees.

Takshaka withdrew his fangs and hovered above Sage Kashyapa. His ruby eyes glinted in his hooded face. 'You see, brahmin? That tree is destroyed! Nobody can save it now!'

But still Kashyapa stepped forward, approaching the skeletal ruin of the once-proud lord of the forest. He knelt down and laid a hand on the base of the trunk. 'So you say, king of snakes. You have shown what you can do with your destructive poison. Now see what I can do through the power of science and knowledge!'

And Kashyapa set to work, chanting mantras and using herbs and unguents of his own making. Soon, a green shoot emerged from the derelict tree's ruin. The shoot grew into a sapling, then the sapling sprouted leaves, then twigs, then branches . . . before the astonished eyes of the snake king, the entire tree rose up again from the earth, every inch as it had been before, glowing with health and vigour. Kashyapa picked a fruit from a low-hanging branch and bit into it, smiling to show that it was delicious.

Takshaka hissed long and hard at the brahmin, flashed his fangs in anger, shook his tail about, raised and dipped his hood. Finally, his anger spent, he subsided sulkily. 'Very well, brahmin. I concede that you possess a great ability. Never before have I seen anyone counteract the effect of my venom in this manner. Truly you must be blessed with great knowledge and power. Tell me, what is your real purpose in going to the palace of Raja Parikshit? What do you seek to gain by saving his life?'

Kashyapa answered honestly, 'I seek to enrich myself. He is a king of the great Kuru line. If I save his life, he will certainly reward me richly.'

Takshaka's ruby eyes gleamed brightly within the shadows of his hood. He lowered his great hood so his face was on the same level as that of the sage. 'Brahmin, you know that the king is under a powerful curse, a terrible shraap. There is no power that can countermand such a shraap, once uttered. Nor has anyone mitigated or circumvented the effect of the curse as yet. It is Raja Parikshit's fate to die today. No matter how great your knowledge or skill, your success is uncertain. If you perchance fail, instead of gaining riches, you will suffer a great loss of reputation. Whatever earnings you presently gain will also cease and you will be penniless.'

Kashyapa considered Takshaka's words and found merit in them. 'Let us assume you are right in your assumption. What do you propose?'

Takshaka hissed sibilantly with pleasure. 'Best of brahmins, if it is riches you seek, I can give you more than you can ever hope to get from Raja Parikshit. Moreover, your gain will be assured as I will give it to you right now. All you need do is turn back and retrace your steps homewards, a rich man!'

Kashyapa meditated on the proposal and saw that Takshaka was right. No matter what he did, Parikshit was doomed to die. It could not be any other way. There was therefore no reason why he should not profit from this proposal.

'So be it,' he answered at last.

Takshaka then produced a great store of riches which he gave to Kashyapa. Burdened with his newly-gained wealth, the sage returned home.

Takshaka continued on his way to Nagasahnya. He disliked referring to the capital city of the Kurus as Hastinapura, for the name meant City of Elephants, and elephants often trampled snakes underfoot and crushed them to death. He preferred the name Nagasahnya: Nest of Snakes!

Reaching the city, he quickly learned from his spasas—the wily snakes who acted as his spies—that Raja Parikshit had taken elaborate precautions to ensure his survival. While it would not be impossible to gain access to the king, Takshaka had no desire to be seen until the very last instant. Because he could only kill the king through a bite, he must get close enough to Parikshit to commit the deed without anyone being aware of his presence. He first dispatched several of his snake spasas to the king, using Maya—the power of illusion—to disguise them as ascetics. They carried with them leaves, water and fruit, allegedly for a rite they were to perform. There were any number of holy men performing similar rites in and around the king's palace that day. Even so, the king's guards searched the ascetics and the things they carried carefully. Not a blade of darbha grass or single fruit did they leave unexamined. Only when they found nothing suspicious did they let the party pass into the palace.

The ascetics performed the rites with due ceremony. When they had finished, they gave the king the fruit that had been consecrated by the ritual. After examining each fruit carefully, the king's advisors pronounced the fruits safe to eat. Raja Parikshit asked his advisors to share the fruit with him for it was late in the day and in moments the sun would set and the time of the curse end.

Lit by the rays of the setting sun that shone in through a window of the raised palace, Raja Parikshit selected a fruit at random from the platter placed before him but did not pick it up. It was a succulent ripe fruit, perfect in every way, the skin unbroken and unblemished. He took it up for a moment then returned it to the platter. Everyone was on edge, waiting eagerly for the sun to pass below the horizon and the curse to end. As the moments passed by and the rays dipped lower, the mood turned from one of great anxiety to one of controlled jubilation for it was obvious by now that Takshaka had failed to complete the curse and the king would be free of the threat.

At that moment, the sun fell below the horizon and the time of the curse was at an end. Cheers began to ring out across the palace—and farther across the city, as the citizenry celebrated the survival of their beloved king. For too many Kurus had already perished in the great Maha Bharata war not long ago, and nobody wished to see yet another of that great dynasty die before his time.

Smiling, Raja Parikshit picked up the fruit and was about to bite into it. But as he raised the fruit to his mouth, the skin broke and the tiniest of black worms emerged from the succulent ripe flesh. Parikshit laughed and held up the fruit, showing it to all his well-wishers.

'Look! The hour of the curse has come and gone and I am still alive and well! The sun has set on the seventh day! Now, Takshaka cannot bite me and kill me with his poison. I have no fear of assassination from him! But because the brahmin cursed me in Takshaka's name, I do not wish to see the words spoken by a brahmin to be untrue. Therefore, I pronounce this little worm to be Takshaka! Let him bite me, if he can, and let the brahmin's words therefore be true to the letter, if not to the deed.'

And so saying, he placed the tiny worm upon his own neck, still laughing at his own wit. Filled with the euphoria of having escaped a certain death, he was obnoxious and arrogant. His advisors too, exulting in their success at keeping the king alive despite all odds, were filled with pride at their achievement, and laughed loud and long as well.

'Come now, Takshaka,' Raja Parikshit said mockingly, clicking his tongue as if addressing a pet, 'will you not bite me now?'

In a flash, Takshaka assumed his true form. Gigantic, jewel-scaled, powerful, he coiled around the king. As the horrified advisors and guards watched, Raja Parikshit was wrapped from head to foot in the mammoth coils of the king of snakes. At once their laughter turned to tears and cries of dismay. Takshaka opened his great maw and showed them his giant fangs, dripping with venom. As they stared, hypnotized like prey before the fascinating gaze of a cobra, he roared at them in fury, demonstrating his power. Droplets of venom sprayed the entire palace, drenching it, bathing everyone present. The stench of the snake king's maw filled the room, turning the stomachs of the advisors and guards.

The roar reverberated throughout the city. Everywhere, people celebrating and dancing stopped still and listened, their hearts chilled by that terrible sound.

The advisors and guards picked themselves up off the floor, staring in dismay at the white specks that dotted their clothes and skin. They could feel the toxin from the venom poisoning their bodies already. Screaming, they ran, tearing off their own clothes, falling out of the palace windows in their haste to get out. Some fell to their death or injury, others succeeded in tumbling out the doors and down the steps, scouring off the venom with mud, leaves, anything they could find. From within the palace, another terrible roar exploded, this one louder and more terrible than the first. They ran in every direction, screaming and tearing at their own skin.

Takshaka roared again and again, spewing his venom across the palace that had been built to keep him out. In moments, the palace lay ruined, its walls, pillars, floor, ceiling, furnishings, all smoking and smouldering as the venom worked its poisonous magic, seeping into the very cracks and crevices, corrupting the very foundations. As the walls began to shake and the pillars cracked, Takshaka rose up and lunged skywards. Bursting out of the roof of the palace, he flew up into the sky, hapless Raja Parikshit clutched in his coils. Below, the palace crumbled and collapsed inwards, leaving only a cloud of dust. Takshaka bellowed loud and long enough to cause riots and panic across Hastinapura, terrifying everyone. People looked up in the dusky twilight and pointed in horror as they saw the king of Nagas holding their king in his coils. As they watched, Takshaka sank his fangs into Parikshit's body, impaling him as a man fallen upon swords. When Parikshit was completely dead,

Takshaka released his body, letting it fall to the ground before his ruined palace and slaughtered advisors. Then Takshaka flew through the sky and disappeared from sight, his goal accomplished.

In time, the people and city completed the mourning period for their beloved king and installed his young son Yuvraj Janamajaya on the throne in his stead. He was thus named for someday being a slayer of many enemies, but he was yet a child then. His early ascension and good Kuru upbringing compelled him to become wiser than his years. With the help of his father's advisors—those who had survived—and preceptor, he attempted to rule wisely over the kingdom as his brave forebear Yudhishtira had not long ago.

When he was of age sufficient to go to war, young Raja Janamajaya's advisors went to the king of Kashi, Raja Suvarnavarman, and asked his daughter's hand in marriage. The alliance of the two kingdoms would benefit both and the match was a suitable one as well. Kashi-naresh Suvarnavarnam agreed readily and his daughter Vapushtama was married to Janamajaya. The Kuru king was so besotted with his young bride, he never loved another woman in his life. Together, Janamajaya and Vapushtama found great love and companionship and were as happy in each other's company as Pururava and Urvashi once were in times of yore. They roamed the lakes and forests, glens and dales, and basked in the pleasure of their mutual love.

||Eighteen||

Around the time that Janamajaya married Vapushtama, the yayavara Jaratkaru was still roaming the earth as a mendicant, sleeping wherever he happened to stop each day, possessing nothing, pursuing great feats of austerity, abstaining even from food and living on little more than air, wasting away his body day by day. It was at this time that he came to the cave where he saw his ancestors hanging upside down from the roof and learned of their misery. When he knew that these were his own forebears, suffering and descending into the earth day by day because of his lack of offspring, he was moved to vow to them that he would marry and raise a son who would continue their line, provided his bride met with certain conditions. Then he went out into the world and sought a suitable girl for a considerable length of time before finally being approached by Vasuki and agreeing to marry the snake king's sister who was also named Jaratkaru. So particular was Jaratkaru to adhere to his chosen path as a yayavara that he even warned Vasuki that if he took his sister as his wife he would never be able to provide for her. 'As my chosen path forbids me from working, I cannot maintain her in any manner. She must be given to me as alms and survive as best as she can, just as I do.' All these and the earlier conditions Vasuki agreed to readily and so Jaratkaru was introduced to his namesake and married her.

Vasuki built a beautiful house with splendid décor and furnishings and gave it to Jaratkaru as a wedding present. Jaratkaru lived there, finally resting his head under the same roof each night for he understood that in order to have progeny and raise a family, he must enter the stage of grihastha-ashrama and become a householder. But even so, he cautioned his new bride: 'Take care that you never do anything that causes me displeasure. If you do, I shall leave you forever and never set foot in this house again.' Anxious to please him as well as to honour her brother's wishes, poor Jaratkaru agreed without protest. Like a shwetakakiya, a fabled white crow, she served him from that day onwards, displaying the dedication and watchfulness of a faithful dog, the timidity of a doe, and the instinct of a crow.

One day, during her time of fertility, she bathed and after preparing herself suitably, lay with her husband. That night she conceived a child from their union, radiant as the flames of the yagna fire, endowed with the heat of tapas, and splendid as Agni himself. As the moon waxed that fortnight, so did her child wax within her womb.

A few days later, she was sitting with her husband when, overcome by fatigue, he lay his head down on her lap and fell asleep. He continued sleeping even as the sun dipped low and began to slip behind the mountains. Vasuki's sister grew anxious with every passing moment. It was vital for her husband to perform his evening rituals at a precise time and that time was rapidly passing. Yet she feared to wake him in case he resented his sleep being disturbed. For several moments, she debated both choices, tormenting herself with anxiety. Finally, she decided that it was better for her to suffer her husband's anger than for him to suffer the loss of dharma that missing his evening rites would bring. Her mind made up and preparing herself for any consequence, Jaratkaru woke her namesake with the sweetest voice she could summon. 'Beloved husband, rise now. See, the sun is setting and soon the great and auspicious moment for agnihotra will pass. Perform your duties before the time dwindles and dusk falls across the world.'

As she had feared, Jaratkaru was not accustomed to being woken by another person. He reared at her in anger. 'You sister of a snake! You dare break my rest? So long as I sleep, even the sun itself dare not set. By suggesting that I am capable of missing the precious hour of agnihotra and failing in my duties, you insult me greatly. How dare you think that I would fail in my dharma? I have warned you before not to displease me for any reason, yet you have done so now! I cannot live with you a moment longer!'

Vasuki's sister's heart shrank with sorrow at her husband's words but she attempted to explain herself. 'Great one, I had no intention of insulting you. On the contrary, as your wife, I desired only that you fulfil your dharma immaculately. That is the only reason why I woke you.'

But Jaratkaru's mind was made up. Rigid and intolerant in his outlook, the mendicant told his wife angrily, 'I told you that if you displease me, I would leave you. As you have displeased me, I must go now. Otherwise, I would prove myself to be a liar and that is an even greater transgression against dharma! I am leaving now.'

She ran behind him, crying out. 'What shall I tell my brother?'

He said, 'Tell him that my time with you was a pleasant time. But then the time came for me to leave.' In a gentler tone, acknowledging the brief period of happiness they had shared, he also said, 'Do not grieve for me.'

Then he continued on his way.

Beautiful Jaratkaru, her womb quick with child, was overwhelmed by great sorrow. Her mouth was parched from pleading, and her face wet from crying. Forcing herself to make one last attempt, she ran after her husband yet again and appealed to him with joined palms. 'If you are a master of dharma, then I too am a queen of dharma! I was given to you for a purpose and that purpose has not been achieved yet. I too have a dharma to fulfil and it cannot be done if you leave me. Will you fufil your own dharma at the cost of mine?'

Puzzled at her outburst, the inflexible Jaratkaru came to a stop. What did the woman mean? What dharma was she speaking of that she had to fulfil? How was he costing her that goal?

Seeing her opportunity, the sister of Vasuki explained in a rush of words, telling her husband the story of her siblings, their mother's curse and their subsequent conception of a loophole that would enable them to subvert the curse and survive extinction, ending with her brother grooming her to become the wife of the wandering yayavara. 'Now, I am with child by your grace, but I must ensure that he is the one desired by my brother and family, the one who will be our salvation. If you leave now, how can I be certain that my purpose has been fulfilled? What if this is not the child? How can I conceive another without your presence?'

After hearing the story, Jaratkaru's heart softened towards his wife. He put his arm around her to comfort her and said, 'Bhagyavan, you are indeed the fortunate one. The child that lies within your womb shall turn out to be one of the greatest of rishis, a follower of dharma and a master of the Vedas and Vedangas. I have seen all this even as my head lay in your lap and I slept. The child you seek, it is there.' When he said this, his wife's heart leaped up with joy for her great purpose was fulfilled. But the woman in her still hoped that he would relent and stay with her, if not to conceive a child, then to extend the period of happiness they had shared so briefly. Clutching at his arm, she appealed to him silently one final time. But his heart was set on returning to the path of austerities and now that he knew he had fulfilled his vow to his ancestors, the yayavara could not justify any reason to stay. The pursuit of happiness and the pastime of love are not sufficient to keep the austere from treading the path of enlightenment. And so Jaratkaru left his namesake and went his separate way.

||Twenty||

After her husband had departed, Jaratkaru went to her brother Vasuki and told him what had transpired. He listened sombrely and when he heard the tone of sorrow and anguish in his sister's voice, his heart grew sorrowful as well. He comforted her as best as he could, saying, 'I feel your grief, sister. But you are truly bhagyavan. For you have accomplished the task you were set to accomplish. You have succeeded in conceiving a son who will be our saviour and salvation. Your husband is a proud and virtuous man and I regret his leaving you thus. But his very pride and austerity mean that he has told the absolute truth. The child within your womb is indeed the one we desire. He would never lie about anything and this means that your son will someday save our entire species. Rejoice in that knowledge and whatever else you desire, I shall bring to you for your pleasure.'

So saying, the king of snakes showered his sister with kindness, praise, love and gifts. He ensured that she was as happy as was possible under the circumstances and that the child within her grew healthy and strong. In time, she gave birth and as promised, her offspring was a son, radiant and perfect in all respects. He grew up in the house of the king of snakes and studied the Vedas and Vedangas under the tutelage of Chyavana, son of Bhrigu. Even as a child, he was disciplined and exact in his actions and words, gifted with great intelligence, spiritual strength and numerous other fine qualities. His mother named him Astika after his father's last word, 'asti' which meant literally 'it is there'. And so Astika, son of Jaratkaru and Jaratkaru, grew up to be a rishi of shining virtue, as noble as the illustrious Lord Shulapati himself, Shiva, the bearer of the sacred trishul.

||Twenty-one||

Around the time that Astika was born and began his journey towards manhood in Vasuki's house, the Kuru king Janamajaya learned for the first time the full story of his father's demise. Because he desired to know every detail that led to Parikshit's tragic end and the reason for the sarpa satra that he himself was conducting, his advisors told him everything.

Parikshit was a well-beloved king known for his fairness and honesty in all matters. He did not distinguish between the varnas and treated vaishyas, sudras, kshatriyas and brahmins alike, caring for all who needed his help, meting out justice where required, extending the state's support to widows, orphans, disabled and poor, and abiding by dharma in everything he said and did. In appearance, he was a handsome man, often described as another moon in his lustre and charm. A shishya of Guru Sharadvata, he mastered the science of war and weaponry as expounded in the Dhanur Veda. He did everything possible to uphold the honour of his dynasty and further the reputation of the Kuru race.

For he was an emblem of hope to a troubled Kuru nation. After the genocide that was the Maha Bharata war, the sole survivor in the Kuru line was the male child in the womb of Uttara, wife of Abhimanyu. After the war was over and Uttara gave birth, the world hailed the last of the Kuru line. In acknowledgement of the weakening of the once-great dynasty and the dwindling of its number to this solitary heir, the boy came to be known as Parikshit after the Sanskrit word Parikshina, or emaciation. Keenly aware that the hopes of an entire nation and the future of a dynasty rested on his slender shoulders, young Parikshit worked constantly to build up those shoulders so they could carry the great burden of history forward. It was said of him that he conquered the six vices that plague mortal men—kama, krodha, lobha, mada, moha and matsarya. In other words, desire, anger, greed, ego, self-delusion and envy. For sixty years he ruled Hastinapura wisely as a king. But despite all his efforts, he was undone by a single act of pique, committed in a moment of exhaustion and deprivation-fuelled anger. The moment he placed the dead snake upon the shoulders of the sage Shamika, his doom was sealed. Thus was another great son of the Kuru dynasty cut down before his time through tragic circumstances.

After extolling the virtues of Parikshit and lamenting his premature demise, the king's advisors told Janamajaya everything that transpired after his father went on the deer hunt, leaving no detail unsaid. While they were speaking, Janamajaya was troubled by a question: How did they come to know of the encounter between Sage Kashyapa and Takshaka on the road to Hastinapura? Was it from the lips of Kashyapa himself? For surely Takshaka never stayed to boast of the whole tale? They explained that the account had been related by a man, an ordinary citizen who had climbed a large and ancient fig tree, to break off dry twigs that could be used as kindling. Concealed by the profuse branches and leaves, he went unnoticed by both the snake king and the rishi. When Takshaka destroyed the tree with his venom, the poor man was killed as well, poisoned by the fiery venom through contact with the branch on which he sat. He was then revived through Kashyapa's power and herbs, again through contact with the same branch on which his corpse still lay. Terrified of being seen by the snake king, he remained in the tree long after both he and the brahmin had left the spot. When he returned to the city that night, he heard the news of the king's demise and immediately knew what had happened. He came forward and bore witness to the incident, and thus it was included in the history of Janamajaya's dynasty. Thus are the histories of kings founded upon the testimonies of countless nameless witnesses.

After listening to the entire tale, and learning of the awful, needless death that befell his father, Janamajaya was overcome by grief. A young boy when his father died, he had possessed little understanding of the event at the time and the ministers had deemed him too innocent to know the full story. Now, he finally knew everything, he resolved not to rest until every last snake in the world was destroyed. But most of all, he sought to kill Takshaka himself, along with his closest brethren and kin. Thus, the sarpa satra of Janamajaya was undertaken with great vehemence and intensity.

One small incident occurred at the outset of the sacrifice which in hindsight proved to have great significance: A suta who was also wise in vaastu shastra, and in the building and architecture of structures and sites, examined the plot of land measured out and marked by the brahmins and purohits for the sacrifice and warned them that the site on which they meant to perform the yagna was such that it indicated that the sacrifice would not be completed and that a brahmin would be the cause of this non-completion. Janamajaya heard of this man's warning and installed strict security measures, ensuring that nobody except the authorized priests and attendants could enter the yagna site without his permission. This was the reason why Sarama's son was beaten off so brutally by the king's brothers, who were overseeing the task at the time.

As the sarpa satra gained momentum, the time approached for the yagna's accumulated power to draw in the beings targetted for extinction.

The hotar of the yagna was the brahmin Chandabhargava, a descendant of Chyavana in the Bhrigu line. It was his job to recite the mantras. The udgatar or priest who recited and sang along was a wise old brahmin named Kautsarya Jaimini. Bodhapingala was the adhvaryu, the officiating priest of ceremonies. And Sharngarava was the chief priest. The main sadasya or resident of the ceremony was the illustrious Krishna Dweipayana Vyasa himself, along with his sons and disciples Uddalaka, Shamathaka, Shvetaketu, Panchama, Asita, Devala, Narada, Parvata, Atreya, Kundajathara, and the senior brahmins Kutighata, Vatsya, Shrutashrava the old scholar, Kahoda, Devasharma, Maudgalya and Samasaurabha. Apart from these main priests there were many other reputed brahmins who also attended as sadasyas at the great sacrifice.

As the energies of the ritual increased in potency, snakes began to be drawn from all corners of the earth. From far and wide they were sucked into the vortex of brahman energy created by the sacred ritual. On and on the priests chanted their mantras and poured great quantities of ghee into the satra agni, resolute in their vows and intent in their purpose. One by one the snakes were summoned against their will, compelled to come flying through the air, up into the sky, thence to fall directly into the sacrificial fire. As the chanting increased in intensity, and the oblations were poured in greater quantity, the fire roared higher and louder, filling the air with Agni's bellow. The heat was tremendous as was the height of the flames. The tongues of Agni reached up as if they would scorch the bellies of the clouds themselves. And down came the snakes in a never-ending torrent, until they appeared to descend like a waterfall that melted instantly in the heat of the yagna fire. The great square tank of the yagna began to fill with the fat and marrow of the snakes, crackling and spitting and hissing like a nest of serpents. It was impossible to tell if the sounds that emerged were from snakes that suffered as they were burned to death or merely from the fluids they turned into after they were dead. Either way, the sounds were horrible to hear. The stench would have been too great to tolerate but for the oblations the priests poured into the fire in copious quantities.

Down fell the torrent of snakes, never-ending and relentless, to be consumed instantly by the ravenous mouth of Agni.

Never before or since that time have so many snakes been seen by human eyes. There were snakes of every hue, length, thickness and description. There were two-headed snakes, five-headed snakes and seven-headed snakes. There were snakes a full yojana in length, and there were snakes twice as long. Of Vasuki's lineage, many great snakes, their bodies red, white and blue and filled with virulent venom, died: Kotika, Manasa, Purna, Saha, Paila, Halisaka, Picchila, Konapa, Chakra, Konavega, Prakalana, Hiranyavaha, Sharana, Kakshaka, Kaladanta. Of Takshaka's bloodline, Pucchandaka, Mandalaka, Pindabhetta, Rabhenaka, Ucchikha, Surasa, Dranga, Balaheda, Virohana, Shili, Shalakara, Muka,

Sukumara, Pravepana, Mudgara, Shasharoma, Sumana and Vegavahana perished in that yagna.

Of Airavata's lineage, Paravata, Pariyatra, Pandara, Harina, Krisha, Vihanga, Sharabha, Moda, Pramoda, Samhatangada died. Of the Kaurava line Aindila, Kundala, Mundo, Veni, Skandha, Kumaraka, Bhuka, Shringavega, Dhurtaka, Pata and Patara were the casualties.

Of the line of Dhritarashtra were Shankukarna, Pingalaka, Kutharamukha, Mechaka, Purnangada, Purnamukha, Prahasa, Shakuni, Hari, Amahatha, Komathaka, Shvasana, Manava, Vata, Bhairava, Mundavedanga, Pishanga, Udraparaga, Rishabha, Vegavana, Pindaraka, Mahahanu, Raktanga, Sarvasaranga, Samriddha, Pata, Rakshasa, Varahaka, Varanaka, Sumitra, Chitravedika, Parashara, Tarunaka, Maniskandha and Aruni.

Thousands upon thousands perished. Then hundreds of thousands. Then millions. Then tens of millions. And still the rain of snakes continued unabated, pouring from the sky into the heart of the fire, where each snake died at once, scorched to ashes by the supernatural power of the yagna fire.

Afraid now for his own well-being, King Takshaka of the Nagas rushed to Indraloka, the heavenly abode of Lord Indra, king of the devas. Standing before Purandara, he tearfully confessed all his transgressions and begged the great one for protection. Indra smiled at the unexpected sight of Takshaka begging for mercy, and assured the snake king that his fate had already been decided. Both Brahma and Indra had conferred on the matter and it was clear that Takshaka was not going to perish in the yagna of Janamajaya. Takshaka was greatly relieved but asked for sanctuary until the yagna was ended. Indra granted him leave to stay in his own palace so that he might not be drawn into the fire.

Meanwhile, Vasuki was experiencing the effects of the sarpa satra. Yet, unlike his brother Takshaka, Vasuki was more concerned over the millions of snakes that were being slain by the yagna than with his own survival. 'At this rate,' he thought, distressed, 'our entire species will be extinguished.' Appealing to his sister Jaratkaru who still lived in Vasuki's house with her son, he pleaded, 'Now is the time of which we were warned. That terrible day of doom has arrived at last. Now that it is here, I have lost all strength to resist. I myself feel the powerful pull of the mantras chanted by Janamajaya's priests. It requires all my strength to keep from being pulled to the fire myself! I can barely stand erect, my senses are in turmoil, my vision blurs, my heart pounds as if about to burst, and I cannot control the direction of my movements. Soon, I fear, I too will be drawn to my destruction. If I, a king of snakes, cannot resist, then imagine the plight of my fellow Nagas! Surely they will all be destroyed in no time at all now. We have only one chance of survival. This is the very reason why we gave you to the yayavara in marriage. Sister mine, you alone can ensure the survival of our species now. Brahma himself has prophesied that your son Astika will halt this sacrifice and save us all. Now is the time to put his words into action. Go seek out your son and send him to undertake this task for the sake of the survival of his own kind.'

Jaratkaru left her brother in this state of anxiety and hurried to find her son. She took him aside and told him the story of his birth in full detail and the purpose for which he had been created. Astika listened solemnly to the extraordinary history of his family and when his mother was done, he bowed before her and took her blessings before undertaking his given task. Vasuki came out and was relieved to see his nephew prepare to depart on his journey.

Astika addressed his uncle, although his words were intended for his own mother as well. 'I shall ensure the survival of our species. I shall go to the site of Raja Janamajaya's sarpa satra at once and stop it. This I promise.'

Saying this, Astika left and set out for Samantapanchaka.

||Twenty-two||

Astika arrived at the site of the sacrifice and was awed by the scale of the event. A vast area of the plain had been taken over for the yagna, with literally hundreds of priests officiating and thousands of ritvijas assisting in the numerous tasks, all clad in sombre black as befitted the nature of the sacrifice. And in the centre of that vast theatre of activity was the enormous square where the sacred fire burned. He could hear its roar all the way here, where he stood, hundreds of yards away, and feel its heat. And from the sky, descending out of apparently nowhere, the torrent of snakes rushing down to be consumed by the fire, the most extraordinary sight he had ever witnessed in his brief youthful life. He watched in morbid fascination as the morass of writhing, screaming snakes poured down continuously like water from a pipe, dissolving instantly in the tremendous supernatural and physical heat of the sacred flames. Resolved to do as he was meant, he moved towards the fire, knowing that the king would surely be close to the sacrificial Agni. By dint of his being a brahmin, he managed to come within hearing distance of the king himself. Several burly guards barred his way, preventing him from going further. Seeing Janamajaya just ahead, he immediately began singing the praises of Parikshit's son.

'I come to praise Janamajaya, son of Parikshit, best of the

Bharatas! In ancient times, many great sacrifices were held in Prayaga by Soma, Varuna and Prajapati. The sarpa satra of Janamajaya ranks among those great sacrifices! This great event is equivalent to the hundred sacrifices performed by Indra. It is equal in greatness to those conducted by Yama, Harimedha and Raja Rantideva. It also measures up to the rituals performed by Gaya, Raja Shashabindu and Raja Vaishravana. I compare it to the rites of Nriga, Ajamida and Dasaratha-putra Rama Chandra himself! There I see Satyavati's son Krishna Dweipayana, which is fitting because this great event compares favourably even when matched against the one conducted earlier by Vyasa. Is there a ritvija in all the worlds who can compare to Krishna Dweipayana? Even his disciples are great ritvijas, constantly in demand to perform yagnas! The scale and size and success shall be historic. Agni appears to rival even the mighty sun himself, earning the title of Vibhavasu and the title of Chitrabhanu, displays a golden heart of perfect purity, points his head due south and exudes great clouds of black smoke—all auspicious signs! Raja Janamajaya, you impress me with your achievement and persistence. Truly, you are no less than Varuna, or Dharmaraja Yama, or vajra-wielder Shakra in your influence. In your qualities, you are like Khatvanga, Nabhaga and Dilipa. In your power you are like Yayati and Mandhata. In your splendour you are the sun incarnate. In the rigidity of your vows, you are Bhishma. In your eloquence and sophistication you are Valmiki. In your self-control you are Vashishta. In your sovereignity, you are Indra. In your radiance you are Narayana. In your adherence to dharma you are Yama. You are Krishna. You are the vasus. You are the place where Lakshmi dwells. You are the epitome of all sacrifices. In your strength you are Dambhodbhava. In your prowess at arms you are Parashurama. In your energy, you are Ourva and Trita. In your awe-inspiring appearance you are Bhagiratha.'

When Astika continued to praise Janamajaya and the other priests officiating at the ceremony with such passionate eloquence, they were charmed and pleased.

Deferring to the brahmins, Janamajaya said, 'This is but a child, yet he speaks as eloquently as a wise old sage. I am impressed by his eloquence. Grant me permission to have him brought before me that I may reward him for his talent.'

The sadasyas replied, 'Certainly, for any learned one deserves the praise of kings, though he be but a child. But you must wait until we have accomplished the chief goal of this sacrifice. Once your father's assassin, Takshaka, is summoned here to die in this sacrificial fire, you may do as you please. Until then, all our energies must be focussed on bringing the lord of snakes down.'

Through all this, Astika continued his chant of praises without pause. For hours on end, he stood reciting beautiful shlokas praising Janamajaya, the brahmins, the sacrificial fire, the line of the Kurus, the Bharata race . . . his eloquence and innocence were irresistible. Time and again, Janamajaya's heart went out to him, and he was eager to thank the boy and bid him join him in the sacrifice. But each time he tried to summon the boy, the brahmins surrounding him objected. Finally, he tried to catch the boy's attention and summon him directly. Seeing this, hotar Chandabhargava said severely, 'Raje? Have you forgotten what we discussed? Until Takshaka is destroyed, all our attention and energies must be focussed solely on this sacrifice. This is an immense task that demands every ounce of our ability.' Janamajaya, distracted by the continual chanting of the brahmin boy, replied, 'In that case, let us bring Takshaka here now and destroy him at once. Why delay?' At that moment, the hotar was compelled to continue his ritual chanting and did so, glaring disapprovingly at Janamajaya. The ritvijas spoke up then: 'O King, we have done all that we could to summon Takshaka to the fire but he has taken refuge in Indra's palace. Even our best efforts are unable to pry him loose from that sanctuary.' The suta Lohitaksha was present and he confirmed what the brahmins said, 'It is so. The shastras confirm this fact. Indra has granted Takshaka sanctuary in his own house. This fire can no longer burn that king of snakes.' Hearing this, Janamajaya forgot about the brahmin boy and his chanting and grew angry at Takshaka once again. Determined to avenge his father's cruel death, he resumed his own part in the satra and dedicated himself to chanting along with the brahmins and pouring oblations into the fire to add his own soul's strength to the effort. Then the intensity of the fire grew even greater and the torrent of snakes increased to a blurring downpour. The earth grew depleted of every crawling snake and serpent and even the depths of the ocean yielded up their kin, all to perish in the inexorable fire of the great yagna of Janamajaya.

Meanwhile, in Indra's palace, Takshaka was unable to resist the pull of the yagna's power. He cried out in agony as the sacred mantras compelled him to fly to his doom and fainted dead away, helpless. Seeing his plight, Indra realized he could no longer protect Takshaka simply by keeping him here. He picked up the snake king, intending to keep his promise of sanctuary. As soon as he did so, he too felt the pull of the mantras drawing him downwards to earth.

Moved by the power of the yagna, Indra himself was forced to descend from his heavenly abode of Indraloka. Concealing Takshaka upon his person, hidden within the folds of his anga-vastra, he emerged from boiling clouds, accompanied by a great congregation of vidyadharas and apsaras. This heavenly host descended and landed upon the plain of Kurukshetra, approaching the site of the yagna.

'Look, Raje!' cried the brahmins of the yagna to Janamajaya. 'Takshaka has been summoned by the power of our ritual. He can no longer resist or escape. Mighty Indra himself is compelled to bring him here, concealed in his garments. Soon you will accomplish the goal of this sacrifice and slay your father's assassin!'

At this, Astika sent up a great shout of praise and broke into a song praising Janamajaya even more lavishly. So moving was his eloquence, and so pleased and relieved was Janamajaya at the success of his enterprise, that the king of the Kurus resolved to invite the young brahmin to join the yagna in time to participate in the slaying of Takshaka. In a sense, it was his presence that had provoked and motivated Janamajaya to put in the extra effort that had resulted in Takshaka's summoning.

Astika was permitted at last to enter the last square and brought into the presence of the king. As he greeted the great liege, Janamajaya said, 'Youth, the beauty and perfection of your singing has inspired me. I am greatly impressed by such talent in one so young. See for yourself. Takshaka, king of snakes, has been forced to come to the fire through the power of our mantras, carried by Lord Indra himself. In another moment, the Naga who killed my father will be dead at last. Will you participate in his demise? Come, sit beside me, and join the rite! Your singing has earned you the right to share in this great moment of my triumph!'

Astika joined his palms together, thanking Janamajaya for such a great honour. 'Hastinapura-naresh, king of the Kurus, son of Parikshit, as you are pleased with my recitations and wish to thank me, and as I am a brahmin and you a kshatriya, I ask you for a gift. Do not refuse me.'

Janamajaya was in a magnanimous mood and answered, smiling, 'Ask me anything and you shall have it.'

Astika bowed his head. 'Then grant me only this boon. Halt this sacrifice this instant. Kill no more snakes.'

Janamajaya reacted as if struck by a sword. 'Brahmin! What are you saying? I meant to thank you for your praises and talent. This is not what I had in mind! Ask me for anything—gold, silver, kine, anything you desire. But I cannot stop this sacrifice at this crucial juncture! We are about to fulfil our chief purpose! Soon Takshaka will be dead and the last of his kind will be exterminated!'

But Astika was firm. 'You offered me a gift and you cannot refuse me now. Stop the sacrifice instantly. I will accept nothing less.'

Agitated and stricken by anxiety, Janamajaya begged and pleaded but to no avail. Astika remained resolute. Finally, the sadasyas present rose and came to Janamajaya, speaking to him sympathetically. 'You have no choice now. You must concede to the young brahmin's wish. We are stopping the sacrifice.'

||Twenty-three||

At this point, an extraordinary thing occurred. Rendered senseless by the power of the mantras, Takshaka was drawn forth from the folds of Indra's garments. Pulled by an invisible force, the snake king's inert body flew through the air, destined for the sacrificial fire where he would perish on contact with the flame. Indra reached out his hand to grasp the tail of the snake, but it slipped from his grasp. Janamajaya, harried by the brahmin boy's demand and his own priests' pronouncement, stared at the assassin of his father, flying through the air, an instant from his death. In another moment, Takshaka would fall into the flames and perish and his own goal would be accomplished. All Janamajaya need do was delay his answer by another heartbeat and he would succeed, despite the turn of events.

But Astika held out one small hand and spoke with a power belying his youth and innocence: 'STAY!' he cried.

The passage of the unconscious snake slowed visibly. Takshaka's sleeping form continued to float but at a much slower pace, still moving toward the yagna fire.

'STAY!' Astika cried a second time.

Takshaka's body slowed almost to a halt but still it crept toward the fire, as if even in his unconscious state, the king of snakes was compelled by the mantras and the tapas heat of the fire to proceed towards his own destruction.

'STAY!' Astika cried a third time.

And this time even the sky reverberated with his command. The vast plain of Samantapanchaka echoed with the single word, so powerfully uttered. For an instant, everything on that plain, man, beast, insect, wind, even the birds of the sky, paused motionless before continuing on their way.

But Takshaka hung rock-still in mid-air, only yards away from the pit of fire which had been designed chiefly to draw him and slay him. The senseless snake neither moved nor budged, but merely stayed suspended there.

Then Janamajaya, like all others present there, including the great Vyasa and Indra, turned to look at this young brahmin boy who possessed such spiritual power that he could stop the snake in mid-air, defying both the law of gravity as well as the combined spiritual power of all the thousands of brahmins present. He remembered the warning issued by the suta Lohitaksha who had studied the vaastu of the sacrificial site and cautioned him that the sacrifice was destined to be thwarted by a brahmin. The king of the Kurus knew then that this was what was meant to be. Regardless of what had gone before, of how righteous his own desire for vengeance, how powerful his yagna, he was meant to spare Takshaka and yield to the demand of a young brahmin boy.

He raised his hand and declared, 'You have your wish, boy. Stop the yagna!'

As the chanting of the hotar and other officiating brahmins died away, a deafening silence fell across the site of the sarpa satra. The torrent of snakes stopped in mid-air, just as Takshaka had stopped.

Then with a great roar of exultation, the snakes broke free of the tractor beam of the brahman that controlled them. The sky exploded with colours as hundreds of thousands of snakes flew back to their respective abodes and habitats across the earth. Takshaka revived, opened his ruby-bright eyes, his hood rising, expanding himself to his fullest. Hissing with renewed vigour, the snake king shepherded his people away from the place where they had been brought to perish. Fleeing as rapidly as possible, in moments, all the snakes vanished from sight. The air was clear, the sky bright blue and cloudless and only the crackle and hiss of the yagna fire remained; even that slowly faded as the priests no longer poured oblations and the sadasyas ceased their activities.

Janamajaya was a righteous king who always obeyed dharma. Despite the abrupt cessation of the yagna and his failure to avenge his father's assassination by killing Takshaka, he upheld his duties and responsibilities. Richly rewarding and compensating every single sadasya, purohit, hotar, and ritvija brahmin attendant at the satra, he sent them home enriched and smiling. He gave a special reward to the suta and builder Lohitaksha for his prediction had indeed come true. And then, in accordance with the steps prescribed by the shastras, he concluded the ritual formally. The sacred fire was banked, the site cleared. At last, after everyone had left, the king turned to the young brahmin boy who had single-handedly saved the line of snakes from extinction. Other kings might have been wroth at the boy for bringing the yagna to a halt before its chief aim was achieved. But Janamajaya had accepted the turn of events with magnanimous grace. Rather than be upset with Astika, he praised him for his boldness and spiritual strength. If he could achieve such a feat at this tender age, what might he not achieve when he had attained his full maturity? 'I shall perform the rajasuya someday,' Janamajaya told Astika, 'for as king of the Kuru, I must reassert my dynasty's dominion when the time is right. It would honour me if you consent to be a sadasya in that horse sacrifice.' Astika smiled and agreed at once. Brahmin boy and Kshatriya king, neither bore ill will towards each other. Then both went their separate ways.

Returning home, Astika touched his mother's and uncle's feet and was warmly embraced by both in turn. Vasuki took him out of the house to show him the grassy slopes of the mountain on which their house rested. The mountainside was covered with snakes of every description, hue, and size. At the sight of their saviour, the snakes set up a tumultuous clamour. 'These are some of the snakes you saved today,' Vasuki told his nephew proudly. 'You have saved our entire species from extinction. They wish to grant you a boon. Name anything you desire and you shall have it.' Astika smiled and bowed with joined palms, greeting his kith and kin. 'From this moment on, let no brahmin or mortal man, woman or child who reads this history of our species and the triumphant conclusion, ever have any reason to fear one of us. This account should be read with a calm disposition either in the morning or the evening for maximum benefit. The reader shall never have reason to fear being bitten by one of us, no matter the cause or provocation.' As one, the Nagas replied, 'It shall be so, exactly as you say, Astika son of Jaratkaru and Jaratkaru! All those who invoke your name, Astika, will be protected from our bite. In addition, those who remember the great sages Asita, Artimana and Sunitha at any time, day or night, shall also be safe from our venom always.'

Astika went on to become a great sage, magnificent in austerities, perfect in dharma, and engendered many children and grandchildren of his own, furthering his line prodigiously. In due course, after a long illustrious life, when his time was ended, he found a peaceful death.

||Paksha Seven||

THE BIRTH OF VYASA

||One||

Rishi Krishna Dweipayana Vyasa, hearing that Raja Janamajaya had instated himself at the sarpa satra, proceeded to grace the yagna with his august presence. The greatest of storytellers, even the three parts of his name told three stories. Krishna, the Dark One, because he was exceptionally dark-skinned even for our race, after his mother, the virgin Kali, so named for her ebony skin, later known as Satyavati. Dweipayana, Island-Born, because he was indeed born on an island in the river Yamuna. And Vyasa, because he collated the one great body of vedic shlokas and invocations into four distinct Vedic books, literally by division or vyasa. Arriving at Samantapanchaka, he was received with great joy and respect by his descendant Janamajaya, who offered his forebear a seat of gold, as the great Indra had once offered Brihaspati, preceptor of the gods. Janamajaya then performed the arghya ritual for his ancestor, offering the sage water to wash his feet and mouth, then greeting him with all due ritual and ceremony, ending with the gift of a cow as befitted a visiting brahmin. Vyasa graciously accepted all with pleasure, blessing his descendant. Janamajaya then sat on a seat lower than Vyasa and enquired after his great-grandfather's health. After they had exchanged various pleasantries and the other ritvijas had interacted as well with the august personage, Janamajaya enquired, 'Great father, I hear that you have composed an epic poem narrating in full the account of the great Maha Bharata war involving our family. In that work, I have been told, you have recited the great exploits of the Kauravas and the Pandavas and their histories. What was the reason for the great conflict between the two lines of our family? Why did my grandfathers, such great men all, go to war against their own blood-brothers? What were the terrible events that led to the downfall of the great Kuru dynasty and the deaths of countless Kuru? Pray, tell me all. Narrate if you will, your great poetic composition. I dearly wish to know the itihasa of my family.'

Vyasa turned to his foremost disciple who was seated by his side. 'Vaisampayana, relate exactly as you heard me recite, the brief history of the Maha Bharata war, which I composed.' Vaisampayana bowed to his guru first, then to all present, invoked the appropriate blessings and epigrams, then narrated an outline of the main events of the great conflict for Janamajaya's benefit. The Kuru king listened with great interest, then said, 'This is a brief history of the chief events. I now wish to know the entire history in all its details.' Vyasa said, 'You shall know it. The whole epic is one hundred thousand shlokas. It has many beginnings and many ends. Let us begin with one such beginning.' He then instructed Vaisampayana to tell the story.

||Two||

There once lived a king named Vasu of the Kuru line. A great warrior, his exploits were renowned across all the worlds, and even mighty Indra the storm-thrower learned of him and came to befriend him out of respect. After many wars and campaigns, he tired of violence and began to meditate on his actions. In time, he grew engrossed in austerities and pursued a hermit's life with the same intensity that had driven him to so many military successes. Observing his rapid spiritual progress, Indra feared that if Vasu continued in this vein, he might someday gain enough power to rival the king of gods himself! Seeking to prevent such a possibility, the thunder-wielding god appeared before Uparichara one day. 'Lord of the world. Your dharma requires you to protect others. Only through the protection of others can you fulfil your dharma. This alone is the righteous path that you must follow if you wish to attain to other worlds more sacred than this mortal realm.' Indra then told his friend of a place which rivalled even the heavenly realms. A place of indescribable beauty, perfect climate, ample food, natural resources, animals, beautiful sights, and great cities filled with righteous people, it was a paradise on earth. In that place, nobody ever told a lie. Children never turned against their parents, not even to claim their inheritances, and served their elders respectfully and diligently. The cows were always healthy and no farmer lacked a strong ox to draw his plough. All people went about their work without complaint or disagreement and performed their duties immaculately. This place was named Chhedi.

To entice Vasu further, and turn him away from the dangerous path of austerities, Indra gave him gifts that would aid him in his campaign to conquer the paradisiacal kingdom. First, he gave him a resplendent flying chariot, a vimana made wholly of crystal. Around his friend's neck he hung a magical garland of perennially fresh lotus blossoms, called Vaijayanti, which literally meant the garland of victory. And finally, he gave him also a staff made of bamboo that he might plant it in the earth of the place he conquered, as a sign that Indra himself guaranteed protection to the new king of that realm. Vasu did as Indra said, reassembled his army, and set out to conquer Chhedi. After a year, he planted the bamboo staff in the ground. After decorating it with garlands, perfumed incense, ornaments and baskets, his people worshipped Indra in his form of Shakra by bowing to that symbol of his protection. Pleased with Vasu's actions and by his subsequent show of homage, Indra blessed the people of Chhedi, prophesying that so long as the kings and people of that kingdom worshipped him and celebrated his annual festival, they would enjoy prosperity and victory forever. At this generous blessing the people gave Indra the epithet, Maghavan, the Generous One.

In time, Vasu had five sons. Blessed as they were with infinite valour and might, he granted each of them their own kingdom to rule. His son Brihadratha earned the title of Maharatha through his exploits, meaning a warrior capable of facing ten thousand warriors single-handedly; Brihadratha was given the kingdom of Magadha.

His other sons were given territories where they established their own city-state kingdoms, named after them: Pratyagraha Manivahana, Kushamba Macchilla, Yadu, and a fifth son, ruled the great kingdom of Chhedi. Vasu travelled where he pleased in the crystal vimana given by Indra, sweeping across the earth like a god. For his ability to travel in the upper realms, he earned the epithet Uparichara and was thereafter known as Uparichara Vasu.

Near the city of Chhedi, capital of the kingdom, flowed a river named Shuktimati. So beautiful was this river that a mountain on its course named Kolahola was overcome with lust for her. Unable to bear his unrequited longing, the mountain finally seized hold of the river, preventing her from flowing past him. When Vasu saw the river's plight, he dealt the mountain a powerful kick, breaking it open, and freeing the river. Shuktimati had conceived from the mountain's embrace and the result of their union was a pair of twins. In return for saving her, she gifted the twins to Uparichara Vasu. One was a beautiful boy, the other a stunningly alluring girl. He made the son his senapati, general of his armies. The daughter was named Girika and when she came of age, he married her. Girika's beauty was legendary and the king took great pleasure in their union. He looked forward to their time together in the marital chamber. Girika dearly desired to have offspring and welcomed his embraces, even choosing the suitable time for their coition and sending for him on these occasions, that they might benefit from their joining.

On one occasion, Girika adjudged that the time was perfect for her to conceive. Desiring to make love to her husband, she sent for him urgently. Uparichara Vasu received the missive and at once knew what his wife desired him to do. He was most eager to go home to indulge his wife, but he was required to hunt deer to appease his ancestors first. Even while he was on the hunt, his thoughts turned constantly back to his wife, as beautiful as Sri herself, waiting eagerly for him to come home and please her. Deep in the jungle, he was overcome by his desire and spilled his seed in the forest. Not wishing to let his semen go waste, he collected it in a leaf. Now that the semen had been discharged, it occurred to him that if he could not go home to make love to his wife, he could at the very least send home his semen that she might conceive from it. A knowledgeable man, he saw a hawk perched on a branch nearby and addressed the bird in its own language. 'Amiable friend, do me this great favour. Take my semen home to my wife Girika. She is in season now and dearly desires a child.' The hawk consented and flew off with the rolled leaf containing Uparichara Vasu's semen clutched firmly in his claw.

While the hawk was flying, another hawk saw it and misjudged what it was carrying. Mistakenly assuming it was meat, the second hawk flew at him, demanding a share. The two hawks fought and in the struggle, the first hawk dropped Vasu's semen which fell into the waters of the river Yamuna. An apsara named Adrika had been cursed to live as a fish in the river and she happened to be looking up when the hawk dropped the leaf containing the semen. In a trice, Adrika swallowed the semen before it could be spilled into the river for she knew that it would be her salvation. She conceived from the seed of Vasu and in time her womb grew heavy with twin human children. But she was still a fish, and when she was in her tenth month, she was caught in a fisherman's net. When she was cut open, the fisherman found the human twins, perfectly formed and beautiful in every respect but one: they smelled exactly like fish. The fish which had been cut open sighed with relief as she turned back into her true form. Adrika had been promised by Brahma that the day she gave birth to two human children, she would be freed from her curse. She died happily, rising up to heaven in the footsteps of siddhas, rishis and charanas.

Marvelling at this miracle, the fisherman took the babies to the king who was delighted and accepted the male child of the pair, permitting the fisherman to keep the female. The male child became Vasu's fifth son who came to be better known as Matsya because of his birth from a fish. The girl child born of Adrika from Vasu's semen grew up to be Kali, whom the fishermen later called Satyavati. Pitch-black in colour and beautiful in every other aspect as well, she was much admired and loved by everyone. Her only drawback was that she smelled constantly of fish. When she grew old enough to do her own chores, she began to ply a boat on the river Yamuna to help her father. In time, she became a familiar sight ferrying travellers across the river and back in her rowboat. She often sang the songs of the fisherfolk as she rowed, her sweet voice charming even the fish in the river.

One day, the great sage Parashara started on a pilgrimage. Coming to the river Yamuna, he boarded Satyavati's boat in order to cross to the other side. While in the boat, he was drawn to Satyavati's extraordinary beauty. Overcome by lust, the sage could think of nothing else but the urge to make love to her. Satyavati grew aware of the sage's desire and was flattered that such a great rishi desired her. But there were many other brahmins in sight, on both banks of the river. Surely they could not engage in intercourse in full view of them all? Undaunted, Rishi Parashara summoned up a dense fog, so dark and impenetrable that the entire river was shrouded in pitch darkness. Surprised and realizing that she could not refuse the rishi's advances, Satyavati was overcome with shyness. 'Mahadev,' she pleaded, 'I am the virginal daughter of a humble fisherman. If you commit this act with me, with what face will I go home to my father's house? I will never be able to live among my people again, nor will they forgive me this lapse. I beg of you, consider my situation.'

Parashara was a powerful brahmin possessed of great abilities. 'Beautiful Kali, what you say is true. I will ensure that your reputation is not sullied. Even if you conceive from our union, yet you shall remain a virgin, and your child shall be birthed within this very day and grow instantly to manhood, so that none may ever suspect that you engaged in intercourse with me. In time, you may marry any man of your father's choosing with a clear conscience for you have my word that you will be as pure and unsullied as any untouched virgin. What is more, in exchange for granting me my desire, ask me for any boon and I shall grant it.'

Still modest and shy, Satyavati could think only of the perpetual smell of fish that always clung about her, dissuading all potential suitors. 'Dispel my malodour, lord. I ask nothing more.'

'So be it,' Parashara said.

Then, under cover of the dark fog he had conjured, the rishi engaged in an immensely pleasurable union with Satyavati in the boat. After his pleasure was spent, the rishi dispelled the fog, was rowed to the far bank, and continued on his way. The instant she was touched by the rishi, Satyavati's fish smell disappeared completely and was replaced by a natural floral odour so sweet and redolent that henceforth, she was known by the name of Gandhavati, or even Yojanagandha on account of the fact that her enticing scent could be smelled from as far as a full yojana away. From their union, she instantly conceived a child and her belly grew heavy with growth within moments. Rowing herself to a deserted island in the middle of the river, she climbed ashore just in time to deliver the baby. Though it emerged newborn, within moments, before her astonished eyes, it grew to become a full-grown man, as dark in aspect as herself. What he lacked in beauty, her son gained richly in knowledge and wisdom. She named him Krishna for his black skin, Dweipayana for being born on an island and in time, through his dedicated efforts and genius, he came to divide the great Book of Knowledge, the Veda, into four distinct parts, earning himself the additional title of Vyasa. Thus was Krishna Dweipayana Vyasa born, composer of the great epic the *Mahabharata,* forebear of the Kauravas and Pandavas, witness to the great conflict that destroyed the Kuru line and left countless millions dead. On gaining full manhood, scant hours after his birth, and after his mother's conception through Parashara, Krishna Dweipayana stood before his mother clad in garments she had given him, and joined his palms before her. 'Maatr, I wish to dedicate myself to a life of ascetism and study. Grant me leave to do so.' Satyavati was overcome with emotion by the suddenness of events, but her own unusual origins and ancestry made her stronger and more accepting of such things than most persons. She was proud of her tall and impressive son. His intelligence glowed from his eyes and face and she felt certain he would go on to achieve great things in life. She felt a pang of regret that she had not the opportunity to raise him as her son, and share in his life, but nonetheless she felt great love and affection toward him. 'Go with my blessing, son. Do as you see fit, live long and prosper.' At his mother's words, Krishna Dweipayana bowed long and low. 'Maatr, at any time if you have need of me, you need but think of me and I shall arrive before you instantly. Whatever the purpose, do not hesitate to call on me.' Satyavati understood then that despite the strangeness of the conception and his birth, the bond between her son and herself was a powerful one ordained by great forces and served some higher purpose that she could not fathom at that time. She wished him well and he went on his way. She climbed aboard the rowboat and rowed herself back to the far bank where already passengers waited to be ferried across the Yamuna. The day had not yet ended and she had work to do.

||Three||

Janamajaya then asked Vyasa, 'Gurudev, I know that you are my great-grandfather and engendered the present line of Kuru kings. I would hear the full account of how that came to pass as well as the history of the great Maha Bharata war between my ancestors. But first answer this question that troubles me. These were all great warriors, perhaps the greatest that ever lived on earth. Yet I have heard that the brahmin Parashurama had embarked on a campaign of vengeance and cleansed the earth of all kshatriyas. Not once did he massacre the warriors but thrice seven times! How did the warrior varna arise again if all those born of that caste had been extinguished? How did the four varnas regain their normal structure and things come to be as they are today? Most of all, how was it that even after Parashurama's genocide, such great warriors arose again as were present at the time of the Maha Bharata war? Surely there was some higher purpose served by this phenomenon? What was the real reason behind the revival of the kshatriya class and the rise of a new breed of great warriors?'

Vyasa instructed his disciple to answer the king. Vaisampayana said, 'O King, the questions you ask are great ones that even most gods would be hard pressed to answer correctly. Yet my great preceptor in his infinite wisdom has included the answer in this seminal epic of our Bharata nation. Listen now.'

||Four||

Twenty-one times in all did Jamadagni's son Rama of the Axe wipe out every last kshatriya on earth. Finally, when his task was done, he retired to the peak of Mount Mahendra where he meditated for an untold length of time. The world was quiet and peaceful, with every warrior gone and none left to wage war or inflict violence.

But the widows of countless kshatriyas remained, childless and husbandless. Bereft and grieving, these proud women had accepted the loss of their menfolk, but still desired to bear children that their line might continue. Since no men of their varna remained and since it was by a brahmin's hand that their men had died, they came therefore to the brahmins, asking them to seed their wombs and engender progeny. The brahmins consented but were rigid in their vows and austerities and could not relinquish them to husband the kshatriya women. They agreed to have intercourse with them only at their time of fertility, to fill their wombs, not to satiate lust or desire. This was a firm rule of the brahmins and under no circumstances would they copulate with the kshatriya women other than for the purpose of creating offspring, nor when they were out of season. With this condition, the brahmins of the world fathered upon the widowed kshatriya women thousands upon thousands of offspring, male as well as female, for the vengeance of Parashurama had been sated, and it was deemed acceptable for the kshatriya race to flourish once more. Thus, the present kshatriya race originated from kshatriya women and brahmin men, bringing about a balance of qualities.

The new generation of kshatriya children were equitable and filled with the best of both their parent varnas. They were righteous in dharma and never resorted to violence without just cause or reason, and also engaged in the pursuit of knowledge. The world flourished. The four varnas lived in perfect harmony with one another. Following the example of their brahmin fathers, even the kshatriyas engaged in copulation only with their wives, and only when they were in season, and did not succumb to lust impulsively. All four varnas did the same, and influenced by the dharma of mortals, even the non-human denizens of the world followed the same path. By adhering to dharma in every respect, all creatures of the world lived long and prospered. Humankind was free of all disease and experienced no calamities. The earth showered them with blessings and did not cause calamities such as earthquakes, floods, and other natural disasters. All beings lived free of anger, lust, covetousness, and were swift to mete out righteous justice to those who transgressed against their fellows. The population of the earth swelled to enormous proportions and great civilizations and cities flourished everywhere, with people occupying even the highest mountains, the remotest valleys, the deepest forests, even the boundaries of the ocean. People lived for hundreds and thousands of years. Kshatriyas governed the earth and protected all, including the brahmins. Kings and rulers of men were free from avarice, greed or lust, and governed wisely and justly. Their subjects prospered and profited and nobody wanted for anything. No children died. No man or woman engaged in coition before they had attained maturity. The kshatriyas performed great sacrifices and presented alms liberally. Brahmins were free to spend their lives studying the Vedas, Vedangas and Upanishads. No brahmin ever sold his knowledge for money or personal gain. Brahmins retained their knowledge with proprietorial pride, never once reciting their Vedic knowledge in the presence of sudras, who lived blissfully unconcerned with the higher state of knowledge. Vaishyas engaged in farming and tilling the earth with the willing aid of cattle. They did not need to yoke cows to ploughs or force any beast to bear burden, for those that helped them did so willingly. Those that were too frail, old or sick and thin to work were allowed to rest and were well cared for. Cows were never milked during their period of nursing and calves were free to drink as much as they pleased. No merchant tipped his scales or used wrong weights or cheated people. Everyone performed their given tasks and took pleasure in them, births occurred naturally and always at the right time, trees bore flowers and fruit in the right season, and all was paradisiacal on earth. This was the golden age of Krita Yuga.

But even in this age of plenty there arose a dark spectre. During the time that the kshatriyas were absent from the world, the asuras had seized their opportunity to regain their advantage. This time, the sons of Diti were shrewd and did not attempt to proliferate in the heavenly realms where their increase in numbers would be noted by their arch enemies, the devas. Instead, they took birth on earth, in the royal dynasties of mortals, and as a variety of different beings—cows, horses, asses, camels, buffaloes, predatory creatures, elephants, deer. So great were the number of beasts and mortals on earth then, and so long were their lifespans and few their deaths, that the earth herself laboured to provide for her children. Some of Diti's and Danu's children grew up as the offspring of royals at this time, taking advantage of their positions to raise armies and force conflicts. With the earth populated from shore to shore, every step they took encroached on someone's domain, and once begun, a sequence of conflicts was easy to maintain and escalate. Malevolently, they set out to invade, conquer and attack without provocation or need, oppressing people everywhere. They did not discriminate between varnas—brahmins, kshatriyas, vaishyas, sudras, they terrorized all people equally, as well as other living creatures. Roaming the earth in great numbers, they violated dharma at every opportunity, persecuted even the highest maharishis in their own ashrams and gurukuls, and indulged in sickening displays of violent subjugation. Then the golden age turned to ashes and blood as the misdeeds of the asuras exceeded all bounds and they embarked on a campaign of butchery and genocide. Even the elements of the earth, the wind, the rain, the mountains, the great Shesha Naga upon whose coils the world rested, could not bear this slaughter and injustice and trembled with unhappiness.

Stricken by the cries and laments of innocent mortals, the devas appealed to mighty Brahma. Great was the congregation that thronged Brahmaloka. Devas, brahmins, maharishis, gandharvas, apsaras, all began to chant and sing and recite their woes. Then Prithvi Maa, the goddess that was Earth herself, appeared before the celestial court and wept for her children. Brahma, the all-knowing, all-seeing, already knew of the woes they suffered. How could he not know? But he heard each complaint patiently and sympathetically.

Then the great Creator who is also Prajapati, Isa, and Shambhu, and lord of the world entire, addressed the goddess Prithvi Maa. 'O Vasundhara,' he said, for that was another of her names. 'It is clear that the asuras have taken the war against us to the mortal realm. Because they could no longer hope to triumph against us here in the heavenly realms, so they have descended to terrorize the innocent earthlings. Under these circumstances, there is only one recourse. We devas must also descend to earth in suitable forms, amsas and avataras, and join in conflict with them, halting their reign of terror. To avoid their learning whom we choose to become on earth, whether as a disguise, an altered form, or a partial or full incarnation, we shall each choose our own manner of descent and appear on earth to pursue individual agendas and campaigns of war against them. Choose your time and place and form and descend. Let us take the war to their doorstep now! Live long and triumph!'

Indra and all the devas were pleased with Brahma's proposal. They left Brahmaloka excited and impatient to begin the new campaign against the asuras at once. But before they embarked on that venture, they visited Vaikuntha, the celestial abode of Narayana. There they were received warmly by that Wielder of the Chakra and the Gada, dressed in his trademark yellow, his personage glowing radiantly, a lotus blooming from his navel and his eyes soft, wide and sloped downwards and mesmerizing to behold. Bowing before him, they announced that as the greatest of them all, it was only fitting that he should be the first to incarnate on earth. They would then follow and do their respective tasks. Hari smiled and raised his open palm in acceptance and declared that it would be as they asked.

Thus, the stage was set for the greatest conflict of all between the gods and the races of demons.

||Paksha Eight||

ANSHAVATARNA

||One||

Then began the campaign of the devas versus the asuras, a war so terrible and far-reaching in its consequences that some believe that even today all mortal conflict stems from that primal enmity.

These are the accounts of the births of devas, danavas, gandharvas, apsaras, mortals, yakshas, rakshasas, and other beings. Anshavatarana: a record of the reincarnations.

Through the power of his mind, Brahma created six sons—Marichi, Atri, Angiras, Pulastya, Pulaha and Kratu. Marichi had a son named Kashyapa and all mortals were subsequently descended from Kashyapa. Prajapati Daksha was blessed with thirteen daughters—Aditi, Diti, Danu, Kala, Anayu, Simhika, Muni, Krodha, Prava, Arishta, Vinata, Kapila and Kadru. All living species on earth, human or otherwise, are descended from Daksha's daughters. Do not confuse some of these names with the names of various devas or personages as they are quite distinct.

From Aditi were born the twelve rulers of the world, the Adityas—Dhata, Mitra, Aryamana, Shakra, Varuna, Amsha, Bhaga, Vivasvana, Pusha, Savita, Tvashta and Vishnu.

Diti was blessed with only one son, Hiranyakashipu. He sired five sons—Prahlada, Samhrada, Anuhrada, Shibi and Bashkala. Prahlada in turn had three sons—Virochana, Kumbha and

Nikumbha. Virochana's son was the powerful Bali and Bali's son was the famous asura Bana.

Danu had forty sons—the eldest and most famous was Viprachaitti. The others were Shambara, Namuchi, Puloman, Asiloman, Keshi, Durjaya, Ayahshira, Ashvashira, Ashvashanku, Gaganamurdhana, Vegavan, Ketuman, Svarbhanu, Ashva, Ashvapati, Vrishaparva, Ajaka, Ashvagriva, Sukshma, Tuhundu, Isripa, Ekachakra, Virupaksha, Hara, Ahara, Nichandra, Nikumbha, Kupatha, Kapatha, Sharabha, Shalabha, Surya and Chandrama—the last two bearing no relation to the Sun and Moon gods of the same names—Ekaksha, Mritapa, Pralamba, Naraka, Vatapi, Shatrutapana, Shatha, Gavihstha, Danayu and Dirghajihva. Their offspring were innumerable.

Simhika birthed a son named Rahu, who was indeed the same asura who swallowed the Amrit and was exposed by the devas Surya and Chandra and had his head cut off, as well as three other sons—Suchandra, Chandraharta and Chandravimardana. Krodha was as her name suggested: the very meaning of the word Krodha derives from her qualities; cruel, angry, wrathful—and so were all her offspring, earning great notoriety in their persecution of innocents. In contrast, Anayu's four sons were asuras only in name and were filled with the best qualities—their names were Vikshara, Bala, Vira and Vritra. Four of Kala's sons—Vinashana, Krodha, Krodhahantra and Krodhashatru—were, as their names suggest, destroyers and anger-wielders who crushed their enemies on earth. Kala had many other sons whose names are not known but are collectively termed as the Kaleyas.

Guru Shukra was the preceptor of the asuras and a great brahmin in his own right. Also known as Ushanas, he had four sons, who performed all ceremonies and rites for the asuras—Tvashtavara, Atri and two unnamed ones. Their knowledge of mantras was prodigal, their ability to manipulate the brahman unequalled.

Apart from Garuda and Aruna who was also known as Tarkshya, Vinata had three other sons named Arishtanemi, Aruni and Varuni. Of Kadru's one thousand sons the best-known were Shesha, Ananta, Vasuki, Takshakaa, Kurma and Kulika. Muni was a divine gandharva. His sons were Bhimasena, Ugrasena, Suparna, Varuna, Gopati, Dhritarashtra, Suryavarcha, Pattravan, Arkaparna, Prayuta, Bhima, Chitrakaratha, Shalishira, Pradyumna, Kali and Narada and all were justly famous as munis in their own right.

Prava was also a gandharva and she birthed Anavadya, Anuvasha, Anuranuna, Priya, Anupa, Subhaga, d Bhasi, Siddha, Purna, Barhi, Purnayu, Brahmachari, Ratiguna, Suparna, Vishvavasu, Bhanu, Suchandra. Through the Sage Kashyapa she birthed the race known as apsaras, starting with Alambusha, Mishrakeshi, Vidyutparna, Tulanagha, Aruna, Rakshita, Rambha, Asita, Subahu, Suvrata, Subhuja and Supriya. Of the race of gandharvas, the four most famous were Atibahu, Haha, Huhu, and Tumbura.

||Two||

Shiva in his identity as Sthanu also birthed eleven great sons through the power of his mind, just as Brahma had done—Mrigavyadha, Sarva, Nirriti, Aja, Ekapada, Pinaki the famous destroyer of enemies, Dahana, Ishvara, Kapali, Sthanu and Bhaga. Collectively, they were known as the Rudras.

The six sons of Brahma engendered many powerful beings. Maharishi Angiras sired Brihaspati, Utathya and Samvartha. Maharishi Atri had many sons, all maharishis in their own right. Maharishi Pulastya sired the rakshasa race, the vanaras and the kinnaras, those wondrous hybrid beings with the bodies of humans and heads of horses. Maharishi Pulaha created the deer, the lions, the tigers, and the kimpurushas who were akin to the kinnaras in most respects. Maharishi Kratu's sons were the valakhilya sages, sixty thousand in all, born of his own body, each the size of a man's thumb or smaller, and their task was to precede the chariot of the sun and be Surya's companion.

Daksha himself, a great prajapati in his own stead, was born from Brahma's right toe. From the left toe of Brahma was born Daksha's wife, through whom the Prajapati had fifty daughters, all with eyes like the lotus and perfect in feature and aspect. Daksha sired no sons so he declared his daughters putrikas, for eventually even a daughter becomes a son and a son becomes a daughter—when either marries, their spouse becomes as one's own son or daughter. Of his fifty daughters, Prajapati Daksha gave ten to Dharma, twenty-seven to Indu who was also Chandra the moon, and thirteen to Kashyapa. Brahma then decreed that the ten wives of Dharma would themselves be the doorways to dharma. The wives of Soma, also known as Indu or Chandra, the moon, were appointed the task of measuring the passing of time and were known as nakshatras or constellations of stars which mark the movement of worlds and the growth of the universe.

Grandsire Brahma's son Manu sired the eight Vasus. Note their names: Dhara, Dhruva, Soma, Aha, Anila, Anala, Pratyusha, and Prabhasa. Dhara and Dhruva's mother was Dhumra, Soma who is also named Chandra or Indu, was born of Manasvini. Anila was also known as Shvasana as his mother was Shvasa. Aha's mother was named Rata. Anala, also known as Hutashana, for he was fire itself, was born of Shandilya. Pratyusha and Prabhasa were born of Prabhata.

Dhara in turn engendered Dravina and Hutahavyavaha. Dhruva's son was the mighty Timelord Kala, controller of the great Samay Chakra, the eternal Wheel of Time that regulates all worlds. Soma had a son Varcha and Varcha's sons were Shishira, Prana and Ramana. Aha's sons were Jyoti, Shama, Shanta and Muni. Anala who is also known as Agni had a son named Kumara. Born in a bed of reeds, because he was raised by the krittikas, he became famous as Kartikeya. Anala's other sons were named Shakha, Vishakha and Naigamesha. Anila married Shiva and on her sired Purojava and Avijnatagati. Pratyusha's son was the renowned Rishi Devala who had two sons. Sage Brihaspati, preceptor of the devas, had a sister named Vivasvat who chose to remain celibate and walked the path of self-renunciation through yoga for many years. Eventually, Vivasvat became the wife of Prabhasa, the eighth vasu, with whom she begot Vishwakarma, the first craftsman, who created all arts on earth. Artisan to the devas themselves, jeweller, designer, builder, engineer and chariot-maker, he bestowed on humankind the knowledge and skill of all crafts.

Dharma was born of a cleft in Brahma's right breast and assumed human form. This bringer of happiness to all beings, had three sons—Shama, Kama and Harsha. Their energy supports the world. Kama married Rati, Shama took Prapti as his wife, and Harsha wed Nanda. Together, they sustain worlds.

Now, of Marichi was born Kashyapa. And from Kashyapa were born the devas and asuras themselves, the gods and the demons. Therefore Kashyapa engendered both races that ruled and begat the world. This is their genealogy.

Vivasvat's son Vishwakarma, in the form of a mare, Tvashtri, became wife to Savita and gave birth to the celestial horse twins, the Ashwins. Aditi bore twelve sons, among them Shakra the eldest who became famous as Indra, king of the gods, and Vishnu the youngest, preserver of worlds.

These were the thirty-three gods; now here are their progeny classified by pakshas, kulas and ganas.

Rudras, saddhyas, maruts, vasus, bhargavasand vishvadevas are counted in groups or pakshas.

Vinata's son Garuda, his brother Aruna and Brihaspati are considered to be part of the adityas. The twin Ashwins along with all species of flora and fauna are numbered among the guhyakas, the attendants who wait on Kubera, lord of wealth.

The great Bhrigu, founder of the Bhargavas, emerged from Brahma's body by cleaving open his heart. His son was Shukra, who is also the planet of the same name. Celibate, austere, a master yogi and supremely wise, he became the preceptor to both the devas and the asuras. His given task was to seek out new knowledge and preserve that which had been obtained. Bhrigu's other son Chyavana, who emerged from his mother's womb to slay her abductor, wed Arushi, daughter of Manu, and together they begat Aurva, who birthed himself by ripping open his mother's thighs. Even as an infant, Aurva's energy was immense and in time he sired Richika, who then sired Jamadagni, one of whose four sons was Parashurama. Jamadagni then went on to sire thousands of offspring, thus propagating the Bhrigu race. Brahma's two other sons were Dhata and Vidhata who lived with Manu. Their sister is the resplendent Lakshmi, who lives in the lotus flower and whose sons, born of her mind, are the horses that race across the sky. Shukra begat the devi named Jyeshta who married Varuna, lord of the oceans, and birthed a son named Bala and a daughter named Shura, both of whom were much beloved by the devas.

When animals began to feed upon one another for sustenance, instead of surviving on the inert foods of the world, Adharma was born. This was the beginning of sin, destroyer of all living creatures. Adharma was sin manifest, and he fathered the race of rakshasas upon his wife Nirriti, because of which rakshasas are also know as nairritas. Of the many sons of Nirriti from Adharma were Bhaya, Mahabhaya, and Mrityu—Fear, Terror and Death. Goddess Tamra bore five daughters—Kaki, Shyeni, Bhasi, Dhritarashtri and Shuki. Kaki created the species of owls, Shyeni the hawks, Bhasi the cocks and vultures, Dhritarashtri the ducks, swans and geese, and Shuki the parrots.

Krodha, whose name is synonymous with Wrath, had nine daughters, all manifesting aspects of their father—Mrigi, Mrigamanda, Hari, Bhadramana, Matangi, Sharduli, Shweta, Surabhi, and Surasa. Mrigi begat the species of deer, Mrigamanda the bears and some varieties of deer and yaks, Bhadramana, the elephant Airavata, from whom all pachyderms descend, Hari the tawny and dextrous vanaras who are now evolved as monkeys as well as the golangulas—those cow-tailed monkeys with dark bodies and red parts, Sharduli the great cats—lions, tigers, leopards, panthers, Shweta, the swift elephants of the same name that guard the cardinal points of the compass, Surabhi, the beautiful Rohini and Gandharvi, with Rohini engendering cattle and Gandharvi, horses. Surasa created the Nagas, Kadru the Pannagas or snakes and serpents. Anala created the seven varieties of tree that bear rounded fruits. Aruna and his wife Shyeni, the falcon hawk, birthed Sampati and Jatayu, lords of birdkind.

||Three||

These are the accounts of the asuras who assumed human form.

Viprachitti, a bull among danavas, took the form of a great warrior-king named Jarasandha. Hiranyakashipu, son of Diti, became Shishupala. Prahlada's younger brother Samhrada became Shalya, chief of the Bahlikas, and their youngest brother became Dhrishtaketu. Shibi took birth as a king named Druma. Bashkala became Bhagadatta. Five asuras—Ayahshira, Ashwashira, Ayahshankhu, Gaganamurdha and Veghavan—took birth in the Kekaya lineage as great kings. A mighty demon named Ketumana was reborn as the raja named Amitouja. Svarbhanu became King Ugrasena. Ashwa became King Ashoka, while his younger brother Ashwapati was born as King Hardikya. Vrishaparva became King Dirghaprajna, his younger brother Ajaka became King Malla. Ashvagriva was reborn as King Rochamana. Sukshma became King Brihanta. Tuhunda became King Senabindu. Isripa became King Papajit. Ekachakra became Prativindhya. Virupaksha, famous for being capable of fighting in myriad modes, was reborn as King Chitravarmana. The danava Hara, famous for abducting and killing his enemies, took birth as Suvastu. Ahara, capable of destroying entire armies, became King Bahlika. Nichandra, so named because his face was like the moon, became King Munjakesha. Nikhumbha became Devadhipa. Sharabha was birthed as Rajarshi Paurava. Shalabha was reborn as King Prahrada of the Bahlikas. Chandra, so named because his beauty was equal to that of the moon god, incarnated as Rajarshi Rishika. Mritapa was reborn as King Paschimanupaka. Gavishtha turned into King Drumasena. Mayura transformed as Vishwa while his younger brother Suparna became King Kalakriti. Chandrahanta became Rajarashi Shunaka. Chandravinashana became Rajarashi Janaki. The danava Dirghajihva was birthed as king of Kashi. Rahu, the bodiless asura with the immortal head, took birth as Kratha. Vikshara, son of Anayu, became King Vasumitra, while his brother became king of Pamsu. Balavira became Paoundramatsyaka. Vritra became Rajarshi Manimana and his younger brother Kroshdahanta took the form of King Danda. Krodhavardhana became Dandadhara.

The eight sons of the asura named Kalaka were reborn as eight powerful kings: the eldest became King Jayatsena of Magadha, the second King Aparajita, the third became king of the Nishadas, the fourth the great Rajarshi Shrenimana, the fifth King Mahuja, the sixth Rajarshi Abhiru, the seventh Samundrasena, and the eighth was known as King Brihata.

From krodhavasha asuras—the race who are enslaved by their own anger—many took rebirth on earth as the kings Nandika, Karnaveshta, Siddhartha, Kitaka, Suvira, Subahu, Mahavira, Bahlika, Krodha, Vichitya, Surasa, Nila, Viradhama, Dantavaka, Durjaya, Rukmi, Janamajaya, Ashada, Vayuvega, Buriteja, Ekalavya, Sumitra, Vatadhana, Gomukha, Karushaka, Kshemadhurti, Shrutayau, Uddhava, Brihatsena, Kshema, Ugratirtha, Kuhara, and Ishvara, king of Kalinga and Matimana. Devaka, as resplendent as any deva himself, was born on earth as the lord of the gandharvas.

Not all took birth from mortal wombs. Drona, son of Bharadvaja, emerged whole from the body of Devarshi Brihaspati. This great master of weapons was the supreme teacher of weaponry and warcraft who ever lived. Ashwatthama was born from the body of Mahadeva, Shiva himself, and formed when three separate parts of the great god—Yama, Kama and Krodha: Destruction, Desire and Wrath—merged into one being.

The eight vasus chose to be reborn as sons of Shantanu, through Ganga, according to a pact they made with the goddess of the river. The youngest among them grew up to be the famous Devavrata, better known later in life as Bhishma Pitama, the great Kuru regent who was able to equal even the legendary Parashurama in combat. Brahmarishi Kripa was in fact one of the rudras reborn. As for the notorious Shakuni, a Maharatha among warriors, why, he was Dvapara himself in human form! Satyaki the Vrishni was in fact one of the maruts. Rajarshi Drupada was also an asura reborn on earth. Kritavarma and Rajarshi Virata were also maruts. Arishta's son Hamsa, king of the gandharvas, was reborn as Dhritarashtra, son of Krishna Dweipayana and lord of the Kurus during the time of the historic Maha Bharata war. We shall know his story in due course. Vidura, born in the house of Kurus, sired by Krishna Dweipayana upon a maid, was in fact the son of Atri himself. Duryodhana, eldest of the Kuru princes, was an amsa of Kali, that notorious asura after whom the fourth and last Yuga of the world is named. His siblings, the Kauravas, were in fact Pulastya's sons and daughter. Yudhishtira was but Dharma in mortal amsa, Bhimasena an amsa of Vayu, Arjuna part of Indra, Nakula and Sahadeva the twin Ashwins. Suvarcha son of Soma became Abhimanyu, son of Arjuna on earth. Maharatha Dhrishtadyumna was an amsa of Agni, or Anila. The hermaphrodite Shikhandi was a rakshasa reborn. Draupadi's five sons were in fact five of the vishvadevas, the ten sons of Vishva Devi. Karna, the greatest warrior of all, was an amsa of Surya, the sun god. Narayana incarnated himself on earth as the mighty Vasudeva Krishna. His half-brother Baladeva was an amsa of Shesha Naga, on whose coils Hari Vishnu rests eternally. Pradyumna was an avatara of Sanatkumara. Thus were many other gods also born in Vasudeva's line, to aid him in his mission upon earth against the asuras.

The apsaras took birth under instruction from Vasava. Sixteen thousand of them were born as princesses, to be rescued by and married to Vasudeva Krishna. Sri, the goddess Lakshmi, herself took birth as a daughter of King Drupada. Rising up out of a yagna chaukat—the sacrificial square—she was perfectly dark as dusk, just like Lakshmi herself, of perfect height, perfectly formed and shaped, with long lush black hair, black eyes shaped like lotus leaves and the fragrance of a blue lotus. Her lustrous black skin gleamed and glittered like Vaiduryamani, lapis lazuli. The goddesses Siddhi and Dhriti became the queens Kunti and Madri. Mati became Gandhari, daughter of Subala.

||Four||

'Raja Janamajaya was pleased at this great accounting of incarnations. Having heard it in all its detail, he then requested his great-grandfather's disciple Vaisampayana to recite the history of his own lineage. Vaisampayana gladly complied.' Sauti paused and looked around. His audience was enraptured as always. When he had begun, he could see the far end of the lines of brahmins and brahmacharyas of Naimisha-sharanya, then a considerable gap, and then, at the far end of the clearing, the treeline resumed again. Now, he could see nothing but a forest of faces. Due to the infrequent pools of dim light, after a few score yards, even his keen eyes could not discern individual faces. The forms blurred one into the other until all he could make out was an audience that surely exceeded all the denizens of the ashram of Kulapati Shaunaka. Even if the kulapati lived up to his name and gathered together every last one of the ten thousand acolytes he had trained in his entire lifetime, they would still not have formed as vast an assemblage as now sat before Ugrasrava Lomarsana Sauti. The suta felt no disquiet or sense of alarm, merely a fascination at this supernatural occurrence. Was it true then? Were the souls of the millions killed in the Maha Bharata war truly lost and wandering the deep jungles of Naimisha? And were they now gathered around the ashram to listen to his recounting of the great conflict as well as the numerous histories that led up to the war itself?

He was accustomed to requests from his listeners. Already, he had indulged the kulapati several times by delving into this history or that lineage, or recounting a certain story first, then another. Vyasa himself had done the same on numerous occasions, as had Vaisampayana at the sarpa satra of Janamajaya, within earshot of Ugrasrava himself. That was the beauty of such a masterpiece: one could begin at any point and one would always be able to find one's way to the ending. Of course, if a person heard all these pre-tales and histories before he heard the actual tale, it did help a great deal. For one thing, it prepared one with some background of the underlying forces that were at work, invisibly aiding and abetting the escalation of the conflict and its tragic resolution. Therefore, when the reader actually came to the core story of the Bharata epic, he or she already possessed a knowledge of the cultural and historical background against which that core story unfolded.

He wondered how his audience felt, listening to the names of so many familiar personages cited, their genealogy, their family history, their divine origins . . .

But that was not his task. His task was to tell the tale, as simply yet effectively as possible, in a manner that was pleasing and memorable.

After all, if Krishna Dweipayana Vyasa, a forebear to the main protagonists of the tale and one of the principal participants in that great epic, could compose a poem about himself and his family and narrate it professionally, why should Ugrasrava Lomarsana Sauti have any hesitation or doubt? That was the greatness of itihasa. One simply did one's task: of telling the tale. What the listener took away depended on the listener. It was certain that the deep understanding Kulapati Shaunaka and some of the other maharishis here gained from his account was nowhere near the superficial and peripheral glimpse gained by the young brahmacharyas. For a great story was like a river. One could return to the river at any time, but in fact each time one came back, the river was changed and you were different as well. Never again could you repeat the same visit exactly as it had occurred before. That was the power of Kala, the lord of Time. Just as the water flowing in the river was not the same that had flowed on your last visit, so also you had grown since that visit, changed in some way or other, small or substantial. So also each time one heard a tale as massive and epic as the *Mahabharata* of Krishna Dweipayana Vyasa, the tale itself reshaped itself with the telling or due to the change in the person reciting it, as well as the listener hearing the poem.

This was starting to happen now. At certain points in his narration, he had experienced a strange phenomenon: As if the particular story he was reciting had begun to take shape before his very eyes, real-life figures and structures rising up around him in three-dimensional reality, horses neighing, chariots pounding, swords clashing, men shouting hoarsely, brahmins chanting, fire roaring . . . as if the story had begun to come alive, to take on a life of its own making. Like a coal feeding off air alone, he felt the words leave his mouth to ignite into something greater than mere sounds and symbols. Sanskrit incarnated. Poetry made flesh. An epic carved of sound and light and fury, signifying everything that mattered.

And as he continued, he knew that soon, in the next few shlokas, he himself would begin to disappear like a wraith, along with all the denizens of this great ashram, leaving only the living coal of story itself, the flame that fed on air to sustain itself, blaze and flare into an inferno that consumed this entire great jungle of lost souls, blazing not with real flame and ash and heat, but with the tapas of meditation and contemplation, the intellectual power that had sparked this great epic into existence over years of effort. For three years the great Krishna Dweipayana Vyasa had risen each morning to compose this history of the greatest human conflict ever waged, then he had taught it to his disciples who in turn had taught it to others, and so the pilot flame of culture was passed on from hand to hand, kept alive by the force of mind alone, generation to generation . . . And soon, he, Ugrasrava, would disappear. For as time passed, all narrators must die. Only the tale itself lives on. Eternally.

Listen. Now he heard a gentle sigh deep within the belly of the dark woods. A sigh of expectation and anticipation.

A sigh of longing and becoming. As the countless listeners, past, present and future, dead, living and yet-to-be-born, all sat together in this vast infinite forest of stories, listening to every syllable of every shloka. Until the real and unreal, living and not-yet-living and once-living all merged into one vast audience, drinking together from the deep well of itihasa. Warmed by the same eternal fire. Soon he would be gone. But the story would remain.

With a soft sigh of his own, he resumed the story.

||Paksha Nine||

SHAKUNTALA AND DUSHYANTA

||One||

A great king entered a vast jungle. He was accompanied by his army, hundreds of horses, elephants, warriors armed with swords, spears, balas, maces, javelins, lances and other weapons. They roared and cheered as they rode through the forest to show their might. Conch blowers sounded their shell trumpets, dhol drummers pounded their kettle drums. The chariot wheels rumbled, the elephants trumpeted, the horses neighed. All the denizens of the forest, animal, insect and human, wondered at this great noise and stopped still in fear.

The king was exceedingly handsome and well loved. The women of his kingdom showered flowers and praises—and coy invitations—upon him when he rode through the streets. Wealthy and powerful, he wanted for nothing. His enemies feared him enough to show great respect and avoid confrontations—those that were foolish enough to oppose him in battle met with devastation and ruin, and were massacred or enslaved. Brahmins paid homage to his greatness; kusalavyas sang his praises. After he had conquered all the realms he desired to possess and partaken of all the fruits of pleasure, he grew restless of kingship and sought new thrills and pursuits. His favourite pastime was the hunt. But unlike earlier kings of his line who preferred to ride out alone or in small packs, hunting stealthily, he rode out with small armies, making a great show of it so that everyone knew that the king's hunt was passing by. All heads turned to watch the glamour of his entourage. Many of the citizens even ran behind his train or followed on horse or by wagon. But each time he went farther and farther into the deep jungle, and eventually, all fell back and turned homewards. Finally, only he and his retinue continued, making their way noisily forward, with great merriment and clash of music and voices. Even his chariot was designed to produce the loudest sound, its heavy iron-clad wheels rumbling ominously, the effect intended to strike fear into the hearts of his enemies; it had become his trademark as a king at arms. Despite its ponderous rumbling, the chariot was drawn by powerful bhoja stallions and capable of achieving great speeds, often compared to the swiftness of Garuda, by those who observed it from afar.

That day, the king came to a new place, a forest within the great aranya, the unexplored wilderness that still covered much of the earth. It was a beautiful grove comparable to Nandana itself, the fabled garden of the king of gods in his heavenly realm Indraloka. Magnificent bilva, arka, khadira, kapitha and dhava trees grew in great profusion. The landscape was varied, and ranged from mountains and valleys to vast plains spotted with great boulders. There was no sign of water or human habitation. The king and his retinue rode on for several yojanas, marvelling at this new place they had discovered, so far removed from civilization. In the forested parts of this country within a jungle, they were amazed at the profusion of game. The greatest herds of deer they had ever seen abounded here, as did every other species of forest creatures. So unaccustomed were these beasts to the sight or scent of humans that they stood still at first and stared in puzzlement at the new arrivals, unafraid and unshy. With great enthusiasm, the king and his best men embarked on their hunt. They slaughtered deer by the score. Entire families of tiger were massacred by arrowshot alone. Those that were only wounded, he dismounted from his chariot and slew with his sword. The hunt continued for days and he had recourse to every manner of weapon which he employed in the killing of all manner of beasts. He brought down lions with spears, smashed the skulls of wild boars with maces, flung javelins into the thick hide of elephants. Roaring with exultation like the very predators he killed, he took pleasure and pride in his kills, massacring the animals of that unspoiled forest. At last, in alarm and panic, the creatures of the region began to flee before the thundering advance of this manic herd of two-legged killers, entire herds dispersing and stampeding, deer crying out and leaping in all directions to flee their tormentors, even the long-fanged cats slinking away silently to hide in the deep shadows and glare balefully at their new rivals.

At night, while the king and his jubilant band of followers feasted on the choicest portions of the meat they had hunted, some predators worked their vengeance. Men were dragged off screaming into the darkness, heads chomped to pulp and limbs crushed between iron jaws, bones smashed by rampaging elephants or bellies ripped open by razor-sharp boar tusks. But these losses were minor compared to the slaughter of the animals. As always, man was the cruellest predator of all, hunting for pleasure rather than need. The carcasses they piled up could have fed a force a hundred times their size for weeks. Most would rot uneaten, beautiful beasts slain for man's cruel pleasure.

The forest had its revenge on the invading force. The riverbeds grew parched, the ponds dry. Not a drop of water was to be found for miles and miles. Search as they may, they could find no trace of water, running or still. Surely, the animals must slake their thirst somehow? But the animals could not speak, nor did the forest yield its secret. And so the king and his entourage thirsted mightily even as they tired of the salty meat of their kills and craved other foods. Yet these deprivations only infuriated the king further and rather than withdraw his men, he drove them further into the new country each day, slaying more and more creatures in prodigious numbers. The sheer scale of the massacre grew to epic proportions. Some say he slew several hundreds at the very least, but most insist the number of slaughtered beasts ran into several thousands. Enraged by extreme thirst and blood-rage, he was like a conqueror possessed, waging war against the animals of that region like a mad buffalo run amok.

||Two||

Ravaged by thirst and exhaustion, its numbers already depleted by the attacks of vengeful animals, the king's retinue dwindled further as men began to drop for want of the most simple succour. Water. By degrees, their bloodlust diminished, as the king's anger waned. His own head pounding for lack of water, body parched and blood heated, he ceased his killing spree. Onward they rode, further into unknown territory. Across plains, over mountains, through valleys, they had no choice but to push on—already they had come too far from the last source of water. Turning back was no longer an option. Men fell like the beasts they had slain, dropped by the invisible arrow of thirst, to lie dying or dead in strange lands. The predators that followed the human force crept up under cover of night and consumed these fallen, often tearing them to shreds while still alive. The angry forest wreaked its own revenge on its ravagers.

Finally, when his force had been reduced to a fraction of its original size, his own strength halved, even the horses and elephants half-dead from lack of water, and it seemed as if every last one of them would die there in that unknown country, the king came to a rise. Goading their mounts, his men and he rode upto a ridge overlooking a vast valley. Reining in their exhausted mounts, they gazed upon an extraordinary sight. Below lay a great forest, lush and beautiful like nothing they had seen before. There was water there in plenty—they could see a great river snaking its way through the valley, waterfalls plunging from the surrounding cliffs, ponds and pools visible through gaps in the trees. The trees were emerald green, filled with a profusion of colourful birds of every description. The air was filled with their calls. There were animals in the woods below as well, roaming freely, even more unspoiled and innocent than the ones they had seen earlier. The sounds of lions roaring could be heard, yet a herd of deer continued to graze unafraid. The sight of ripe fruits hanging from the trees made their parched mouths water, and the pristine unblemished beauty of that arboreal vision brought tears to the eyes of these battle-hardened men.

Riding down a sloping pathway that led down, they entered the valley and cried with relief at the sight of water and nourishment. Slaking their thirst and eating their fill of luscious ripe fruits, they lay on the soft cool grassy mounds, beneath the gentle shade of great trees, and recovered their strength. Their urge to hunt was satiated and all they desired was to regain their energy that they might return home. But the king grew eager to explore further. Wishing to continue alone, he bade all his men except two—a priest and an advisor—remain here and indulge their fill of nourishment and rest until he returned. Then, accompanied only by the brahmin and the minister, he proceeded upon his chariot.

So lush was the grassy undergrowth that it all but muffled the rumbling thunder of the king's war chariot. The sun was warm and energizing yet never harsh, even as the day wore on from morning to afternoon. Cool scented breezes blew and all the animals they saw were innocent and unafraid. They saw lions resting beside grazing deer, and everywhere the trees were dark with swarms of shatapadas, buzzing and busily making their sweet treacly honey. The king knew then that this was the innermost heart of the strange realm they had discovered, and that the first forest they had entered had been the gateway to this heavenly country.

At length, they came to a grove at the delta of the river they had glimpsed from the ridge above. The trees here were as smooth and slender as flagpoles, and nestled within the perfect spot was a vast ashram. From the sight of the numerous yagna chaukats they saw everywhere, and the sheer number of thatched huts of all sizes, it was evident that a great number of rishis resided here. It was an idyllic place, fit for the most austere yatis and valakhilyas.

'What place is this?' asked the king of the brahmin.

The brahmin stared in wonderment, enraptured by the beauty and calm of the place. 'It can be none other than the fabled ashram on the banks of the sacred river Malini. I have heard tales of it from sutas but never thought I would live to see it with my own eyes. It is the domicile of Rishi Kanva, descendant of Kashyapa.'

The king gazed out across the hermitage for a while, but neither he nor his companions saw any living soul in sight.

The king handed the reins of the chariot to his advisor. 'Stay here until I return,' he commanded, then disembarked from the chariot.

Continuing alone on foot, he entered the grove, passing through it to the ashram beyond. The ashram overlooked the river and his attention was diverted by the cries and sight of chakravaka birds frolicking in the water noisily. The ruddy geese sent up loud cries, unafraid of any predators as they thrashed and splashed water with their wings. The king smiled at the sight, wishing now that he had carried his bow and quiver, then continued through the ashram. He found every hut empty, every yagna chaukat cold and unlit, and not a single person in sight. Yet there was no doubt that many lived here, for he found garments and belongings, sacrificial oblations and items for the living and ritual sacrifices of brahmins everywhere. Where were the denizens of the ashram? He saw various items and arrangements that he recognized from his own studies of the Vedas—some he knew to be preparations for rituals spelled out in the Rig Vedic chapters of the great books of knowledge, others related to the Sama Veda, Yajur Veda or Atharva Veda. Clearly, many great rishis resided here and pursued their Vedic studies and rituals with complete dedication. 'This must be what Brahmaloka looks like,' he thought, awed.

Not finding anyone through the entire length and breadth of the ashram, yet certain that many must reside here, the king began to call out as he went. His voice echoed in the woods. Finally, just when he was about to give up and retrace his steps, a voice answered. He was surprised to hear a woman's soft tones respond, coming from the direction of the river.

A vision came into sight, freshly bathed, her long black hair still wet from the river. Clad in the humble attire of an ascetic, she was dark of hair and eye, dusky of skin and beautiful beyond description. Surprised to see him, she was nonetheless the epitome of charm and grace and received him with great honour and respect. Offering him a seat, she gave him water for the arghya, and he washed his feet, hands and face and accepted her offer of refreshment. After observing all formalities, she then enquired who he might be and what he desired. Even though it was evident that she was bursting with curiosity, her questions were brief and polite, which impressed him further.

'I am Raja Dushyanta and I am told this is the ashram of the fabled Rishi Kanva. Is it so?'

'It is, sire,' replied the woman. 'But my father is not presently here.'

'Where has he gone?' asked Dushyanta, doing his best not to stare. Her beauty captivated him and he could feel his heart quicken, his blood race.

'He has gone on an errand,' she replied. 'He may be a while returning but please do us the honour of waiting until he returns.'

'And where are the other rishis who reside here? For I see that there must be many, surely?'

'Aye, sire, indeed. The rishis of this ashram are extremely austere in their vows and dedication. There are yatis, valakhilyas and other devout sages. Presently they are all on pilgrimage and my father and I are here alone.'

Unable to contain his eagerness to know the maiden better, Dushyanta began to ask her questions, always polite and courteous, but also enquiring more than any casual visitor might. He learned that her name was Shakuntala, and that she lived here in service to her father Rishi Kanva and the other rishis of the ashram. While she spoke, Dushyanta kept stealing glances at her, admiring her beauty, her youth, her perfection. For her part, she seemed unaware of her own beauty and wore it casually, unselfconsciously, unlike the apsaras of his court who preened and primped themselves all day. Her damp hair hung by her side, waist-long, and it drew his attention time and again to her voluptuously undulating body and shapely hips. He listened as she praised her father and described his qualities and reputation as a man of great self-sacrifice and dedication to the brahman.

Dushyanta could not help ask. 'Yet how is it that a rishi of such severe vows happened to father a daughter, especially one as beautiful as yourself? And how is it that you live here with him in this remote wilderness far from civilization? After all,' he added teasingly, 'a flower so radiant in beauty should not conceal its lustre in the deep forest!'

She blushed shyly at these comments but replied sincerely, 'My lord . . .'

'Dushyanta,' he said quickly. 'I am lord only to those who serve me. You are by no means my servant nor could you ever be. Pray, address me simply as Dushyanta.'

She seemed to contemplate this for a moment. 'I have been raised always to address people correctly, my lord. I cannot disobey my father's order and simply address a king by his name. It would not be right.'

He smiled. So innocent and pure of heart, yet so extravagantly beautiful too. He had never known such a woman before. 'Then I shall have to call you Rani.'

Her doe eyes flashed up, staring at him. 'My lord? I do not comprehend your meaning.'

'If you call me lord or king, I shall call you lady or queen. It is only right.'

She covered her mouth with her hand. 'But that cannot be. I am but a rishi's humble daughter, with no possessions or property to my name. I am no lady, far from a queen!'

'You are possessed of regal bearing, rich in intelligence and wit, a jewelled smile, precious voice, an aspect fitting of the goddess of wealth herself, almighty Lakshmi . . .' he let his words trail off, enjoying her startled expression. 'Queen is barely sufficient. Perhaps I should call you Devi. For you are no less than a goddess in body and mind!'

Her hand shot out as if to cover his lips before he could say more, the innocent instinctive reaction of a child, but she stopped herself before her hand could touch his mouth, withdrew it, and lowered her eyes to the ground shyly. 'Nay, my good Lord Dushyanta. You cannot call me, a simple brahmachari, a goddess! You might anger Sri herself!'

He laughed. 'Then resolve this at once. Agree to call me Dushyanta and I shall call you Shakuntala.'

She glanced up at him. And he saw the fire of energy spark in her eyes. Not quite mischief but it showed that she had great force of will.

He smiled winningly. 'It is the only way.' He added softly: 'Shakuntala.'

Swallowing nervously, she bobbed her head once, then said in barely a whisper, 'Aye, Dushyanta . . . sire.'

He wagged a finger in warning. 'Just Dushyanta, nothing more. Or I crown you Sri on earth incarnate!'

'No!' she cried, genuinely distressed. 'Dushyanta. Please do not.'

At the sound of his name spoken by that nightingale voice in that passionate tone, his heart stirred powerfully. It was all he could do to keep himself from taking her in his embrace and demonstrating his passion for her right there and then. But Dushyanta knew that this was no palace chattel or serving maid. This was indeed a lady, even if she did not know it. He would treat her as such. 'Thank you, Shakuntala.' He resumed his seat calmly, with an effort. 'Pray, continue. You were about to explain to me how your illustrious father Rishi Kanva came to sire a daughter and why you continue to live in this remote if beautiful forest with him like any shaven-head brahmacharya—though you are clearly not one.'

She nodded, taking his words at face value and seeming not to hear the irony in his phrasing—or the subtle innuendo. 'I shall tell you, for it is no secret.'

||Three||

In times of yore, the great brahmarishi Vishwamitra began to practise great austerities. The tapas power he accumulated grew to a great store, enough to dislodge even mighty Lord Indra from his seat if he chose to rise against the devas. Purandara summoned the apsara Menaka, fabled for her beauty, and requested her to seduce Vishwamitra that he might cease his powerful penance. Menaka was afraid of Vishwamitra's legendary temper. 'Great Shakra, you know that when provoked he is capable of unleashing destruction even against one as powerful as thee. I dare not disturb him during his meditation. He once caused the death of the great Vashishta. On another occasion, he created the river Kaushiki from the force produced by his penance, and to this day, it rages so wilfully that few can cross its tempestuous waters. Later he renamed it Para. Do you recall that sacred river? On its banks lived Vishwamitra's own wife, cared for by the righteous rajarshi Matanga who became a hunter to survive the great famine. After the famine ended and Vishwamitra returned home, he thanked Matanga for maintaining his wife by officiating at his ceremony, an event which you yourself attended, Lord Indra, and I saw you drinking soma there in Vishwamitra's presence. Vishwamitra is a nakshatra, and he is possessed with the energy of an entire constellation of stars. He created the constellation Shravana through his own energy. If he brings down his foot on the earth hard, earthquakes ripple throughout the world. If he wishes, he can uproot the great Mount Meru and whirl it around like a mace. Every aspect of his features is as brilliant as the sun, and as deadly as Yama. How can a mere apsara such as I dare to interrupt his great tapasya? Speaking of Yama, the lord of death and dharma himself fears Vishwamitra. As do Soma, the maharishis, saddhyas, vishvadevas and valakhilyas.'

When Shakra pressed Menaka, entreating her to undertake this chore, she continued to argue thus. Finally, she agreed reluctantly on certain conditions. 'If you would have me do this, then you must guarantee me your protection and use your own powers to make me seem innocent. I shall go before Vishwamitra. Let Marut the wind god strip me of my garments. Let Manmatha, lord of love, use his power to entice the brahmarishi. Create an environment that seduces him and makes him receptive to my charms. I shall act innocent. Let him be seduced by me rather than I seduce him wilfully.'

Indra saw the sense in Menaka's suggestion. He enlisted the aid of Vayu and Kama, the lords of the Wind and Love. Menaka entered Vishwamitra's ashram where the great sage sat absorbed in his meditative trance. Pretending to be innocent of his presence, she moved coquettishly around him, dancing and cavorting playfully. From the fruits and trees around, Kama drew fragrances and scents that evoked passion while Vayu swirled them into Vishwamitra's senses, stroking the sage's body with arousing caresses. His senses provoked, the brahmarishi opened his eyes for an instant, and his gaze alighted on Menaka. At exactly that instant, Marut sent a sudden gust of wind to snatch the filmy garment from the apsara's body, leaving her unclothed and exposed in all her radiant beauty. Menaka gasped, then reached for her stolen garment, but even as she stretched out her hand for it, it was whipped further away from her by another puff from the same wind. She had to bend low and reach far to pick it up and as she did so she struck a pose that no man could look upon without feeling a great surge of passion. Given a perfect view of the naked apsara, flawless in body and grace, masterful in movements, filled with the strength and glow of youth, Vishwamitra was overcome with desire for her. Unable to stop himself, he proposed to her that they cohabit. Genuinely awed by the power and reputation of the great brahmarishi, Menaka agreed coyly. Without reclaiming her stolen garment, she came into his arms and he clasped her to himself as a starved man clasps food.

For an untold length of time the apsara and the brahmarishi indulged themselves in that solitary place, losing their wits completely to the act of procreation, until the days and weeks and months melded into each other and seemed to form but a single endless day. All the great tapas energy accumulated by the brahmarishi, which could have given him power enough to dislodge the king of gods had he so desired, was emitted in the act of coition and absorbed in the form of seed by Menaka. Of that act and energy was conceived a female child. When her womb grew heavy, Menaka went to the banks of the river Malini, in the Himalayas. There she stayed until her time came to give birth. Leaving the child on the banks of the Malini, Menaka returned to Indra's assembly, her task accomplished.

Left alone on that desolate Himalayan plain, by the river, the baby's presence attracted numerous predators. Growing bolder by the passing hour, they crept closer to the child, and would have surely consumed her in moments. But the shakuna, the birds who view all from their vantage point high in the sky, floating like kites suspended on invisible string, saw her plight and descended to protect her. They took it upon themselves to keep the predators at bay. Soon after, Rishi Kanva, who had gone up to the Himalayas to meditate, chanced upon her when he went down to the river for his ablutions. Seeing her alone there in that desolate place, he knew that she would not survive long if left unattended. He brought her home, and raised her as his own daughter. The shastras say there are three kinds of parents. One gives a body. The second protects. The third kind provides food. Therefore Kanva adopted the child he sought to protect and nourish as his own daughter. Because he found her surrounded by shakuna birds, he named her Shakuntala.

||Four||

Dushyanta was simultaneously thrilled and inspired by Shakuntala's narration of the circumstances leading to her own birth. More than a little aroused by her frank account of the seduction of her biological forebear by the alluring nymph, he saw that she exhibited no coyness or signs of mischief. To her, it was merely a factual account which she had narrated as best as she knew. There was no attempt on her part to arouse or titillate. He could hardly blame her if the facts of the account themselves were provocative. Now he was even more enamoured of her. For it was clear to him that her beauty was matched by intelligence, wit and a noble spirit. Unable to stop himself, just as Vishwamitra was possessed of desire for her mother Menaka, Dushyanta clasped Shakuntala's hands in his own. She reacted naturally, trying to pry herself free, but he held on. Looking into his eyes, she saw his passion and the force of his desire and was overwhelmed.

'Shakuntala, I was right at first. You are no less than a princess or noble woman in your own right. The story of your birth confirms it. Your very aspect speaks of your high origins and breeding. I am overcome with longing for you. From the instant I first laid eyes on you, your hair wet from the river, your hips sinuous in your simple hermit's garment, your eyes doe-like and bright in the shade of the jambu tree, your innocence, your sincerity, your intelligence, your beauty, all have charmed and overcome me. I cannot resist my senses a moment longer. Consent to marry me. I will shower you with gold necklaces and garments, ornaments and gems, treasures from a dozen faraway nations, wealth and furs, whatever your heart desires you shall possess. My entire kingdom shall be at your disposal, and I myself your servant. Marry me this instant.'

Shakuntala took a moment to recover from the shock and surprise of this passionate outburst. Trembling a little, she finally managed to say, 'Raje, great king that you are, I cannot answer you myself. I beg of you. Wait until my father returns and ask him for my hand in marriage if you desire me.'

Dushyanta's heart was filled with joy for her answer meant that she herself was not averse to the union. It was all he needed to know. 'I cannot wait a moment longer, my love. Let me take you in the gandharva rite of marriage. It is one of the eight accepted forms of marriage and recognized by all civilized people. In this rite, you only need to consent and we can join together willingly as man and wife. It is a marriage of love.'

Shakuntala shook her head. 'I do not know of this gandharva marriage. I am unaware of such matters. How can I agree independently? I ask you again, wait until my father returns. Ask him for my hand in marriage. If he consents, I shall not refuse you.'

But Dushyanta's passion overflowed and he could not bear to wait. 'Shakuntala, I would not mislead you. Let me explain to you the eight kinds of marriage that have the sanction of dharma. They are brahma, deva, arsha, prajapatya, asura, gandharva, rakshasa and paishacha. Manu, the first mortal creator and formulator of the natural laws by which all mortals abide peaceably, has set out in no unclear terms what each of these forms entails. The first four are sanctioned for brahmins, the first six for kshatriyas. Kings may resort to all eight forms freely. The asura form is only sanctioned for vaisyas and sudras. Of the last five of the eight forms, three are in keeping with dharma but the last two—rakshasa and paishacha—exceed the boundaries of natural law. Yet some indulge in their practice and therefore they are also known to us and recorded by Manu. The form of marriage I propose, the gandharva vivah, is eminently acceptable provided both participants are willing and feel genuine passion for one another. Tell me that you do not feel passion for me and I will stop persisting. But I know that the emotion I see in your eloquent eyes mirrors my own desire. I feel the pulse of your blood in the vein of your wrist. I feel your warm breath on my cool palm now. I see all the signs of passion and desire awakened in you, just as they are in me. Therefore, the gandharva form of marriage is most appropriate for us and in keeping with dharma. Tell me if I am wrong in any way.'

Shakuntala regained control of her breathing and admitted: 'Great king of the Kurus, I do not deny the truth in what you say. I am satisfied also by your explanation of the forms of marriage and the righteousness of this form. It is true that I am willing and therefore nothing else prevents us from joining together in this mutual union.'

Dushyanta moved to take her in his arms, his face revealing his delight. 'Then speak no more, my love. Let us be man and wife this instant.'

'Wait,' she said firmly. 'I shall agree to be your wife, Dushyanta, on certain terms and conditions. Only if you agree to them will this union occur. Are you willing?'

'Of course. Did I not say that you may demand anything of me that you desire? Even without naming your conditions, I have agreed to them!'

'Then, give me your word that even though there is no one else to witness our covenant, you will still honour it as a sacred and secret pact. Promise me only this one thing, Dushyanta. If I bear a child by you, and if it is a son, then give me your guarantee that our son will succeed you as king.'

Dushyanta stared at her, unable to believe his ears. 'Is that all? My beloved, it would be the greatest joy of my life to make our son the heir to the Kuru throne! What more could I desire? You shall be cared for as a queen deserves, surrounded by all the wealth and comfort of the world. Our child, when he or she is born, shall want for nothing. All this is my dharma as a husband, it is your right to demand as the wife of a king!'

With those words, Dushyanta dispelled any shred of doubt that might have remained in Shakuntala's mind. Unable to resist him any longer, overcome by her own emotions and her joy at such a fine mate, she succumbed to his embraces and returned his passion tenfold.

After they had dallied together in mutual delight for awhile, Dushyanta lay with Shakuntala. Had the choice been left to him, he might never have left her presence or that idyllic grove.

But in his absence, his men had received word from the capital that a political rebellion was brewing. It had taken a great deal of time and effort to seek him out, but finally the message reached his advisor and priest who were waiting at the outskirts of the grove, and they entered that sanctum to bring him the urgent missive. Dushyanta knew that he must return at once or risk endangering his entire kingdom and throne. He told Shakuntala to come with him but she could not leave without meeting her father and telling him all that had transpired. Unsure when Rishi Kanva would return, Dushyanta felt he had no choice but to leave alone for the present time. But he promised that he would send fresh forces to bring her to the capital at once.

'My love, I shall dispatch a four-fold army, with infantry, cavalry, elephants and chariots, to fetch you in royal style. You shall enter the city of the Kurus like a queen. Then we shall live together the rest of our lives in perfect love.'

So saying, he climbed aboard his chariot and rode away. Shakuntala's heart ached to see him leave and she felt bereft. The same heated passion that had brought her such joy and fervour only hours earlier now left her feeling cold and lonely. Before Dushyanta came, she had stayed alone here in this desolate grove in perfect happiness, never feeling the lack of anything or any person. But now that she had known the joy of union and the love of a man, the same grove, the same solitary existence, all seemed empty and sad.

Somehow, she passed the time until her father returned. By the time he was back, she had begun to think of the many ways he might react to the news of her unexpected marriage and dalliance. Embarrassed, she would not come before him, and hid in the shadows of her hut. But not for nothing was Rishi Kanva a great sage. Through the power of his divine sight, he saw all that had occurred and understood everything. Then he sought out his daughter and said to her gently, 'Bhagyavan, what you have done is nothing to be ashamed of. What the Kuru king said to you was indeed true. All was in accordance with dharma. Even without mantras recited, a gandharva marriage is acceptable between two willing persons. Indeed, among kshatriyas it is the preferred way! Your choice of husband is distinctive: Dushyanta is a good king and a good man, and does his best to live according to dharma. The son of this union will be an even greater king than his father, mighty in power and wealth and influence, and his sway will extend to the far corners of this earth.'

Shakuntala was overjoyed and overwhelmed with relief. As she washed her father's feet with the arghya water and prepared his repast for him, she asked timidly, 'Does that mean you will grant me your blessings, father?'

He smiled and put a hand on her head, blessing her. 'Always, my fortunate one! Not only that, ask me for any boon you desire. Consider it my wedding gift to you both!'

Shakuntala's mind had been filled with anxiety over the rebellion that Dushyanta's men had spoken of when they came to fetch him. To her innocent mind, it had seemed like the end of his kingdom and the world itself. Her sleep had been filled with nightmares that her newly beloved husband and mate might be slain in battle even before he could send for her, and her entire future would be crushed before it even began. With these fears in her mind, she asked her father, 'Grant that the kings of the Kuru race should always be true to their word and never be dislodged from their thrones, no matter how great the challenge.'

Rishi Kanva saw her concern for her husband and applauded it silently. 'So be it,' he proclaimed. And in his mind, he thought, *This is truly my daughter. Even at such a moment, she did not ask for anything for herself. Only for her husband. Dushyanta is a lucky man to have her as his wife.*

||Five||

Dushyanta returned home to his capital city and was instantly plunged into a nest of political intrigue and powerplay. Taking advantage of his long absence, his rivals had begun a deadly conspiracy against him and all those he relied on. He found he could trust no one completely and that even the most reliable advisors and ministers had formed alliances designed to protect their own interests. The web of political deal-making stretched wide and deep and it was not possible for any king to completely uproot it. Wisdom lay in compromise, acceptance and in making one's own deals to ensure stability for the present. Over time, when the opportunity presented itself, he could eliminate the worst of his rivals and enemies in carefully orchestrated ways, without upsetting the entire applecart of politics. Not for nothing was Hastinapura called City of Elephants. Her politics were as ponderous as a ton-heavy gajagamini.

The battle for political survival and stability as well as the forming of alliances demanded all his energy and time. Forced to use whatever means he possessed, he married into various powerful dynasties of neighbouring kingdoms, ensuring their cooperation and thus eliminating potential rivals. In time, he was sucked into the vortex that is the game of kings and forgot all about his dalliance with Shakuntala. The entire time spent on that trip seemed like a fevered dream. The hunt, the terrible slaughter of countless beasts, the blood-lust that had overcome himself and his men, the deadly thirst that had almost killed them, the beautiful hidden forests within forests, the idyllic valley, the heavenly grove, the unspeakably beautiful maiden all alone in the empty hermitage, the extraordinary tale of her birth, the powerful lust that had overcome him . . . all seemed like fragments from a half-remembered dream in the light of awakening. His memory began to deceive him. He began to think that perhaps it had been Shakuntala herself who had seduced him, just as her mother Menaka had seduced the brahmarishi. She had done it subtly, no doubt, with carefully orchestrated details. Perhaps it had all been planned by some rivals of his throne—misdirecting them into that remote aranya, leading them farther and farther inland into a place where they almost died of thirst. Then finally, when they were almost dead from lack of water, finding that grove. Naturally, it had seemed idyllic and perfect. Shakuntala must have been posed that way, freshly bathed, hair loose and wet, emphasizing her figure and beauty, clad in only that simple transparent garment. The more he thought about it, the more he became convinced that he had been seduced and deceived, that it had been the intention of his rivals and the woman to lure him there and trick him into begetting a child upon her, so that they might claim his throne. Even her condition of marriage: that her son would be heir to the Kuru empire. Why would an innocent unworldly rishi's daughter demand such a condition? Why would she even think of it? No, surely there was mischief at work there. She had been too perfect to be true. He must have been half-deluded by thirst and the strangeness of the forest, and she must have drugged or influenced him somehow, either through the water she gave him to drink or the fruits she offered him to eat. Yes, he had been tricked and she had been the instrument of his enemies to unseat him when all other means failed.

Convinced of this, Dushyanta deliberately ignored his promise to Shakuntala and continued living as before. He grew harder and harsher in his kingship, forced to make hard choices and take difficult decisions in order to retain his power and authority. As time passed, the incredible hours he spent in Shakuntala's arms began to seem more and more dreamlike, less real. Until finally, a day came when he felt he must rid himself of the memory itself, and act as if it had never happened. He sought the advice of his ministers and advisors well versed in law and dharma and they too advised the same course of action. Since only Shakuntala and he had been present when that pact was made, all he had to do was deny any such pact existed. She had no other means of proving her claim. Who would believe the word of some wanton woman from the wilderness against the word of a Kuru emperor?

And so, Dushyanta forgot Shakuntala.

Meanwhile, back in the ashram of Rishi Kanva, Shakuntala did indeed conceive from the union. Her gestation was a long one, for she was determined that she would deliver her child on royal silks in the palatial settings he deserved. A prince, a future king, Kuru emperor, he could not be born here in the wilderness. She extended her gestation through the power of her will, certain that Dushyanta would live up to his promise and send for her. But the months passed, and then a whole year went by with no sign of her husband or his representatives. Still she held the baby in her womb, nursing it within, refusing to birth it anywhere except where she felt it was intended to be born. But still no army came, no escort, not even a messenger from her beloved. She waited and waited, and as the first year became a second, and then the third year loomed, she knew at last that something must have befallen him. Some complex weaving of political forces had prevented him from sending for her. Perhaps he feared that his representatives would lead his enemies to her, that she and the child might be in danger? Perhaps there were other issues at stake that she did not know of, that she could not possibly understand out here in the forest, and he did not wish to send her a message for fear it might be intercepted and used against him? Her mind always found some way to rationalize and justify the delay, never once blaming him for the lapse. It was never Dushyanta who was at fault, merely circumstances, or the weight of kingship, or some unknown cause.

When three years had passed, she permitted her son to be born.

Contained within her womb for such a long time, he had grown strong and powerful. The moment he was born, he began to grow at a prodigious rate. In no time at all, he was the equivalent of any other three-year-old boy. At an age when other children could barely walk, he could run and jump and his bones were strongly knitted and body as large as one years older. His progress continued at the same rapid rate. His teeth and nails and bones were particularly strong. Even falls from heights did not break his bones. His bite could rival that of a lion. Living in a jungle, he was fond of wandering off into the deep woods on his own, at an age when most children could barely walk a few steps from their mothers before falling down. He ran for miles, watching the animals of the forest and growing fascinated with them. He played with lion cubs in the presence of the mother lion, who looked on and yawned indulgently. He climbed on baby elephants and rode foals. In time, his play turned rougher as he grew bolder and more mischievous. He would wrestle with lions, tie elephants to trees, ride wild buffalo, grapple with large tusked boars and force them to the ground, sit upon the backs of tigers and compel them to take him where he pleased. He feared no beast and because of this, the animals came to respect him and let him do as he pleased. They became his companions and friends.

By the time he was six years old he was as strong and well built as any young man. Even if one added the three years he had spent in the womb, he still looked nearly twice his age. Awed by his growth, valour and rapid progress, the rishis of Kanva's ashram called him Sarvadamana, He Who Subjugates Everything. In addition, he had a birthmark on his palm, roughly shaped like a chakra. It was the symbol of a king and every rishi who saw him agreed that he could become nothing less than a samrat, a king of kings.

Finally, the day came when all the rishis and sadasyas of the ashram came to Rishi Kanva and told him that the time had come for young Sarvadamana to be installed as Yuvaraja. Rishi Kanva agreed. 'A married woman cannot stay forever in her parents' home. Sooner or later she must go to her husband's house otherwise people will speak ill of her and her marriage.'

Shakuntala had long since realized that her husband would not send for her. But she had not wished to dishonour her father by saying so and had held her tongue. Now, when he urged her to go to Dushyanta, she made only a feeble protest. 'He said he would send for me.' Her father sighed, 'Nine years is long enough to wait. Now it is time to go to him and confront him with his son.' Shakuntala did not protest further. The very next day, Sarvadamana and she left for Gajasharya, the City of Elephants, accompanied by a contingent of her father's most trusted disciples.

On arrival, she went straight to the palace and sought an audience with her husband. Dushyanta was holding court with the full sabha in attendance. Kings, queens, princes, princesses, nobles of every major house, ministers and advisors, priests and diplomats, emissaries and visiting dignitaries, the cream of Arya royalty was present. When the roughly-clad woman came forward with her son dressed in a garment of fur, he failed to even recognize her.

'Dushyanta,' she said, and at the sound of her voice and at the sight of her appearance, the court's hustle and bustle died down instantly. Who was this woman, dressed in rags, calling the king by his first name? What gumption! What arrogance! What ignorance. Tch tch. 'It is I, Shakuntala, whom you took as your wife in the ashram of my father Rishi Kanva. I have brought before you the fruit of our union, your son. Remember our pact and take him into your house. Crown him your Yuvaraja as promised and make him heir-apparent to the Kuru crown.'

In the great commotion that followed, Raja Dushyanta was rendered speechless. Of course he remembered Shakuntala now. His eyes, accustomed to seeing women with painted faces and bejewelled ornaments and silks like the women of the court, had barely given her a second glance. Yet once she had presented herself, there was no mistaking her. At once, the memory of that passionate encounter, so long buried and forgotten, came to the fore of his mind—and his heart. He was filled with a surge of overwhelming love and joy. *My son? Our son?* He almost ran down the steps to embrace Shakuntala and the handsome young boy who stood beside her, looking unmistakably like a young Dushyanta.

Forgotten were the ravings of his besieged mind about her being part of a conspiracy against him. Forgotten were all his suspicions and doubts. Forgotten were the years he had spent making backroom deals and doing whatever had to be done to hold the Kuru empire together and stabilize his throne. Shakuntala was here! His love, his only true love. And he had a son by her. Together they would live now, as king and queen, with a young strong prince to succeed him. He was weary of the coquettish princesses and spoilt concubines that had paraded through his bedroom over the years. None had meant a fraction of what Shakuntala meant to him. Even after years of being married to so many women, that single day he had spent with her in the forest outweighed them all. He had regained his true love, his only love. Everything would be different now. He could be happy once again.

But then he came to his senses and heard the murmurs of the court. All eyes were on him, awaiting his response. He realized he had begun to stand, his hands still on the armrests of the throne. Hearing the curious whispers of his closest advisors and catching the mood of the comments flying around the hall, he resumed his seat. This could not be. He could not accept Shakuntala or her son. It would undo everything he had worked for these past nine years. The struggles of a decade would be ruined. Rebellions would break out once more, fomented by rumours of the king losing his head and handing over his kingdom to an unknown brahmachari's bastard child. His alliances would be worthless, his marriages and backdoor deals rendered impotent. His allies would turn against him, even the people might revolt, unwilling to accept this unknown heir-apparent whom they had never heard of before. People would ask if a king's every get from the wrong side of town was to be granted a crown and a throne, or if this was an exception. He would be the butt of jokes and vile rumours. The very authority of Hastinapura would be undermined.

His grip tightened on the lion's heads that adorned the ends of the armrests, pressing hard on the delicately inlaid silver.

'Sadhini,' he said coldly, speaking loudly and harshly that all might hear him. 'What nonsense do you spout? I have never seen you before in my life. How dare you come before the throne of Hastinapura and make these wild accusations. Neither by dharma, kama or artha did I ever make any pact with you, marital or otherwise. Now go from here before I have you removed by force!'

At these words, the mood of the court changed at once. He felt the surge of relief and regret that swept across the sabha hall. His rivals and enemies were regretful that he had not committed an error of judgement, giving them cause to vent more complaints against him, while his friends and well-wishers were relieved that he had responded so strongly and clearly.

But on no one else in that court did Dushyanta's response have a greater impact than on Shakuntala. At once her face altered, her beauty shrank. Her eyes turned as red as copper as tears welled up uncontrollably. Her lips trembled. And though she remained decorous and made no aggressive movements towards the king—the armed soldiers around her made such a move ill advised—yet through her eyes she communicated more anger than men might do by brandishing swords. Silent for a long torturous moment, when she spoke again it was with the accumulated pain and sorrow of a decade of patient waiting, thinking no ill, and unshakable faith. In a single moment with a few words, Dushyanta had shattered her expectations and faith, humiliated her and reduced her life to ashes and shame. 'Raje,' she said, addressing him by his proper title, 'Great Samrat of the Kuru empire. Consider your words again. You know that what I say is truth and nothing but truth. You yourself were witness to our pact. I urge you: Do what is righteous under dharma. Do the right thing. By lying to me you lie to your own self. By doing so you steal truth from yourself. You do not sin against me, you sin against yourself! And he who can commit such a transgression against himself, what might he not do to others? Listen to your heart and your conscience. There is a being that dwells within each man, and he dwells within you as well. He knows everything you do, good or bad. He is that which is a part of god within us and which makes us godlike. Not for nothing is Yama lord of dharma as well as death. Those who follow dharma may be excused an error of judgement. But those who deny their errors cannot be forgiven. Yama will hunt him down and punish him. I have been faithful to you in every respect. Patiently and silently I waited nine long years, though you said it would be no more than nine days till you sent for me. You said you would send a four-fold army to bring me with all due pomp and ceremony to this very palace. As befitted a queen, you said! And yet, after keeping me waiting in the forest for nine years, when I come to you without complaint or accusation, you treat me this way? Why do you turn this cruel face to me, Dushyanta? This is your dharma. You have no choice but to obey! If not, may your head be splintered into a thousand pieces! The ancients teach us that a son is a part of the husband's body that is rejuvenated and brought back into this world by the wife. That is why the other word for wife is jaya, for with her by his side a man is ever victorious! Because bearing a son saves one's soul from the realm of hell known as put, therefore a son is known as putra.'

Shakuntala looked around at the court filled with richly clad and bejewelled spectators. She had no friends or well-wishers there. She was an island of dharma in an ocean of injustice. She wept and wrung her hands in misery and appealed to the stranger who sat upon the throne, his cold hard face turned away from her, contemplating some distant pillar or detail of the fine architecture of his hall.

'What shall I say to convince you further?' She went on. 'I am a true wife who follows every word of the shastras. I keep house diligently. I bore you a son. I am devoted to you, even when you were absent for nine years I never once thought ill of you. I am a part of you now, and together we have made a better part of ourselves in this, our son. I am the means by which you can achieve dharma, artha and kama. I am the only friend who will be with you to the very end of your life.'

But still Dushyanta was as unyielding as a stone statue and as unrelenting as iron. Weeping copiously, Shakuntala broke down, retreating into the familiar territory of the shastras and Vedic knowledge and lore with which she had grown up, as the daughter of a maharishi, and keeper of an ashram full of learned brahmins.

'A man who has a wife can pursue grihastha-ashrama. A man who has a wife can find happiness. A man who has a wife has a friend in solitude, an associate in ceremonies, and a caretaker in times of suffering. Even in exile, a wife refreshes her husband when all else is lost. A man with a wife can be trusted. A wife is a man's best means of salvation. When a man dies, the wife will even accompany him to the afterworld, for even after death the marital bond does not end unless you wish it to end. A wife who dies before her husband will not continue on her way but will wait for him to arrive that they might proceed together.'

She continued in this vein for an unknown length of time, her voice growing shriller, her words a litany, her message reduced to a plaintive drone.

Finally, at a gesture from the advisors, the soldiers came forward, intending to escort her out of the palace.

At this, she came to her senses and pushed them away, warning them not to come closer. They stepped back warily but remained close at hand, in case she attempted something more desperate.

Instead, she changed her mode of appeal. She held out her hands, palms joined together, in an appeal to Dushyanta.

'If you will not accept me as a wife, whatever your reasons, then at least accept this, your own son. The Vedas tell us we should utter these words when a son is born: "Born of my body, born of my heart, you are I myself returned to life again. May you live a thousand autumns. You extend my life and lineage infinitely. Therefore live well, live happy forever." Look at him, Dushyanta, this is your son, you can see it in his face, his body, his smile. Just as the ahavaniya fire is kindled from the garhapatya fire, so has his body been kindled from your own. It is as if you divided yourself into two and this is the younger half. Remember how we conceived him? You were on a hunting expedition and lost your way. To my father's ashram you came and begged me to marry you in the gandharva style. I was reluctant but you convinced me it was righteous under dharma and I agreed and we entered into wedlock.'

Dushyanta's voice was quiet in the silent hall. 'Woman, I do not even know you. We have never met before. I do not even know your name.'

'Do not say that!' she cried. 'I am Shakuntala! I told you the story of my birth. My mother was Menaka, the foremost of apsaras. Of all the six supreme apsaras—Urvashi, Purvachitti, Sahajanya, Menaka, Vishvachi and Ghritachi, she was the one born from Brahma and the best of them all. Urged by Indra, aided by Vayu and Kama, she descended from Indraloka to earth and seduced Brahmarishi Vishwamitra. The fruit of their union was I, so named because after being born I was protected by shakuna birds. The sage Kanva adopted me and raised me as his own daughter. It was to his ashram that you came that day nine years ago and we met. What sins did I commit in what past life that you deny me now, I do not know. If you choose to forsake me, then so be it, I shall return meekly to my father's ashram and live out the rest of my life in solitude. But do not deny this boy his legacy. He is your own son!'

Dushantya's face was never crueller than in that moment. 'Shakuntala, if that is your name . . . Even if a trace of what you say were true, even if that were so, yet tell me this. How do I know this son is mine? Should I simply take your word for it? Why should I believe you? Your father was a kshatriya who turned brahmin to achieve his own ends, not because he had some higher goal. Even as a brahmin, he succumbed to lust. You claim he sired you upon Menaka, the celestial courtesan? Look at your state! How can you compare yourself to that legendary epitome of womanhood? And this boy you claim is my son, conceived nine years ago? Look at him. Everyone, look at him. He is not nine years old! He is huge. He is perhaps twice that age. His body is like the trunk of the shala tree, his arms are like a wrestler's arms. What nine-year-old boy could have such a physique? Everything you say is nothing but lies. I do not know you or acknowledge you. Go away from here at once and do as you wish. You are nobody to me.'

||Six||

At this terrible pronouncement, even the collective emotions of the sabha hall seemed to turn to sympathy for the ascetic woman with the young boy. Even Dushyanta's fiercest political opponents within the court smiled thinly, inwardly cursing the king's clarity of purpose. They had been hoping beyond hope that he would have relented and acknowledged the woman, for it was clear that there had been some relationship between them at some time. Ascetics as high-minded as she did not make such claims lightly. Rishi Kanva was a legendary if reclusive brahmin. Nobody from his ashram would lie outright, that too on such a royal scale. Probably the king had indeed encountered the woman during one of his many hunting expeditions. There had even been one such famous expedition nine years ago, where he had gone missing for several fortnights. Everyone recalled it well because it was that absence that had fuelled the crisis in the administrative scene, and changed the landscape of Hastinapura's politics. It was also notable because ever since that day, the king had never once ventured away from the capital for more than a few days, no more than a fortnight, and only in the rarest of emergencies. His iron hand and constant presence here had been the very reason why they were unable to work their machinations and pursue their own agenda as forcefully as before.

So the more the woman had argued, her passion and intensity—and her painful sincerity, above all—had won over their minds, making everyone believe that there was some truth to what she claimed, if not the whole truth. The setting was ripe for a controversy. But by denying her so brusquely and cruelly, the king had eliminated any accusations they might have levelled against him. By himself refusing to acknowledge her or the boy, he had left no room for controversy. By law, the court then had to abide by his decision and ignore the woman and her son. It was an unfortunately missed opportunity.

Now, the soldiers moved forward again, this time authorized to haul the woman and boy out of court and out of the city, never to be seen again. Even they moved slowly, faces revealing mixed emotions. This was not some hardened criminal threatening the king. A brahmin woman of such high birth, with such obviously austere upbringing, she was a person to be respected, admired, not apprehended and exiled. But they had their dharma to fulfil. And so they moved closer, blocking her way to the king in case she should attempt something untoward.

'Is this your dharma?' she asked. Her voice was clearly audible in the hushed hall. Everyone was listening with rapt attention, aware that the unexpected drama was almost at an end. Many were openly shocked at Raja Dushyanta's final words and the uncompromising harshness he had displayed. It was evidence of how much he had changed in these past nine years. No more the playful king who cavorted with concubines and indulged in every fleshly pleasure, leaving the administration of the kingdom to his advisors and allies. This was an emperor in every sense of the word, ruling the empire he had himself consolidated and strengthened in the past decade, with a firm rein and unshakeable resoluteness. Imperial. That was the one word that described his response. The words of an emperor who had once been a king who had once been a man. Thus did kingship change men from flesh and blood to iron and gold with hearts of steel.

'Is this the way you treat your own wife and son?' she asked. The soldiers, only yards from her, looked at one another, unsure what to do. Their leader gestured and they retreated to their earlier positions, remaining close enough to apprehend her instantly should she make any foolish move, yet far enough to allow her a few more moments to speak her mind—and heart. What would be the harm? From the way they looked down at the polished floor of the hall, even they felt sympathy for her, especially after the king's cruel denials.

'You accuse me . . . *me!* . . . of such things, yet what of yourself? Is your moral vision so obscured? You see the faults of others even if they are as tiny as mustard seeds but your own, though they are as fat as bilva fruit, you ignore! You dare denigrate me and deny me the truth of my own birth? Who are you to deny me? My mother was indeed Menaka. It is true that as one of the greatest apsaras to the gods, she was able to keep herself well bathed and cared for, clad in the finest garments and most precious ornaments. I have lived the life of a sadhini, in a humble forest ashram, working with my bare hands, with no comforts or luxuries. I have no fine clothes, no jewellery, and I am covered with the dust and grime of a long journey on foot. But nine years ago, when you saw me for the first time, freshly bathed from the river, my hair loosed by my waist, you claimed that I was no less than an apsara to your eyes! You showered compliments upon my beauty like leaves in autumn.

Perhaps much of my beauty has waned with time, for these past nine years have been very hard on me. Perhaps I was never beautiful and you lied to me that day. But it is not my opinion or claim we are debating, it is your own! By your own admission, you are either a liar or a man without dharma! While I have spoken only the truth, in every single word and detail. The difference between you and me, great Dushyanta, is like the difference between a mustard seed and Mount Meru! For I have abided by dharma in every single respect, but you ignore even common decency.'

Now she took a single step forward, raising her hand accusingly to point at the throne upon the dais. The advisors and ministers nearest to the king cringed, for all knew the wrath of a brahmin could be terrible and feared a brahmanic curse. Even the servants fanning the king and standing by with wine and fruit blanched visibly and stepped aside, seeking to distance themselves from their liege in the event that the sadhini issued some terrible pronouncement. The sabha hall's silence deepened to a deathly absence of sound. Not one person coughed or shifted in their seats or moved so much as a tinkling bracelet. They knew some momentous announcement was about to follow.

'Here me now, O king of Hastinapura. I shall speak and you shall listen. For clearly, you are not schooled in the difference between truth and untruth. I shall tell you what is the difference. The ugly man who insists he is handsome may not be telling an untruth for he may not have seen his own face yet. But once he has seen his own visage in a mirror and adjudged how ugly he looks, he would be telling an untruth if he continues to insist he is handsome. The handsome man, on the other hand, never says he is handsome—he does not need to say it, for he carries the truth on his face for all to see! Yet because he is truly handsome, he has no need to call others ugly. Only an ugly man who is also a liar goes around describing people as handsome or ugly or slandering people in general. As a pig seeks out filth to wallow in, the fool pounces on every error and amusing word in a wise man's speech. He fails to hear all the good words and great wisdom and only picks out the bad, or at least those he thinks are bad, for when one makes it a habit to seek out filth, a time comes when one sees only filth everywhere. The swan, on the other hand, seeks to separate milk from water to drink it. Similarly, the wise seek words of wisdom and quality when listening to other people speak. They ignore the bad or ignoble words and phrases and pluck out only the good, separating them from the rest like wheat from chaff. Fools take great pleasure in berating wise men. Wise men keep silent when confronted by fools, choosing rather to walk away than engage in puerile arguments. It is a fact of life that the truly evil person always insists that he is truly good and that those who are genuinely good are truly evil! Thus do the fools of the world try to separate morality into black and white and shades of grey, insisting always that they themselves are pure white, or at worst, a subtle shade of grey. In fact, grey itself is a shade of black. The truly wise do not grade people at all, they accept all humans as equal and only behaviour as good or evil.

Shakuntala took another step forward, her eyes blazing like rubies in her ebony face. A rumbling sound began to grow as she spoke. The congregation looked around, at each other, then at the walls and pillars and ceiling, wondering at the sound, yet too awed by the sadhini's passion and the power of her eloquence to make any move. Each one feared that by moving he or she would attract the wrath of the brahmin onto himself or herself, and that fear kept them rock still, even as the rumbling built and grew into something ominous, as if a thundercloud had formed upon the ceiling of the hall itself and threatened to unleash a vajra at any instant.

'Your denial of my words hurts me deeply, I do not deny it. But I do not address that. It is your denial of your own flesh and blood that I cannot tolerate. It has been said in our shastras that a man who denies his own son can never ascend to higher worlds. The gods themselves destroy his prosperity! So by denying the son of your own body you are invoking the wrath of the gods themselves and leading your entire kingdom and dynasty into ruin!'

With a crash, the rumbling broke into a boom. A blinding miasma forced everyone to shut their eyes momentarily. When they opened their eyes again, almost at once, nothing had changed, yet clearly some supernatural force had spoken in that sound, expressing its wrath.

Shakuntala continued. 'The pitris, our ancestors, have said that the son establishes the family and continues the lineage, and thus, a son can never be abandoned. Pitr Manu even said that a man need not beget a son through biological conception alone. That is one way, to beget a son upon one's wife. But he also spelled out five other ways in which sons can be had—they can be obtained, bought, reared, adopted, or begotten on women other than one's wife. All these qualify as sons. Yet you who have begotten your own son upon your own lawfully wedded wife, deny him!' The rumbling grew again, this time increasing in intensity and depth, like some great invisible giant gnashing his teeth and growling in anticipation of a death blow. 'Sons support the dharma of men, enhance their fathers' fame, and bring happiness to their fathers' hearts. Sons are the rafts of dharma upon which ancestors are transported to the heavenly realms and steered away from the hellish worlds! The shastras also tell us that one natural pond is better than a hundred dug wells. In turn, a sacrifice is better than a hundred natural ponds. But a son is better than a hundred sacrifices. And truth is better than a hundred sons! Can you estimate then, the extent of your falsehood in denying the truth of your own son's existence?'

Now the mood in the sabha hall began to turn to one of near-panic. For everyone feared that the power of the sadhini's anger would scorch all present. She would at any time unleash the full potency of her tapas energy and all would be turned to ashes. But still none dared move.

Only Dushyanta sat silent and still, staring down from his throne without expression. Neither anger nor sorrow nor fear passed across his face. Only a steadfast expression of a monarch who had seen entire armies ground to dust and empires crumble and fall, the face of a man who looks upon his own certain death and does not fear or thwart it, merely watches it approach.

'Your transgression is not against me, or even your own son,' Shakuntala said in a voice that seemed made of the thunder itself, her eyes flashing with a ruby fire that resembled lightning in the belly of a cloud. 'It is against truth itself! For I can accept your denial, your turning me away, your lack of love for me, everything. What I cannot and will not accept are your lies! You deny the truth of my identity. The truth of our marriage. The truth of our union. The truth of our son's birth and existence. This is unacceptable to me. Truth is greater than all the Vedas, greater than dharma, it is the supreme brahman itself, it is the ultimate godhead. Therefore I pronounce this judgement upon you, king of the Kurus. Once you are dead, my son will rule over your kingdom, sit upon your throne, wear your robes and your crown, eat from the same golden plate and drink from the same silver chalice, and he shall reign undisputed and unrivalled. None will dare challenge his supremacy, none will win in battle against him, none will triumph against him in statecraft. He shall be emperor not just in name but in truth! This, I declare to be true and so shall it come to pass!'

And with a great thundering boom, forcing all present to shut their eyes and cry out in terror, the entire world turned to blinding white. Every mind went blank for an instant, every mouth opened to release an involuntary scream, and it was as if the entire congregation had merged with some celestial congregation, as if the court of the gods themselves had been superimposed upon this court of Dushyanta and those celestial courtiers, the devas themselves, spoke in their rumbling booming voices with one single tone, and all they said was, 'It shall be so.'

Then a single great voice, like a gruff grandfather of all creation, spoke:

'Shakuntala speaks truth. This son is the son of Dushyanta. He must be maintained by Dushyanta, and because of this, he shall be known as He Who Is Maintained, *Bharata*.' The final word resounded forth like a blast of thunder from a thousand thunderclouds, etching the word into the memories of all present.

And then the world flashed again to black and when the blindness passed, all was as it had been before.

||Seven||

Dushyanta descended from the throne dais. All eyes were upon him, all throats silent.

He reached the floor of the sabha hall, the same polished level on which Shakuntala and her son—Bharata, he would henceforth always be known by that name—stood.

He smiled and held out his arms.

'My love,' he said. 'My wife! My son.'

A great gasp of excitement rippled through the congregation.

Dushyanta gestured at the royalty, nobility and aristocracy seated around on gilded thrones of their own, the pride and majesty of the empire gathered together. 'Had I accepted you at your first word, as I dearly desired to do, these same people would have renounced me. Had I embraced you and acknowledged you as my wife and Bharata as our son, they would have turned against me. Sedition, conspiracy, assassination, rebellion, secession, these would all have been the order of the day. For only through a show of cruel strength can an emperor hold an empire together. Such is the way it has always been and so shall it always be. There was no place for you or our son in the life of the emperor of Hastinapura. And Dushyanta the king who loved you at first sight and married you . . . why, he would have been assassinated within days, if not moments, of accepting a simple rishi's daughter as his wife and a boy of such obvious dharmic power as his son and heir. Alliances would have toppled, coalitions collapsed, and war would have broken out over the issue of succession alone. Even the people would have been hard-pressed to accept you as their queen or Bharata as our son and their future king. Therefore I was compelled to lie to you, and deny you. But now, now that all of this great gathering has witnessed my denials, heard your responses and witnessed for itself the great voice of the god who spoke thereafter, and heard what that voice had to say, nobody can dispute your righteousness, nor the veracity of your claims.'

Shakuntala had listened to all this with wide staring eyes. No more tears fell from her face, her anger and grief had begun to dissipate, unveiling the beauty that lay beneath. Yet, she hesitated,, asking doubtfully, 'You . . . you knew this would happen? You . . . deliberately compelled me to speak?'

Dushyanta approached her, bowing his head low, his face expressing regret and genuine pain. 'Never have I had to show such cruelty before, not even when I pronounced a sentence of death or slaughtered innocents in order to achieve a military goal. Yes, I admit it, my beloved wife. I provoked you into speaking out, knowing that as a brahmin's daughter and one brought up in the way of dharma, you would not tolerate lies. Therefore I did not simply deny you and turn you away. For nine years I lived in anguish and self-recrimination. I did not know how to send for you and make you my queen without causing the kingdom to revolt against me. It was a seditious time, a turbulent decade. What would have been the point of making you my queen for a night only to see the kingdom burn and both of us assassinated and our son slain?

My only recourse was through dharma. Therefore I waited for you to come to me. You took a long enough time! And when you came before me, I knew I must provoke you into speaking out, to saying exactly the kind of things you said. The honest person is always predictable for he or she will always do what is right! So did you. And your anger and your righteousness prompted the gods themselves to intervene, when the court of men had failed to speak for you,' he gestured at his own court, 'and to pronounce judgement on your behalf. For we still live in an age when dharma and fidelity are rewarded, not punished or ignored. And now, all the world knows that Shakuntala is my lawful wife and Bharata my lawful son and heir. None dare dispute it,' Dushyanta raised his voice to a menacing baritone, glancing around at his courtiers, 'or they risk incurring not just my wrath but the wrath of the gods themselves!' Not one person met his eyes with a challenge or denial. If anything, all bowed their heads in acquiescence.

Shakuntala smiled then, and in that smile all her radiant beauty was visible for all to see, the beauty of a mortal woman born of the apsara Menaka, most beautiful of all female creations. Dushyanta came to her and embraced her, tentatively at first, then openly, and Bharata, laughing and happy at the reunion of his parents, joined in the embrace, and with one movement, the entire court rose to its feet, and began applauding and cheering. The hall filled with their deafening cries of joy and support, and not a single one dared offer any opposition.

'I love you,' Dushyanta said softly to his wife, clasping her and acknowledging her before the entire world. 'Rule with me and be my queen. It is time to fulfil all my promises to you and for us to resume the marriage we entered into so briefly that auspicious day.'

And Shakuntala was pacified and appeased and filled with love and joy.

Thus was Bharata, son of Dushyanta and Shakuntala, born and made heir to the throne of the Kuru nation. In time, he ascended to the throne, exactly as Shakuntala had predicted, and Dushyanta had desired, and in time he brought about the enduring peace that his father had struggled to maintain. Living up to his name, he maintained and was maintained. He came to be known as Chakravarti, monarch of all realms, and as Sarvabhauma, sovereign of the world. He performed many great yagnas, and his grandfather Rishi Kanva was the officiating priest at all of them. The historical records say that he gave Rishi Kanva a thousand padmas as the brahmin's fee. A padma means a lotus, but it also means one trillion in numbers. The usual fee given to a brahmin after a sacrifice was a cow. Does this mean that Raja Bharata gave Rishi Kanva one thousand trillion cows? Perhaps. Whatever the number, it was great indeed, for Raja Bharata possessed enormous wealth, and so did all the kings of his lineage.

||Eight||

As Vaisampayana finished the tale of Shakuntala and Dushyanta, a wind passed across the plain of Samantapanchaka. All present felt the wind. In the wind, he thought he heard voices, whispering. Their words were inaudible but as the voices of the wind passed over him, he saw in his mind's eye the image of another suta, seated in a gathering in a forest clearing, also narrating a tale. Something told him that it was the same tale he was reciting, the *Mahabharata* of his guru Krishna Dweipayana Vyasa. Even as he realized this, his mind filled with other images, of sutas past, present and future, also reciting the same epic poem in all its beauty and glory, to a variety of audiences. The voices on the wind grew in number and intensity, building to a crescendo. The images blurred even as the voices grew to deafening proportions. Down the ages, throughout time itself, a thousand thousand narrators related a thousand thousand versions of the great epic, their voices melding into one great river of narrative flowing through the forest of stories that was itihasa itself.

Next in the Mahabharata Series

THE SEEDS OF WAR

Book Two introduces us to the elder protagonists of the epic, as well as some of the great loves and lusts, friendships and enmities, politics and self-sacrifice that will lay the seeds that will eventually fester and erupt into the mother of all wars. At first it may seem that the journey is the reward, with seemingly unrelated love stories, fantastical tales of exploits in the heavenly realms, divine pacts and demoniac trysts. But it soon becomes evident that all these form a tapestry revealing the grandeur and glamour of the Kuru Bharata race itself, the growing descendants of the original tribe that established perhaps the greatest and oldest human civilization ever known in recoded history. Their loves and enmities are epic, their stories astonishing, their personalities mercurial. Every page you turn reveals magical new thrills and wonders. As one larger-than-life personality after another strides onstage, the drama ratchets up to thriller level, the arrow swarms begin to fly and conflicts turn ugly as the author of the *Ramayana Series* once again proves himself the master of epics.

Next in the Mahabharata Series

THE CHILDREN OF MIDNIGHT

Book Three brings to vivid, searing life the politics and human drama that led to the greatest war ever waged. Patriarch Bhishma-Pitama and Dowager Queen Mother Satyavati do their best to make the right decisions to ensure the survival of the Puru dynasty of Hasinapura. But fate intervenes, and free will outwits destiny. Blind King Dhritirashtra's hundred and one children are born through the intervention of Sage Vyasa at the stroke of midnight. Yet even this strange batch is reason enough to celebrate for a troubled kingdom. Meanwhile, deep in the forest, rightful heir Pandu defies a curse that forbade him from making love—and dies. Acting on his last instructions, his widowed queens Kunti and Madri use divine boons to summon gods to father sons upon them. The five boys produced in this manner prove themselves to be extraordinary at once: each gifted with the power of his divine sire. Thus are the Pandavas and Kauravas born and the stage set for the great conflict.